Ichigo Takano presents

Dreamin'
Sun

4

volume
four

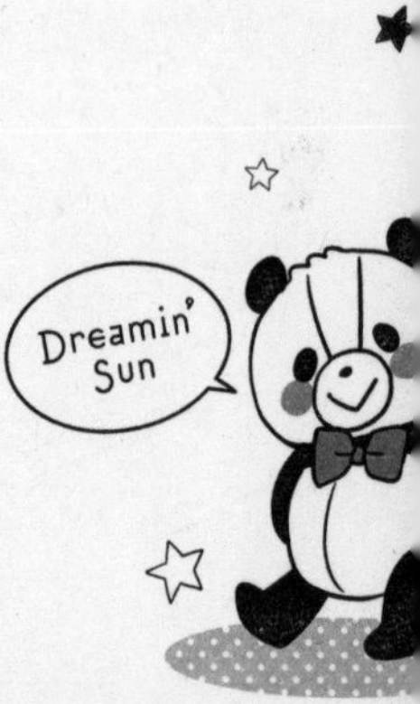
Dreamin' Sun

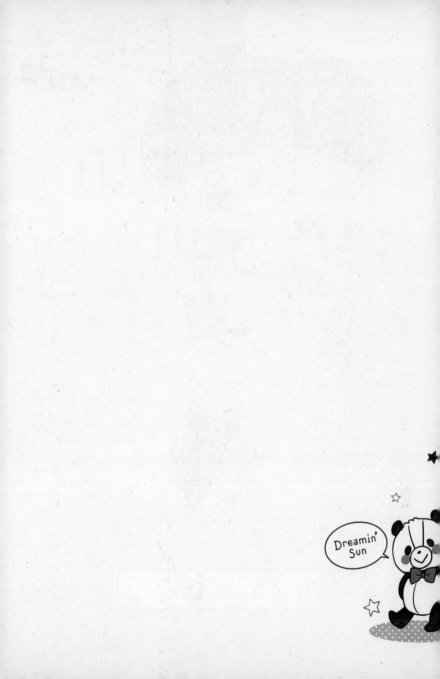

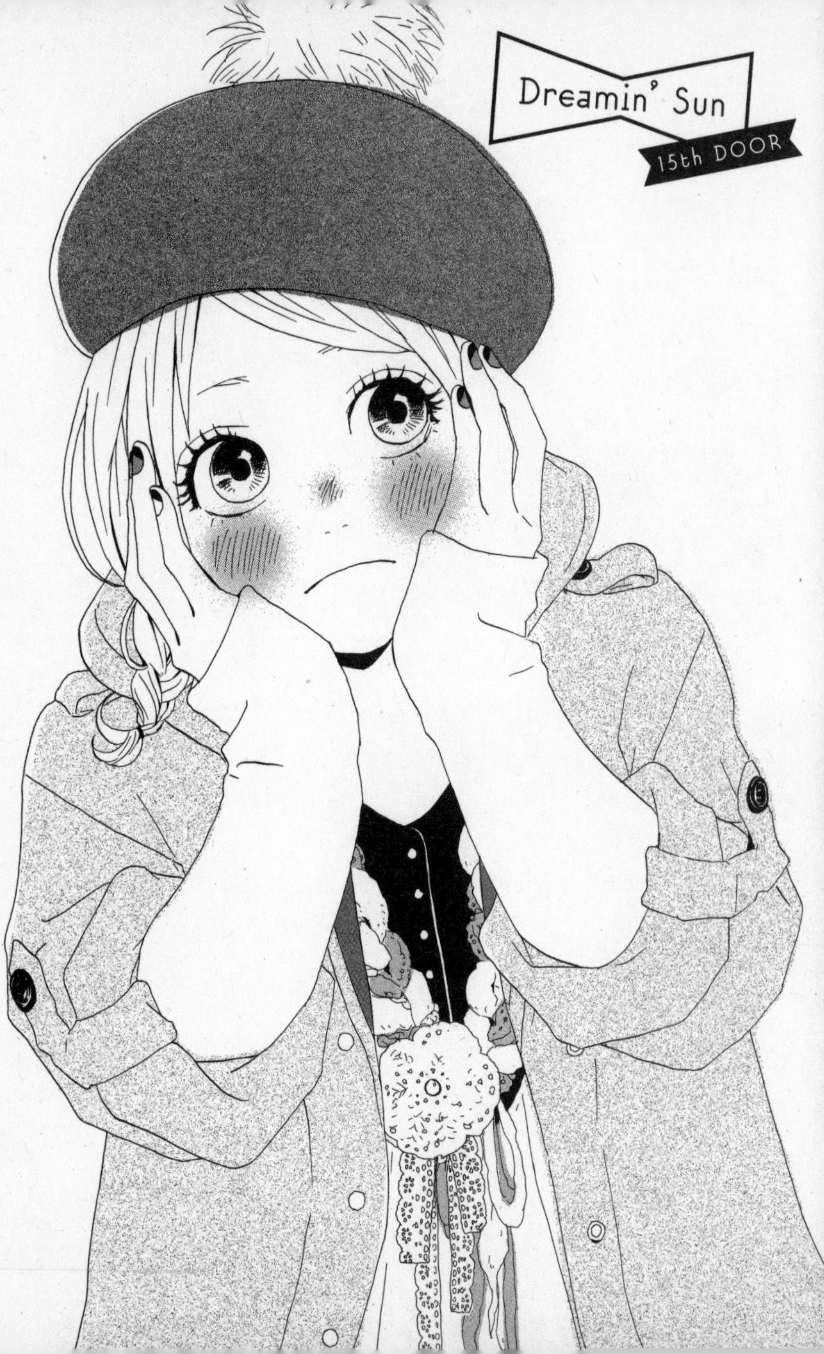
Dreamin' Sun
15th DOOR

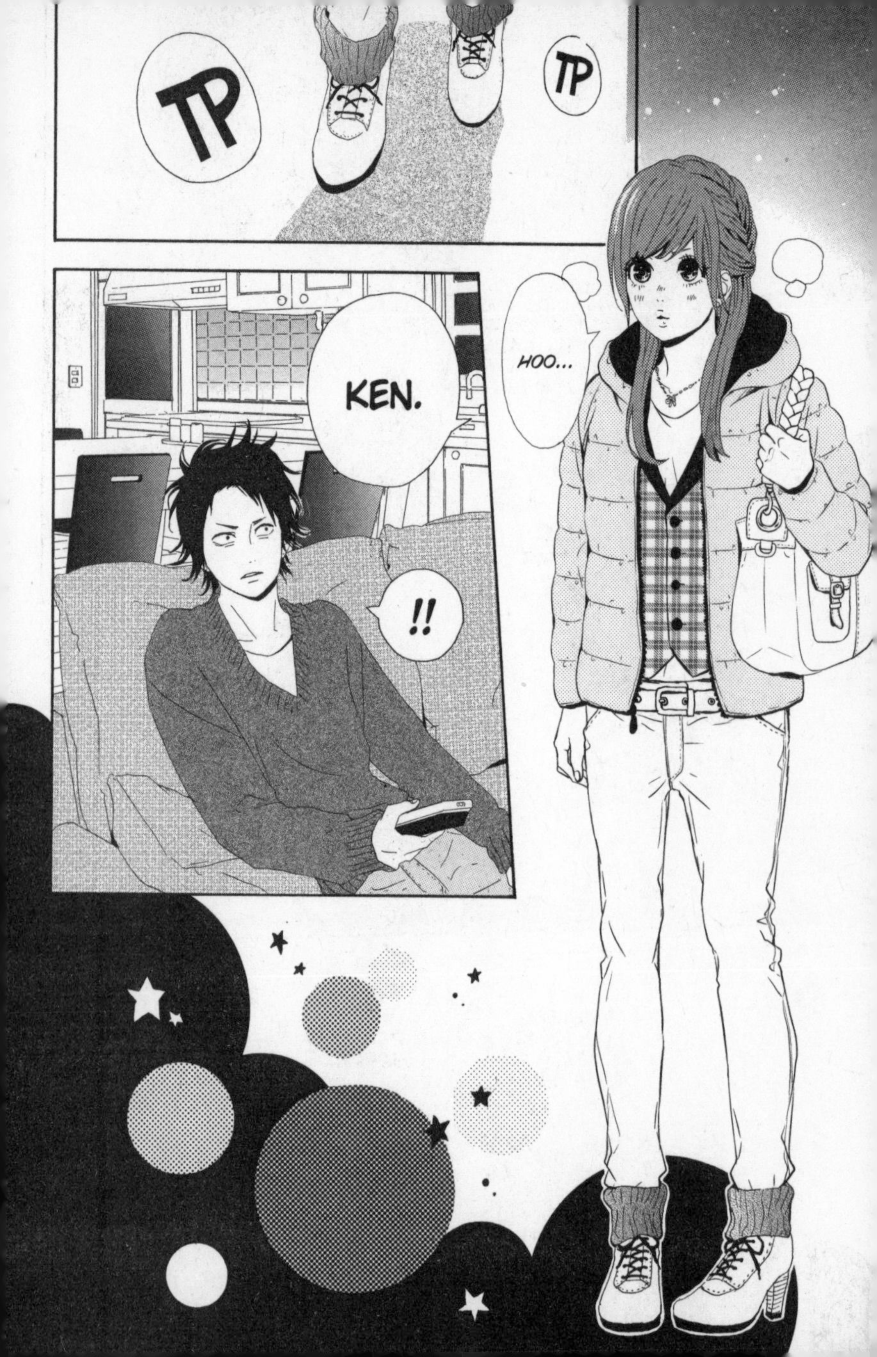
HOO...
TP
TP
KEN.
!!

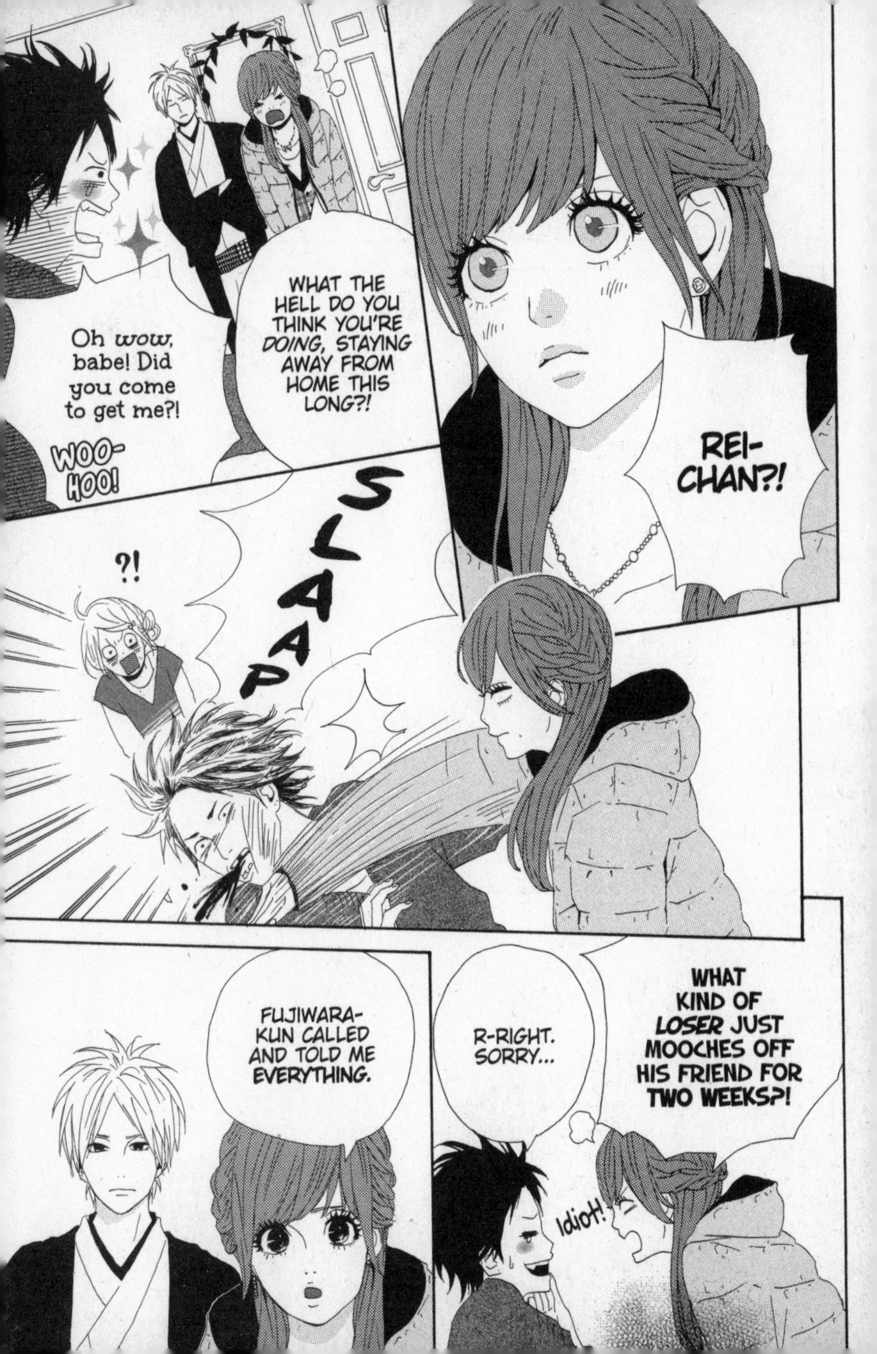

REI-CHAN?!
Oh wow, babe! Did you come to get me?!
WOO-HOO!
SLAAP
?!
WHAT THE HELL DO YOU THINK YOU'RE *DOING*, STAYING AWAY FROM HOME THIS LONG?!
WHAT KIND OF *LOSER* JUST MOOCHES OFF HIS FRIEND FOR TWO WEEKS?!
Idiot!
R-RIGHT. SORRY...
FUJIWARA-KUN CALLED AND TOLD ME EVERYTHING.

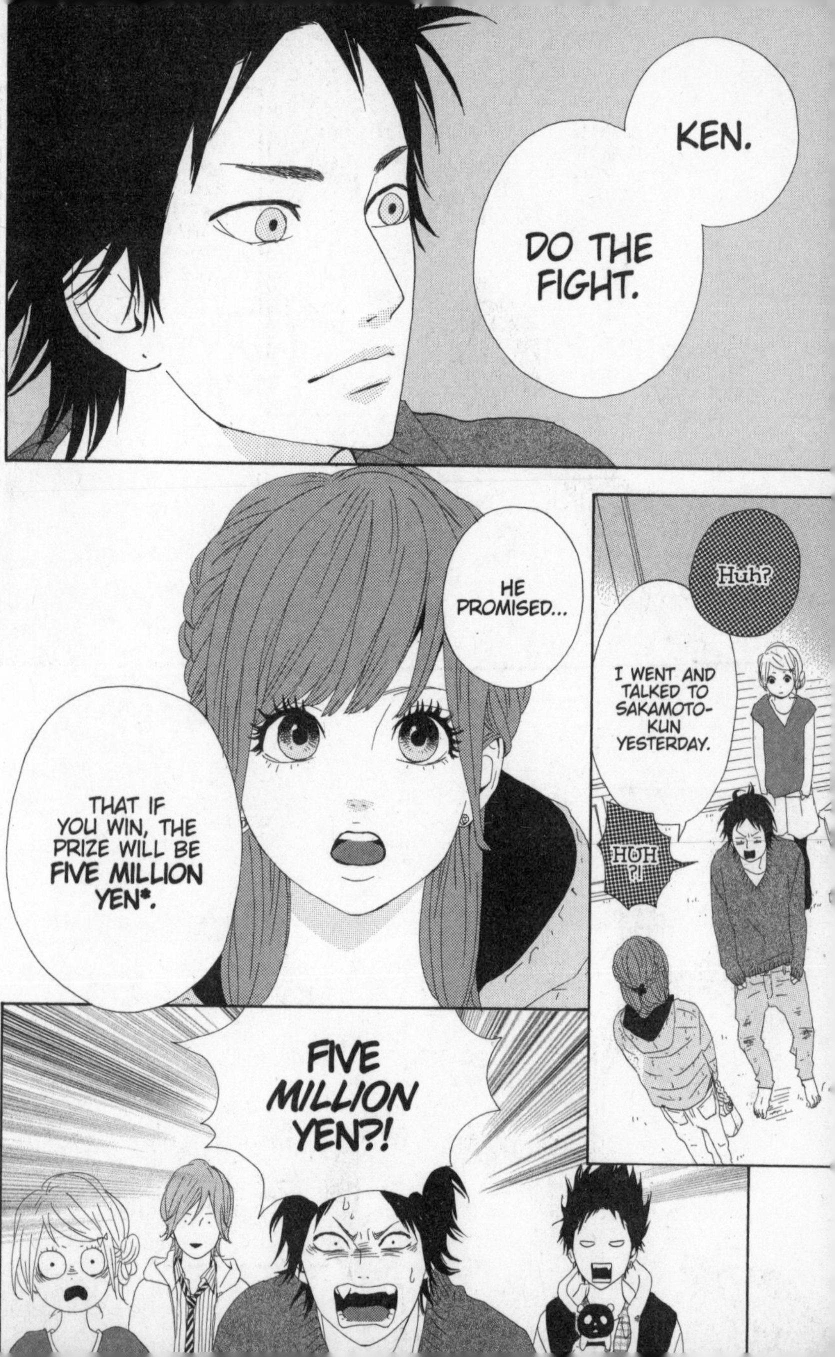
KEN.
DO THE FIGHT.
Huh?
I WENT AND TALKED TO SAKAMOTO-KUN YESTERDAY.
HUH ?!
HE PROMISED...
THAT IF YOU WIN, THE PRIZE WILL BE FIVE MILLION YEN*.
FIVE MILLION YEN?!

*About $44,000 USD.

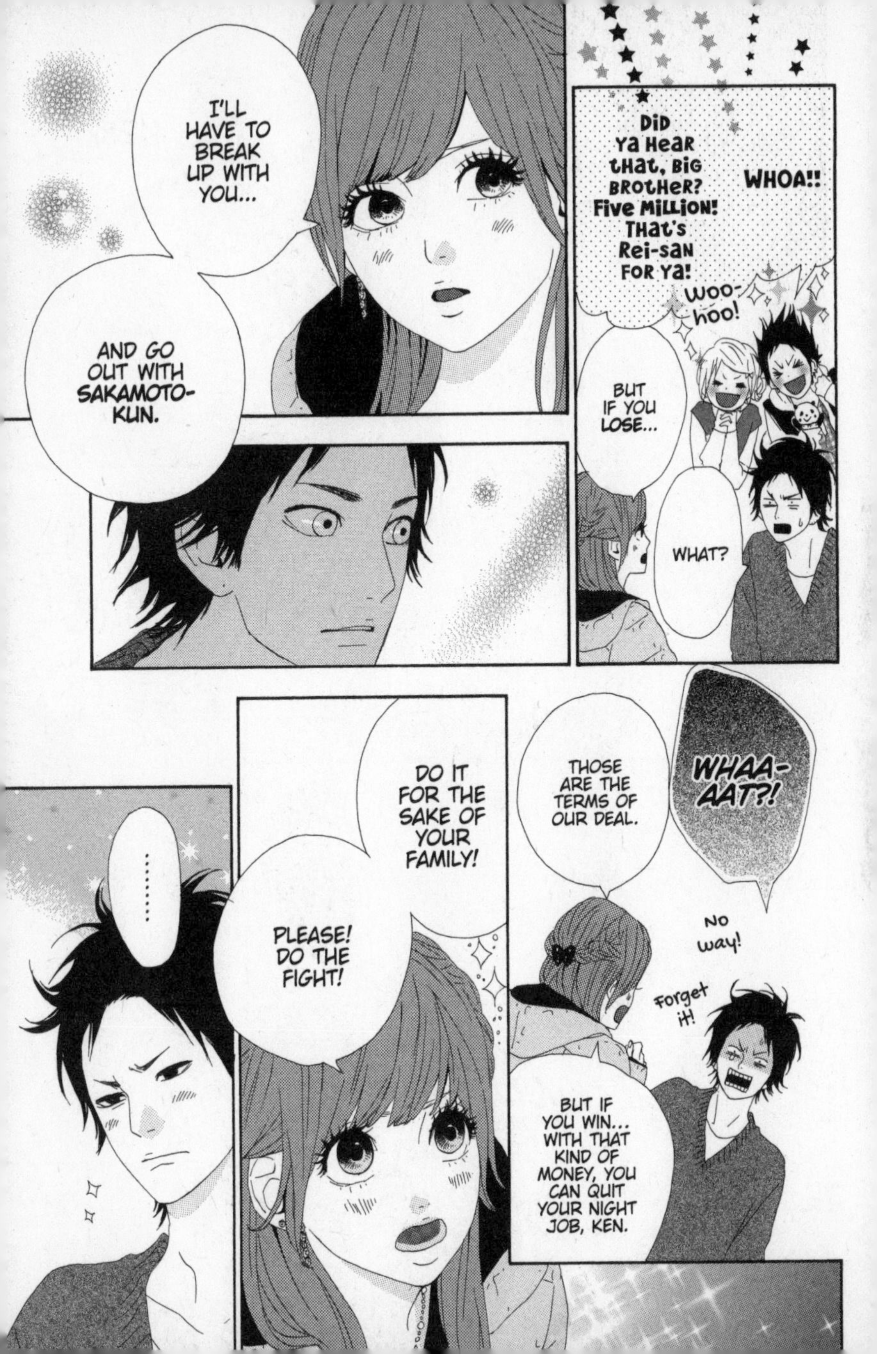
Did ya hear that, big brother? Five million! That's Rei-san for ya!
WHOA!!
Woo-hoo!
BUT IF YOU LOSE...
WHAT?
I'LL HAVE TO BREAK UP WITH YOU...
AND GO OUT WITH SAKAMOTO-KUN.
THOSE ARE THE TERMS OF OUR DEAL.
WHAA-AAT?!
No way!
Forget it!
BUT IF YOU WIN... WITH THAT KIND OF MONEY, YOU CAN QUIT YOUR NIGHT JOB, KEN.
DO IT FOR THE SAKE OF YOUR FAMILY!
PLEASE! DO THE FIGHT!
......

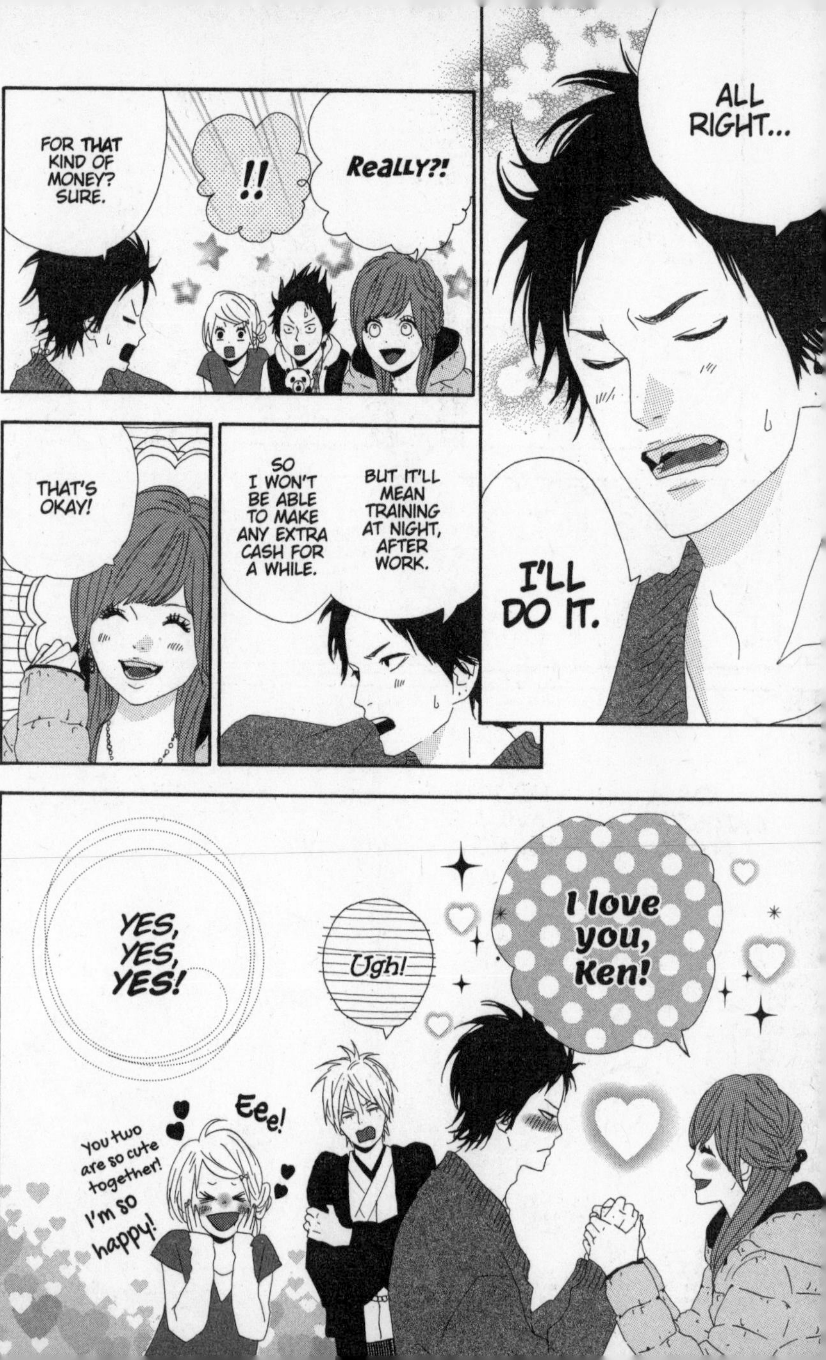
ALL RIGHT...
I'LL DO IT.
Really?!
!!
FOR THAT KIND OF MONEY? SURE.
BUT IT'LL MEAN TRAINING AT NIGHT, AFTER WORK.
SO I WON'T BE ABLE TO MAKE ANY EXTRA CASH FOR A WHILE.
THAT'S OKAY!
I love you, Ken!
Ugh!
Eee!
YES, YES, YES!
You two are so cute together!
I'm so happy!

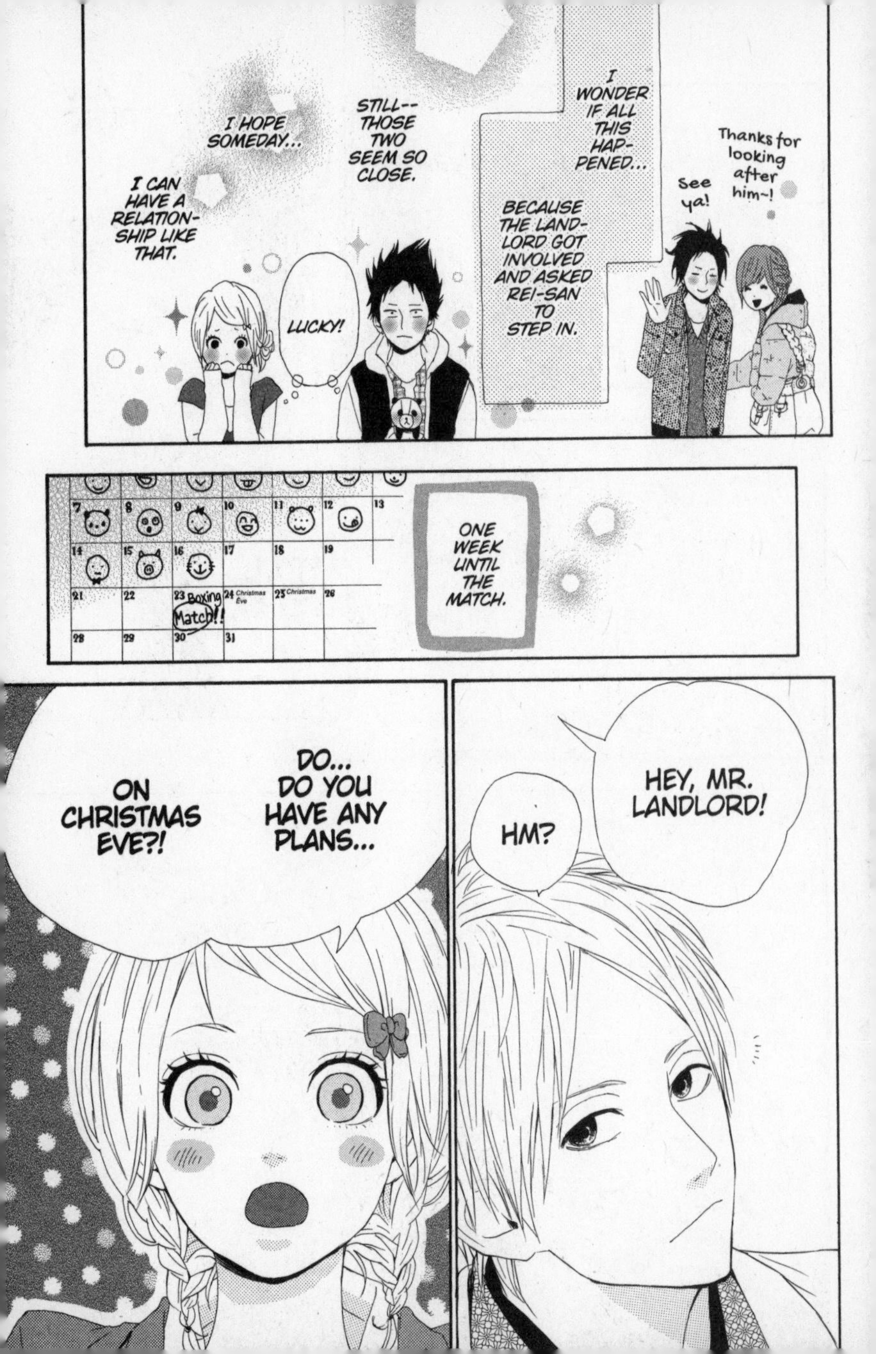
Thanks for looking after him~!
See ya!
I WONDER IF ALL THIS HAPPENED...
BECAUSE THE LANDLORD GOT INVOLVED AND ASKED REI-SAN TO STEP IN.
STILL-- THOSE TWO SEEM SO CLOSE.
LUCKY!
I HOPE SOMEDAY...
I CAN HAVE A RELATIONSHIP LIKE THAT.
ONE WEEK UNTIL THE MATCH.
23 Boxing Match!!
24 Christmas Eve
25 Christmas
HEY, MR. LANDLORD!
HM?
DO... DO YOU HAVE ANY PLANS...
ON CHRISTMAS EVE?!

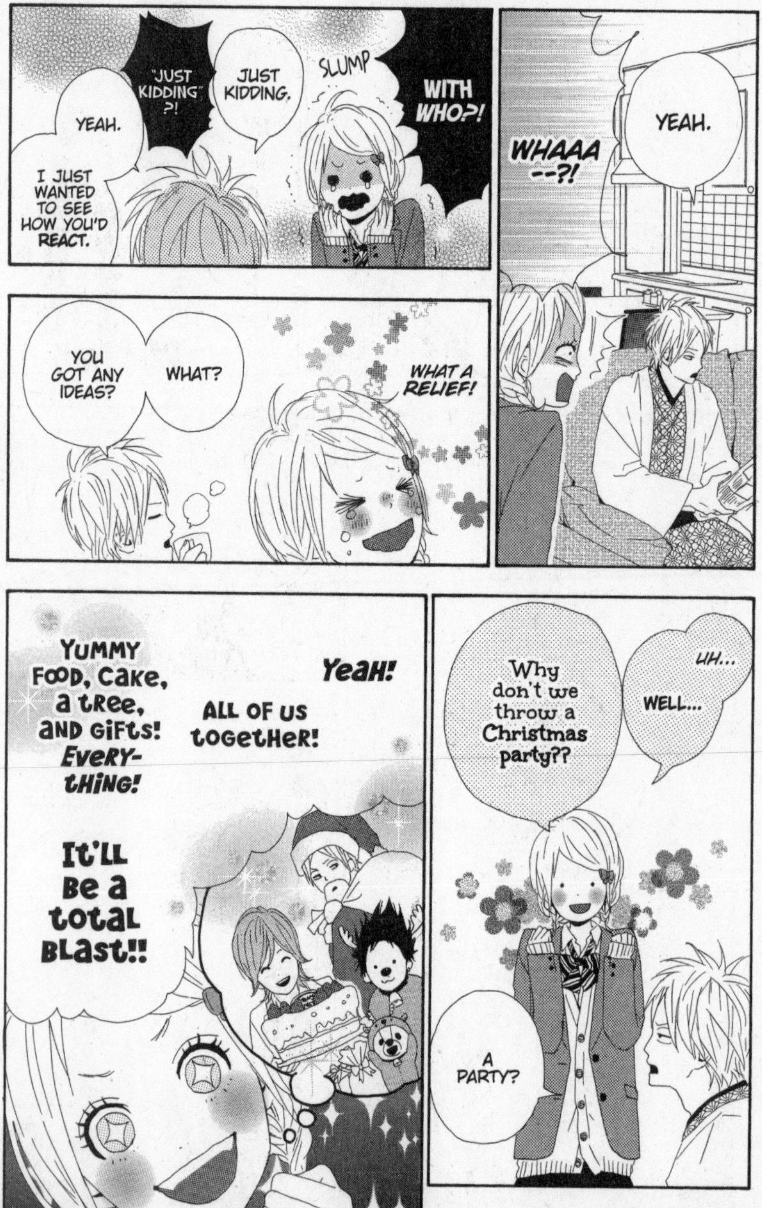
YEAH.
WHAAA--?!
WITH WHO?!
SLUMP
JUST KIDDING.
"JUST KIDDING" ?!
YEAH.
I JUST WANTED TO SEE HOW YOU'D REACT.
WHAT A RELIEF!
WHAT?
YOU GOT ANY IDEAS?
UH... WELL...
Why don't we throw a Christmas party??
A PARTY?
Yeah!
ALL OF US TOGETHER!
YUMMY FOOD, CAKE, A TREE, AND GIFTS! EVERY-THING!
IT'LL BE A TOTAL BLAST!!

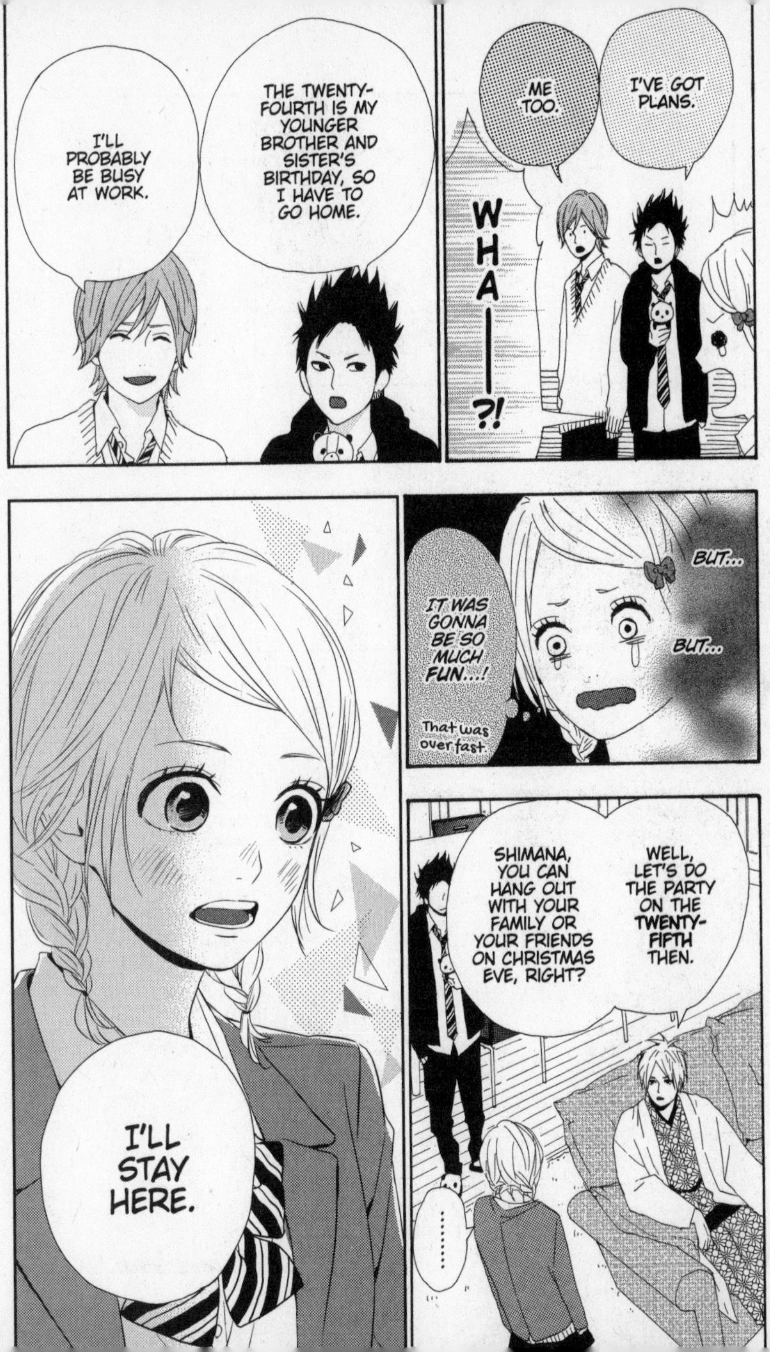
I'VE GOT PLANS.
ME TOO.
WHA—?!
THE TWENTY-FOURTH IS MY YOUNGER BROTHER AND SISTER'S BIRTHDAY, SO I HAVE TO GO HOME.
I'LL PROBABLY BE BUSY AT WORK.
BUT...
BUT...
IT WAS GONNA BE SO MUCH FUN...!
That was over fast.
WELL, LET'S DO THE PARTY ON THE TWENTY-FIFTH THEN.
SHIMANA, YOU CAN HANG OUT WITH YOUR FAMILY OR YOUR FRIENDS ON CHRISTMAS EVE, RIGHT?
....
I'LL STAY HERE.

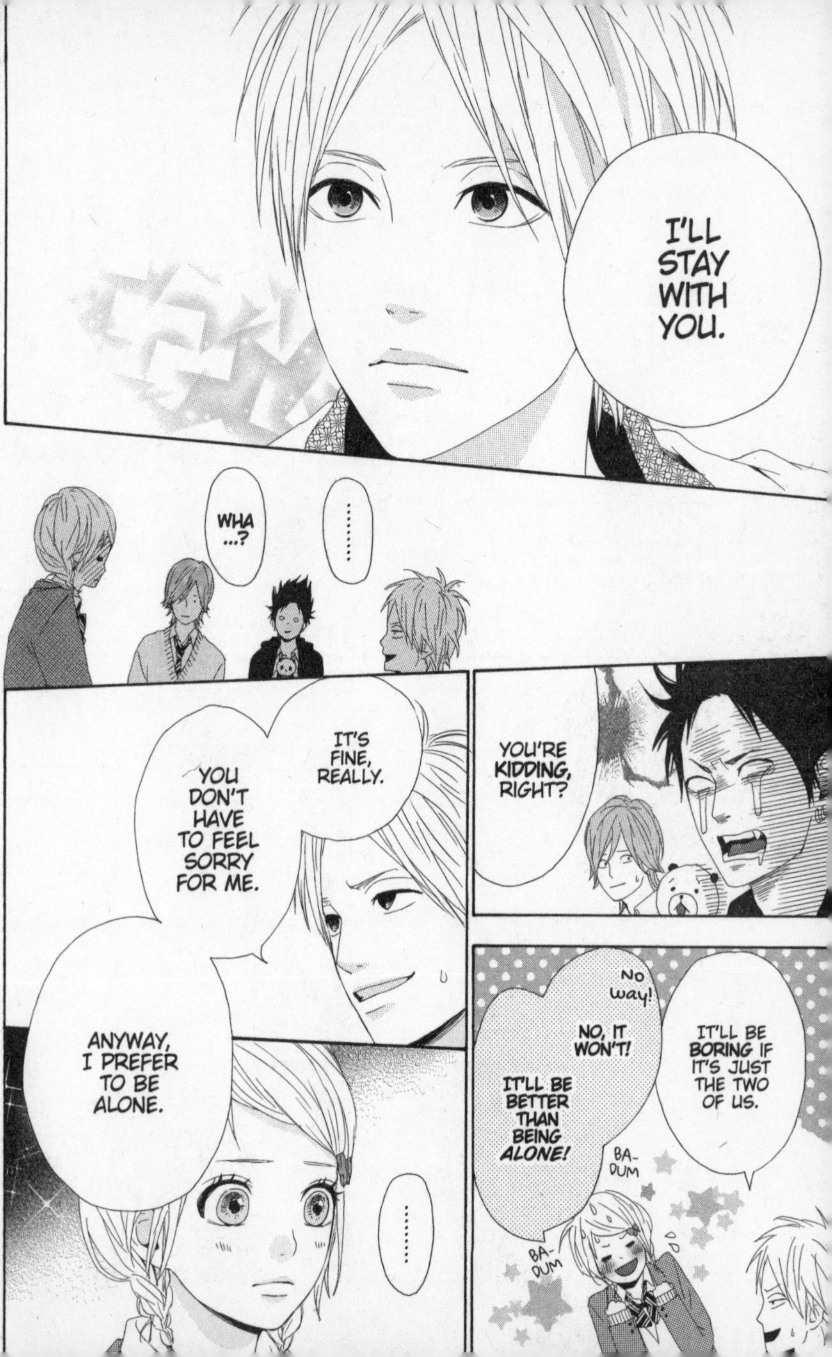

I'LL STAY WITH YOU.
......
WHA ...?
YOU'RE KIDDING, RIGHT?
IT'S FINE, REALLY.
YOU DON'T HAVE TO FEEL SORRY FOR ME.
ANYWAY, I PREFER TO BE ALONE.
......
IT'LL BE BORING IF IT'S JUST THE TWO OF US.
No way!
NO, IT WON'T!
IT'LL BE BETTER THAN BEING ALONE!
BA-DUM
BA-DUM

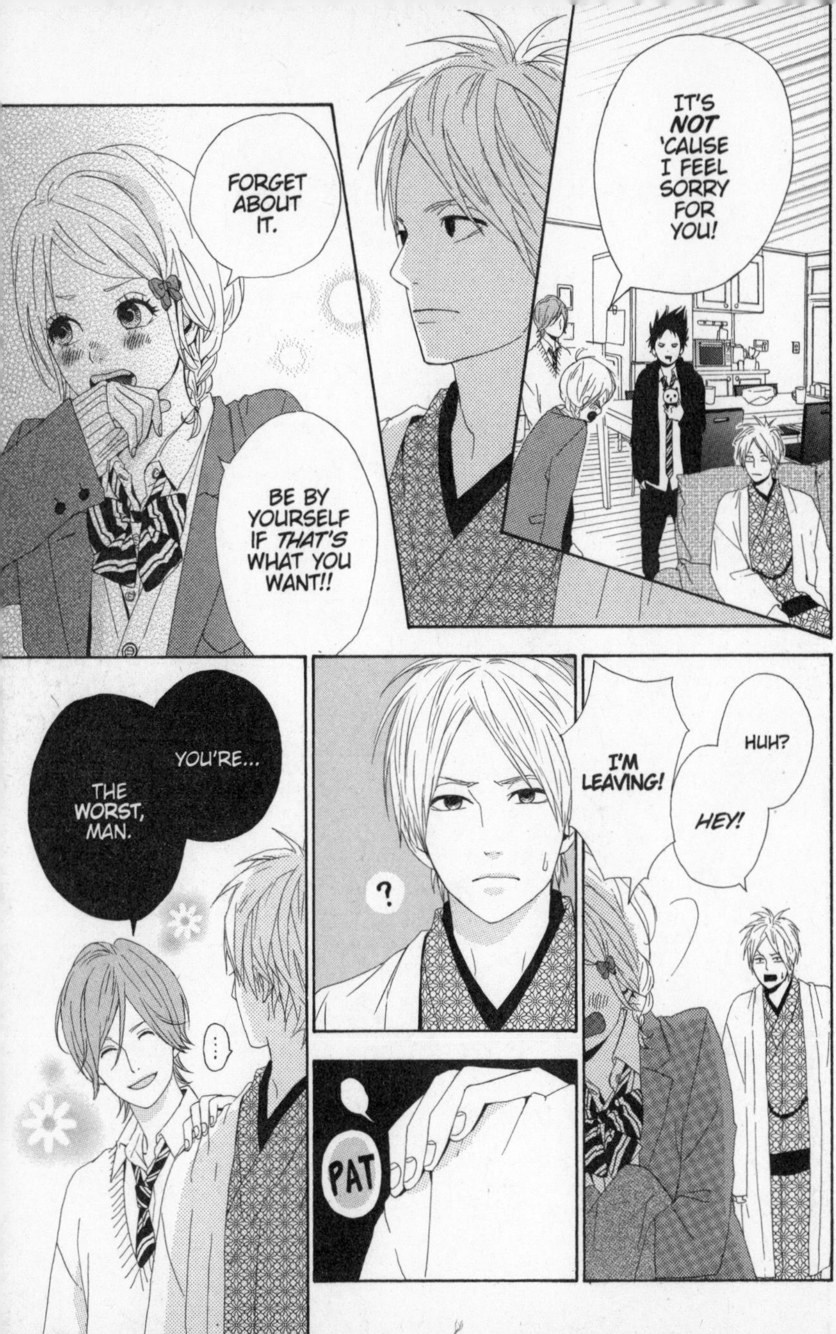
IT'S NOT 'CAUSE I FEEL SORRY FOR YOU!
FORGET ABOUT IT.
BE BY YOURSELF IF THAT'S WHAT YOU WANT!!
I'M LEAVING!
HUH? HEY!
?
PAT
YOU'RE... THE WORST, MAN.
...

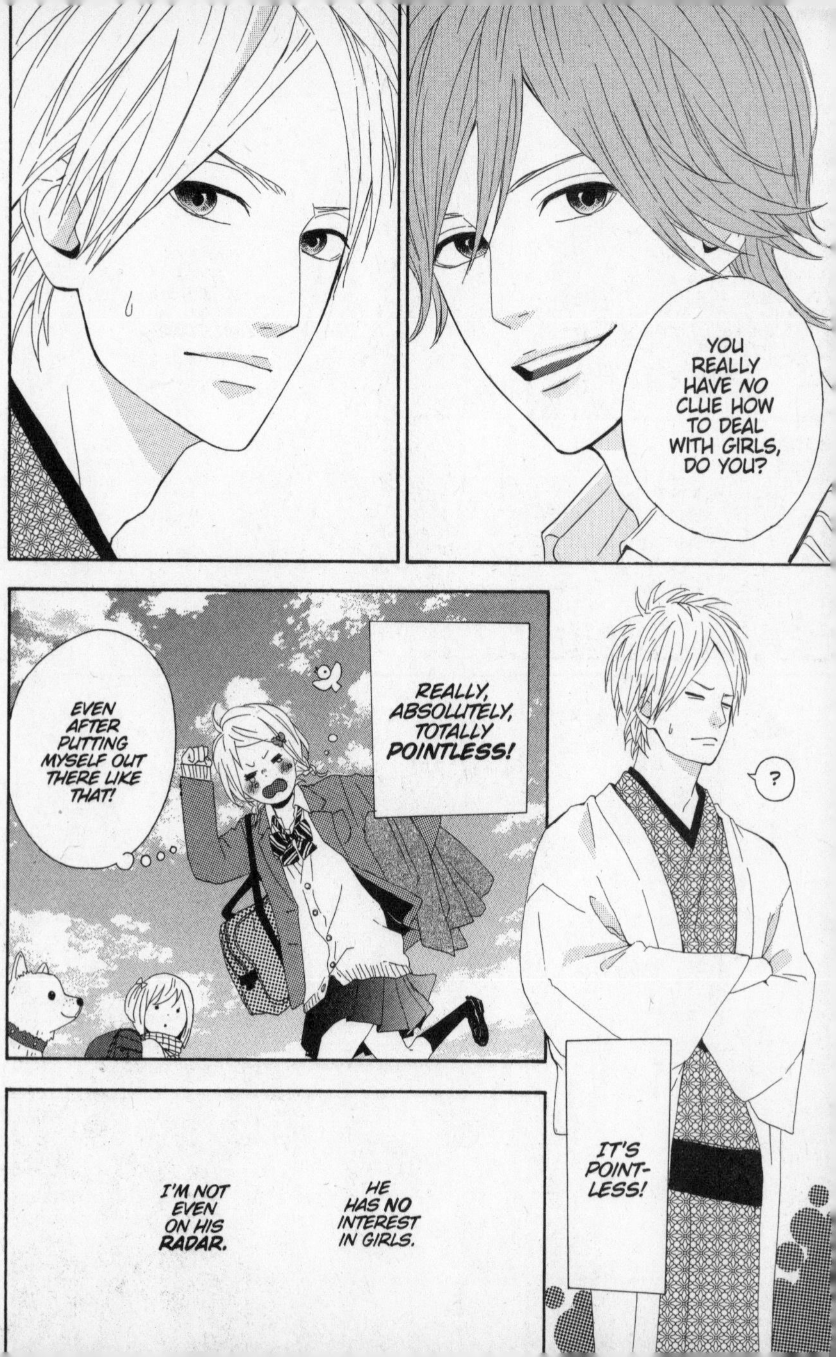
YOU REALLY HAVE NO CLUE HOW TO DEAL WITH GIRLS, DO YOU?
?
IT'S POINT-LESS!
REALLY, ABSOLUTELY, TOTALLY POINTLESS!
EVEN AFTER PUTTING MYSELF OUT THERE LIKE THAT!
HE HAS NO INTEREST IN GIRLS.
I'M NOT EVEN ON HIS RADAR.

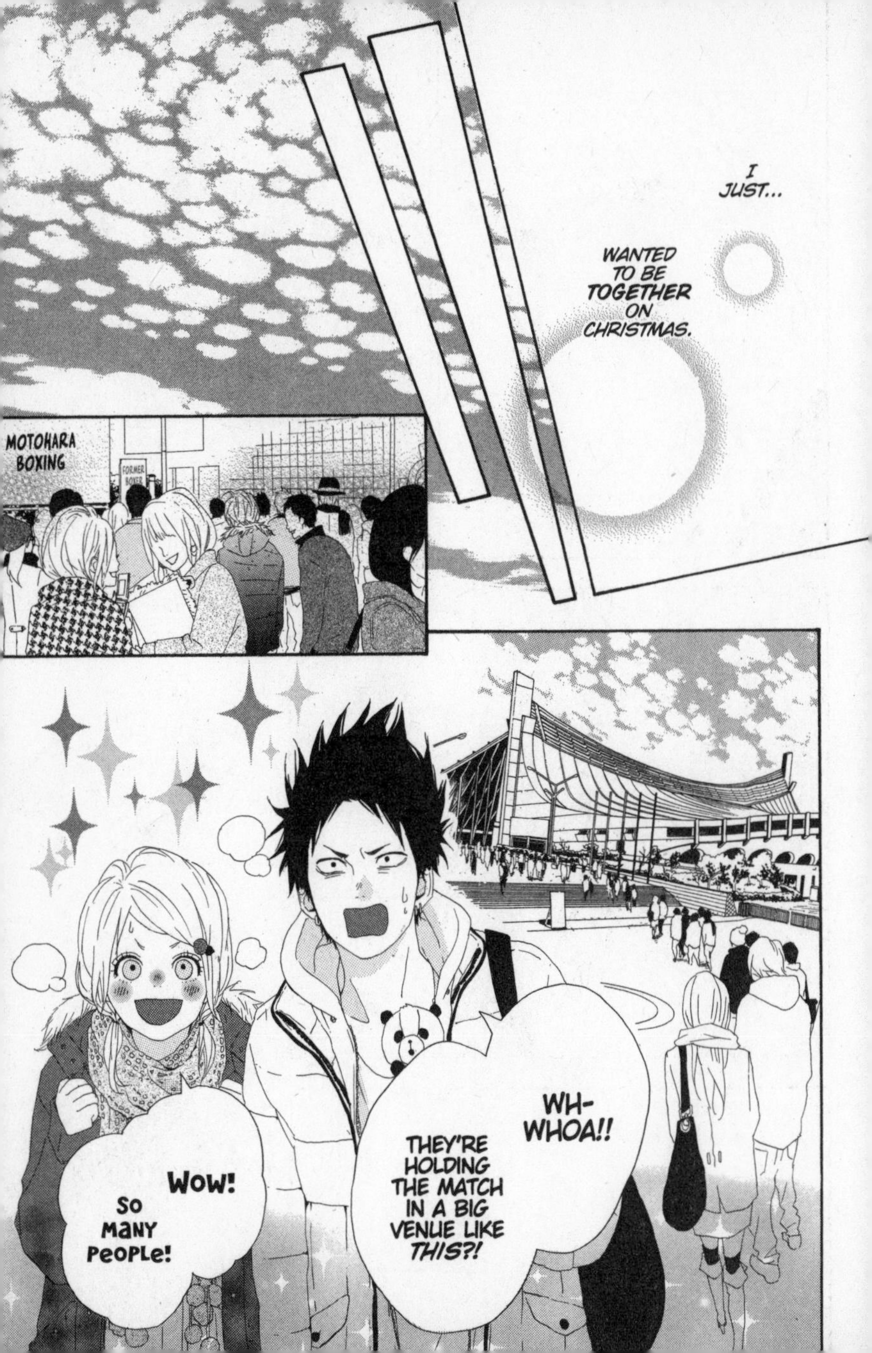
I JUST...
WANTED TO BE TOGETHER ON CHRISTMAS.
MOTOHARA BOXING
FORMER BOXER
WH-WHOA!!
THEY'RE HOLDING THE MATCH IN A BIG VENUE LIKE *THIS?!*
WOW!
SO MANY PEOPLE!

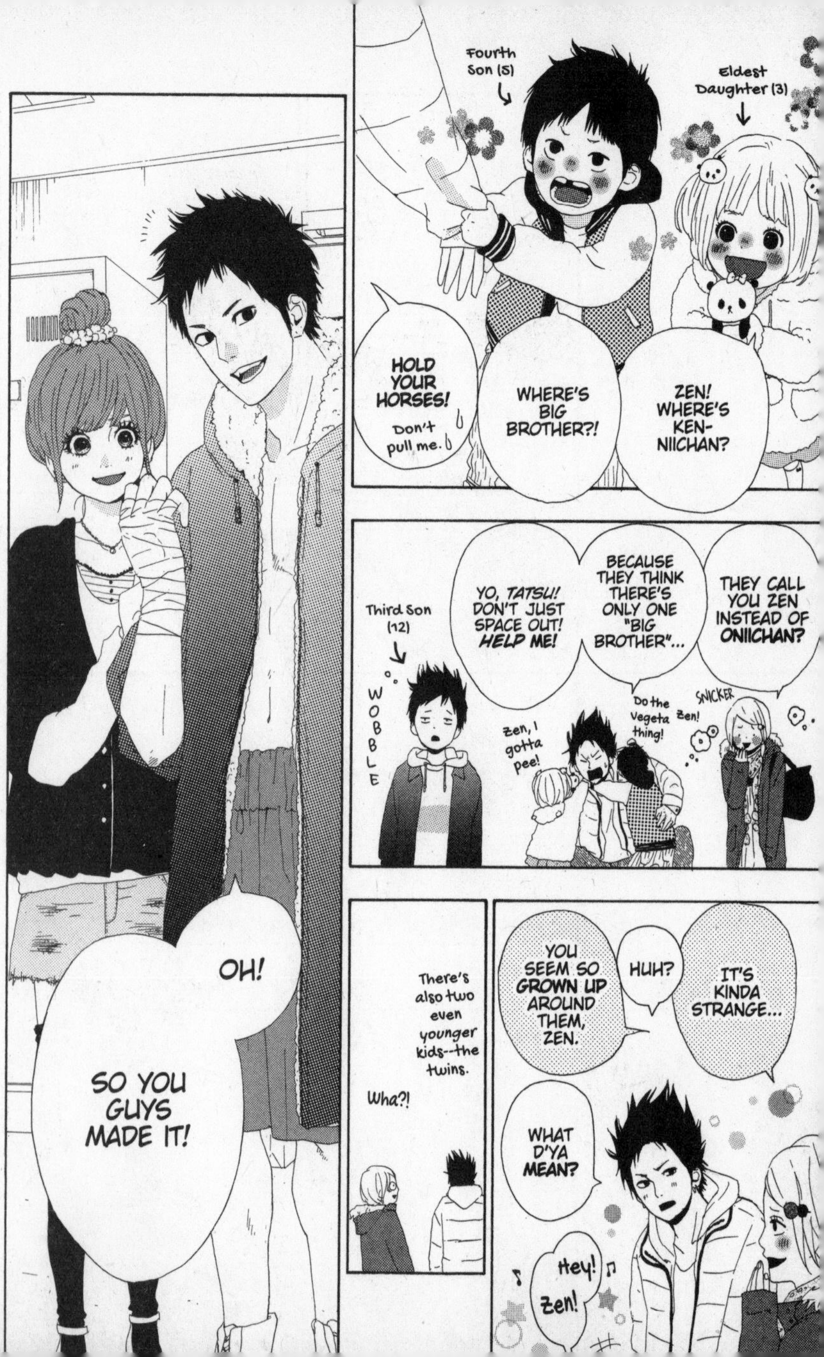
Eldest Daughter (3)
Fourth Son (5)
ZEN! WHERE'S KEN-NIICHAN?
WHERE'S BIG BROTHER?!
HOLD YOUR HORSES!
Don't pull me.
THEY CALL YOU ZEN INSTEAD OF ONIICHAN?
BECAUSE THEY THINK THERE'S ONLY ONE "BIG BROTHER"...
YO, TATSU! DON'T JUST SPACE OUT! HELP ME!
SNICKER
Zen!
Do the Vegeta thing!
Zen, I gotta pee!
Third Son (12)
WOBBLE
IT'S KINDA STRANGE...
HUH?
YOU SEEM SO GROWN UP AROUND THEM, ZEN.
WHAT D'YA MEAN?
Hey! Zen!
There's also two even younger kids--the twins.
Wha?!
OH!
SO YOU GUYS MADE IT!

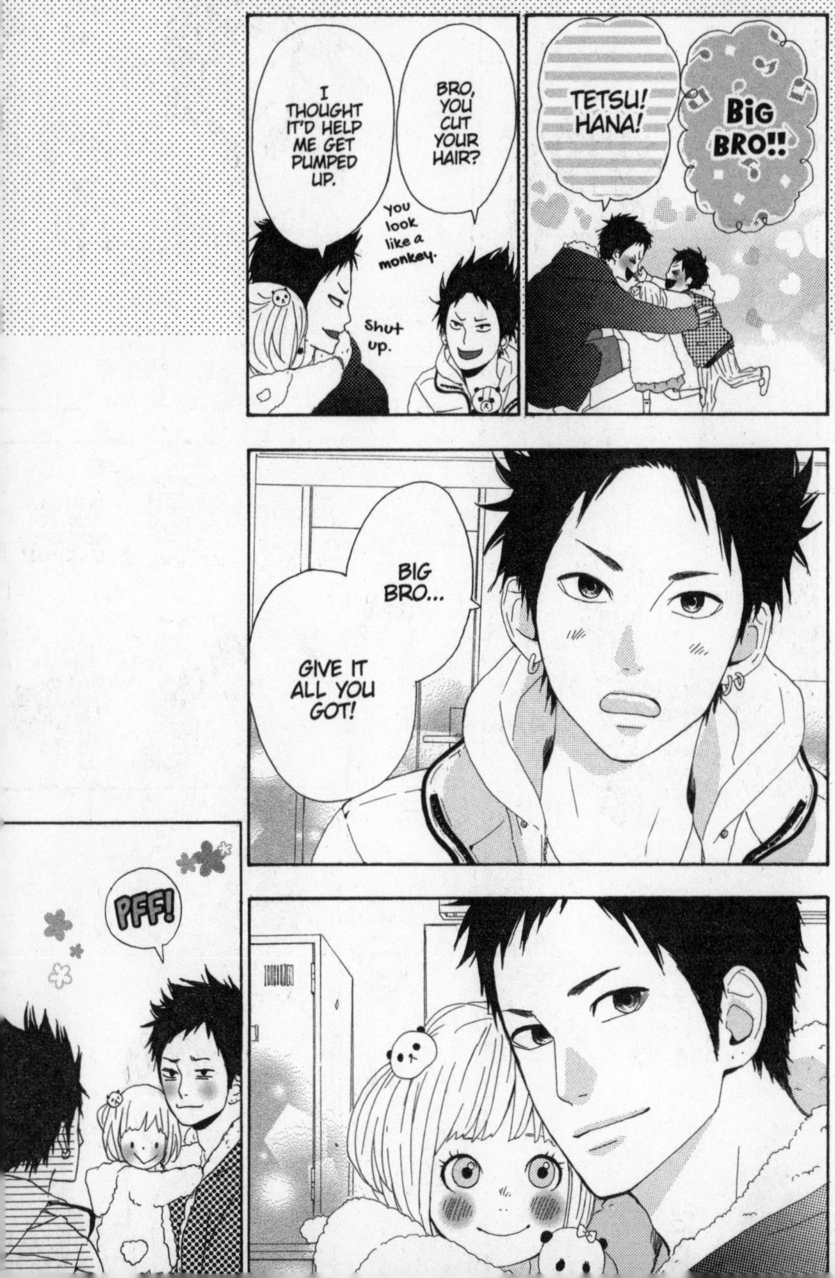
Big BRO!!
TETSU! HANA!
BRO, YOU CUT YOUR HAIR?
I THOUGHT IT'D HELP ME GET PUMPED UP.
You look like a monkey.
Shut up.
BIG BRO...
GIVE IT ALL YOU GOT!
PFF!

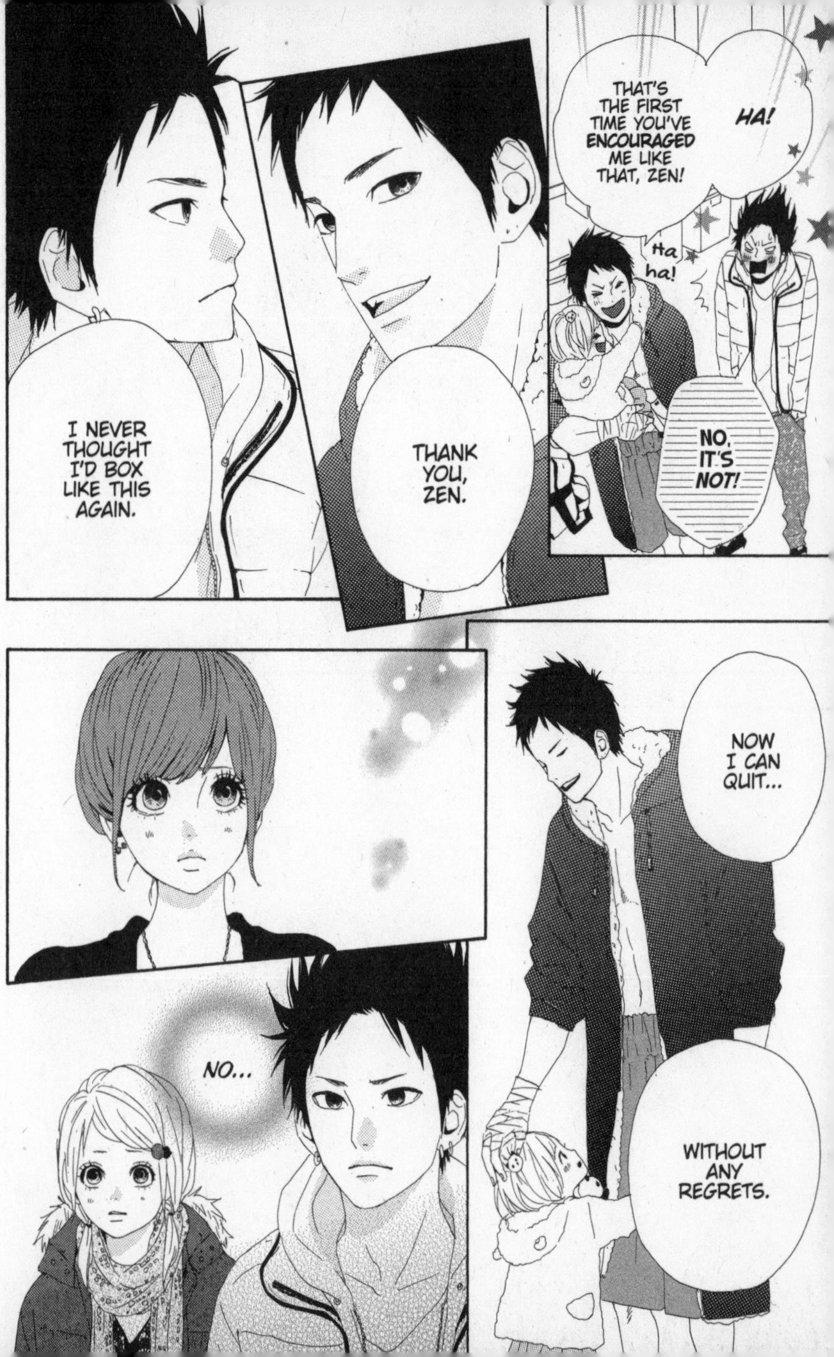
HA!
THAT'S THE FIRST TIME YOU'VE ENCOURAGED ME LIKE THAT, ZEN!
Ha ha!
NO, IT'S NOT!
THANK YOU, ZEN.
I NEVER THOUGHT I'D BOX LIKE THIS AGAIN.
NOW I CAN QUIT...
WITHOUT ANY REGRETS.
NO...

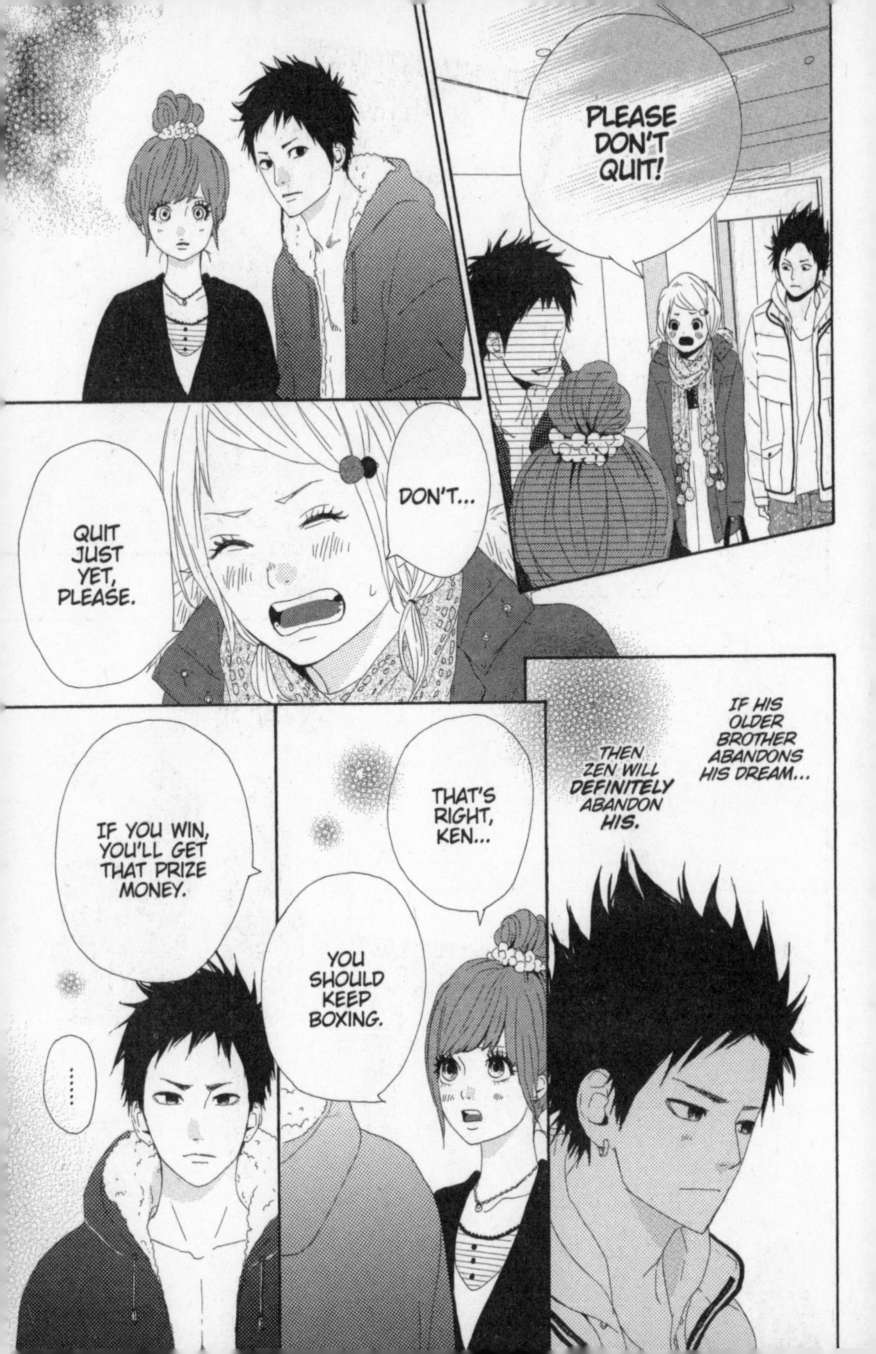
PLEASE DON'T QUIT!
DON'T...
QUIT JUST YET, PLEASE.
IF HIS OLDER BROTHER ABANDONS HIS DREAM...
THEN ZEN WILL DEFINITELY ABANDON HIS.
THAT'S RIGHT, KEN...
YOU SHOULD KEEP BOXING.
IF YOU WIN, YOU'LL GET THAT PRIZE MONEY.
......

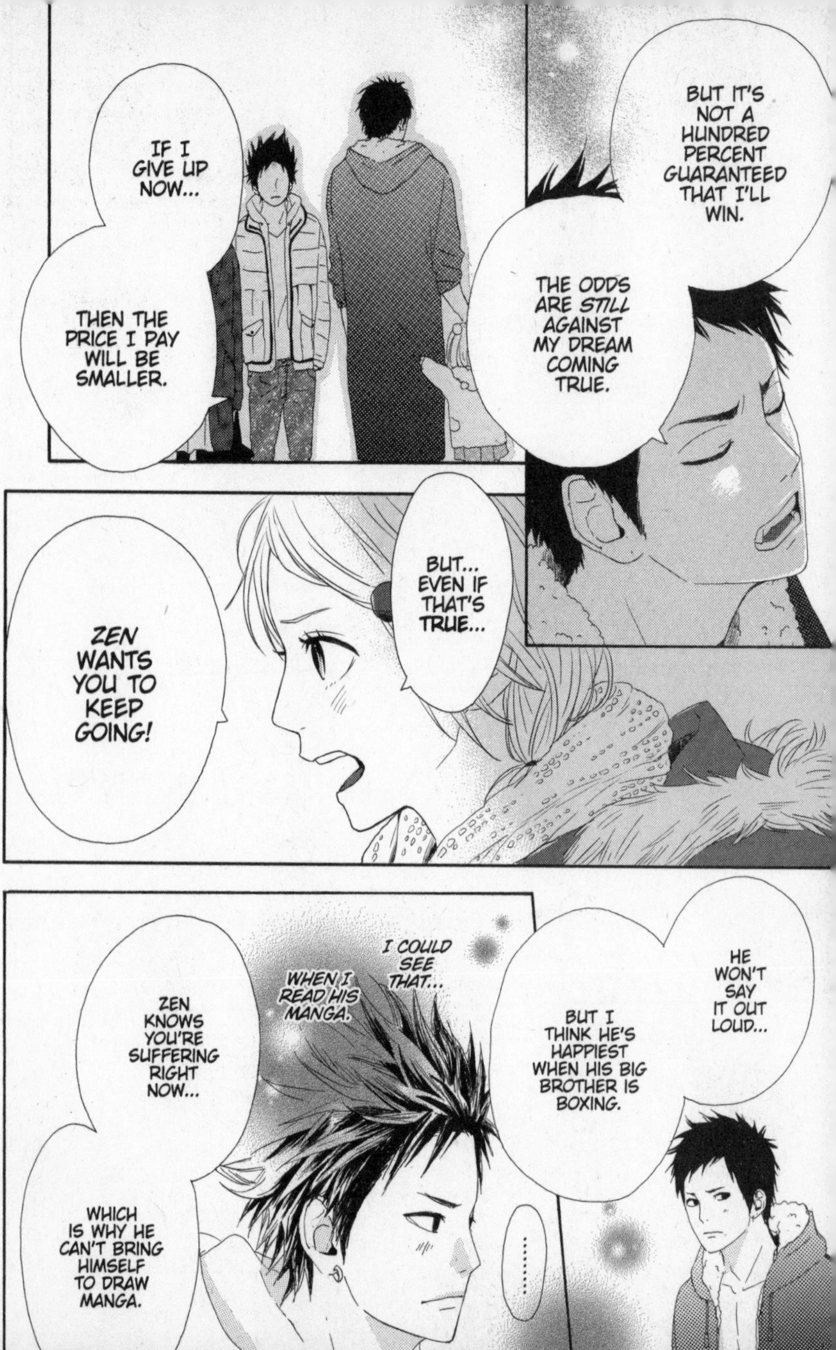
BUT IT'S NOT A HUNDRED PERCENT GUARANTEED THAT I'LL WIN.
THE ODDS ARE *STILL* AGAINST MY DREAM COMING TRUE.
IF I GIVE UP NOW...
THEN THE PRICE I PAY WILL BE SMALLER.
BUT... EVEN IF THAT'S TRUE...
ZEN WANTS YOU TO KEEP GOING!
HE WON'T SAY IT OUT LOUD...
BUT I THINK HE'S HAPPIEST WHEN HIS BIG BROTHER IS BOXING.
I COULD SEE THAT...
WHEN I READ HIS MANGA.
ZEN KNOWS YOU'RE SUFFERING RIGHT NOW...
WHICH IS WHY HE CAN'T BRING HIMSELF TO DRAW MANGA.
......

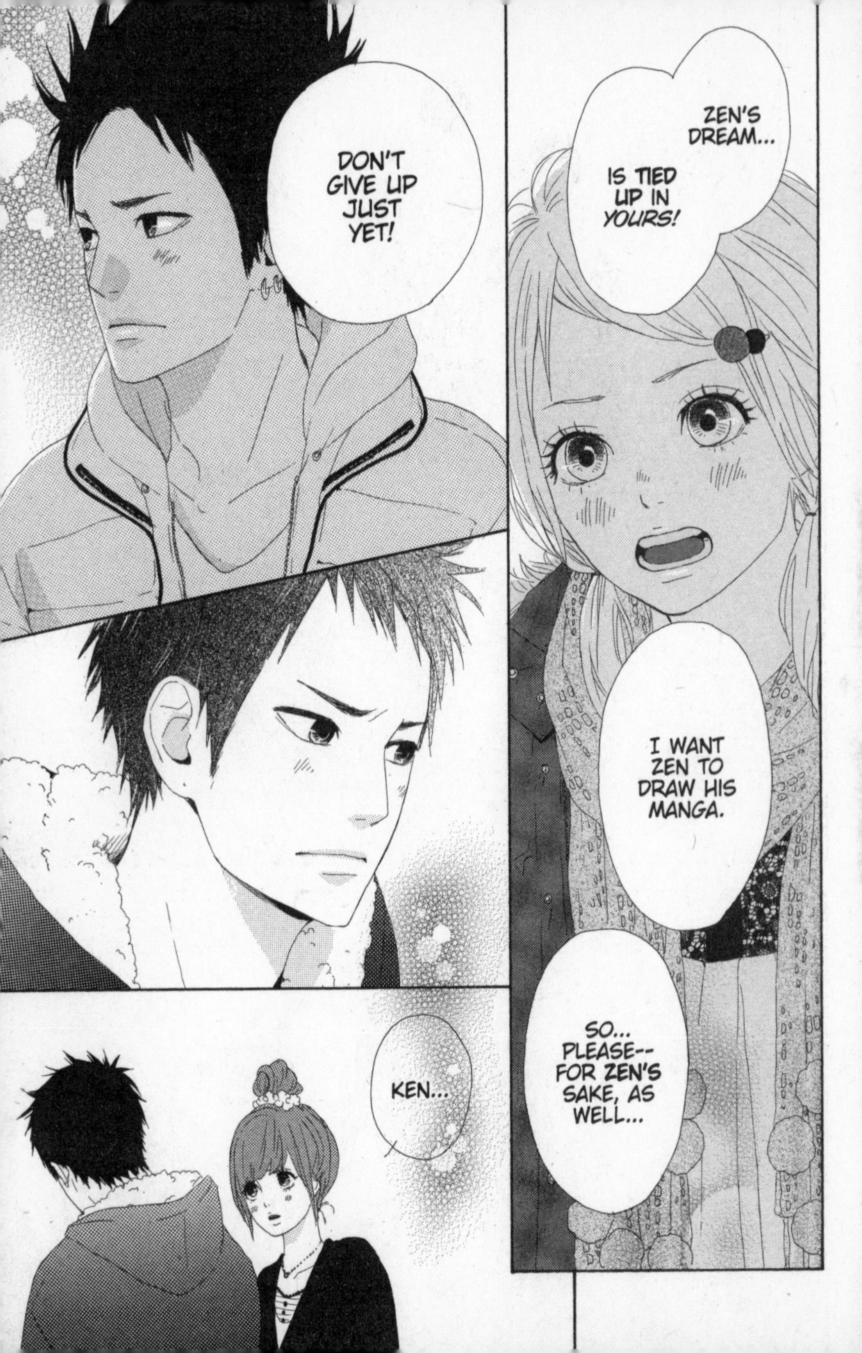
ZEN'S DREAM...
IS TIED UP IN *YOURS!*
I WANT ZEN TO DRAW HIS MANGA.
SO... PLEASE-- FOR ZEN'S SAKE, AS WELL...
DON'T GIVE UP JUST YET!
KEN...

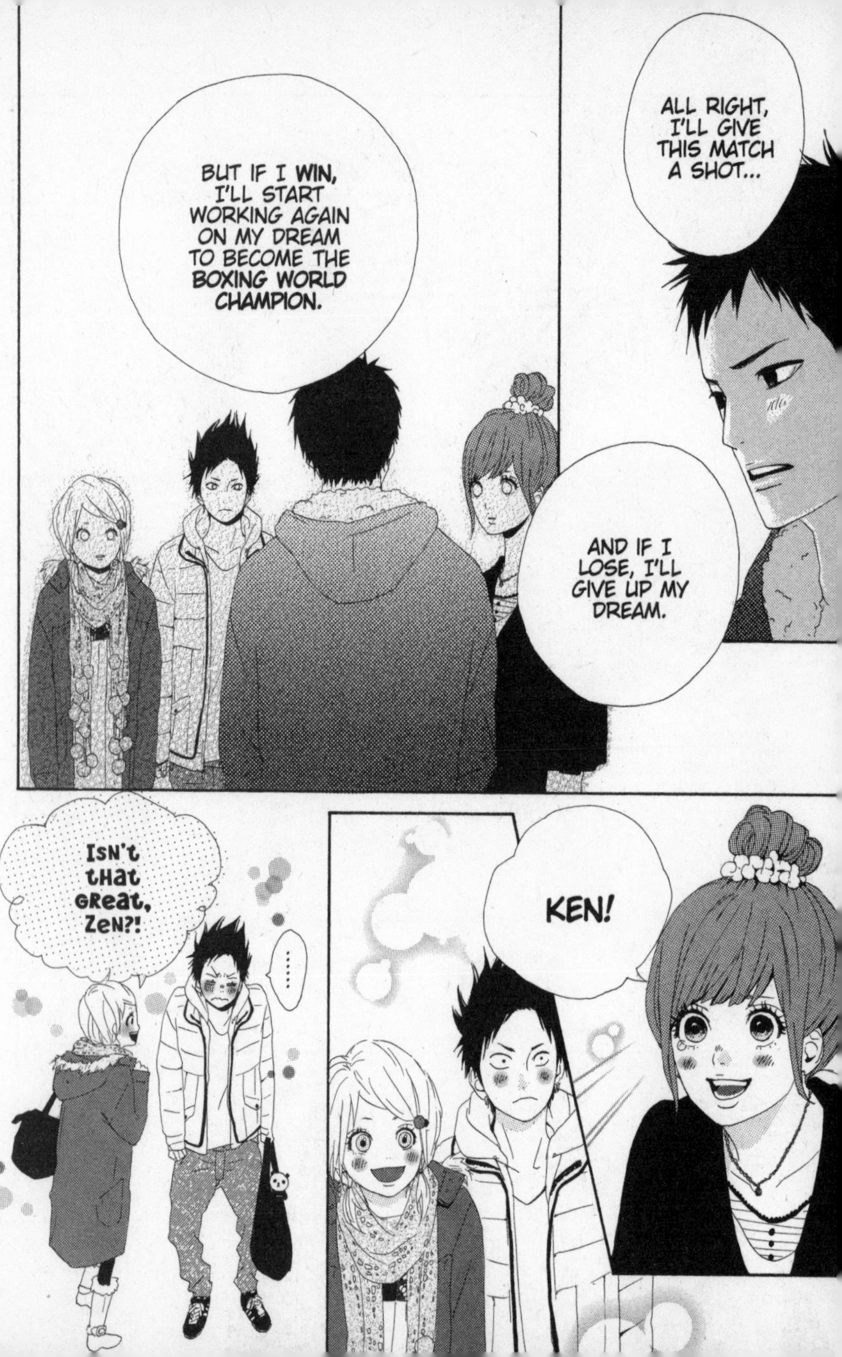
ALL RIGHT, I'LL GIVE THIS MATCH A SHOT...
AND IF I LOSE, I'LL GIVE UP MY DREAM.
BUT IF I WIN, I'LL START WORKING AGAIN ON MY DREAM TO BECOME THE BOXING WORLD CHAMPION.
KEN!
Isn't that great, Zen?!
......

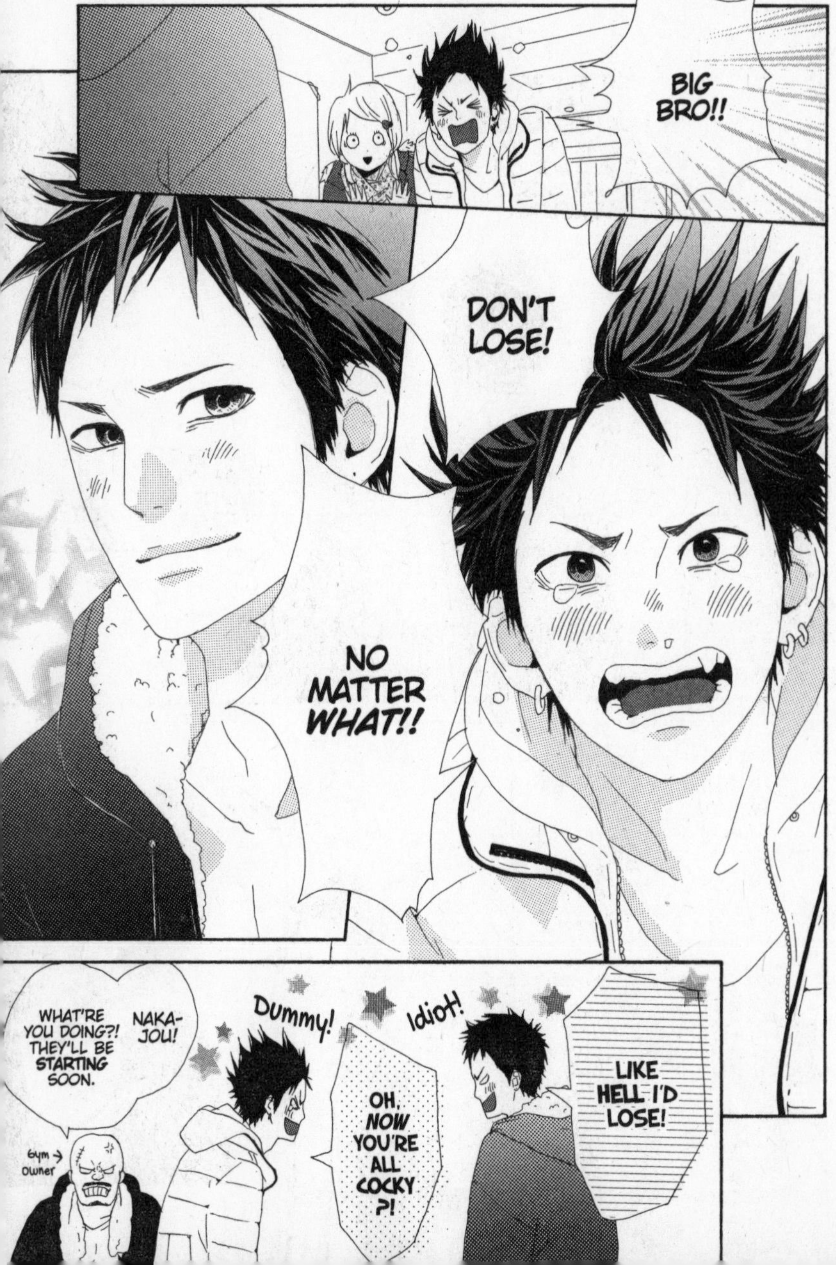
BIG BRO!!
DON'T LOSE!
NO MATTER WHAT!!
LIKE HELL I'D LOSE!
Idiot!
OH, NOW YOU'RE ALL COCKY?!
Dummy!
NAKA-JOU!
WHAT'RE YOU DOING?! THEY'LL BE STARTING SOON.
Gym → owner

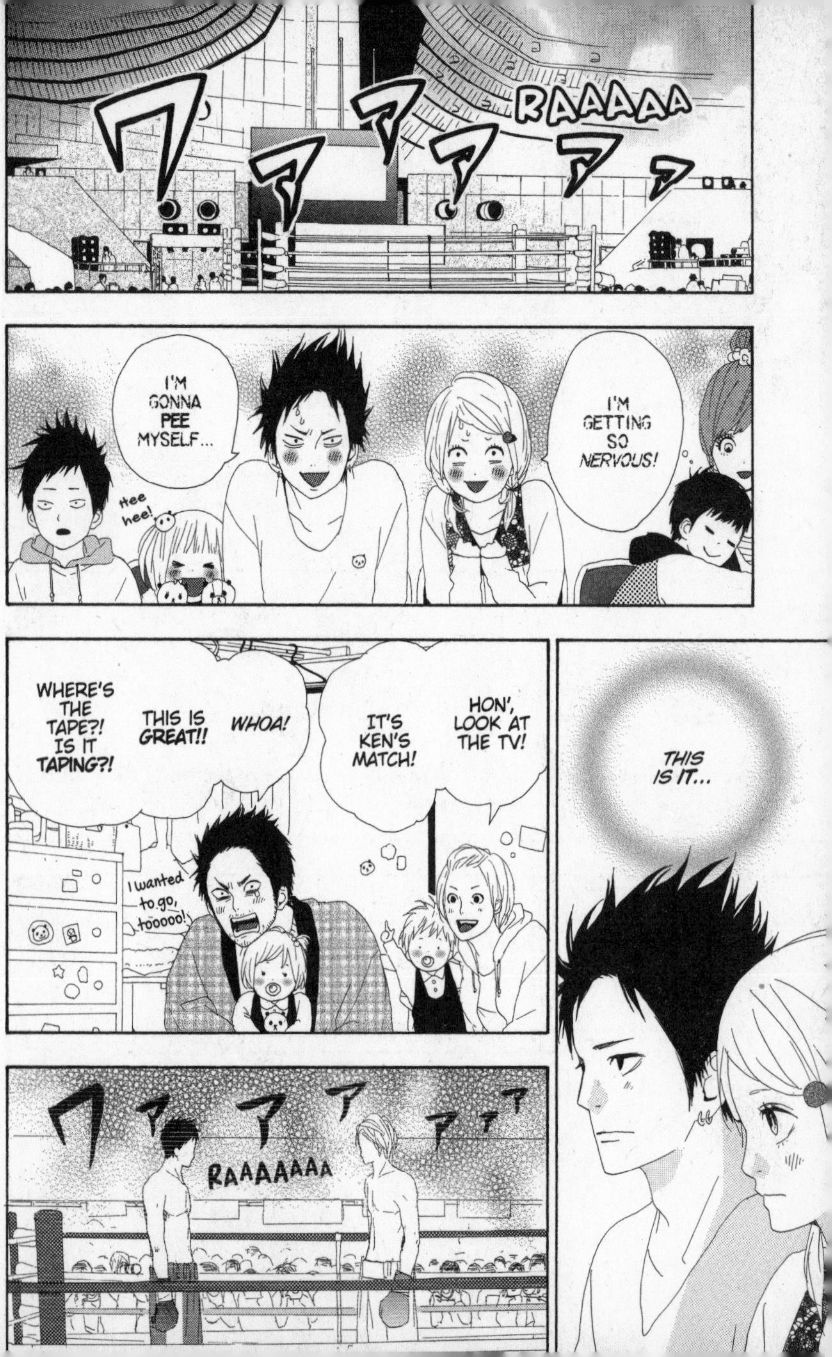
ワァァァァァ
RAAAAA
I'M GETTING SO NERVOUS!
I'M GONNA PEE MYSELF...
Hee hee!
THIS IS IT...
HON', LOOK AT THE TV!
IT'S KEN'S MATCH!
WHOA!
THIS IS GREAT!!
WHERE'S THE TAPE?! IS IT TAPING?!
I wanted to go, tooooo!
ワァァァァァ
RAAAAAAA

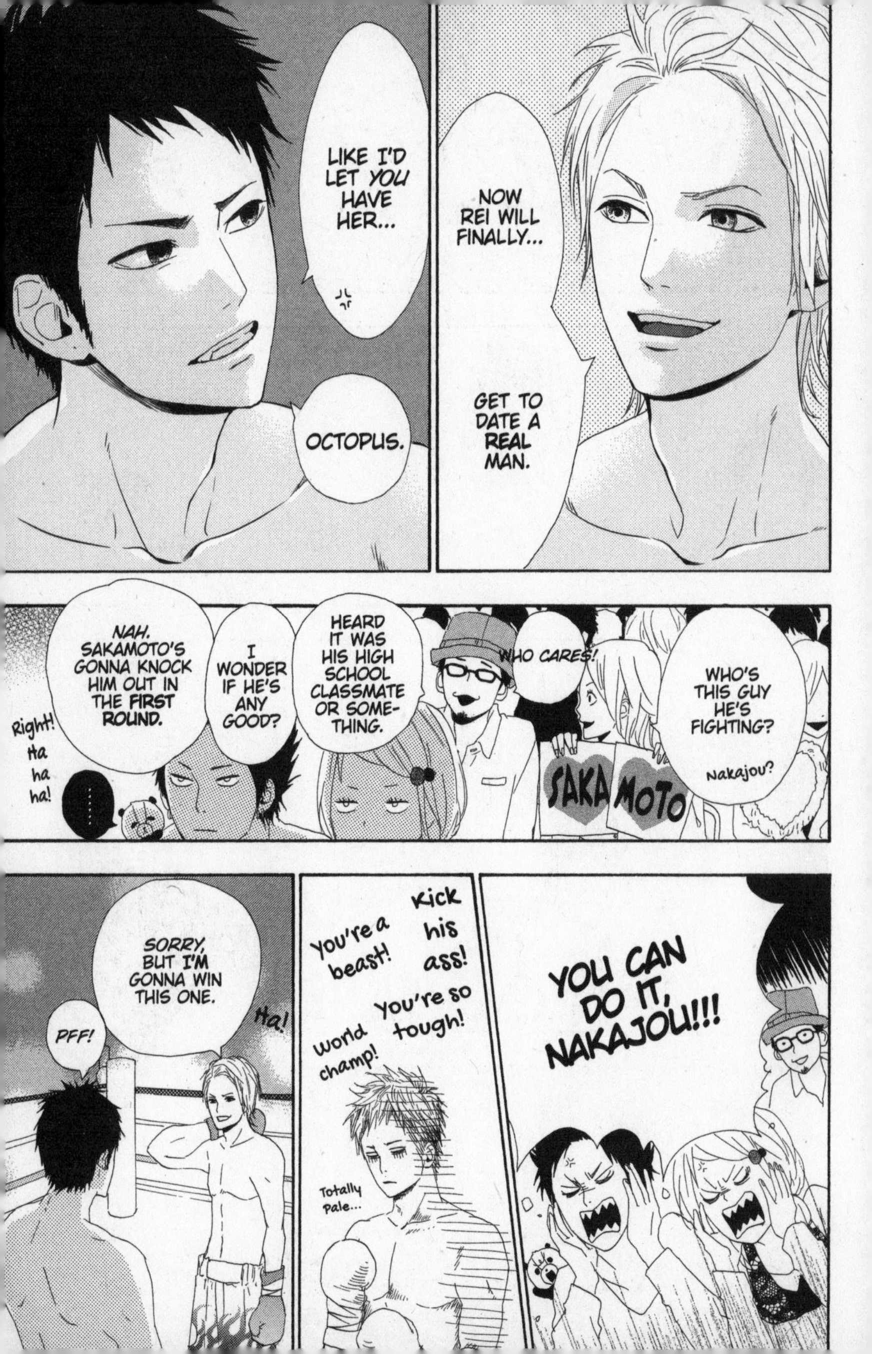
NOW REI WILL FINALLY...
GET TO DATE A REAL MAN.
LIKE I'D LET YOU HAVE HER...
OCTOPUS.
WHO'S THIS GUY HE'S FIGHTING?
Nakajou?
SAKAMOTO
WHO CARES!
HEARD IT WAS HIS HIGH SCHOOL CLASSMATE OR SOME-THING.
I WONDER IF HE'S ANY GOOD?
NAH. SAKAMOTO'S GONNA KNOCK HIM OUT IN THE FIRST ROUND.
Right! Ha ha ha!
......
YOU CAN DO IT, NAKAJOU!!!
Kick his ass!
You're a beast!
You're so tough!
World champ!
Totally pale...
SORRY, BUT I'M GONNA WIN THIS ONE.
Ha!
PFF!

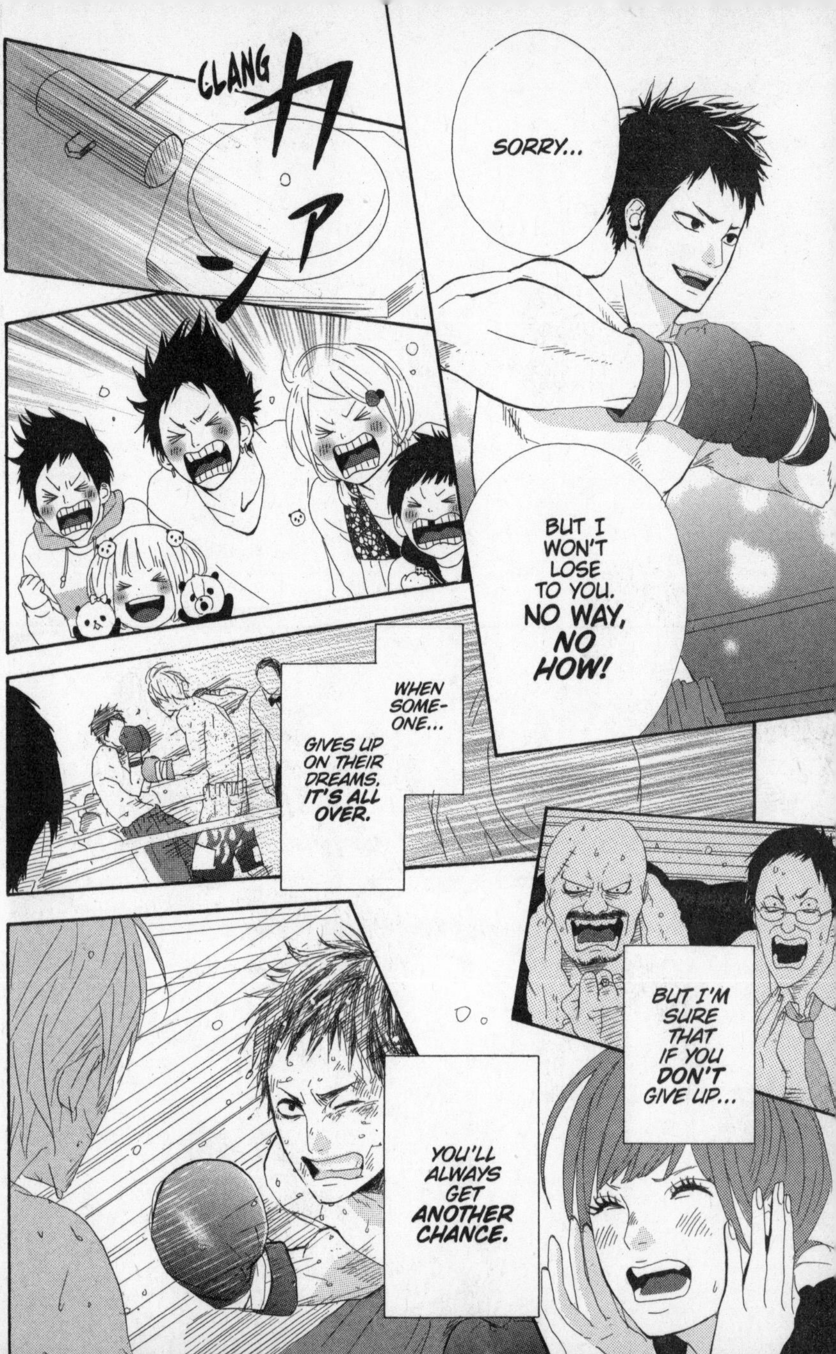
SORRY...
BUT I WON'T LOSE TO YOU. NO WAY, NO HOW!
CLANG
WHEN SOME-ONE...
GIVES UP ON THEIR DREAMS, IT'S ALL OVER.
BUT I'M SURE THAT IF YOU DON'T GIVE UP...
YOU'LL ALWAYS GET ANOTHER CHANCE.

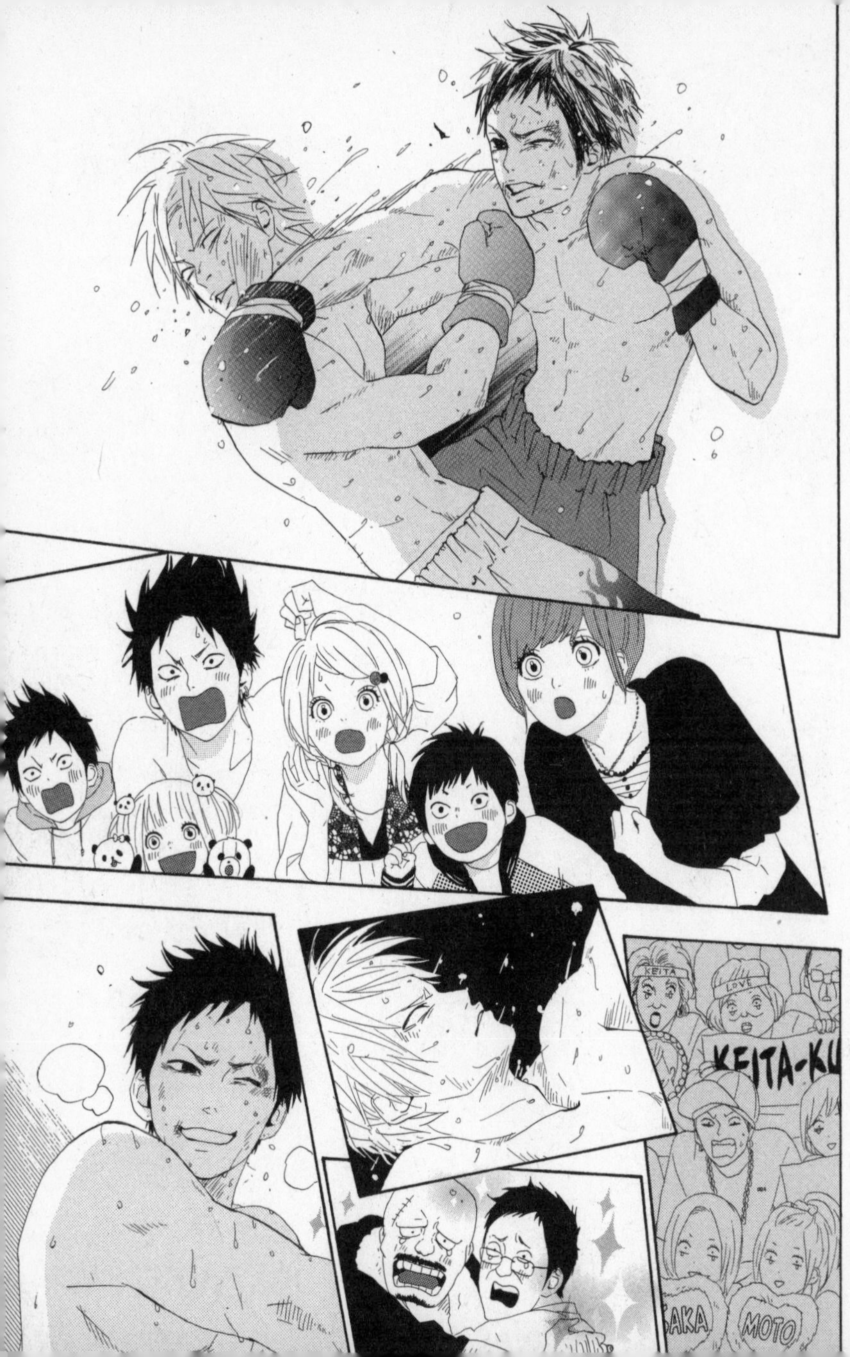
KEITA
LOVE
KEITA-KU
SAKA
MOTO

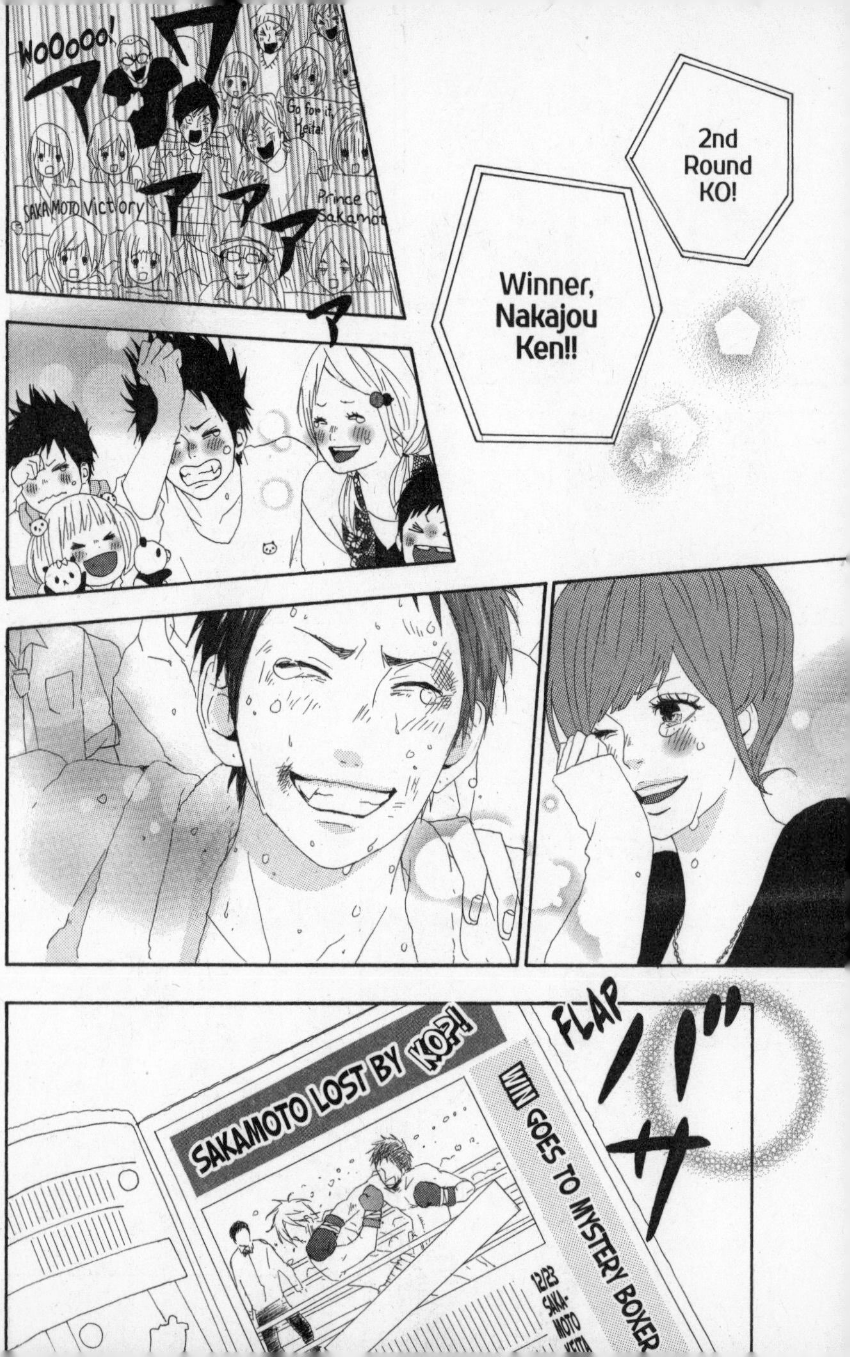
2nd Round KO!
Winner, Nakajou Ken!!
WOOOOO!
Go for it, Keita!
SAKAMOTO Victory
Prince Sakamoto
FLAP
SAKAMOTO LOST BY KO?!
WIN GOES TO MYSTERY BOXER
12/23 SAKA-MOTO

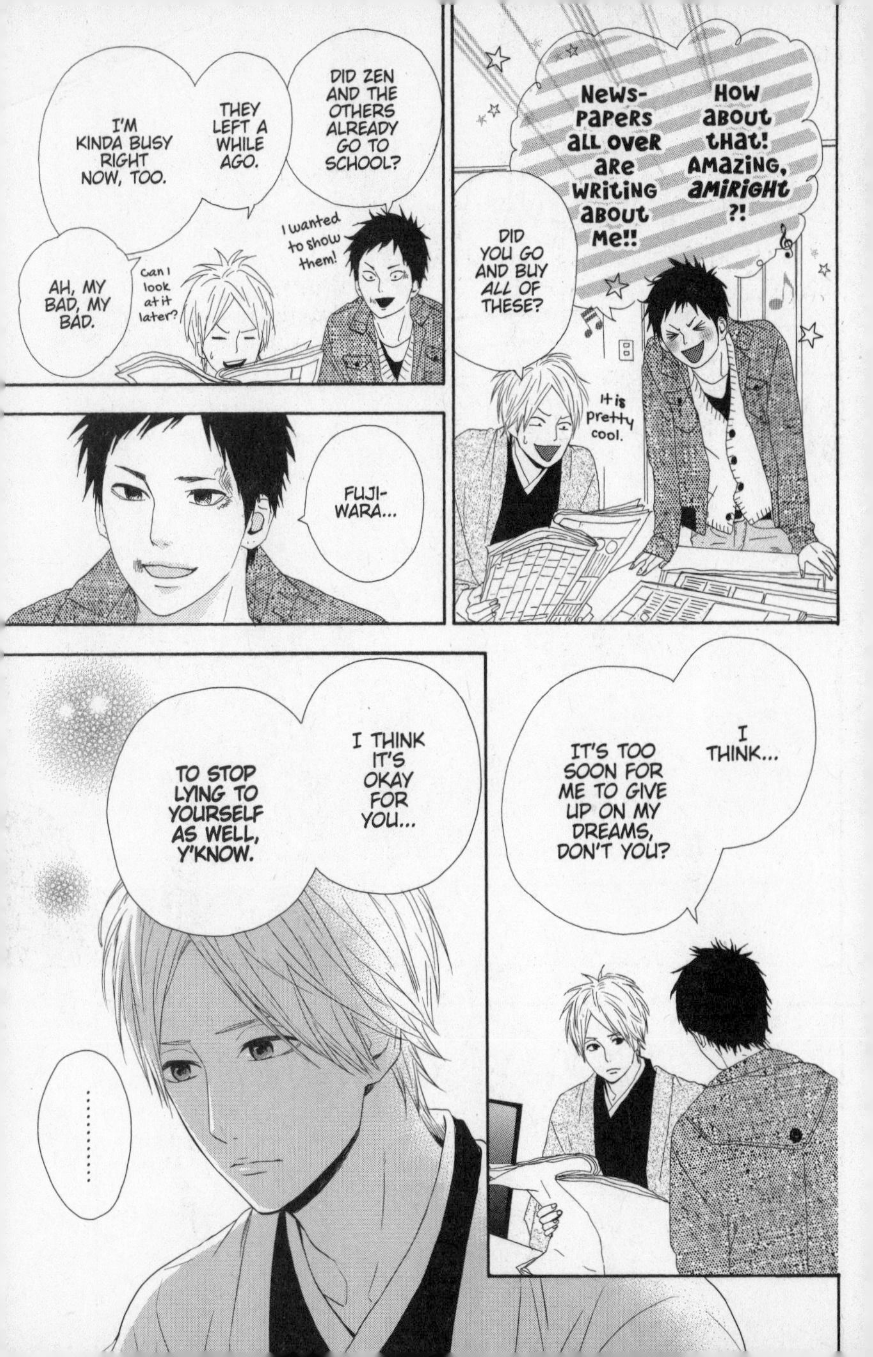
HOW ABOUT THAT! AMAZING, AMIRIGHT?!
NEWS-PAPERS ALL OVER ARE WRITING ABOUT ME!!
DID YOU GO AND BUY ALL OF THESE?
It is pretty cool.
DID ZEN AND THE OTHERS ALREADY GO TO SCHOOL?
THEY LEFT A WHILE AGO.
I'M KINDA BUSY RIGHT NOW, TOO.
I wanted to show them!
Can I look at it later?
AH, MY BAD, MY BAD.
FUJI-WARA...
I THINK...
IT'S TOO SOON FOR ME TO GIVE UP ON MY DREAMS, DON'T YOU?
I THINK IT'S OKAY FOR YOU...
TO STOP LYING TO YOURSELF AS WELL, Y'KNOW.
....

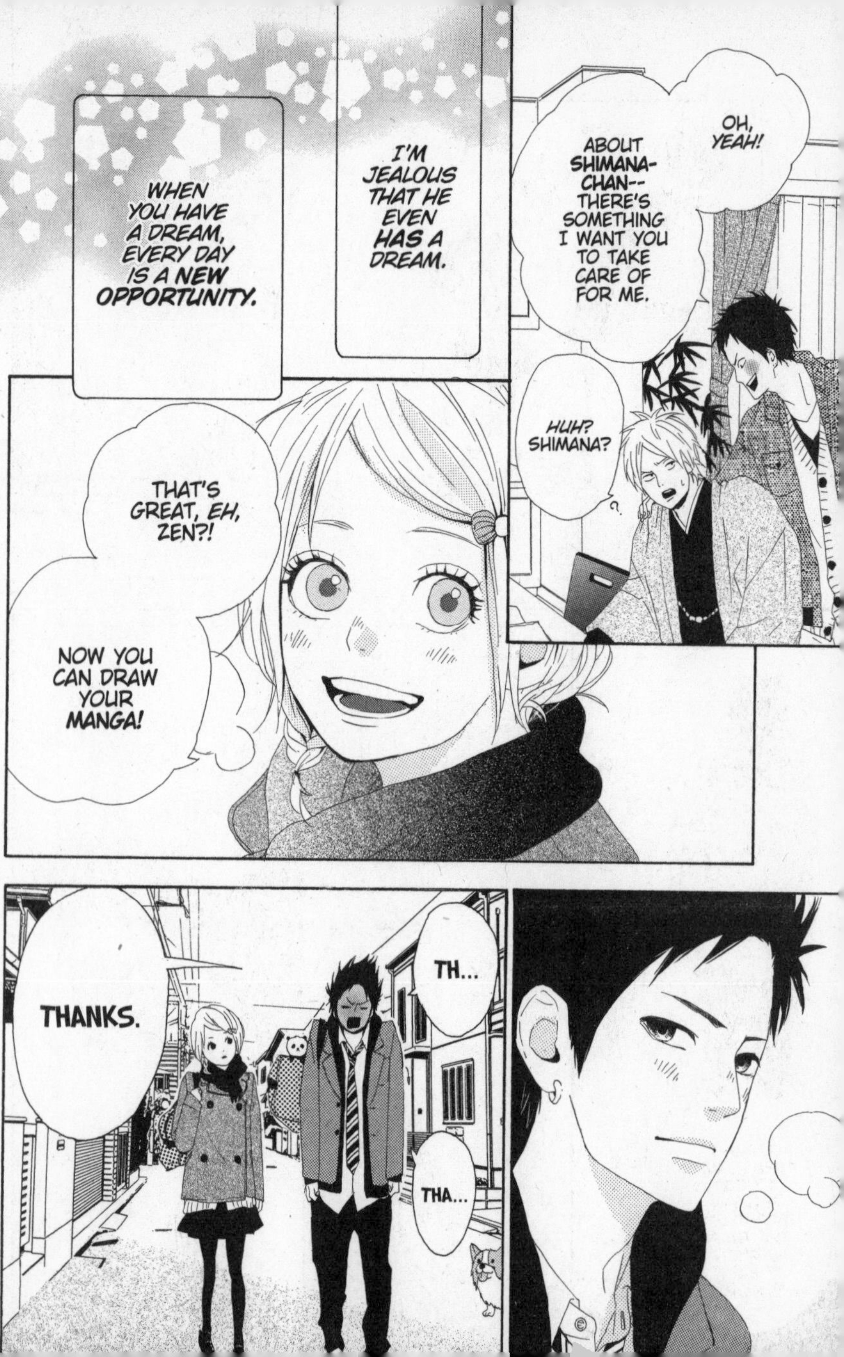
OH, YEAH!
ABOUT SHIMANA-CHAN-- THERE'S SOMETHING I WANT YOU TO TAKE CARE OF FOR ME.
HUH? SHIMANA?
I'M JEALOUS THAT HE EVEN HAS A DREAM.
WHEN YOU HAVE A DREAM, EVERY DAY IS A NEW OPPORTUNITY.
THAT'S GREAT, EH, ZEN?!
NOW YOU CAN DRAW YOUR MANGA!
TH...
THA...
THANKS.

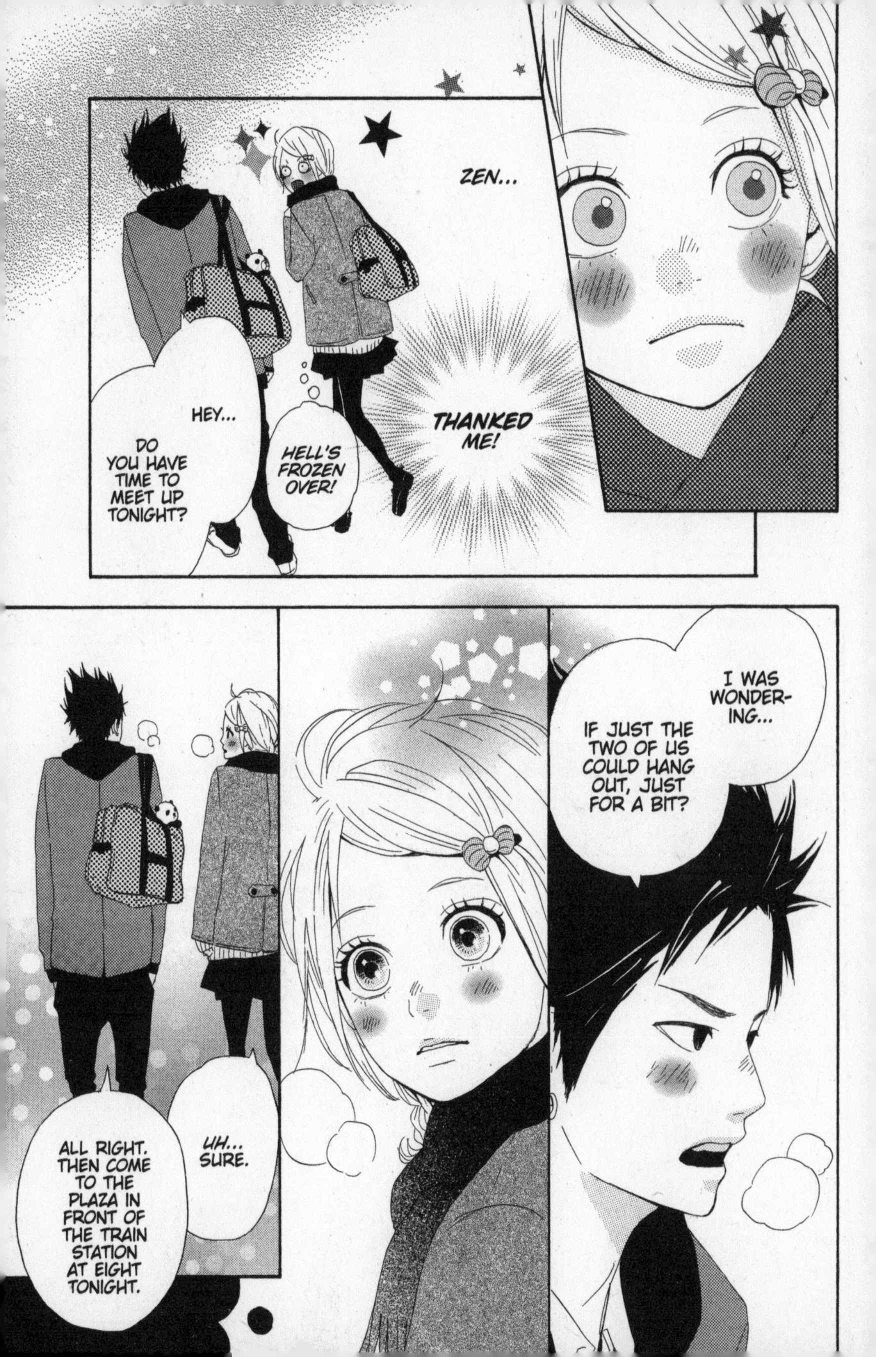
ZEN...
THANKED ME!
HELL'S FROZEN OVER!
HEY...
DO YOU HAVE TIME TO MEET UP TONIGHT?
I WAS WONDER-ING...
IF JUST THE TWO OF US COULD HANG OUT, JUST FOR A BIT?
UH... SURE.
ALL RIGHT. THEN COME TO THE PLAZA IN FRONT OF THE TRAIN STATION AT EIGHT TONIGHT.

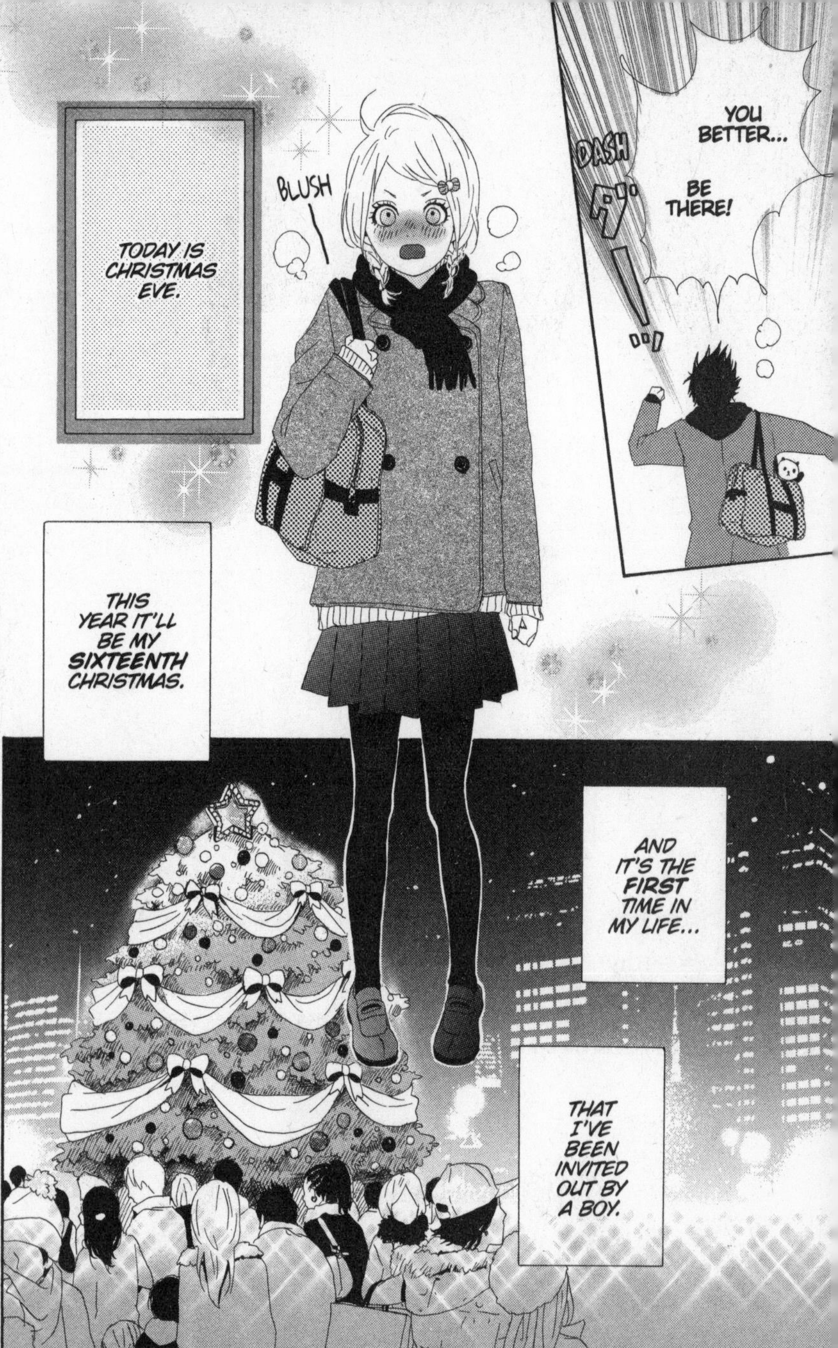
YOU BETTER...
BE THERE!
DASH
TODAY IS CHRISTMAS EVE.
BLUSH
THIS YEAR IT'LL BE MY SIXTEENTH CHRISTMAS.
AND IT'S THE FIRST TIME IN MY LIFE...
THAT I'VE BEEN INVITED OUT BY A BOY.

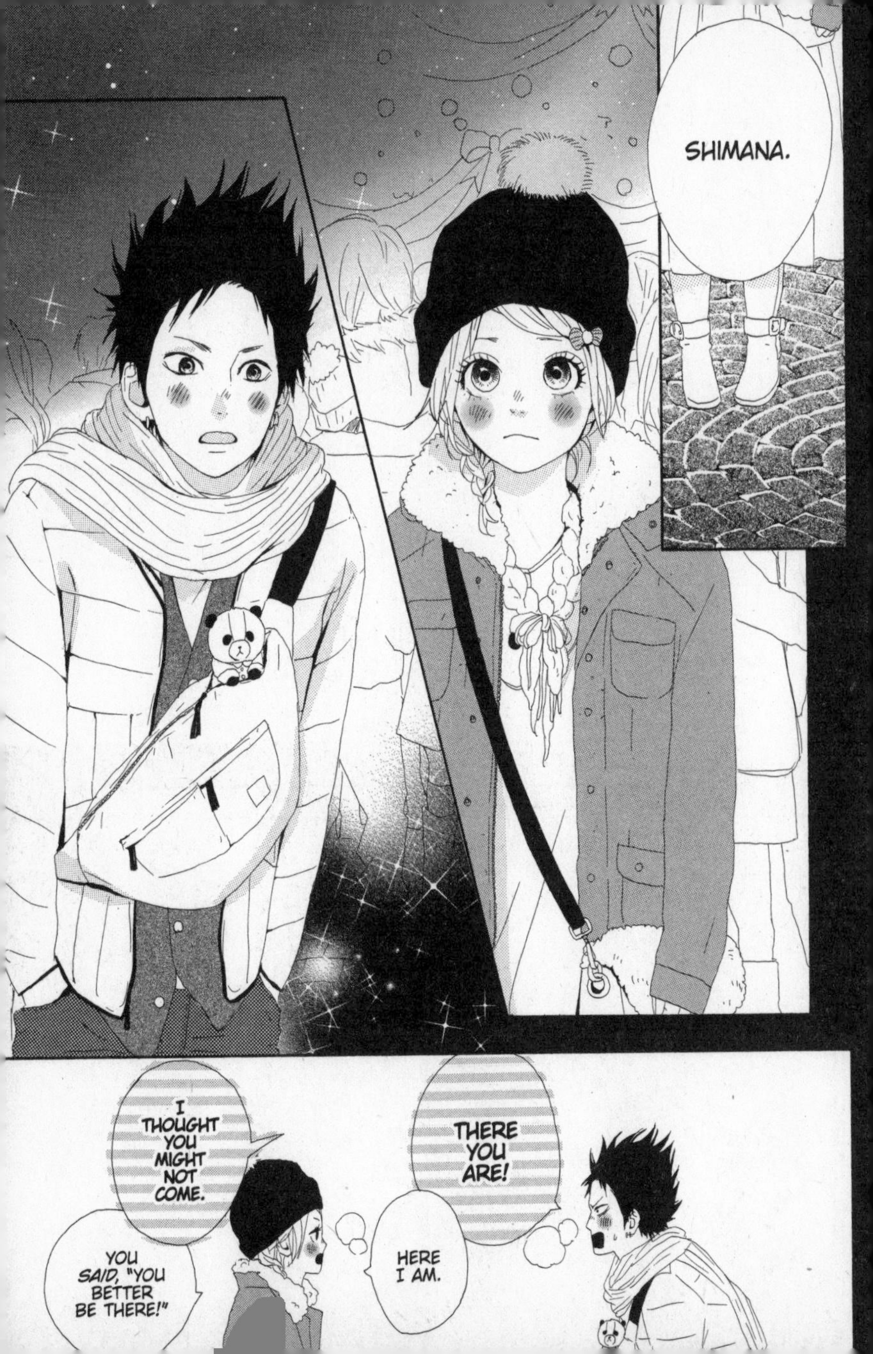
SHIMANA.
THERE YOU ARE!
I THOUGHT YOU MIGHT NOT COME.
HERE I AM.
YOU SAID, "YOU BETTER BE THERE!"

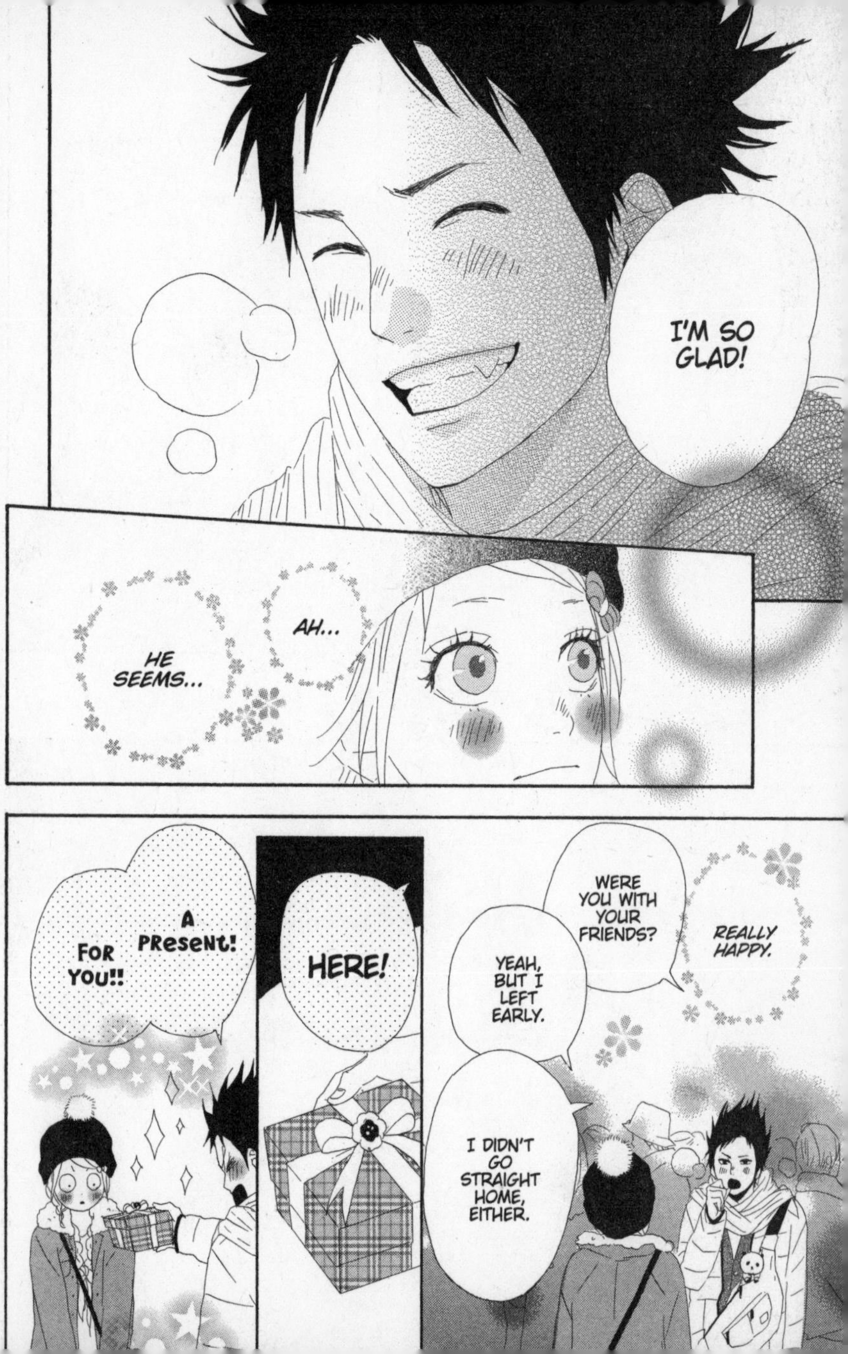
I'M SO GLAD!
AH...
HE SEEMS...
REALLY HAPPY.
WERE YOU WITH YOUR FRIENDS?
YEAH, BUT I LEFT EARLY.
I DIDN'T GO STRAIGHT HOME, EITHER.
HERE!
A PRESENT!
FOR YOU!!

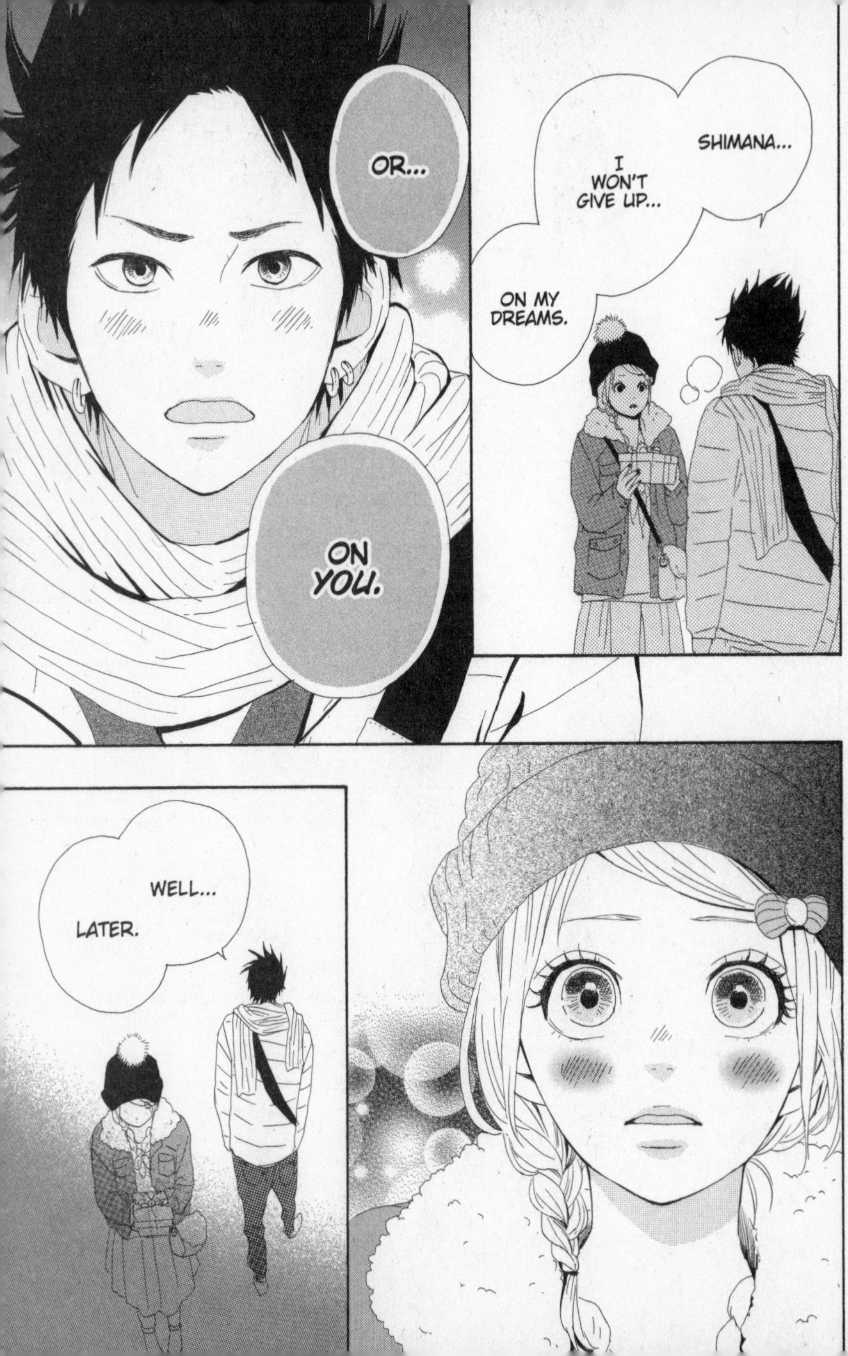
SHIMANA...
I WON'T GIVE UP...
ON MY DREAMS.
OR...
ON YOU.
WELL...
LATER.

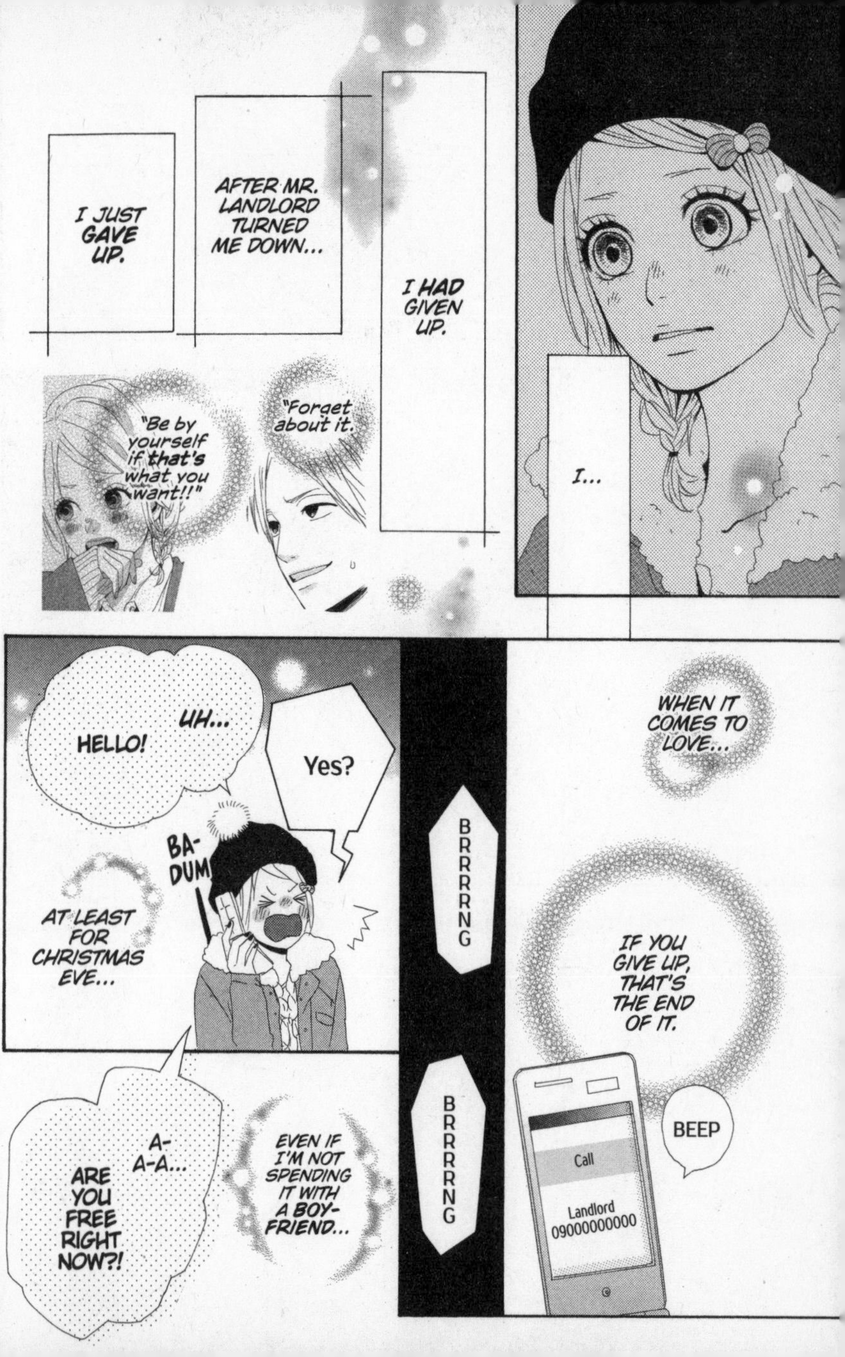
I...
I HAD GIVEN UP.
AFTER MR. LANDLORD TURNED ME DOWN...
I JUST GAVE UP.
"Forget about it.
"Be by yourself if that's what you want!!"
WHEN IT COMES TO LOVE...
IF YOU GIVE UP, THAT'S THE END OF IT.
Call
Landlord
09000000000
BEEP
BRRRRRNG
BRRRRRNG
Yes?
UH...
HELLO!
BA-DUM
AT LEAST FOR CHRISTMAS EVE...
EVEN IF I'M NOT SPENDING IT WITH A BOY-FRIEND...
A- A-A...
ARE YOU FREE RIGHT NOW?!

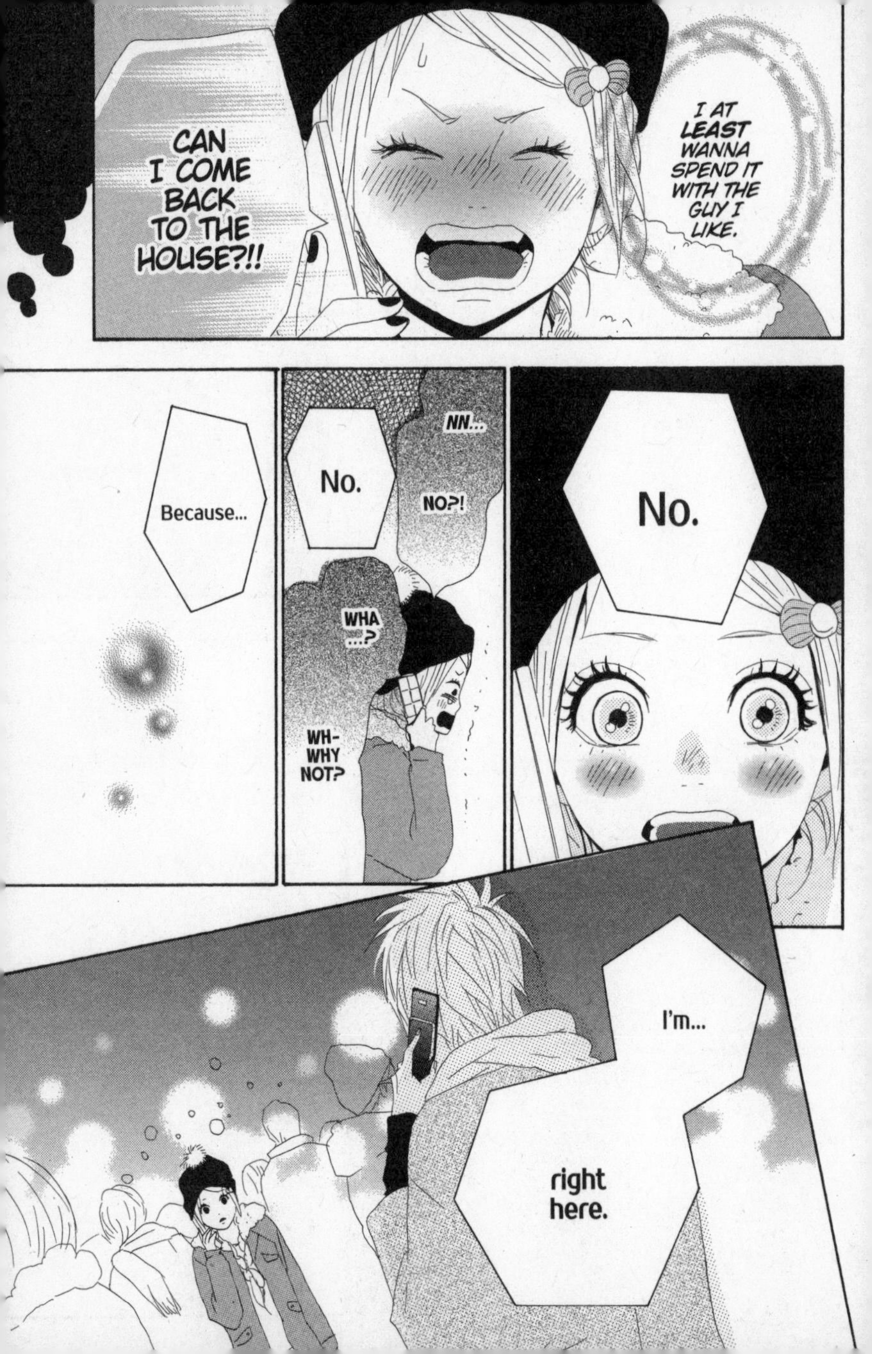
I AT LEAST WANNA SPEND IT WITH THE GUY I LIKE.
CAN I COME BACK TO THE HOUSE?!!
No.
NN...
No.
NO?!
WHA ...?
WH- WHY NOT?
Because...
I'm...
right here.

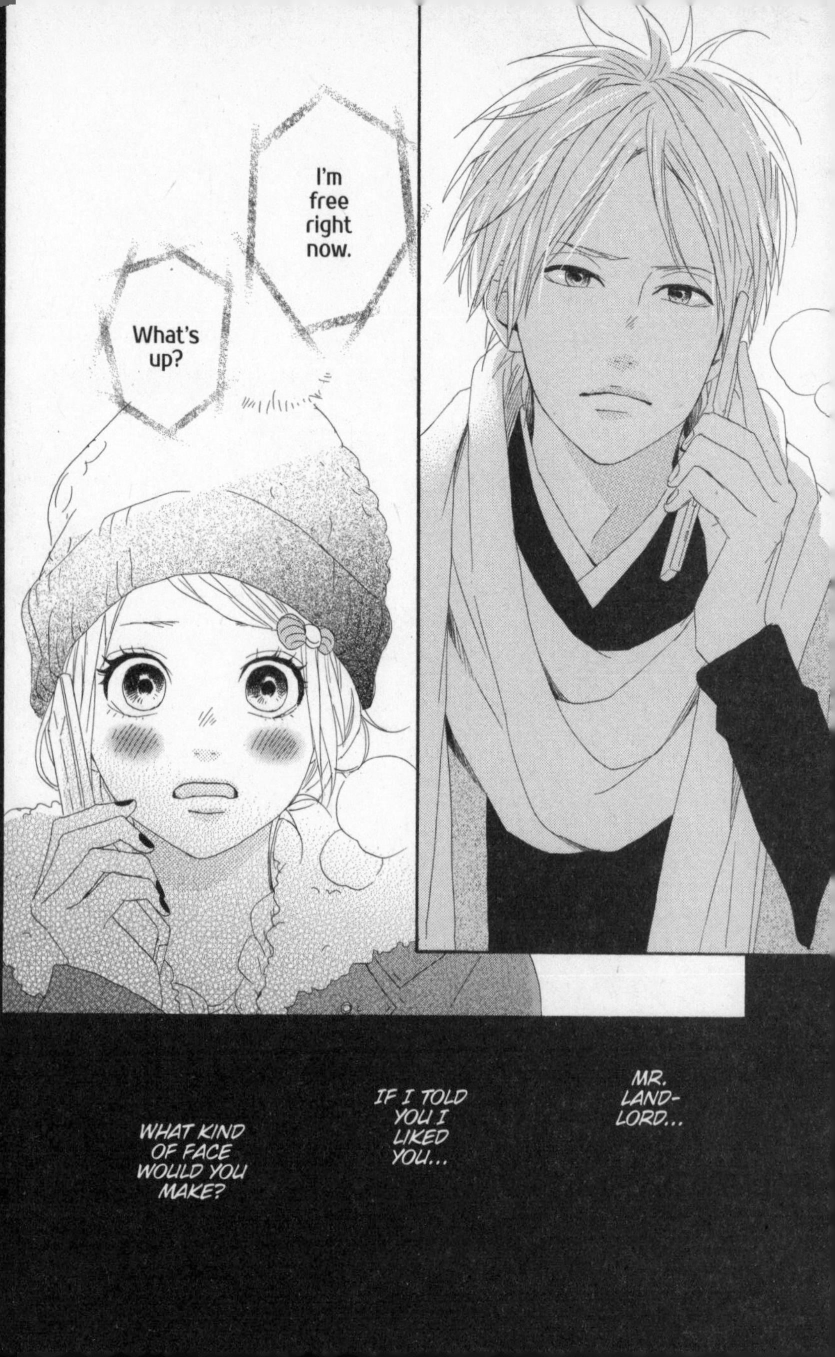
I'm free right now.
What's up?
MR. LAND-LORD...
IF I TOLD YOU I LIKED YOU...
WHAT KIND OF FACE WOULD YOU MAKE?

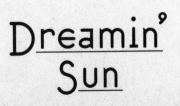

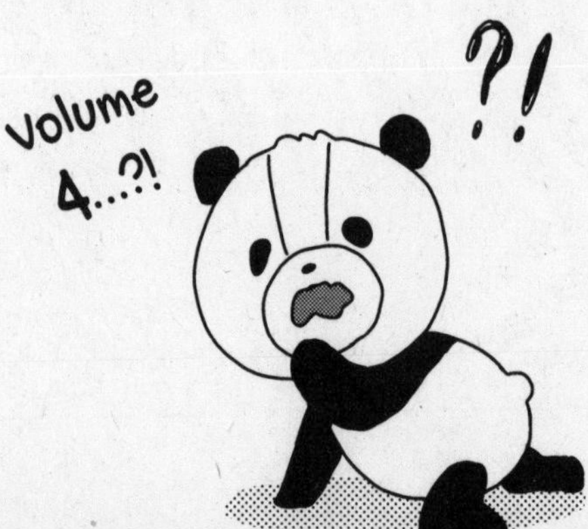
Volume 4...?!
?!

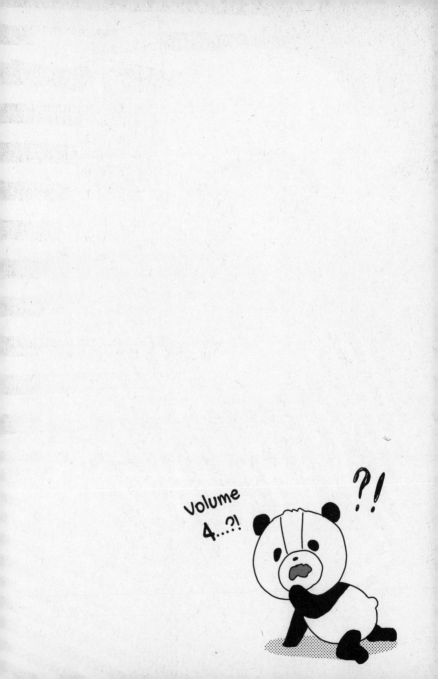

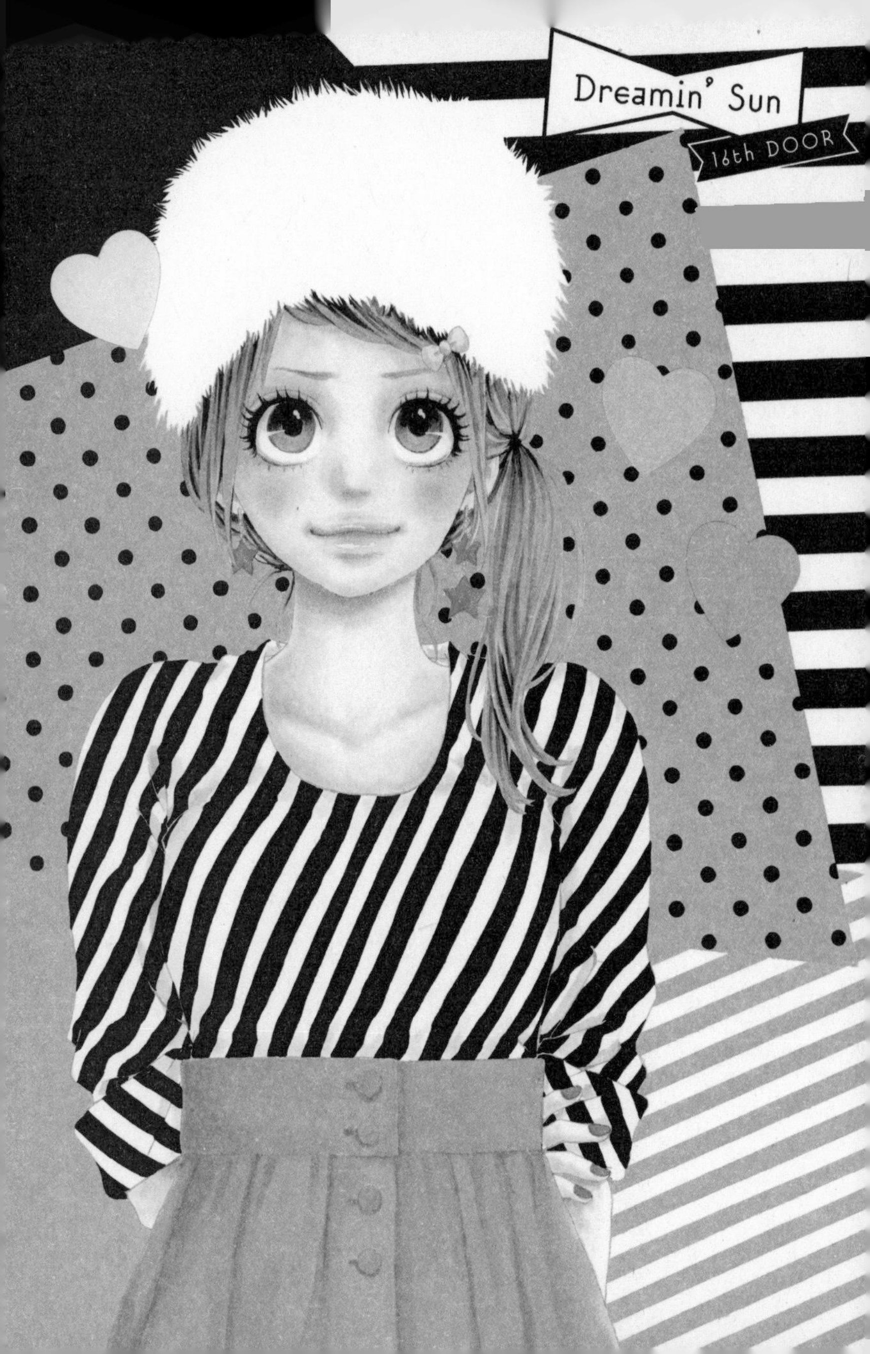
Dreamin' Sun
16th DOOR

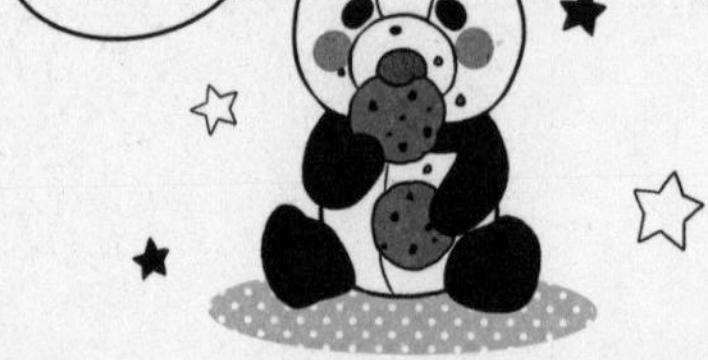
Dreamin' Sun

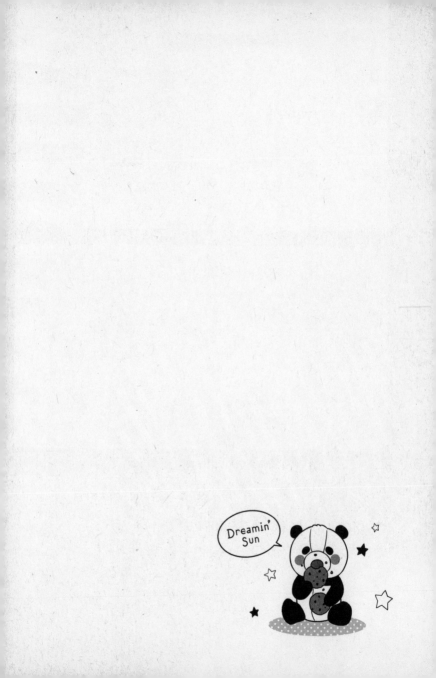

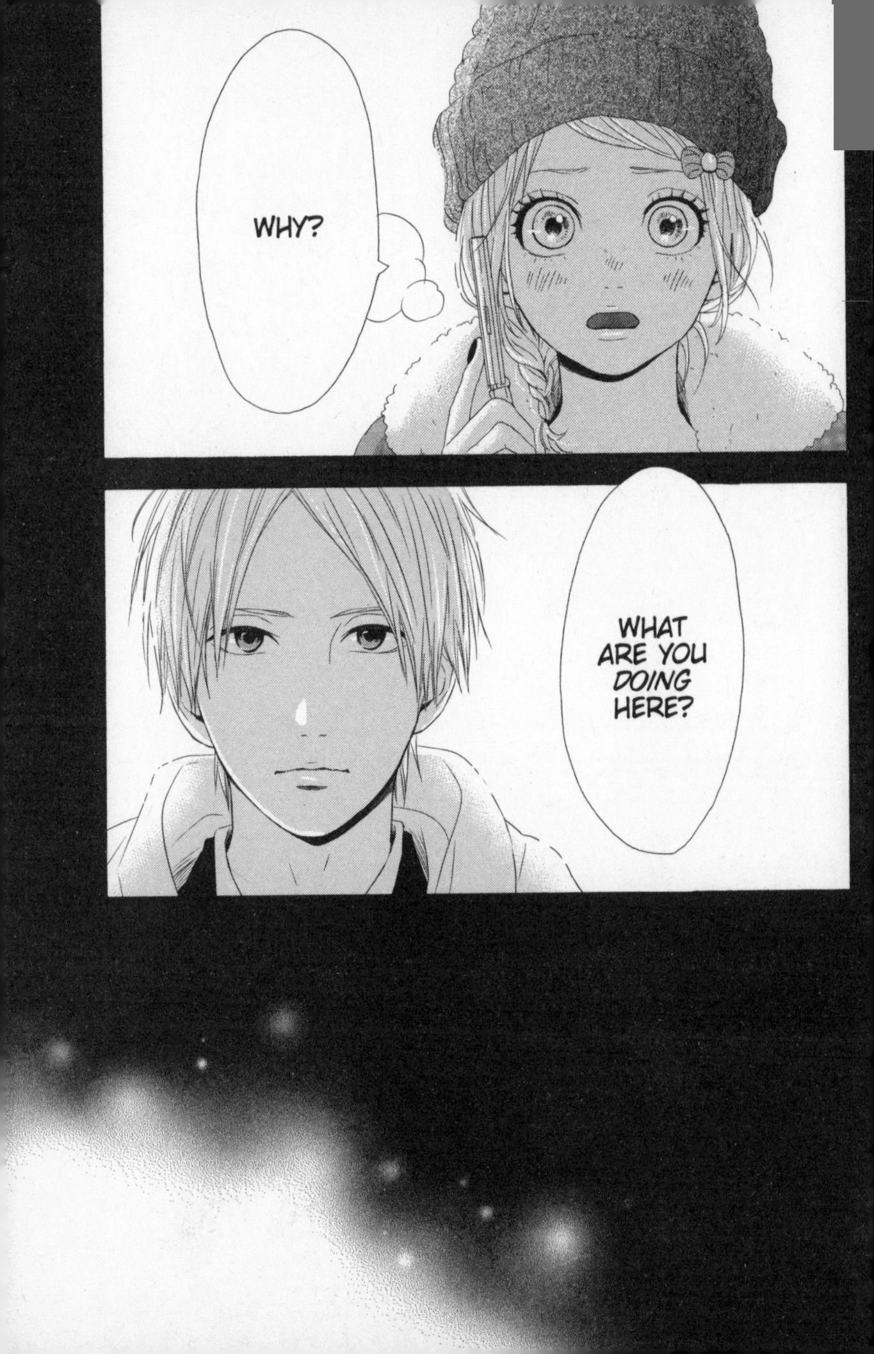
WHY?
WHAT ARE YOU DOING HERE?

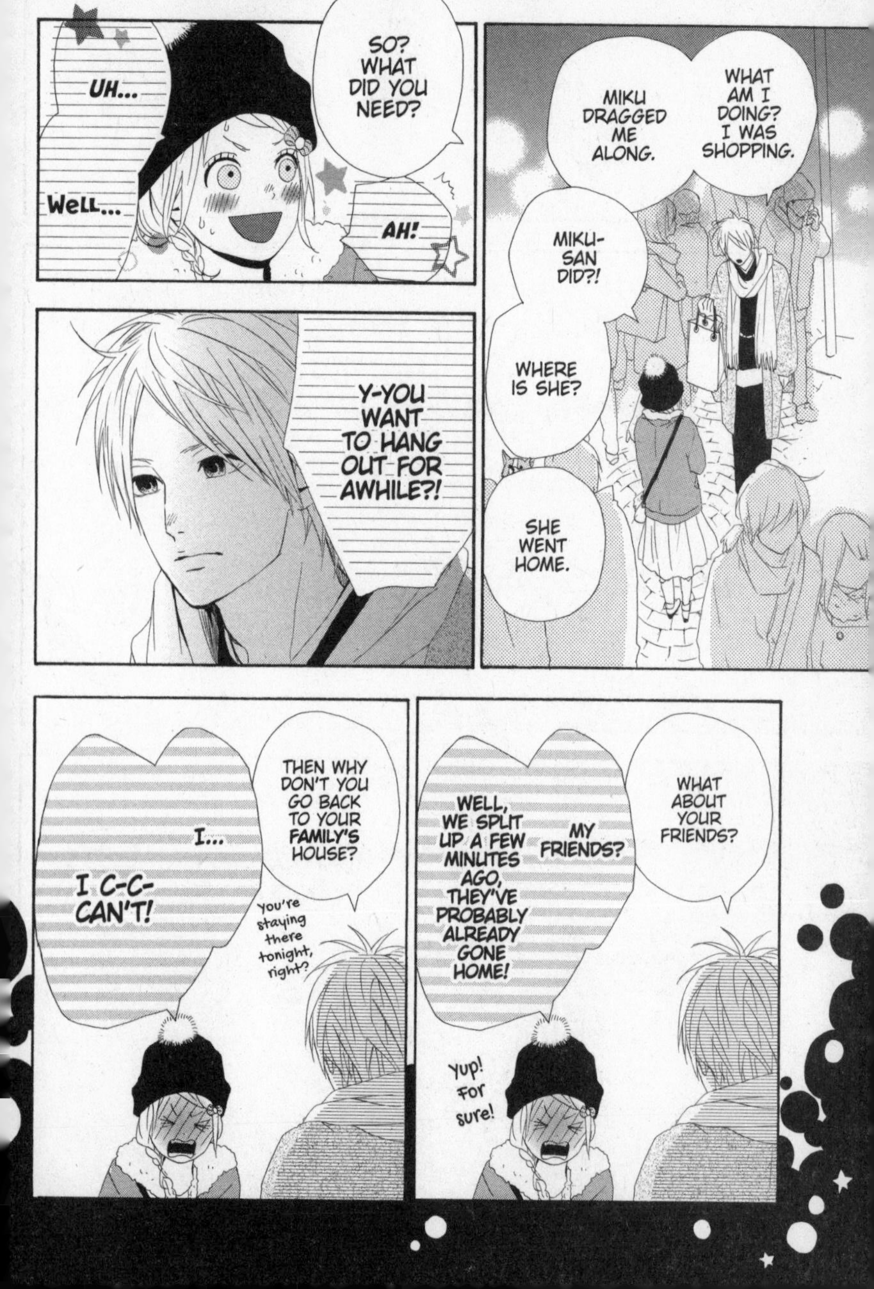
WHAT AM I DOING? I WAS SHOPPING.
MIKU DRAGGED ME ALONG.
MIKU-SAN DID?!
WHERE IS SHE?
SHE WENT HOME.
SO? WHAT DID YOU NEED?
AH!
UH...
Well...
Y-YOU WANT TO HANG OUT FOR AWHILE?!
WHAT ABOUT YOUR FRIENDS?
MY FRIENDS?
WELL, WE SPLIT UP A FEW MINUTES AGO, THEY'VE PROBABLY ALREADY GONE HOME!
Yup! For sure!
THEN WHY DON'T YOU GO BACK TO YOUR FAMILY'S HOUSE?
You're staying there tonight, right?
I...
I C-C-CAN'T!

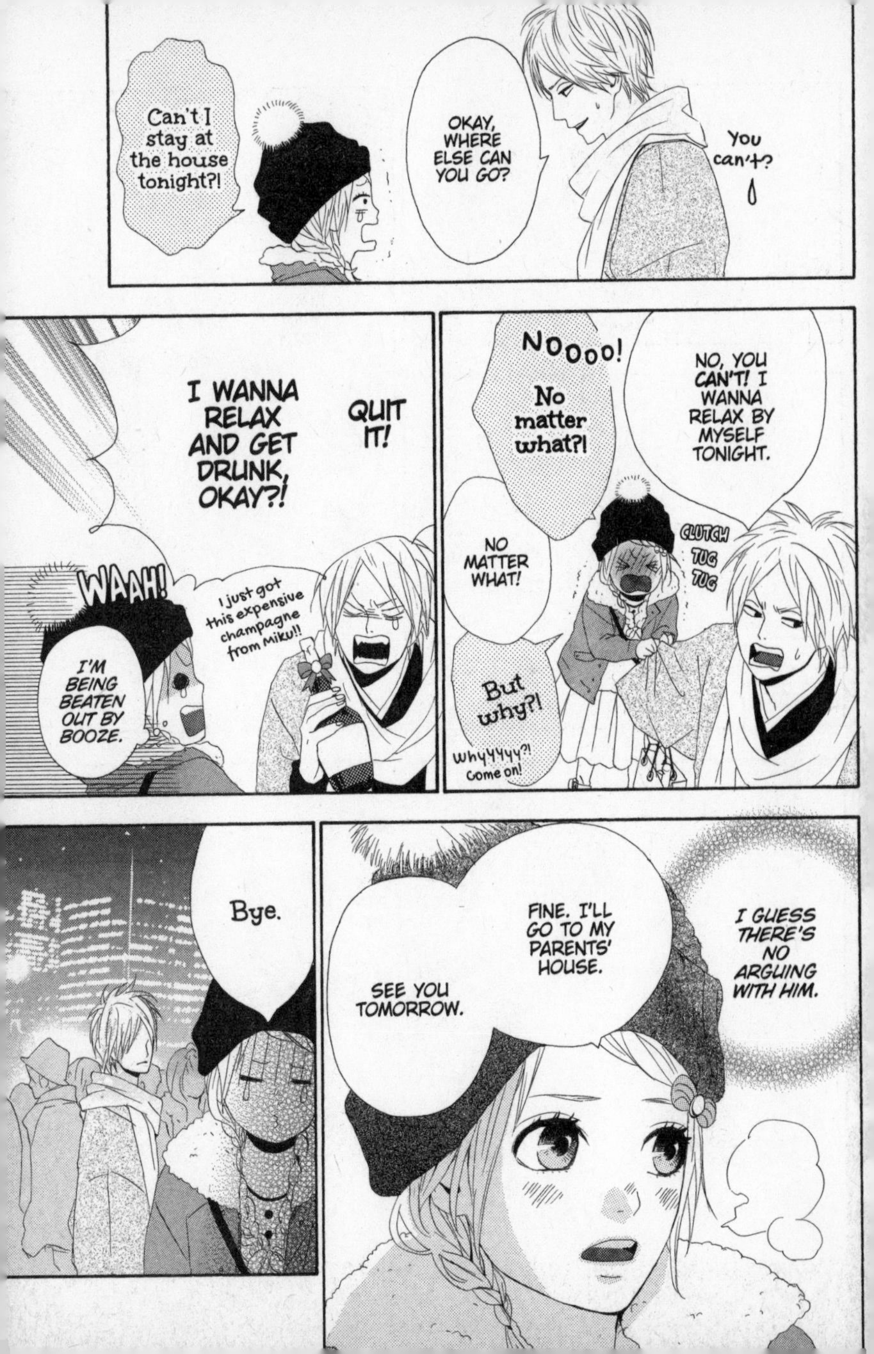
You can't?
OKAY, WHERE ELSE CAN YOU GO?
Can't I stay at the house tonight?!
NO, YOU CAN'T! I WANNA RELAX BY MYSELF TONIGHT.
Noooo!
No matter what?!
CLUTCH
TUG TUG
NO MATTER WHAT!
But why?!
Whyyyyy?! Come on!
QUIT IT!
I WANNA RELAX AND GET DRUNK, OKAY?!
I just got this expensive champagne from Miku!!
WAAH!
I'M BEING BEATEN OUT BY BOOZE.
I GUESS THERE'S NO ARGUING WITH HIM.
FINE. I'LL GO TO MY PARENTS' HOUSE.
SEE YOU TOMORROW.
Bye.

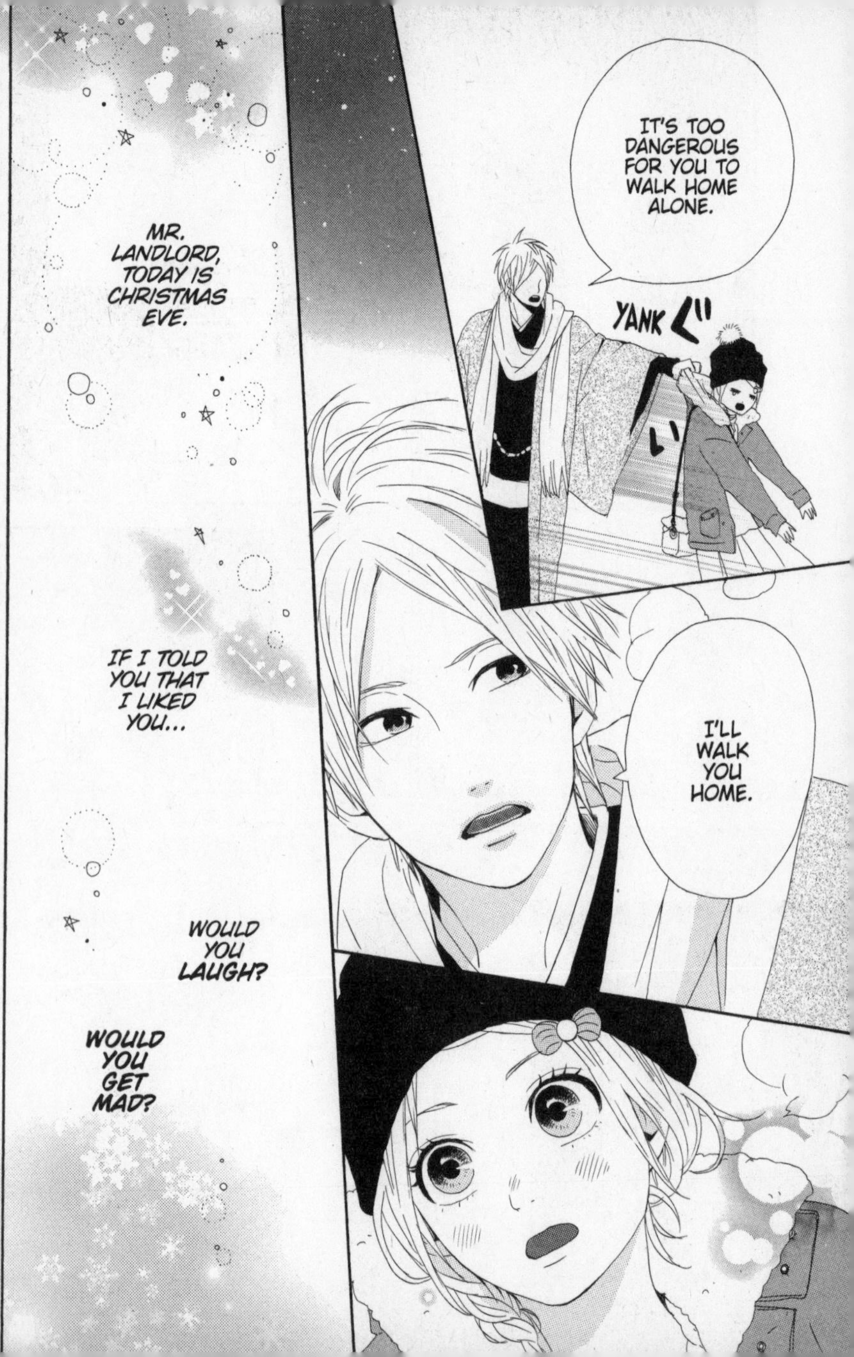
IT'S TOO DANGEROUS FOR YOU TO WALK HOME ALONE.
YANK ぐい
I'LL WALK YOU HOME.
MR. LANDLORD, TODAY IS CHRISTMAS EVE.
IF I TOLD YOU THAT I LIKED YOU...
WOULD YOU LAUGH?
WOULD YOU GET MAD?

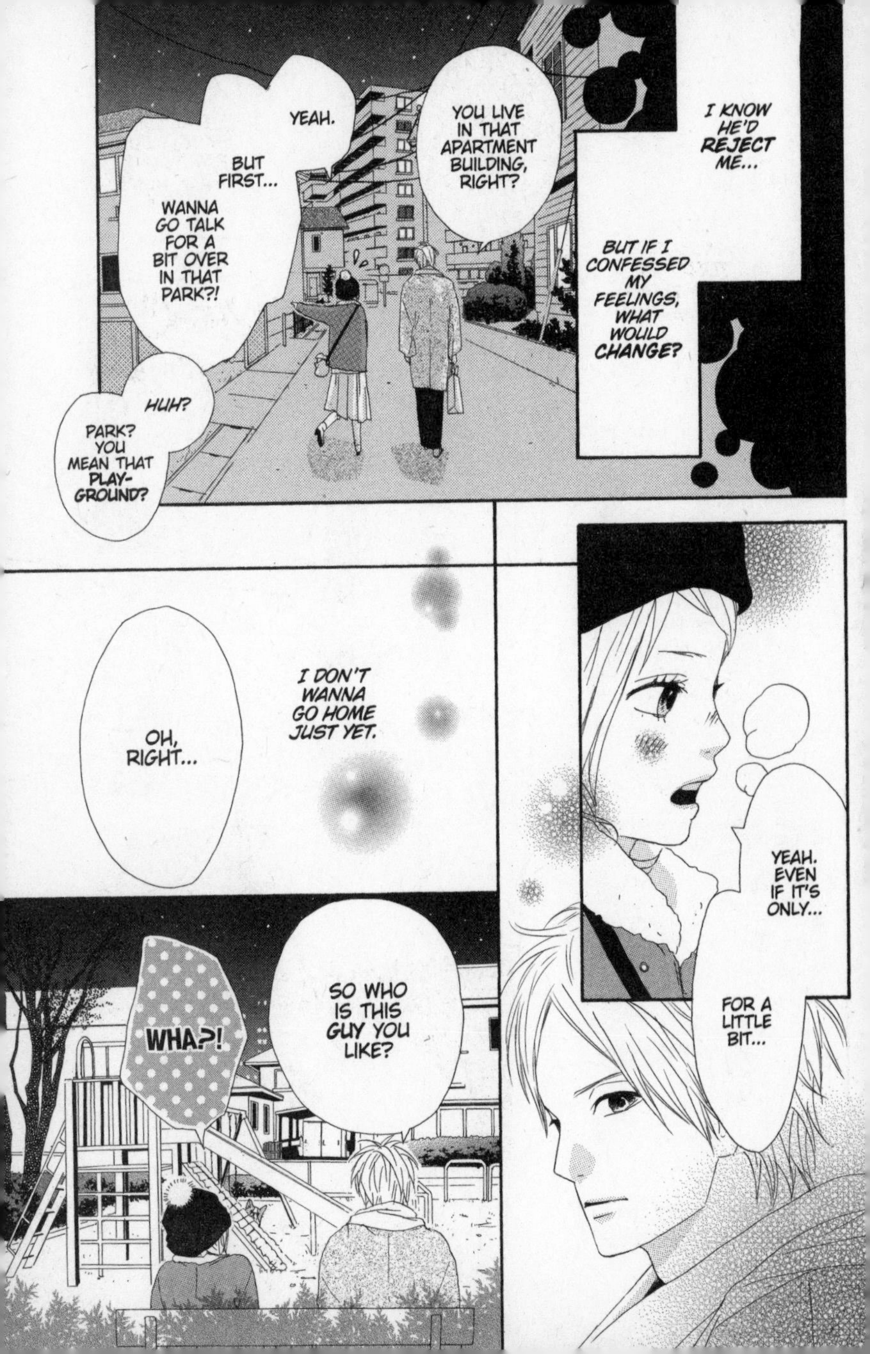
I KNOW HE'D REJECT ME...
BUT IF I CONFESSED MY FEELINGS, WHAT WOULD CHANGE?
YOU LIVE IN THAT APARTMENT BUILDING, RIGHT?
YEAH.
BUT FIRST...
WANNA GO TALK FOR A BIT OVER IN THAT PARK?!
HUH?
PARK? YOU MEAN THAT PLAY-GROUND?
YEAH. EVEN IF IT'S ONLY...
FOR A LITTLE BIT...
I DON'T WANNA GO HOME JUST YET.
OH, RIGHT...
SO WHO IS THIS GUY YOU LIKE?
WHA?!

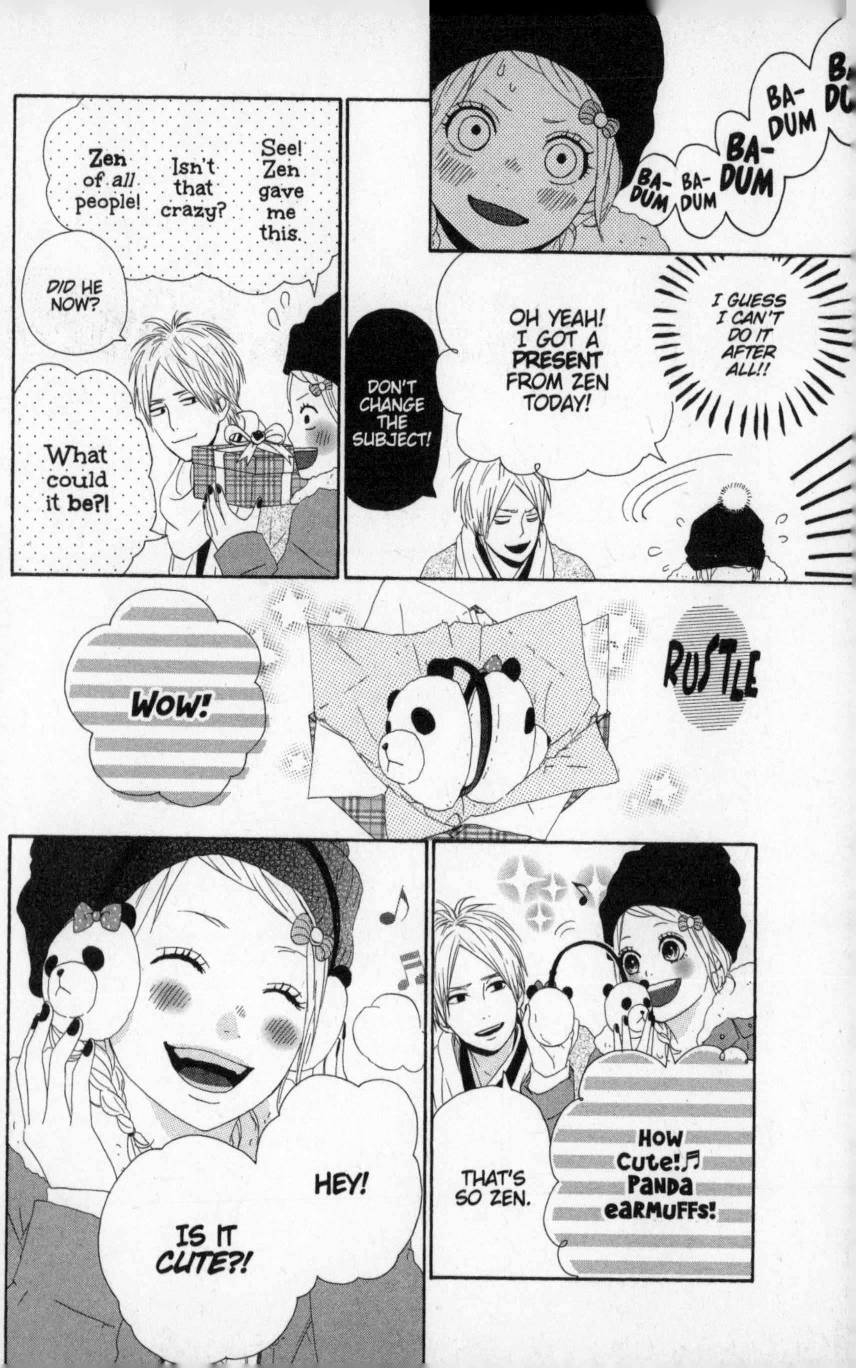
BA-DUM
BA-DUM
BA-DUM
BA-DUM
I GUESS I CAN'T DO IT AFTER ALL!!
OH YEAH! I GOT A PRESENT FROM ZEN TODAY!
DON'T CHANGE THE SUBJECT!
See! Zen gave me this.
Isn't that crazy?
Zen of *all* people!
DID HE NOW?
What could it be?!
RUSTLE
WOW!
How Cute!♬ Panda earmuffs!
THAT'S SO ZEN.
HEY!
IS IT CUTE?!

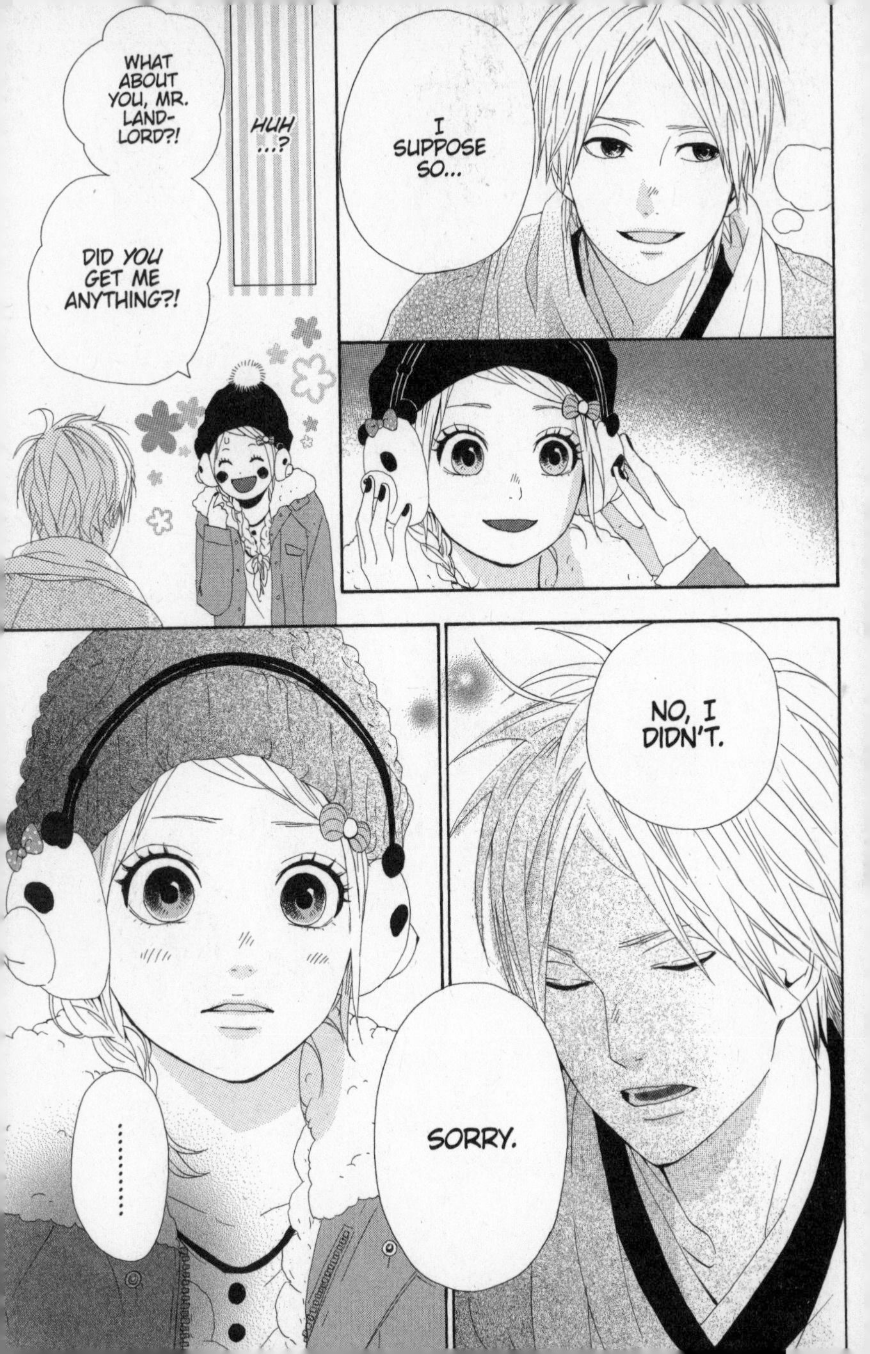
I SUPPOSE SO...
HUH ...?
WHAT ABOUT YOU, MR. LAND-LORD?!
DID YOU GET ME ANYTHING?!
NO, I DIDN'T.
SORRY.
....

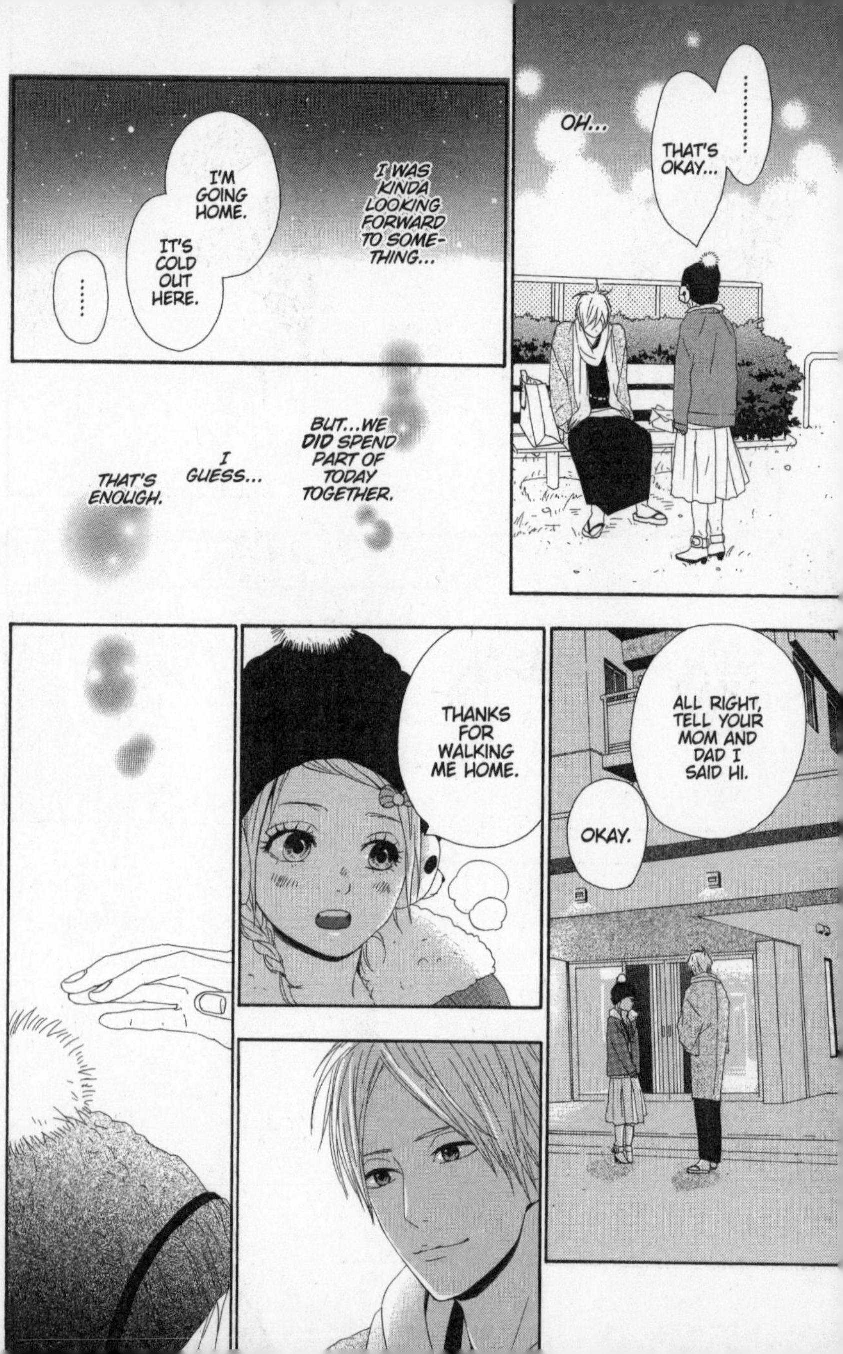
......
THAT'S OKAY...
OH...
I WAS KINDA LOOKING FORWARD TO SOMETHING...
I'M GOING HOME.
IT'S COLD OUT HERE.
......
BUT...WE DID SPEND PART OF TODAY TOGETHER.
I GUESS...
THAT'S ENOUGH.
ALL RIGHT, TELL YOUR MOM AND DAD I SAID HI.
OKAY.
THANKS FOR WALKING ME HOME.

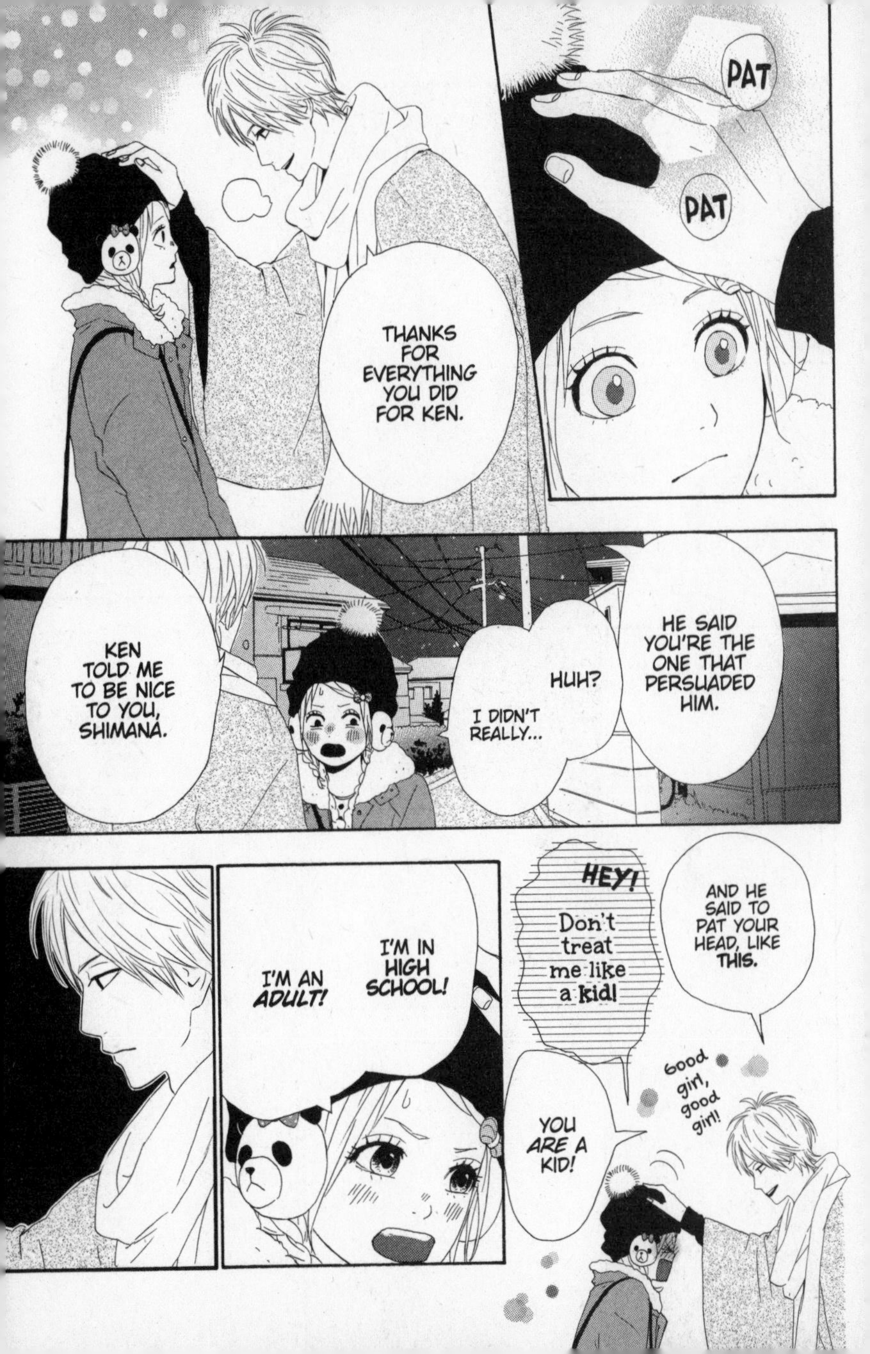
PAT
PAT
THANKS FOR EVERYTHING YOU DID FOR KEN.
HE SAID YOU'RE THE ONE THAT PERSUADED HIM.
HUH?
I DIDN'T REALLY...
KEN TOLD ME TO BE NICE TO YOU, SHIMANA.
AND HE SAID TO PAT YOUR HEAD, LIKE THIS.
HEY! Don't treat me like a kid!
Good girl, good girl!
YOU ARE A KID!
I'M IN HIGH SCHOOL!
I'M AN ADULT!

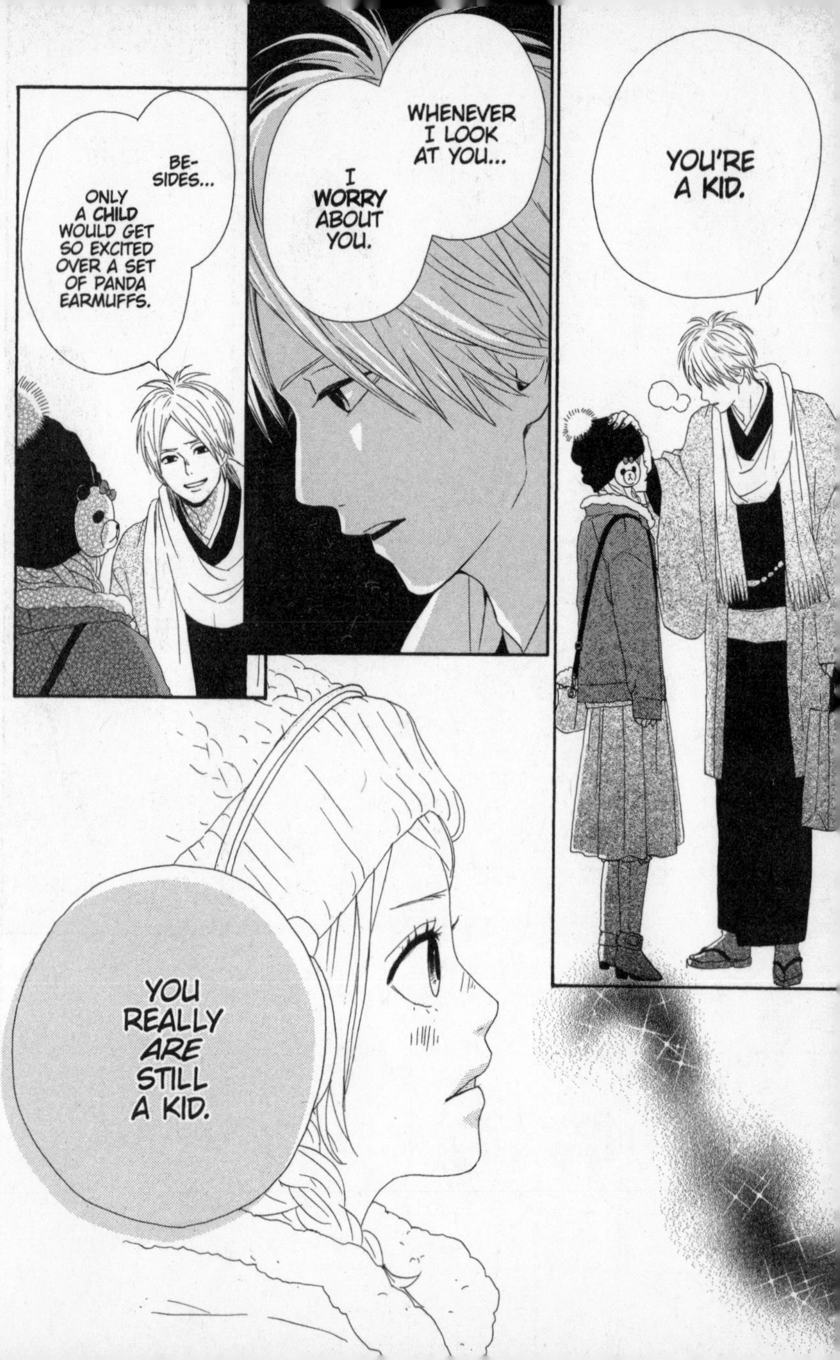
YOU'RE A KID.
WHENEVER I LOOK AT YOU... I WORRY ABOUT YOU.
BE-SIDES... ONLY A CHILD WOULD GET SO EXCITED OVER A SET OF PANDA EARMUFFS.
YOU REALLY *ARE* STILL A KID.

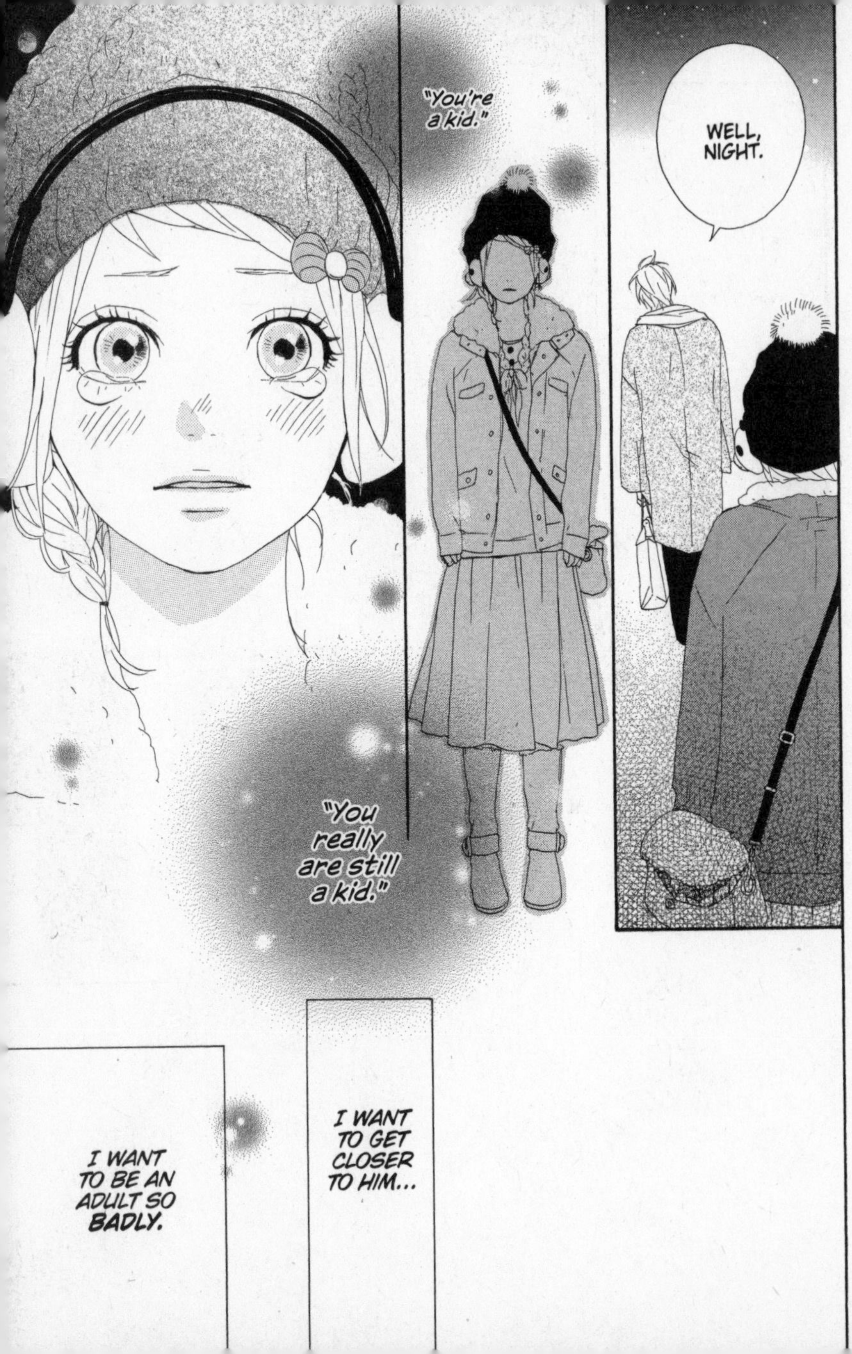
WELL, NIGHT.
"You're a kid."
"You really are still a kid."
I WANT TO GET CLOSER TO HIM...
I WANT TO BE AN ADULT SO BADLY.

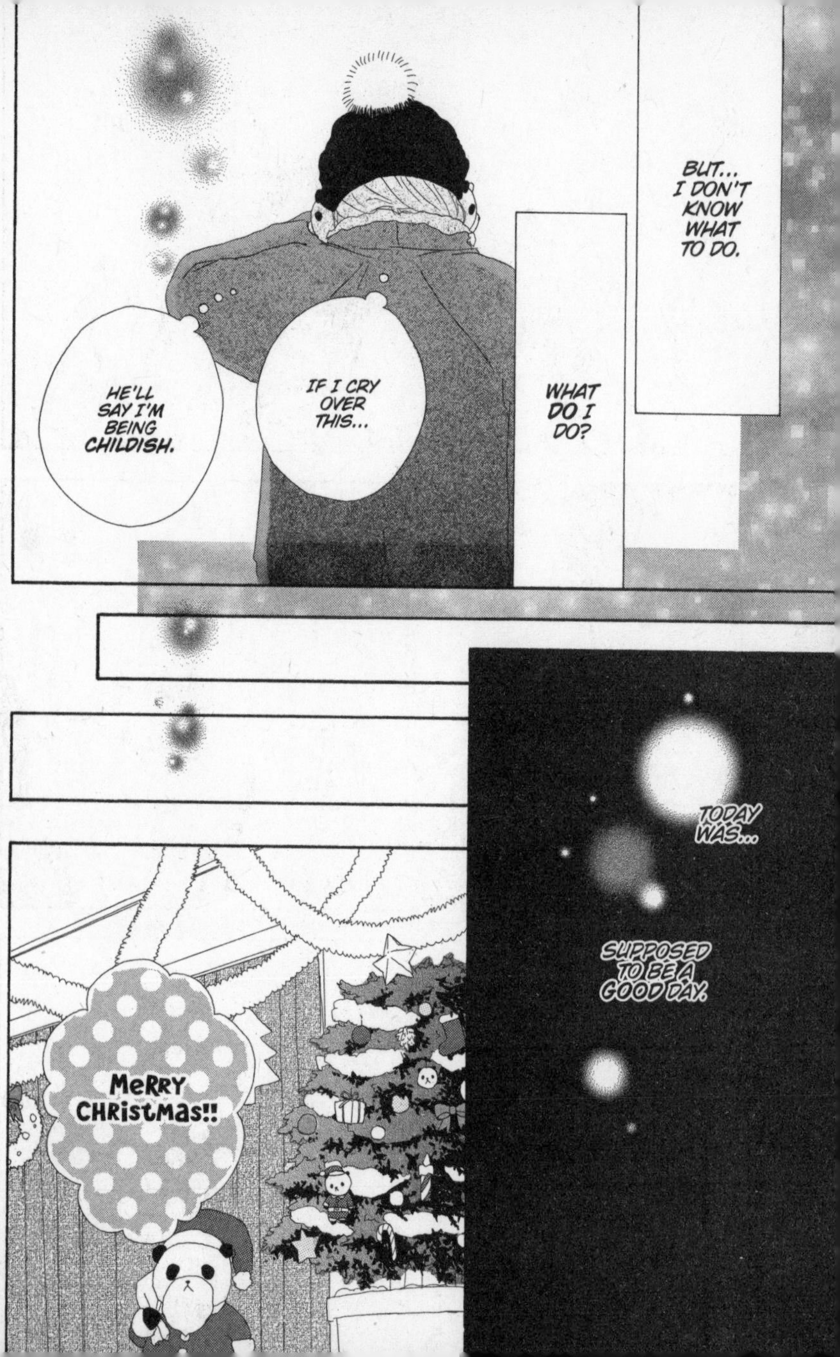
BUT... I DON'T KNOW WHAT TO DO.
WHAT DO I DO?
IF I CRY OVER THIS...
HE'LL SAY I'M BEING CHILDISH.
TODAY WAS...
SUPPOSED TO BE A GOOD DAY.
MERRY CHRISTMAS!!

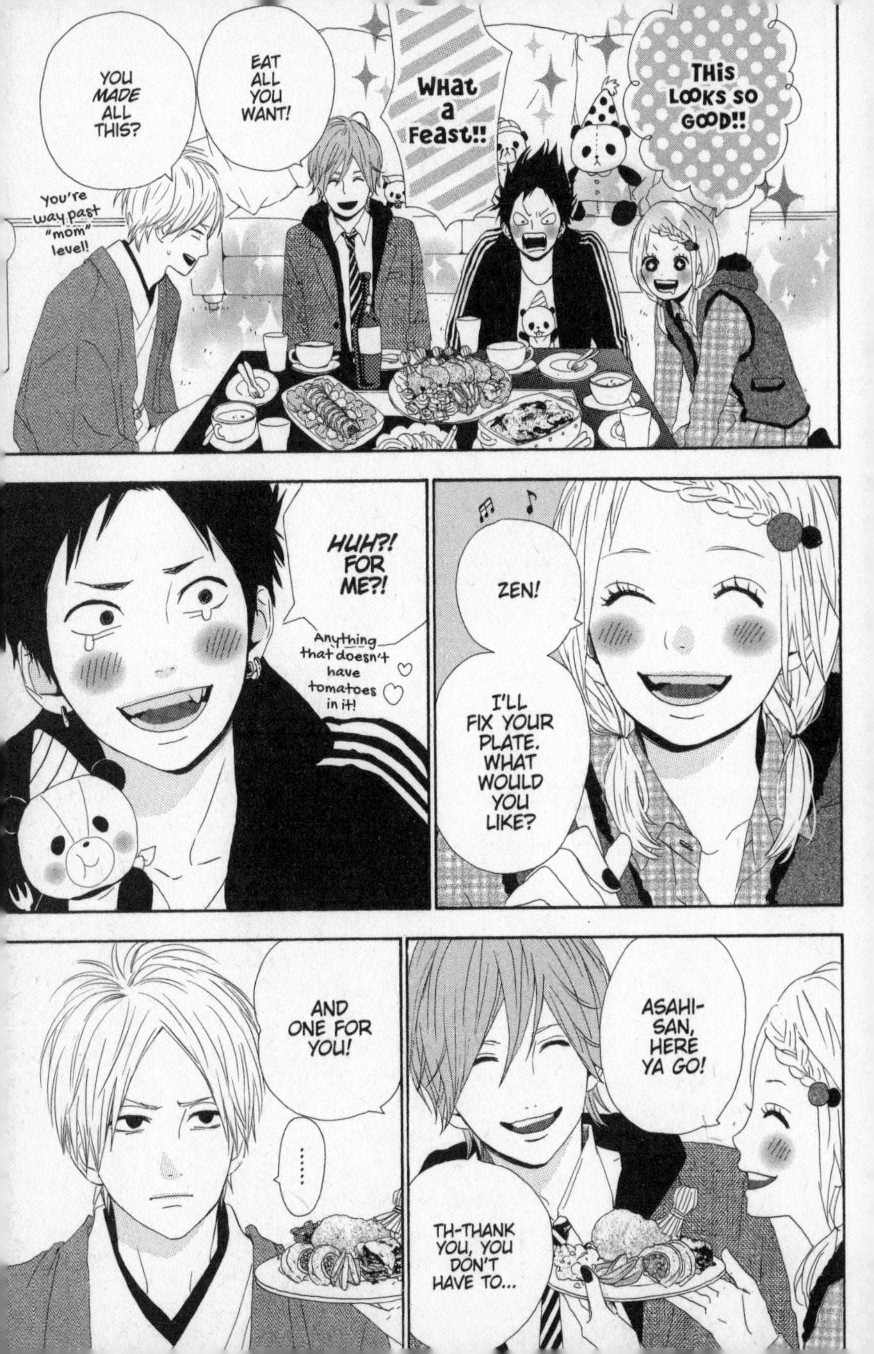
THIS LOOKS SO GOOD!!
What a Feast!!
EAT ALL YOU WANT!
YOU MADE ALL THIS?
You're way past "mom" level!
ZEN!
I'LL FIX YOUR PLATE. WHAT WOULD YOU LIKE?
HUH?! FOR ME?!
Anything that doesn't have tomatoes in it!
ASAHI-SAN, HERE YA GO!
TH-THANK YOU, YOU DON'T HAVE TO...
AND ONE FOR YOU!
......

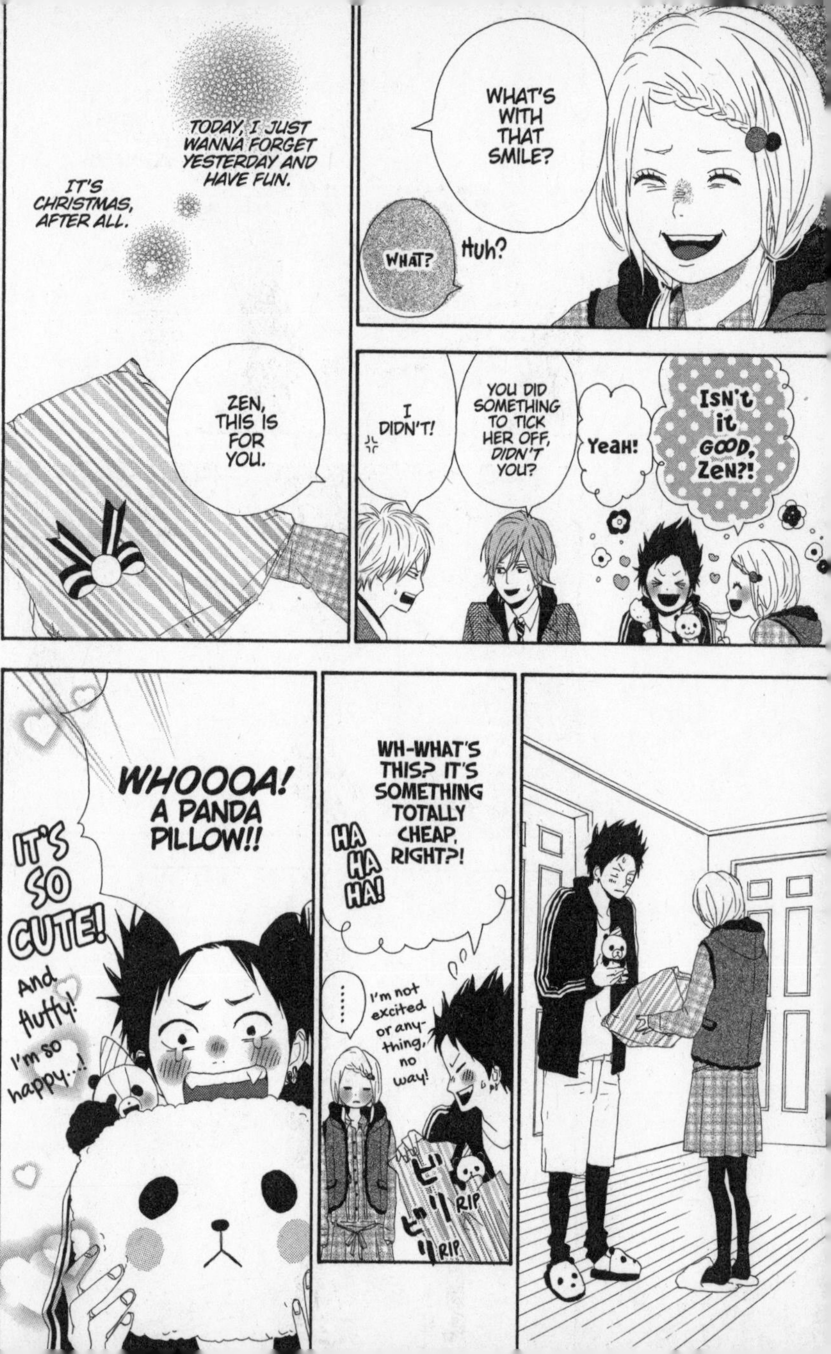
WHAT'S WITH THAT SMILE?
Huh?
WHAT?
ISN'T it GOOD, ZEN?!
Yeah!
YOU DID SOMETHING TO TICK HER OFF, DIDN'T YOU?
I DIDN'T!
TODAY, I JUST WANNA FORGET YESTERDAY AND HAVE FUN.
IT'S CHRISTMAS, AFTER ALL.
ZEN, THIS IS FOR YOU.
WH-WHAT'S THIS? IT'S SOMETHING TOTALLY CHEAP, RIGHT?!
HA HA HA!
I'm not excited or any-thing, no way!
......
RIP
RIP
WHOOOA! A PANDA PILLOW!!
IT'S SO CUTE!
And fluffy! I'm so happy...!

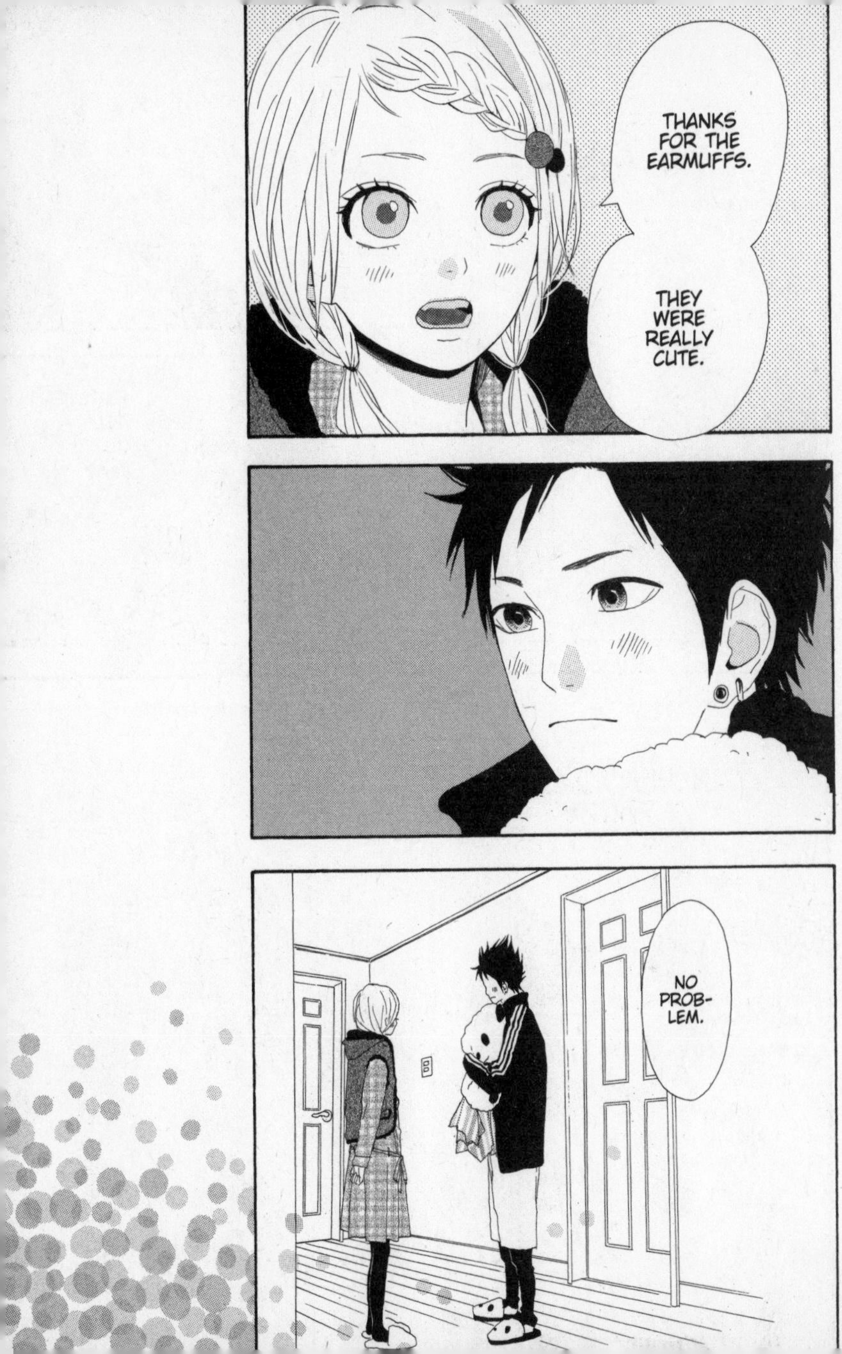
THANKS FOR THE EARMUFFS.
THEY WERE REALLY CUTE.
NO PROB-LEM.

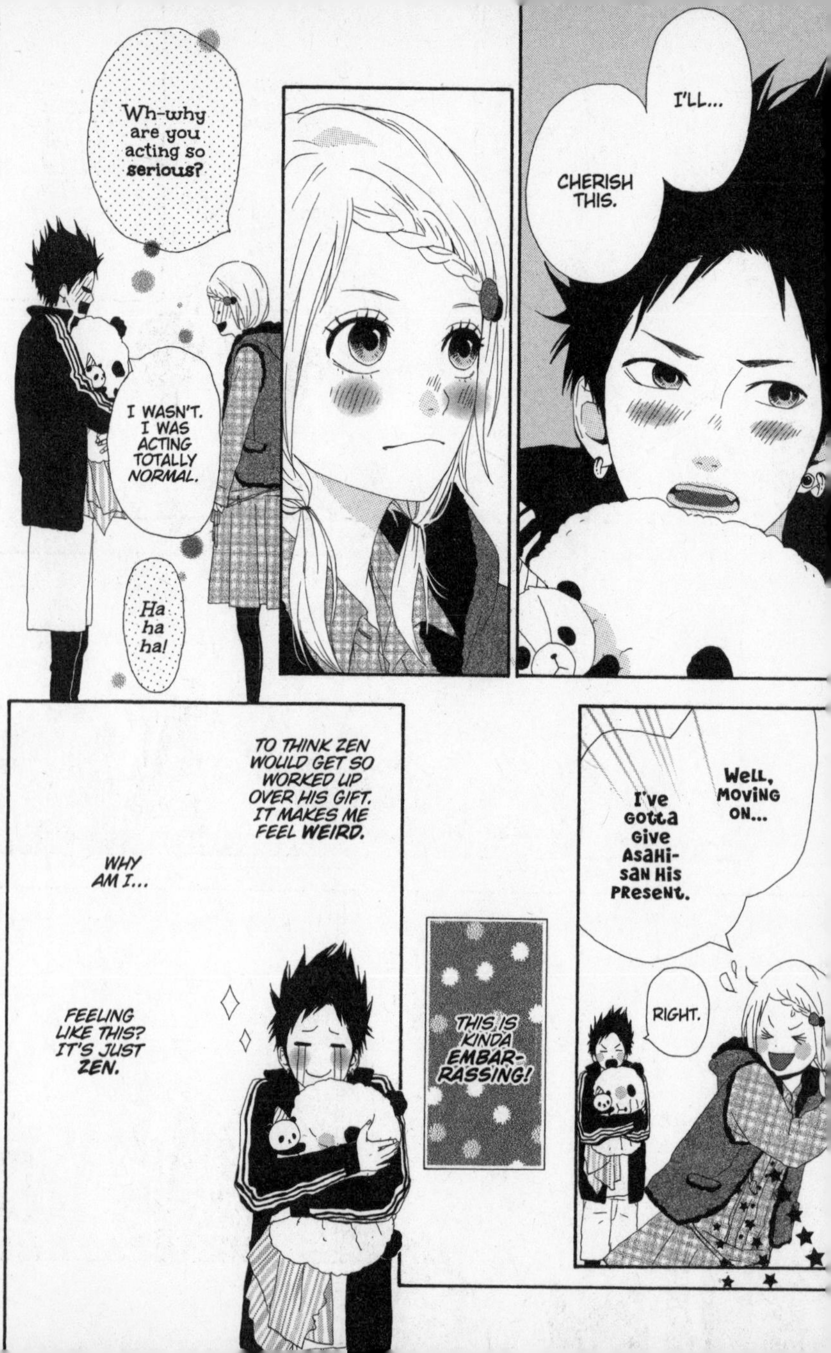
I'LL...
CHERISH THIS.
Wh-why are you acting so serious?
I WASN'T. I WAS ACTING TOTALLY NORMAL.
Ha ha ha!
Well, moving on...
I've gotta give Asahi-san his present.
RIGHT.
TO THINK ZEN WOULD GET SO WORKED UP OVER HIS GIFT. IT MAKES ME FEEL WEIRD.
THIS IS KINDA EMBARRASSING!
WHY AM I...
FEELING LIKE THIS? IT'S JUST ZEN.

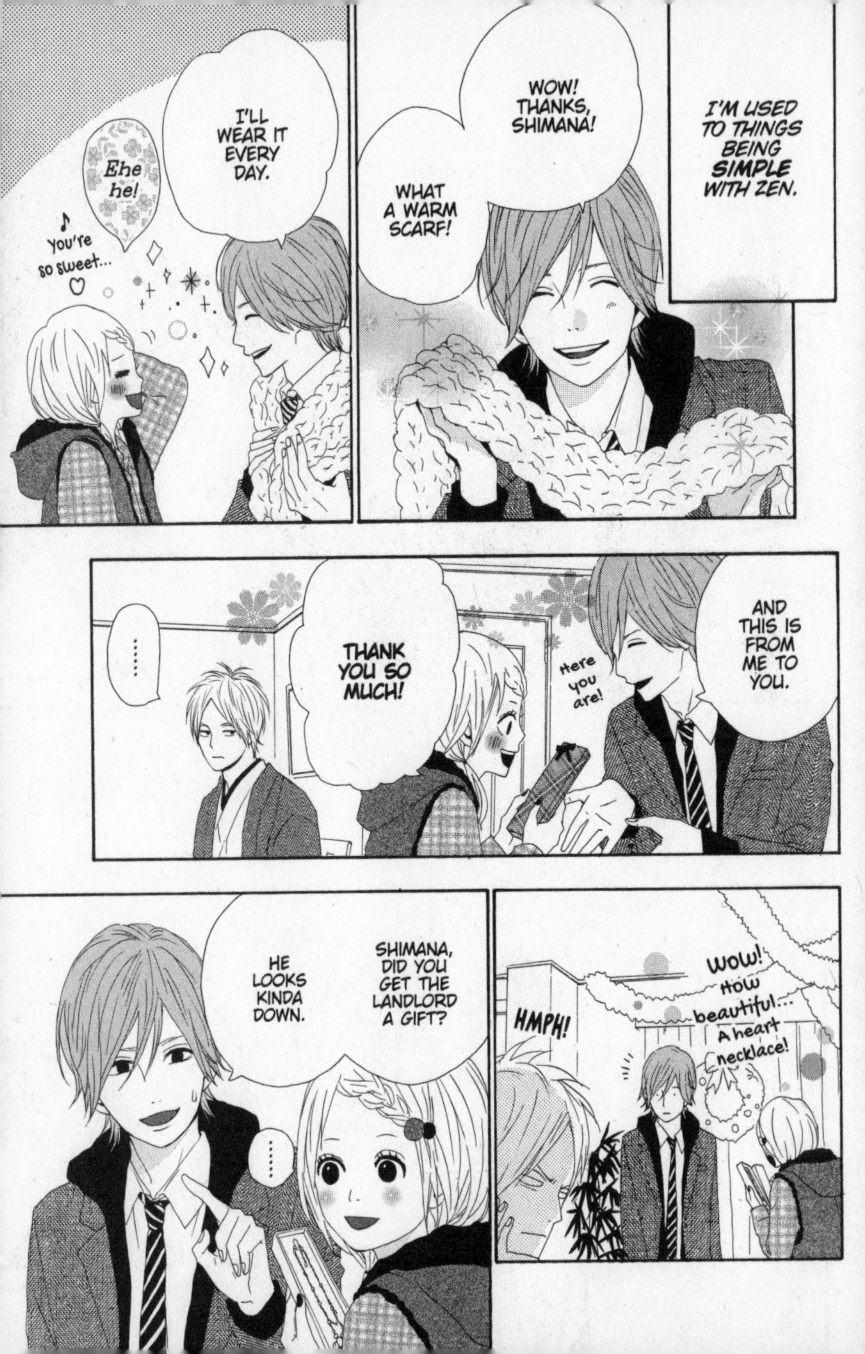
I'M USED TO THINGS BEING SIMPLE WITH ZEN.
WOW! THANKS, SHIMANA!
WHAT A WARM SCARF!
I'LL WEAR IT EVERY DAY.
Ehe he!
♪ You're so sweet... ♡
AND THIS IS FROM ME TO YOU.
Here you are!
THANK YOU SO MUCH!
......
WOW! How beautiful... A heart necklace!
HMPH!
SHIMANA, DID YOU GET THE LANDLORD A GIFT?
HE LOOKS KINDA DOWN.
......

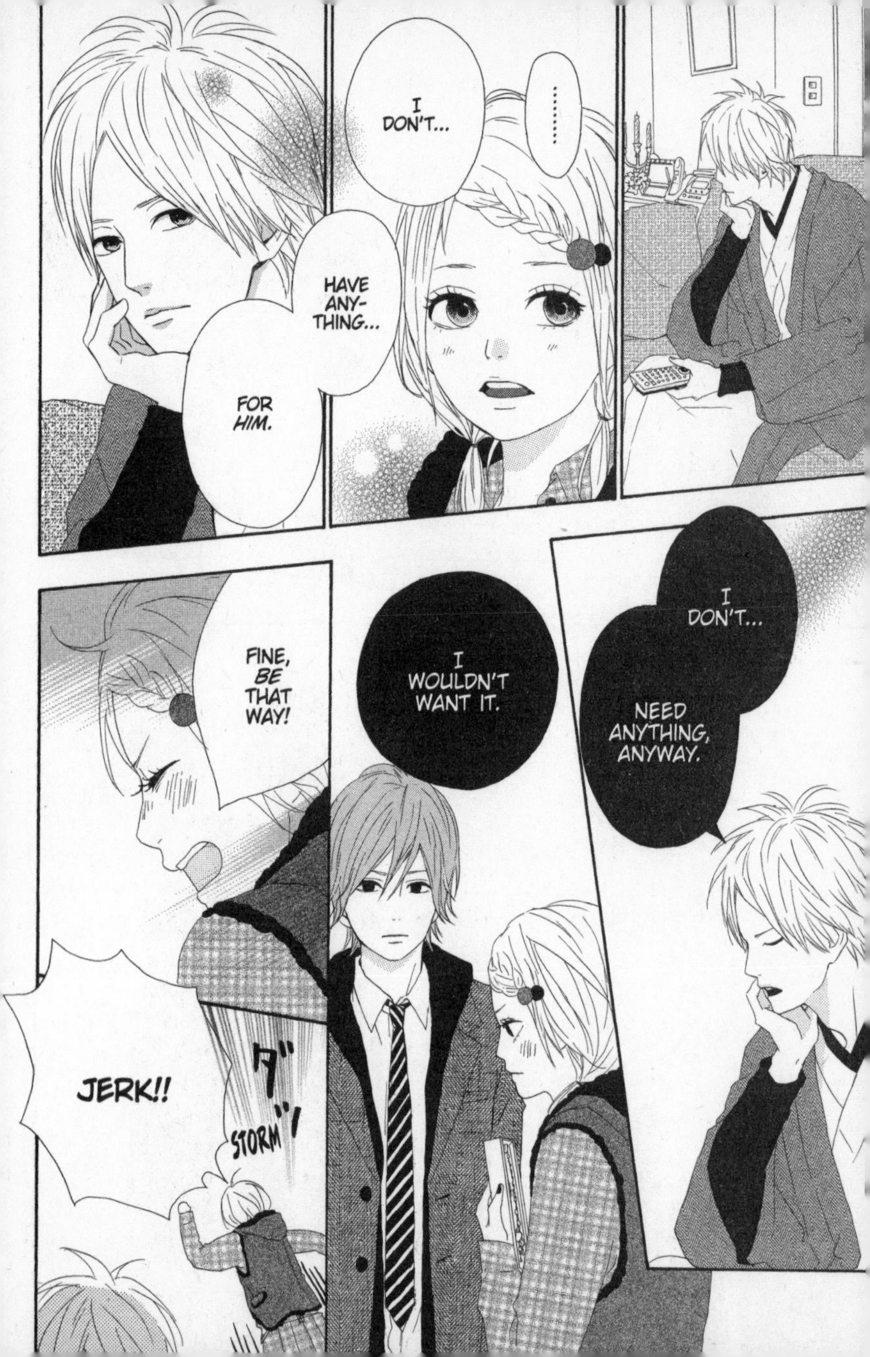
......
I DON'T...
HAVE ANY-THING...
FOR HIM.
I DON'T...
NEED ANYTHING, ANYWAY.
I WOULDN'T WANT IT.
FINE, BE THAT WAY!
JERK!!
ダッ
STORM

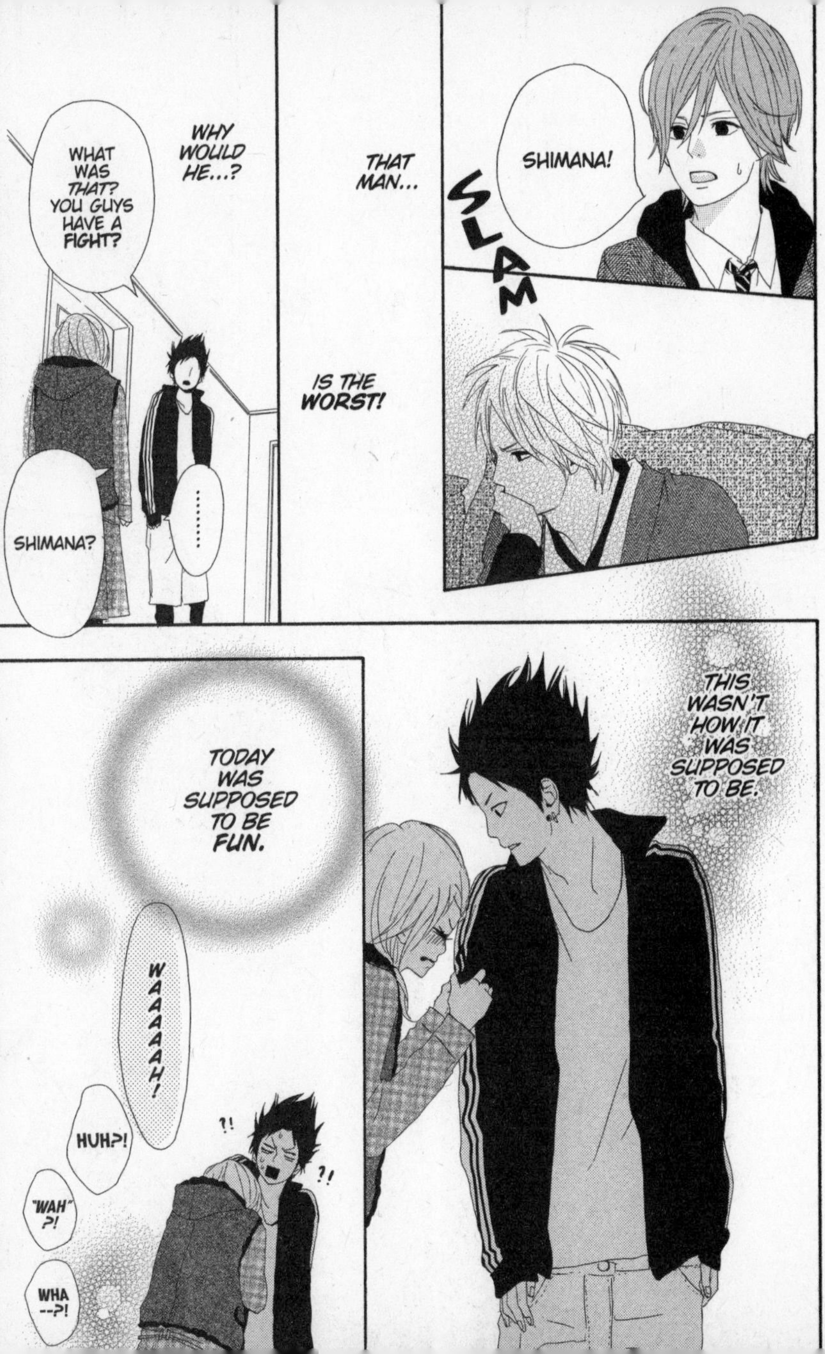
SHIMANA!
SLAM
THAT MAN...
IS THE WORST!
WHY WOULD HE...?
WHAT WAS THAT? YOU GUYS HAVE A FIGHT?
......
SHIMANA?
THIS WASN'T HOW IT WAS SUPPOSED TO BE.
TODAY WAS SUPPOSED TO BE FUN.
WAAAAAAH!
?!
?!
HUH?!
"WAH"?!
WHA--?!

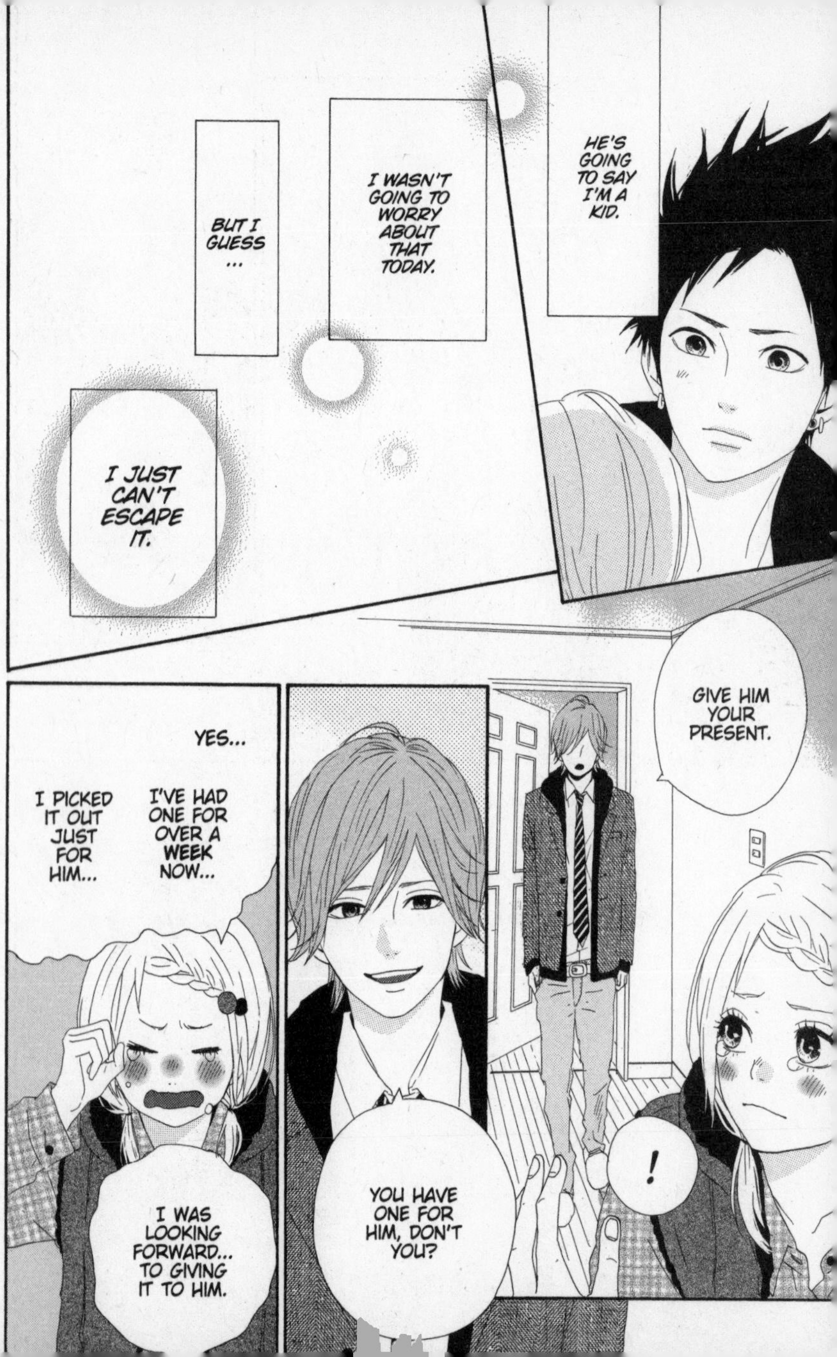
HE'S GOING TO SAY I'M A KID.
I WASN'T GOING TO WORRY ABOUT THAT TODAY.
BUT I GUESS ...
I JUST CAN'T ESCAPE IT.
GIVE HIM YOUR PRESENT.
!
YOU HAVE ONE FOR HIM, DON'T YOU?
YES...
I'VE HAD ONE FOR OVER A WEEK NOW...
I PICKED IT OUT JUST FOR HIM...
I WAS LOOKING FORWARD... TO GIVING IT TO HIM.

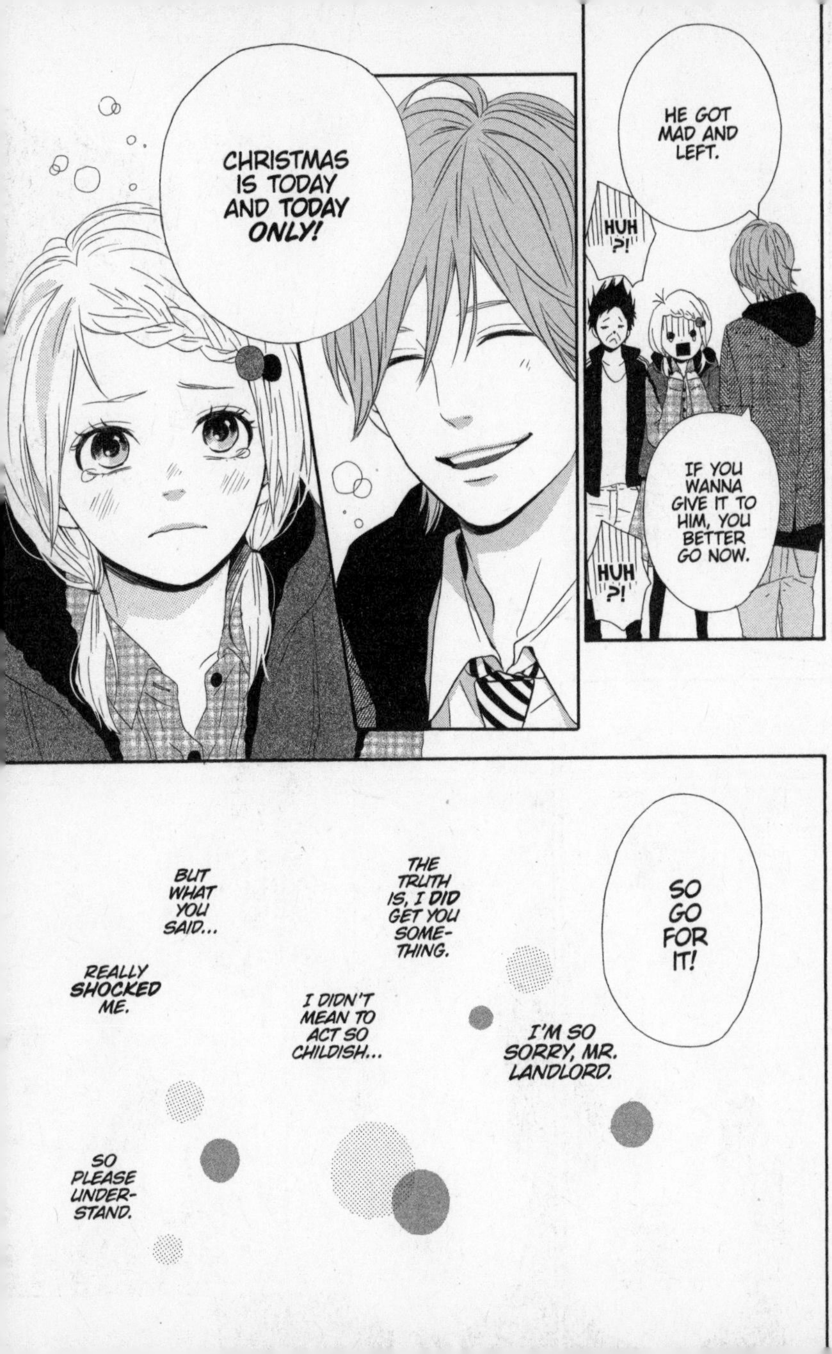
HE GOT MAD AND LEFT.
HUH?!
IF YOU WANNA GIVE IT TO HIM, YOU BETTER GO NOW.
HUH?!
CHRISTMAS IS TODAY AND TODAY ONLY!
SO GO FOR IT!
I'M SO SORRY, MR. LANDLORD.
THE TRUTH IS, I DID GET YOU SOME-THING.
I DIDN'T MEAN TO ACT SO CHILDISH...
BUT WHAT YOU SAID...
REALLY SHOCKED ME.
SO PLEASE UNDER-STAND.

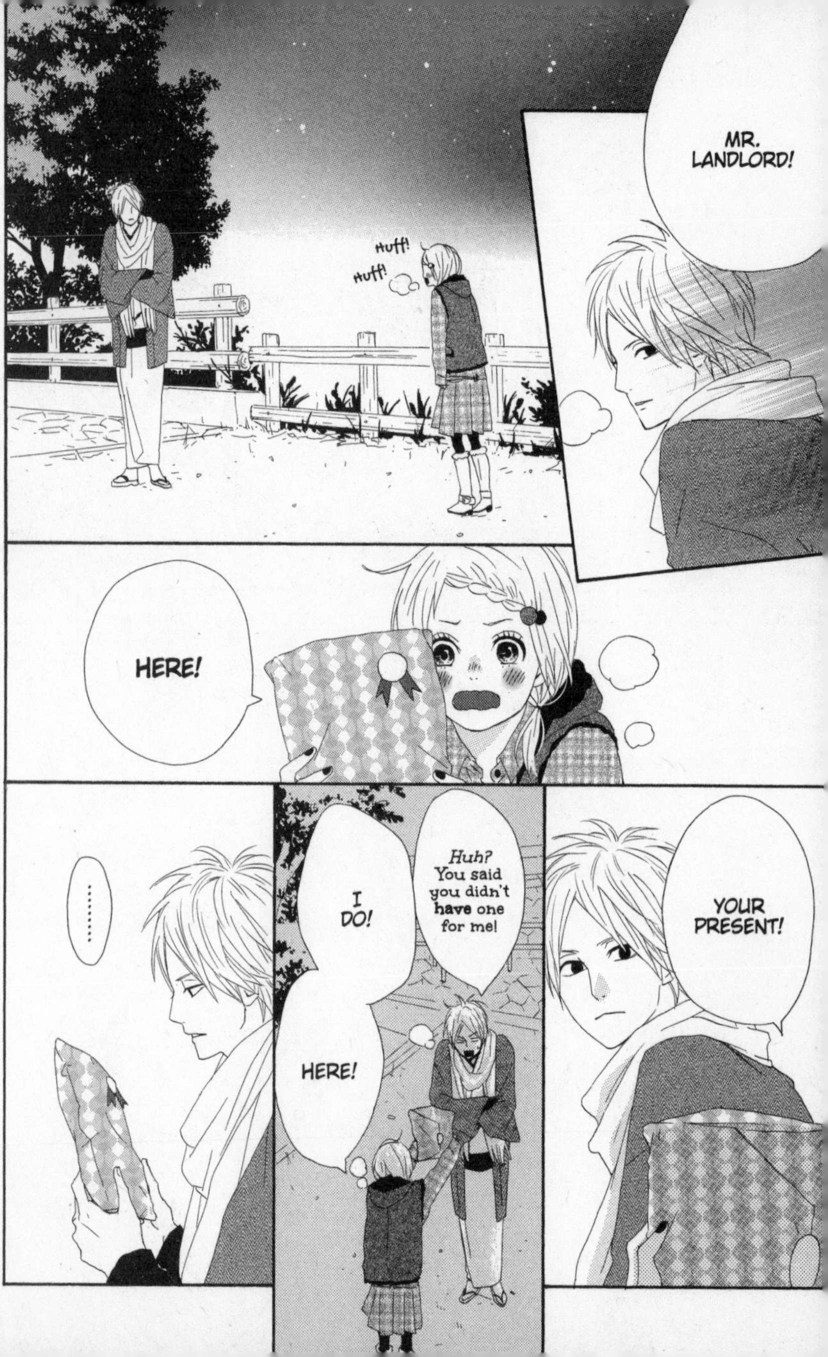
MR. LANDLORD!
Huff!
Huff!
HERE!
YOUR PRESENT!
Huh? You said you didn't have one for me!
I DO!
HERE!
....

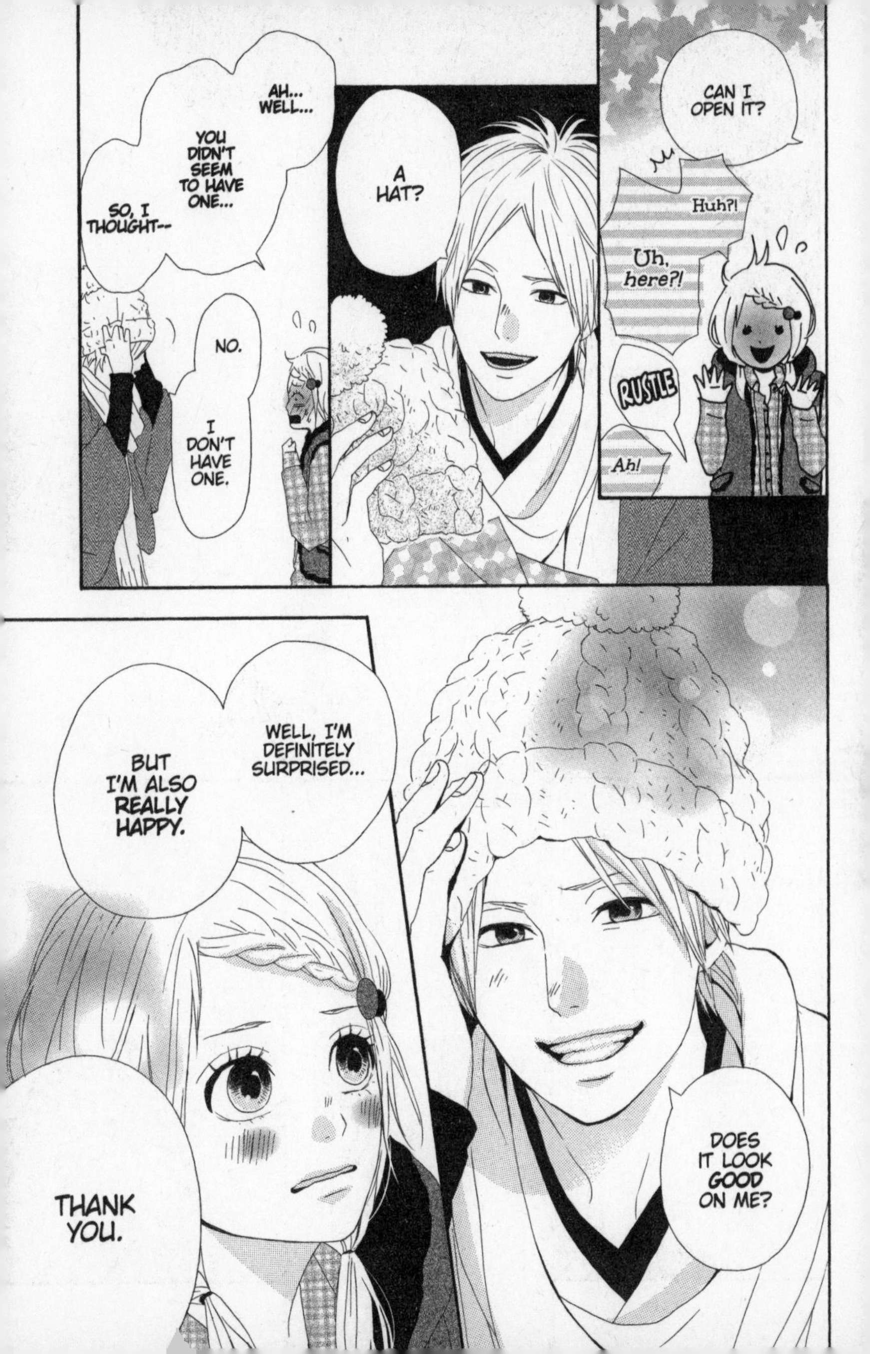
CAN I OPEN IT?
Huh?!
Uh, here?!
RUSTLE
Ah!
A HAT?
AH... WELL...
YOU DIDN'T SEEM TO HAVE ONE...
SO, I THOUGHT--
NO.
I DON'T HAVE ONE.
DOES IT LOOK GOOD ON ME?
WELL, I'M DEFINITELY SURPRISED...
BUT I'M ALSO REALLY HAPPY.
THANK YOU.

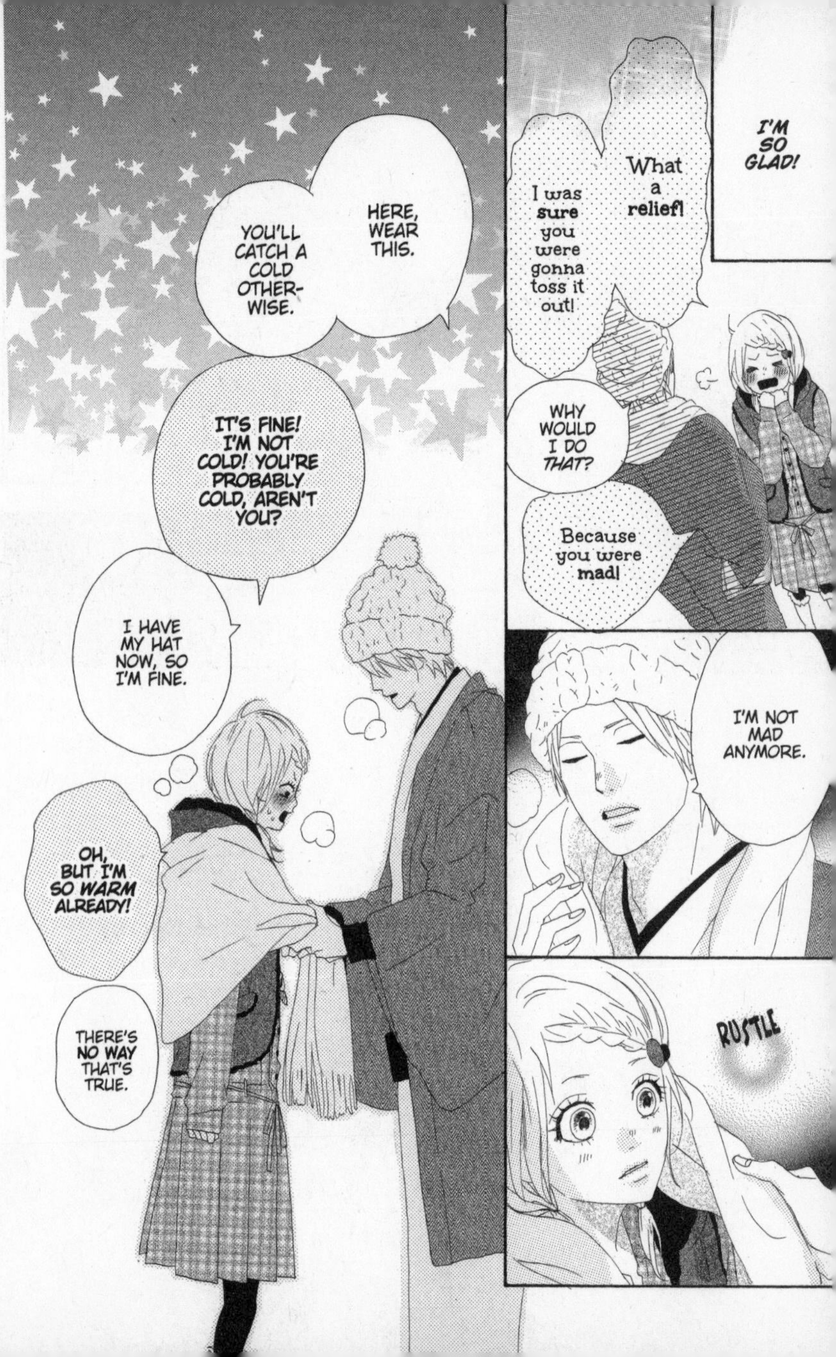
I'M SO GLAD!
What a relief!
I was sure you were gonna toss it out!
WHY WOULD I DO THAT?
Because you were mad!
I'M NOT MAD ANYMORE.
RUSTLE
HERE, WEAR THIS.
YOU'LL CATCH A COLD OTHERWISE.
IT'S FINE! I'M NOT COLD! YOU'RE PROBABLY COLD, AREN'T YOU?
I HAVE MY HAT NOW, SO I'M FINE.
OH, BUT I'M SO WARM ALREADY!
THERE'S NO WAY THAT'S TRUE.

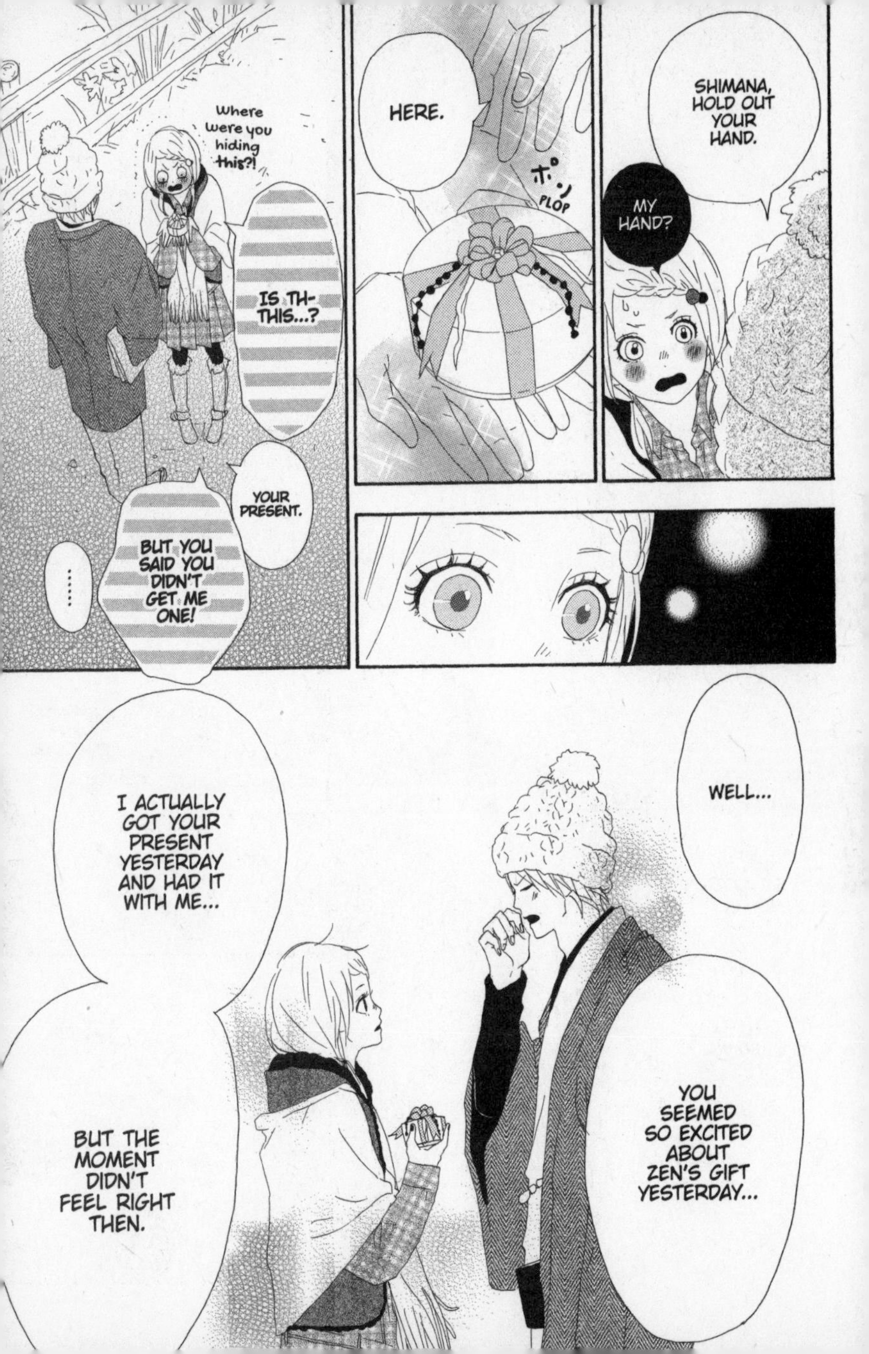
SHIMANA, HOLD OUT YOUR HAND.
MY HAND?
HERE.
ポン
PLOP
Where were you hiding this?!
IS TH- THIS...?
YOUR PRESENT.
BUT YOU SAID YOU DIDN'T GET ME ONE!
......
WELL...
YOU SEEMED SO EXCITED ABOUT ZEN'S GIFT YESTERDAY...
I ACTUALLY GOT YOUR PRESENT YESTERDAY AND HAD IT WITH ME...
BUT THE MOMENT DIDN'T FEEL RIGHT THEN.

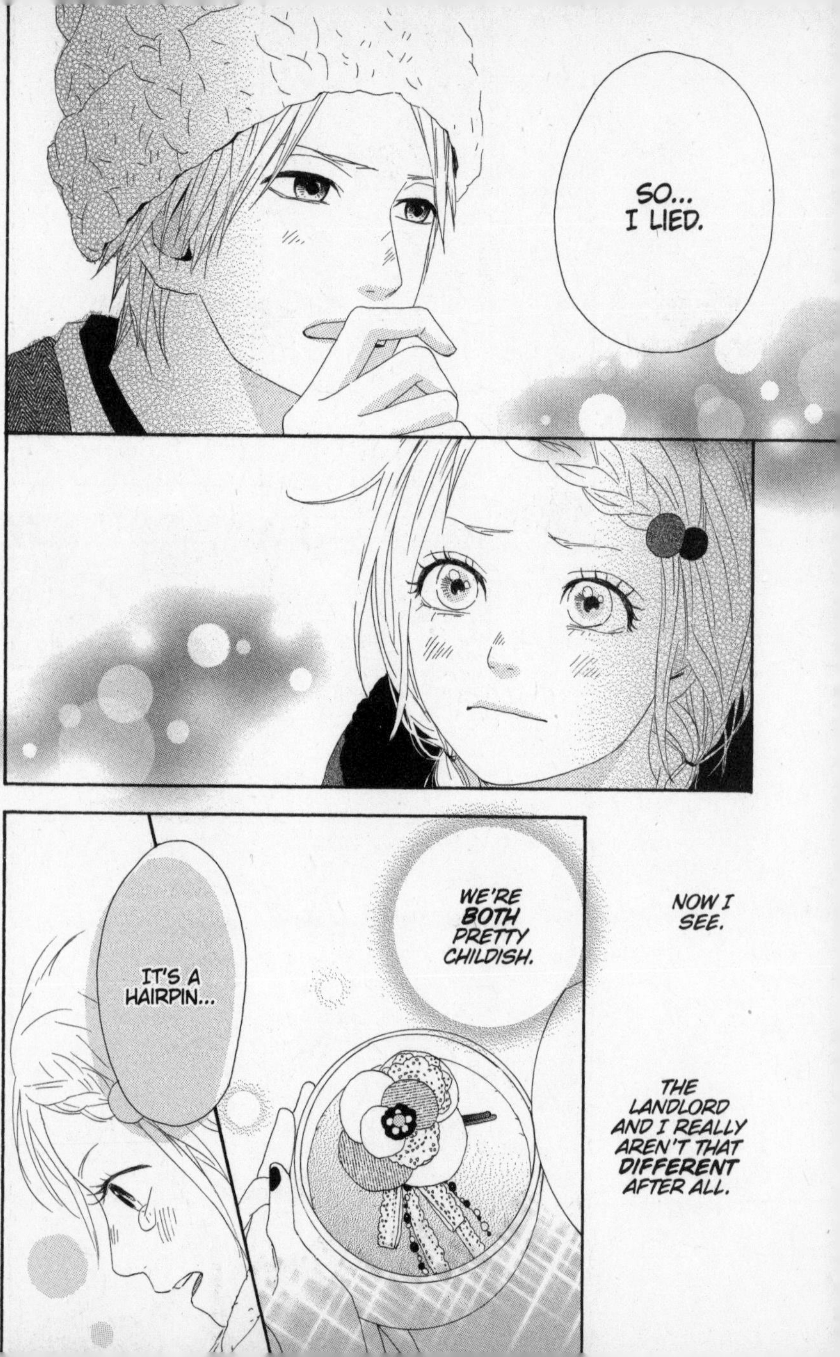
SO...
I LIED.
NOW I SEE.
WE'RE BOTH PRETTY CHILDISH.
IT'S A HAIRPIN...
THE LANDLORD AND I REALLY AREN'T THAT DIFFERENT AFTER ALL.

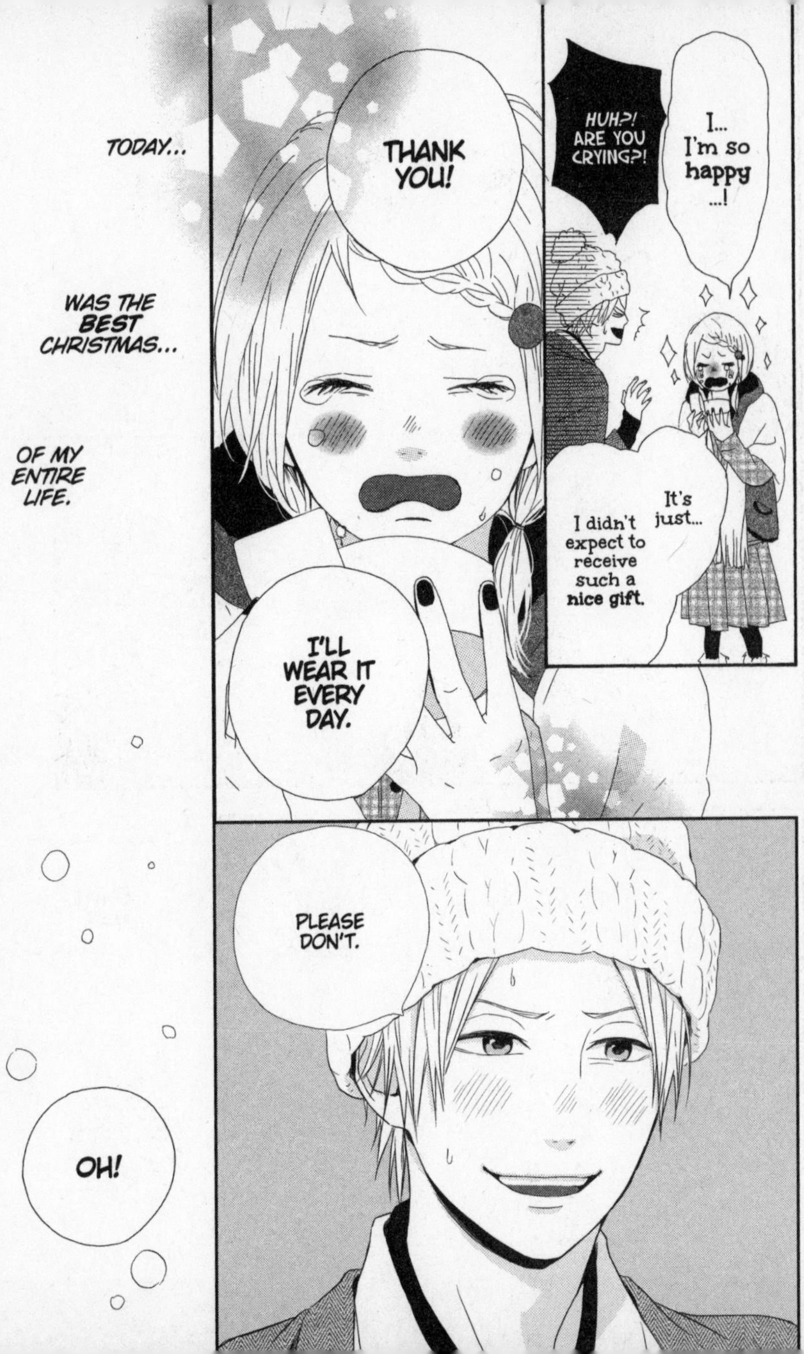
I... I'm so happy ...!
HUH?! ARE YOU CRYING?!
It's just... I didn't expect to receive such a nice gift.
THANK YOU!
I'LL WEAR IT EVERY DAY.
TODAY...
WAS THE BEST CHRISTMAS...
OF MY ENTIRE LIFE.
PLEASE DON'T.
OH!

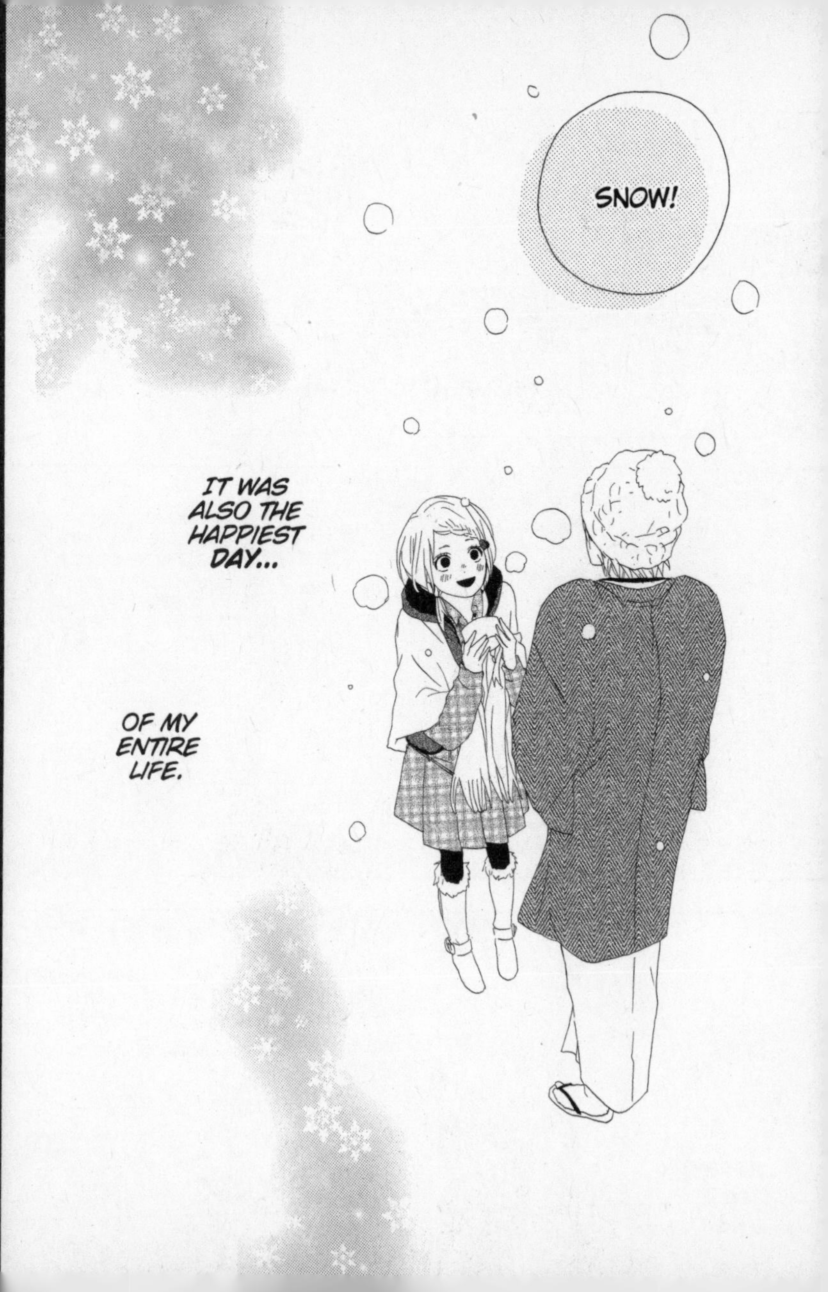
SNOW!
IT WAS ALSO THE HAPPIEST DAY...
OF MY ENTIRE LIFE.

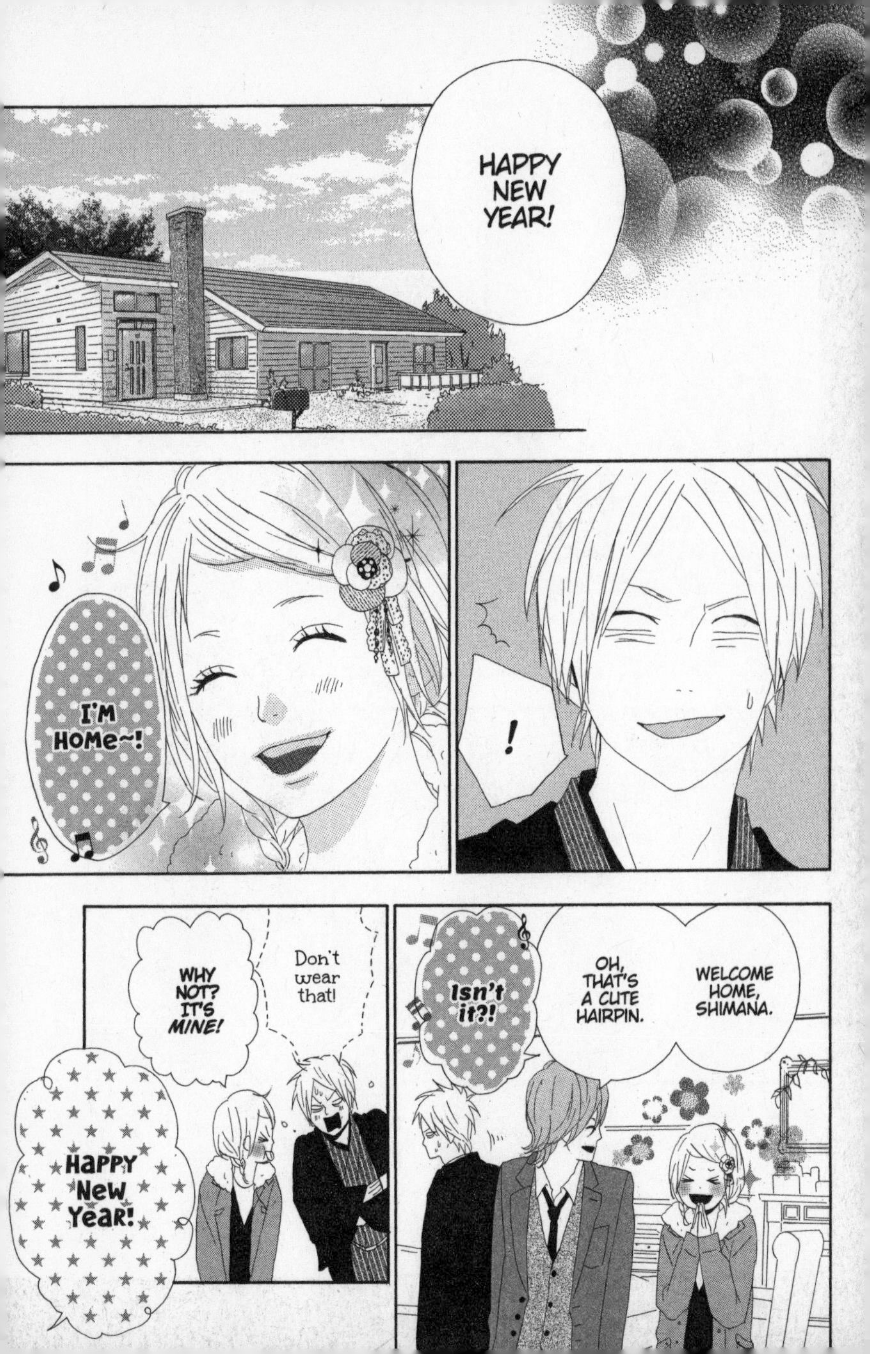
HAPPY NEW YEAR!
!
I'M HOME~!
WELCOME HOME, SHIMANA.
OH, THAT'S A CUTE HAIRPIN.
Isn't it?!
Don't wear that!
WHY NOT? IT'S MINE!
HAPPY NEW YEAR!

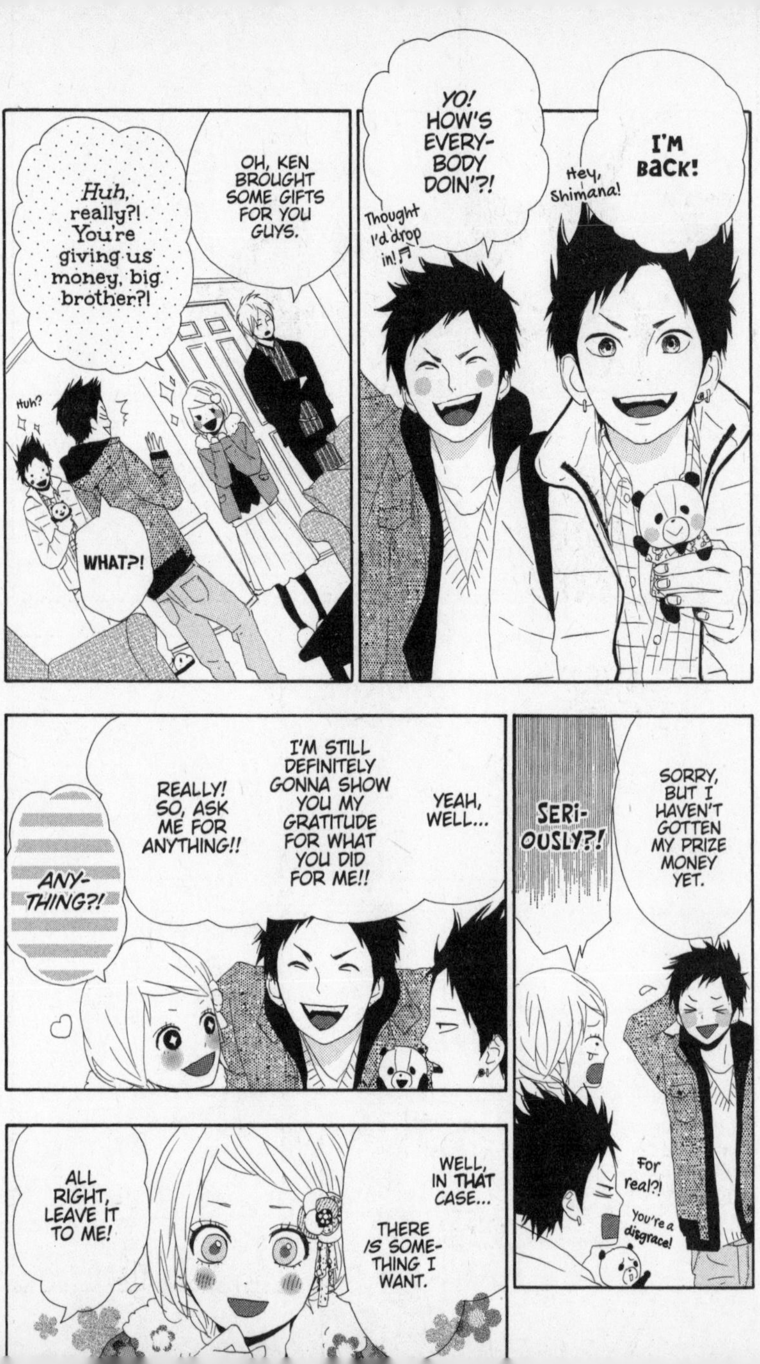
Hey, Shimana!
I'M BACK!
YO! HOW'S EVERY-BODY DOIN'?!
Thought I'd drop in!♪
OH, KEN BROUGHT SOME GIFTS FOR YOU GUYS.
Huh, really?! You're giving us money, big brother?!
Huh?
WHAT?!
SORRY, BUT I HAVEN'T GOTTEN MY PRIZE MONEY YET.
SERI-OUSLY?!
For real?!
You're a disgrace!
YEAH, WELL...
I'M STILL DEFINITELY GONNA SHOW YOU MY GRATITUDE FOR WHAT YOU DID FOR ME!!
REALLY! SO, ASK ME FOR ANYTHING!!
ANY-THING?!
WELL, IN THAT CASE...
THERE IS SOME-THING I WANT.
ALL RIGHT, LEAVE IT TO ME!

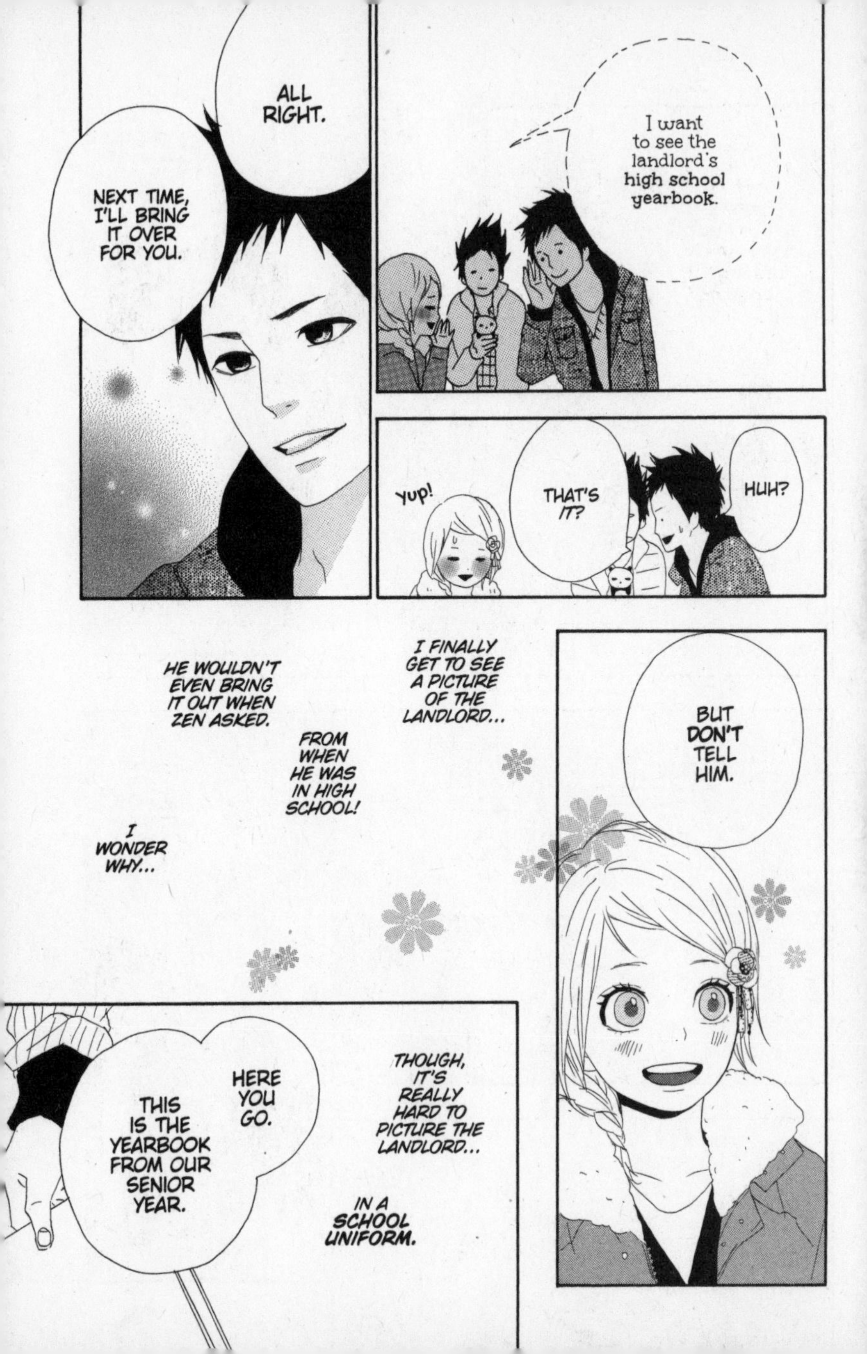
I want to see the landlord's high school yearbook.
HUH?
THAT'S IT?
YUP!
ALL RIGHT.
NEXT TIME, I'LL BRING IT OVER FOR YOU.
BUT DON'T TELL HIM.
I FINALLY GET TO SEE A PICTURE OF THE LANDLORD...
FROM WHEN HE WAS IN HIGH SCHOOL!
HE WOULDN'T EVEN BRING IT OUT WHEN ZEN ASKED.
I WONDER WHY...
THOUGH, IT'S REALLY HARD TO PICTURE THE LANDLORD...
IN A SCHOOL UNIFORM.
HERE YOU GO.
THIS IS THE YEARBOOK FROM OUR SENIOR YEAR.

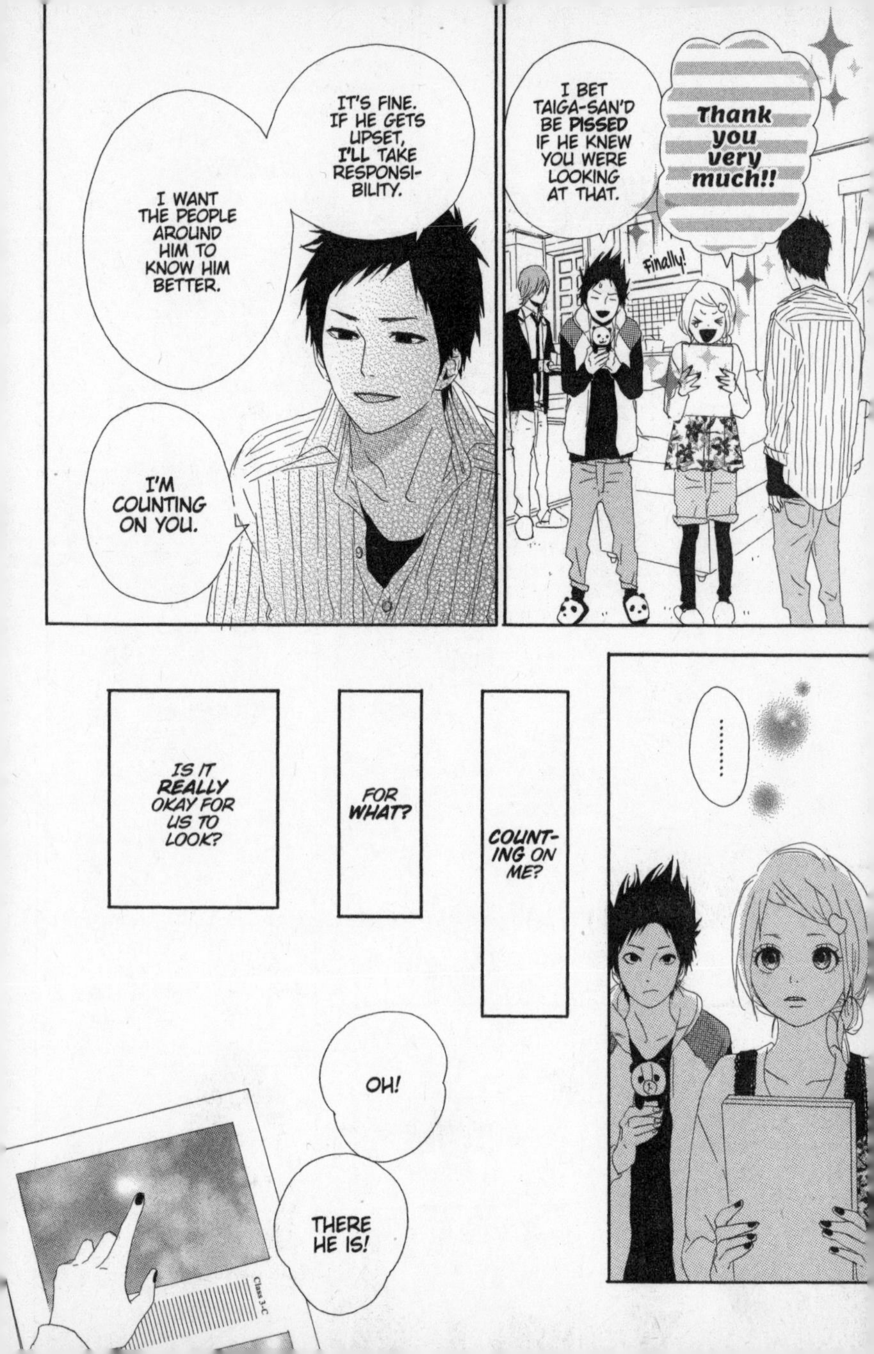
Thank you very much!!
Finally!
I BET TAIGA-SAN'D BE PISSED IF HE KNEW YOU WERE LOOKING AT THAT.
IT'S FINE. IF HE GETS UPSET, I'LL TAKE RESPONSIBILITY.
I WANT THE PEOPLE AROUND HIM TO KNOW HIM BETTER.
I'M COUNTING ON YOU.
......
COUNTING ON ME?
FOR WHAT?
IS IT REALLY OKAY FOR US TO LOOK?
OH!
THERE HE IS!
Class 3-C

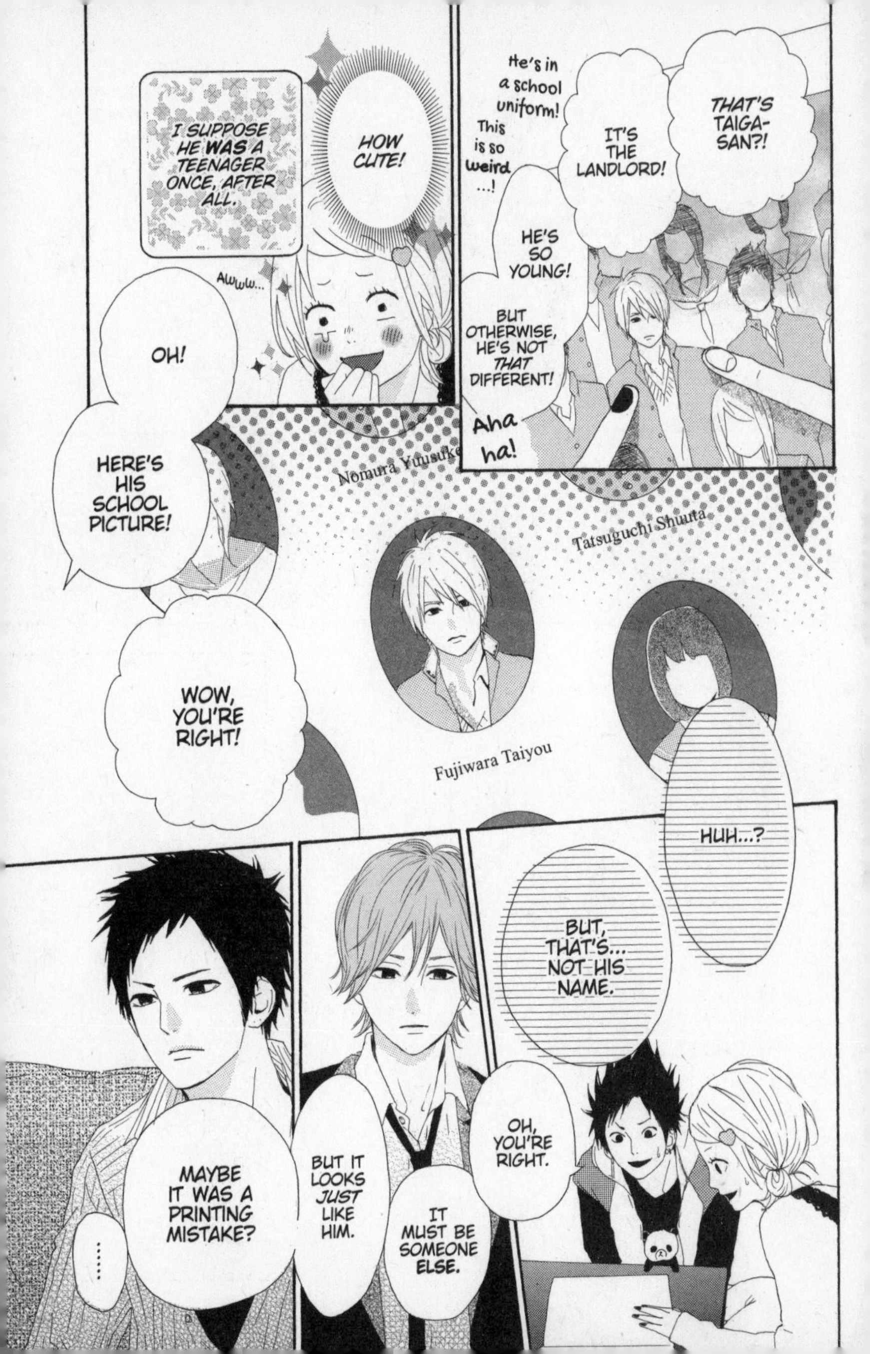
THAT'S TAIGA-SAN?!
IT'S THE LANDLORD!
He's in a school uniform!
This is so weird...!
HE'S SO YOUNG!
BUT OTHERWISE, HE'S NOT *THAT* DIFFERENT!
Aha ha!
HOW CUTE!
I SUPPOSE HE **WAS** A TEENAGER ONCE, AFTER ALL.
Awww...
OH!
HERE'S HIS SCHOOL PICTURE!
Nomura Yuusuke
Tatsuguchi Shuuta
Fujiwara Taiyou
WOW, YOU'RE RIGHT!
HUH...?
BUT, THAT'S... NOT HIS NAME.
OH, YOU'RE RIGHT.
IT MUST BE SOMEONE ELSE.
BUT IT LOOKS *JUST* LIKE HIM.
MAYBE IT WAS A PRINTING MISTAKE?
......

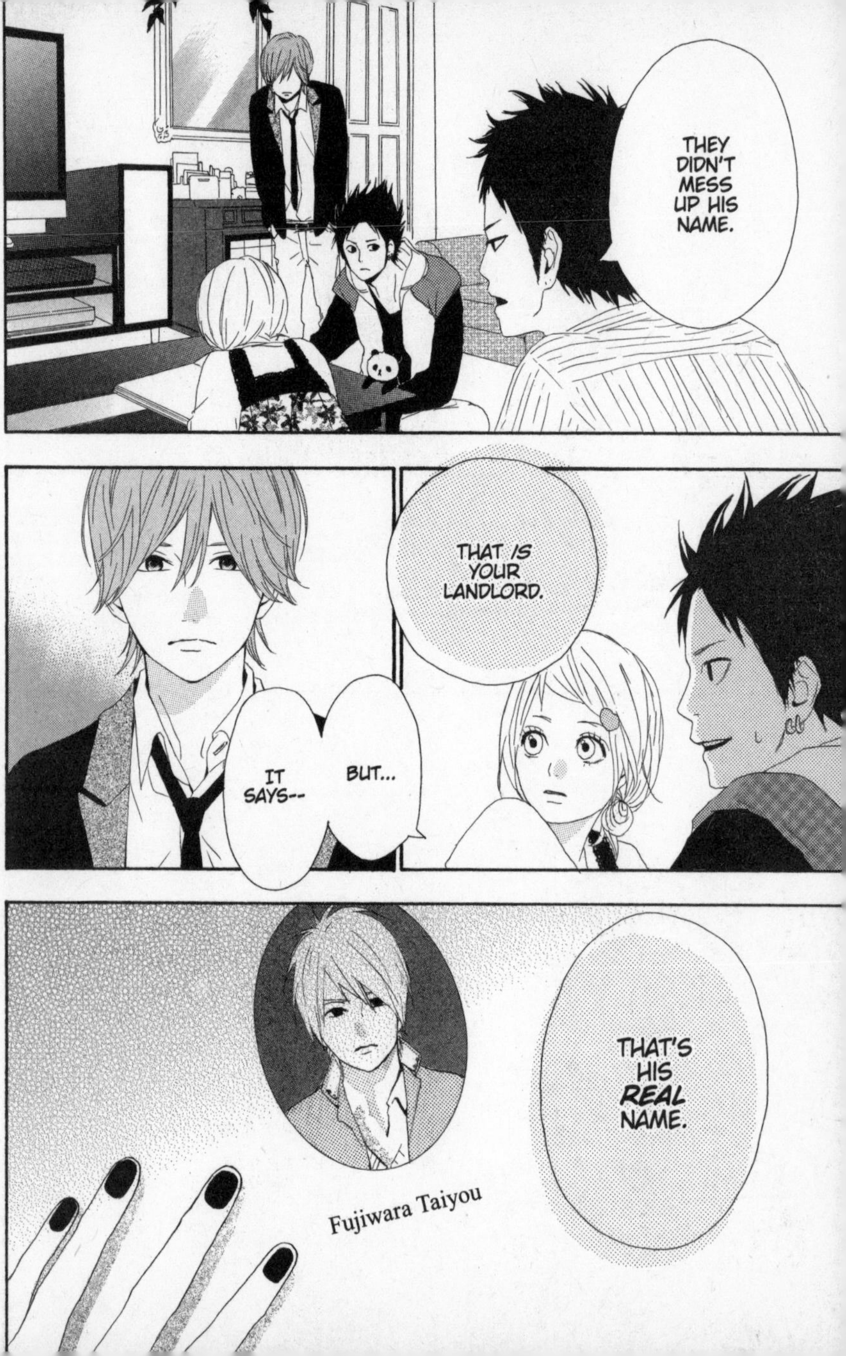
THEY DIDN'T MESS UP HIS NAME.
THAT IS YOUR LANDLORD.
BUT...
IT SAYS--
THAT'S HIS REAL NAME.
Fujiwara Taiyou

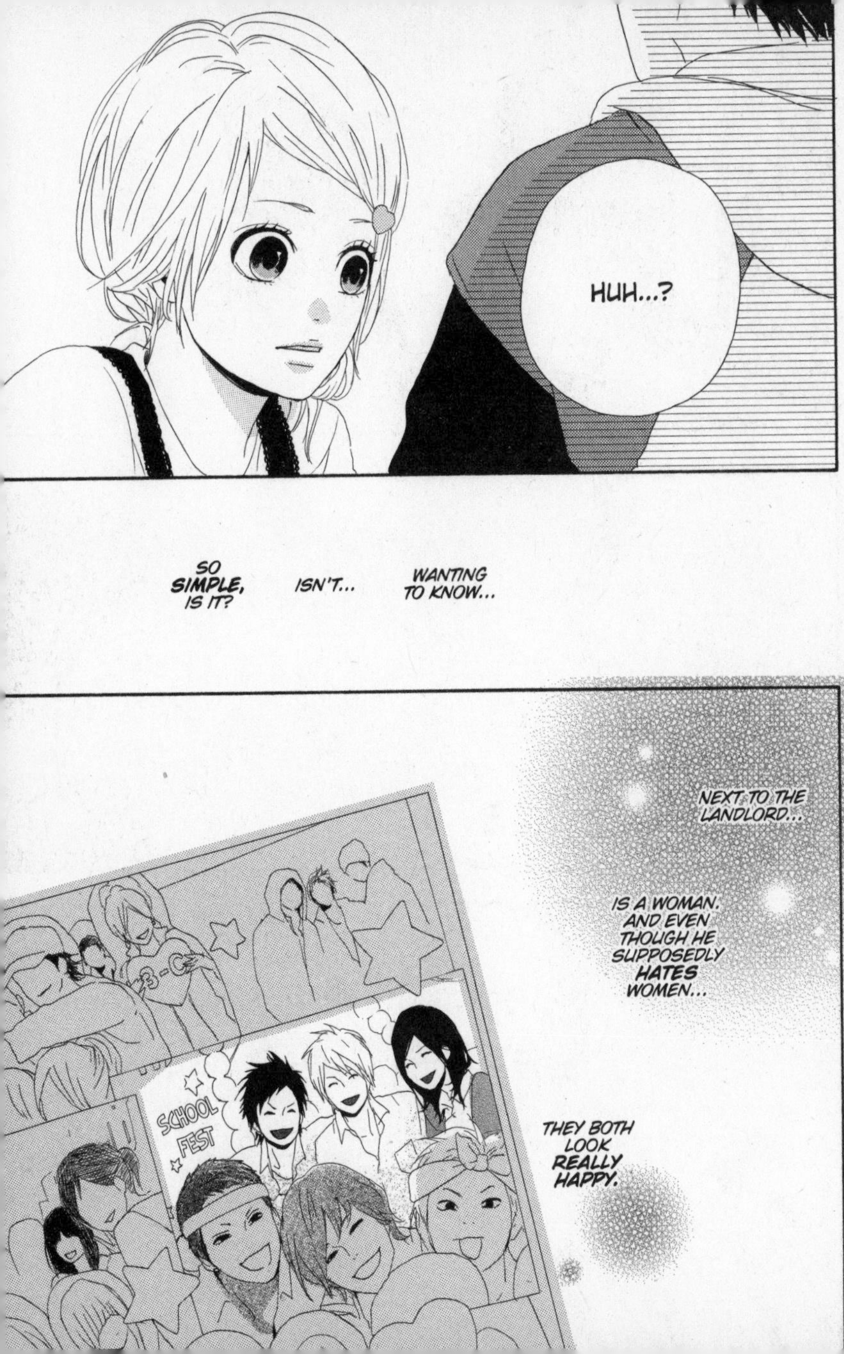
HUH...?
WANTING TO KNOW...
ISN'T...
SO **SIMPLE,** IS IT?
NEXT TO THE LANDLORD...
IS A WOMAN. AND EVEN THOUGH HE SUPPOSEDLY **HATES** WOMEN...
THEY BOTH LOOK **REALLY HAPPY.**
3-C
SCHOOL FEST

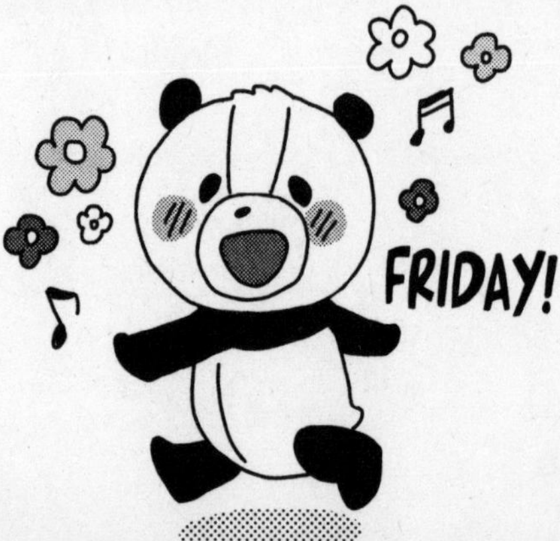
FRIDAY!

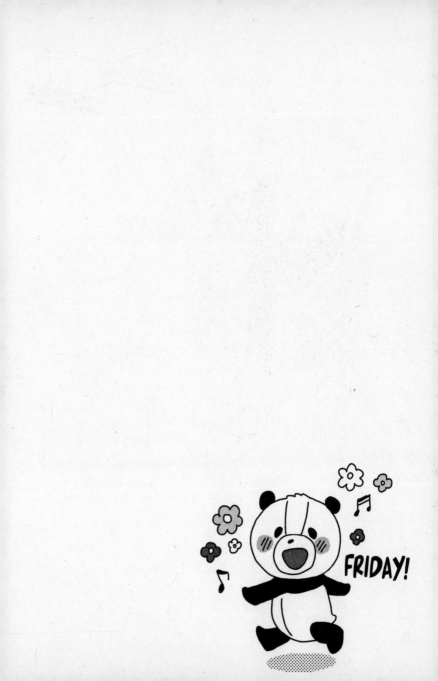

Dreamin' Sun

17th DOOR

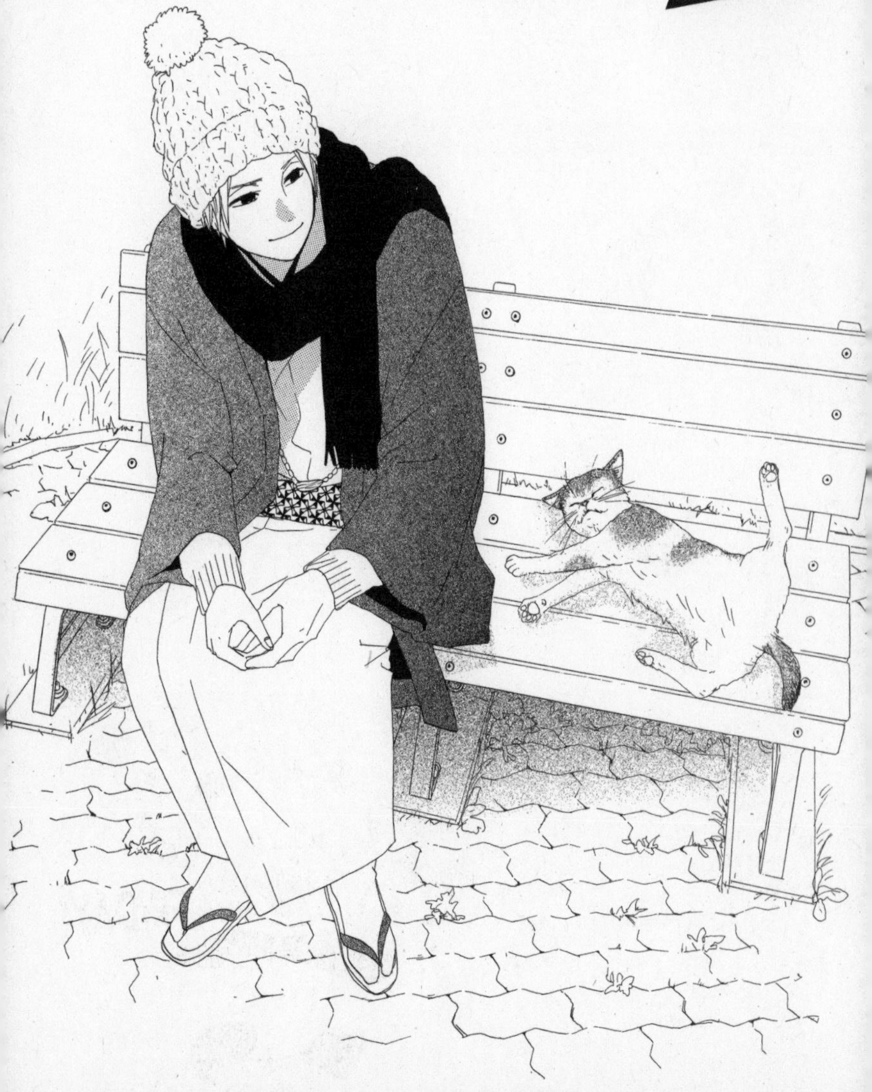

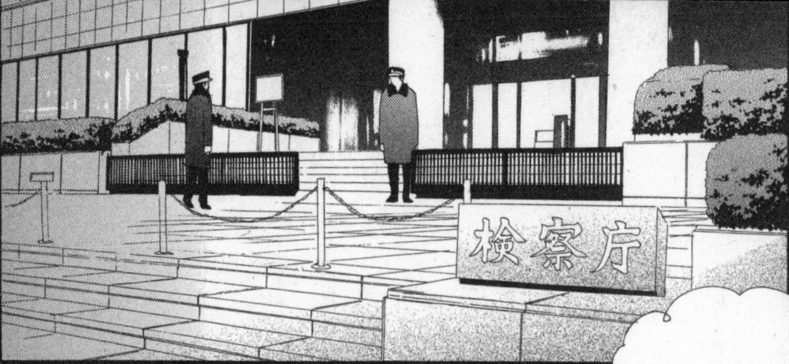
検察庁

Sign: Public Prosecutor's Office

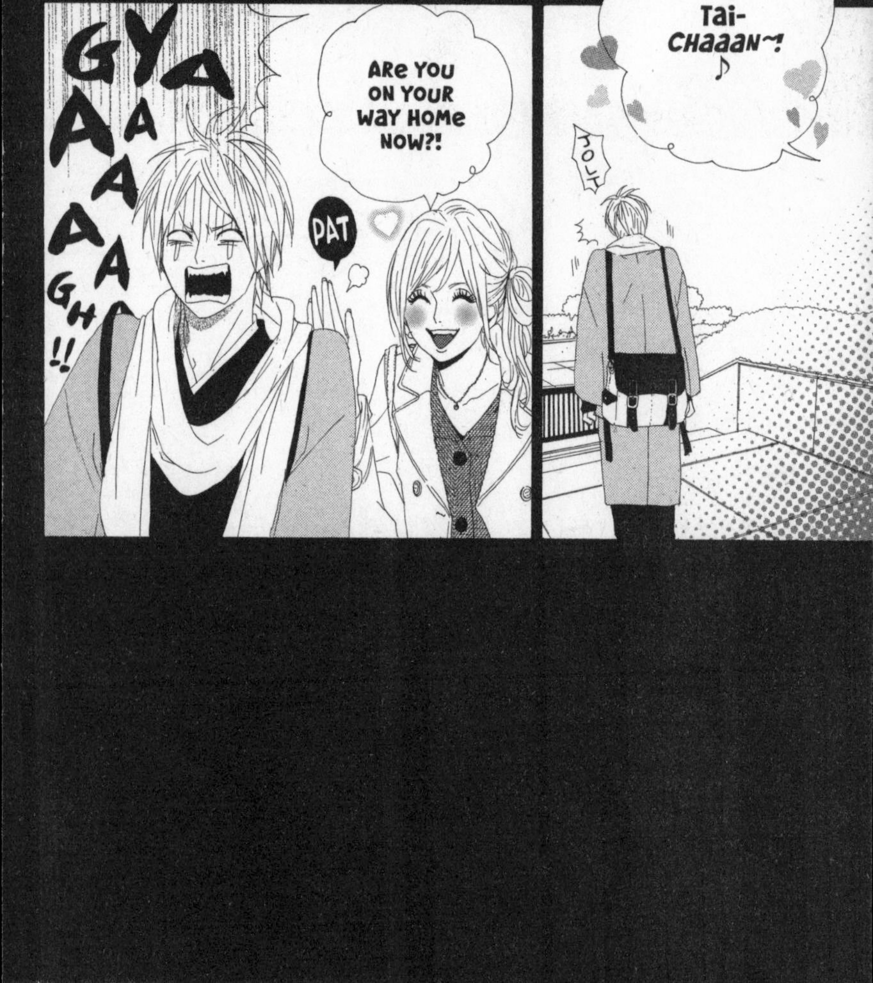
Tai-chaaan~! ♪
JOLT
Are you on your way home now?!
PAT
GYAAAAAAAGH!!

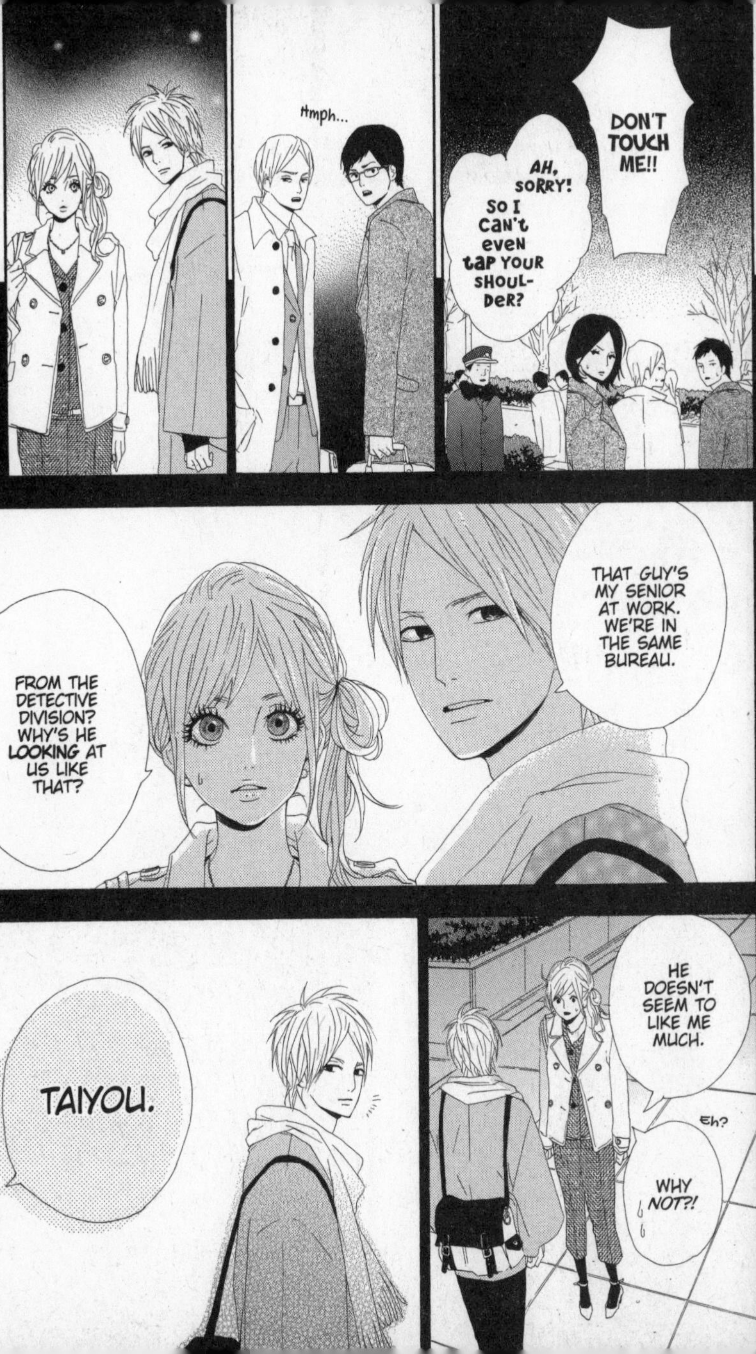
DON'T TOUCH ME!!
AH, SORRY! SO I CAN'T EVEN TAP YOUR SHOULDER?
Hmph...
THAT GUY'S MY SENIOR AT WORK. WE'RE IN THE SAME BUREAU.
FROM THE DETECTIVE DIVISION? WHY'S HE LOOKING AT US LIKE THAT?
HE DOESN'T SEEM TO LIKE ME MUCH.
Eh?
WHY NOT?!
TAIYOU.

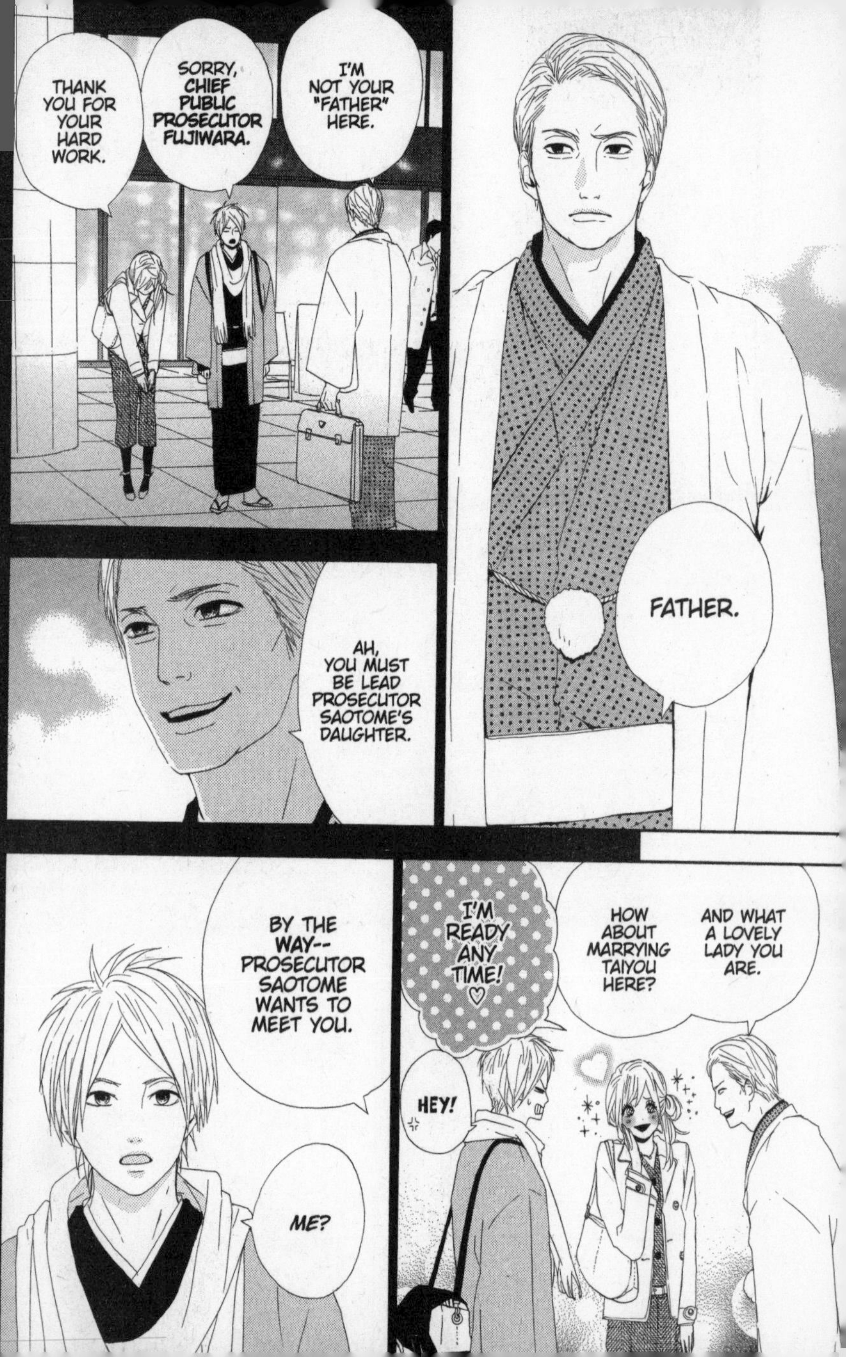
FATHER.
I'M NOT YOUR "FATHER" HERE.
SORRY, CHIEF PUBLIC PROSECUTOR FUJIWARA.
THANK YOU FOR YOUR HARD WORK.
AH, YOU MUST BE LEAD PROSECUTOR SAOTOME'S DAUGHTER.
AND WHAT A LOVELY LADY YOU ARE.
HOW ABOUT MARRYING TAIYOU HERE?
I'M READY ANY TIME! ♡
HEY!
BY THE WAY-- PROSECUTOR SAOTOME WANTS TO MEET YOU.
ME?

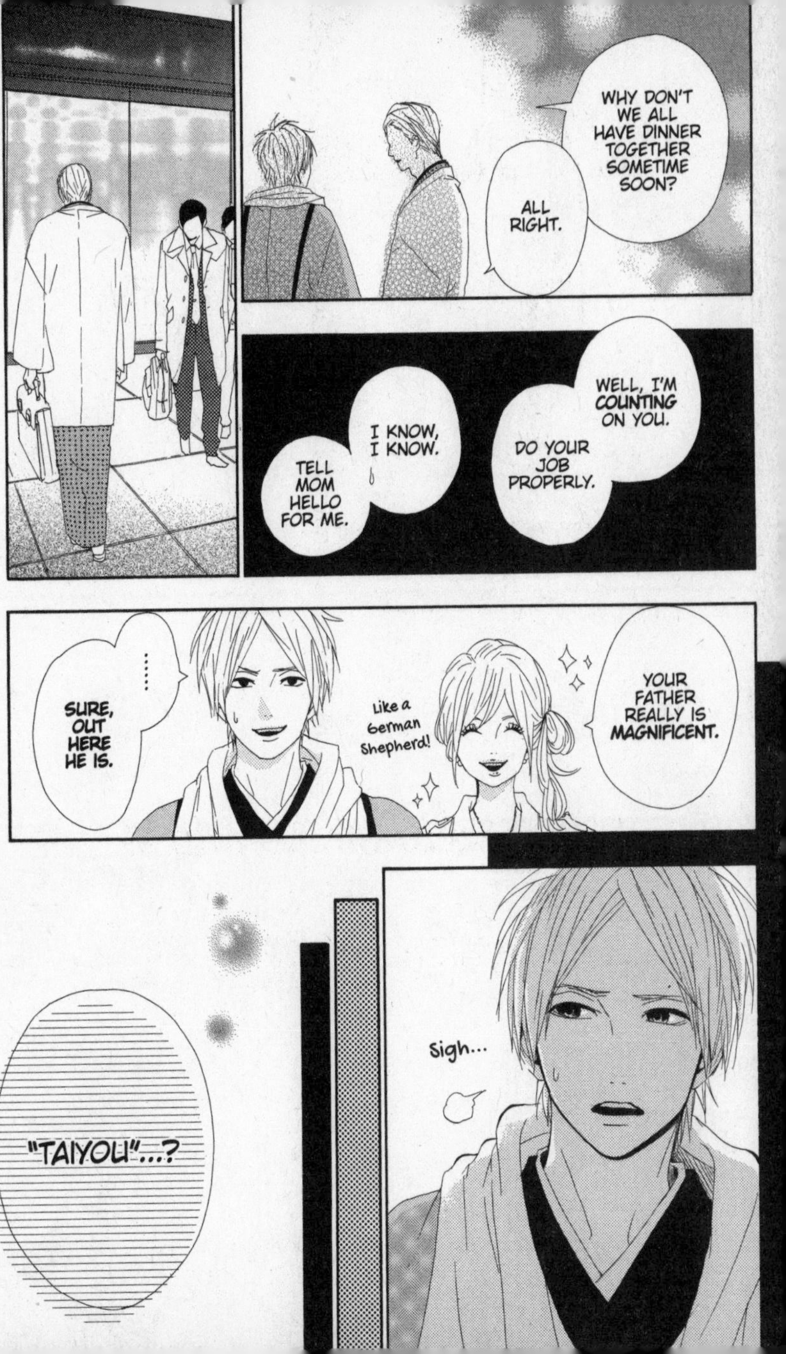
WHY DON'T WE ALL HAVE DINNER TOGETHER SOMETIME SOON?
ALL RIGHT.
WELL, I'M COUNTING ON YOU.
DO YOUR JOB PROPERLY.
I KNOW, I KNOW.
TELL MOM HELLO FOR ME.
YOUR FATHER REALLY IS MAGNIFICENT.
Like a German Shepherd!
......
SURE, OUT HERE HE IS.
Sigh...
"TAIYOU"...?

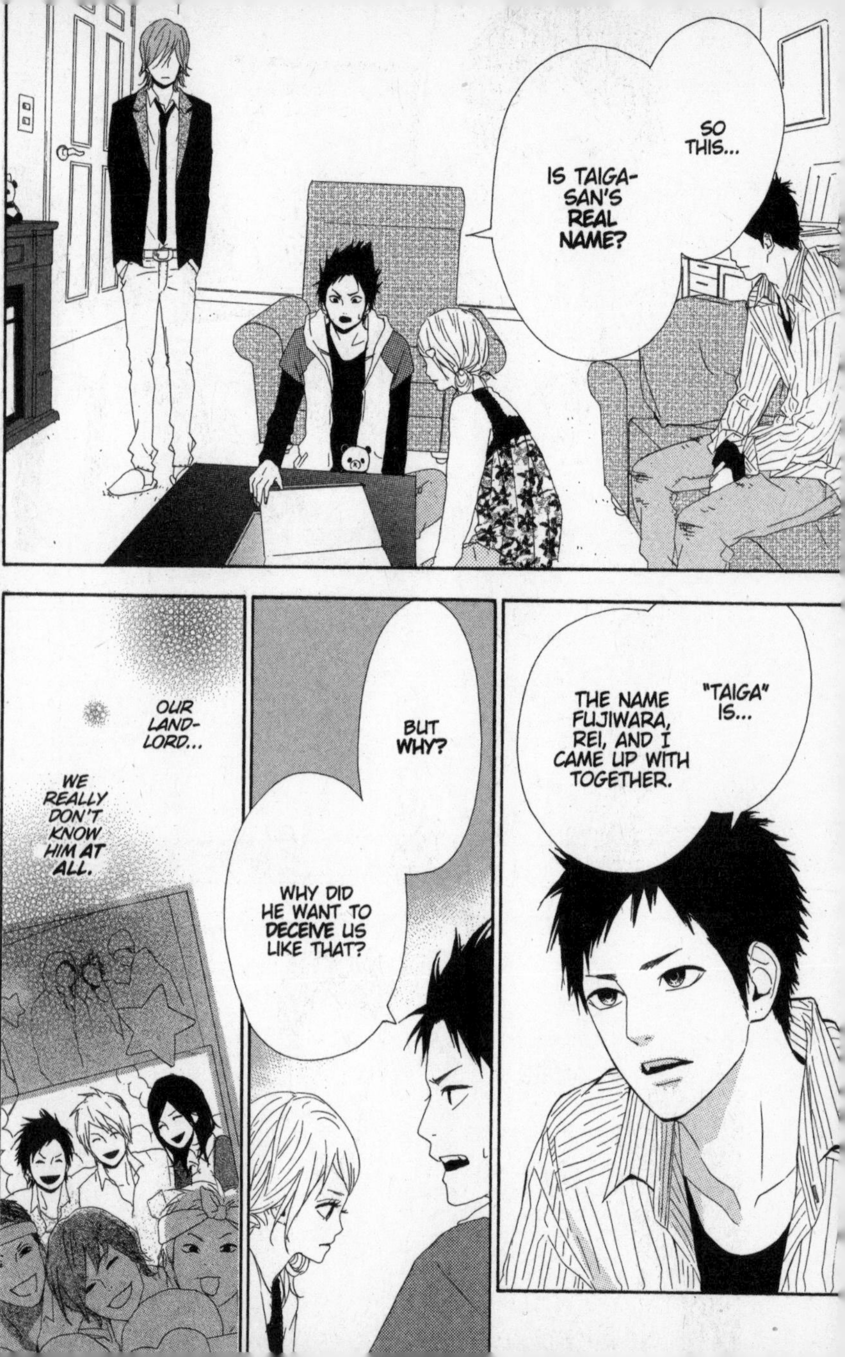
SO THIS...
IS TAIGA-SAN'S REAL NAME?
"TAIGA" IS...
THE NAME FUJIWARA, REI, AND I CAME UP WITH TOGETHER.
BUT WHY?
WHY DID HE WANT TO DECEIVE US LIKE THAT?
OUR LANDLORD...
WE REALLY DON'T KNOW HIM AT ALL.

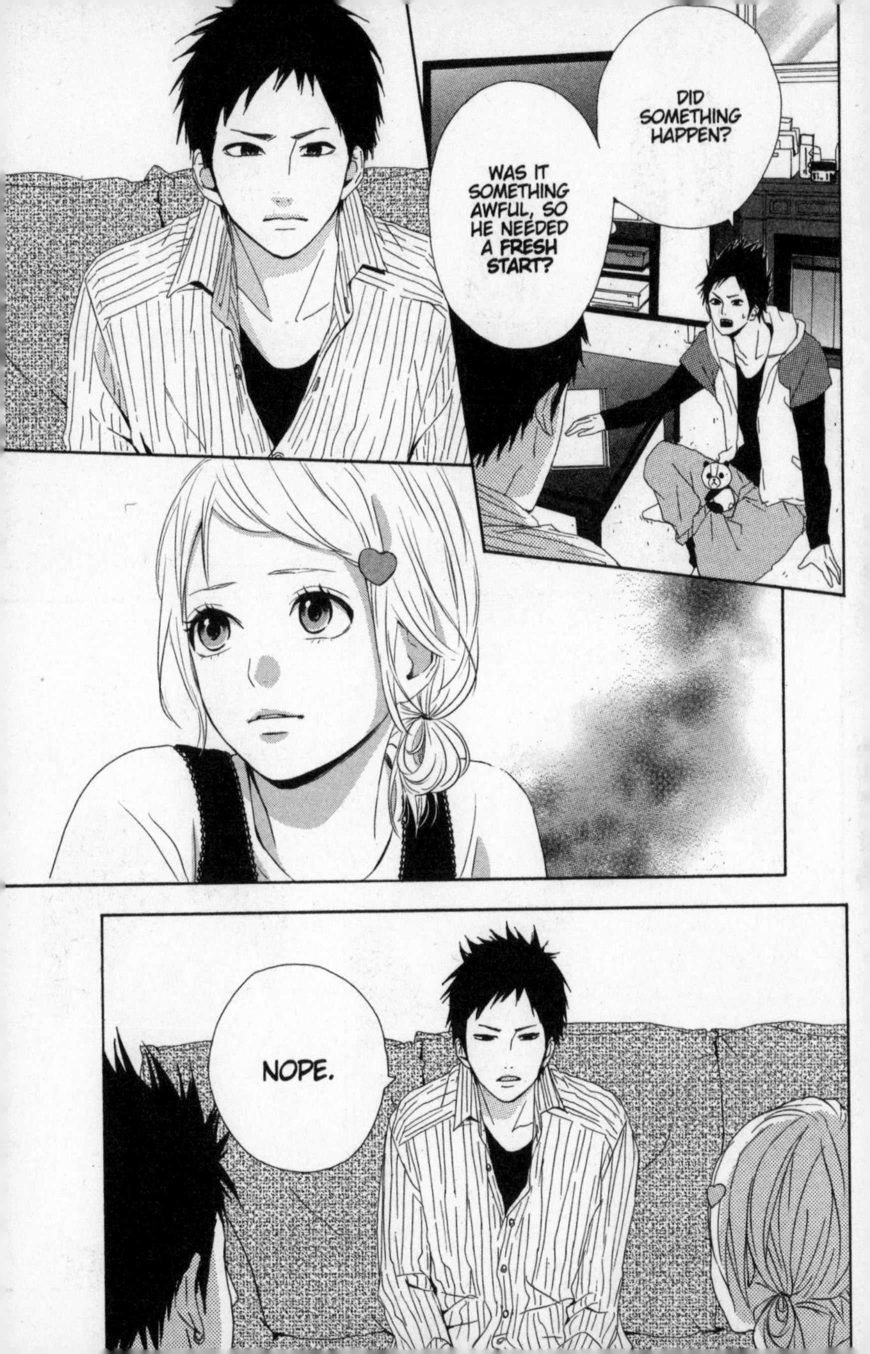
DID SOMETHING HAPPEN?
WAS IT SOMETHING AWFUL, SO HE NEEDED A FRESH START?
NOPE.

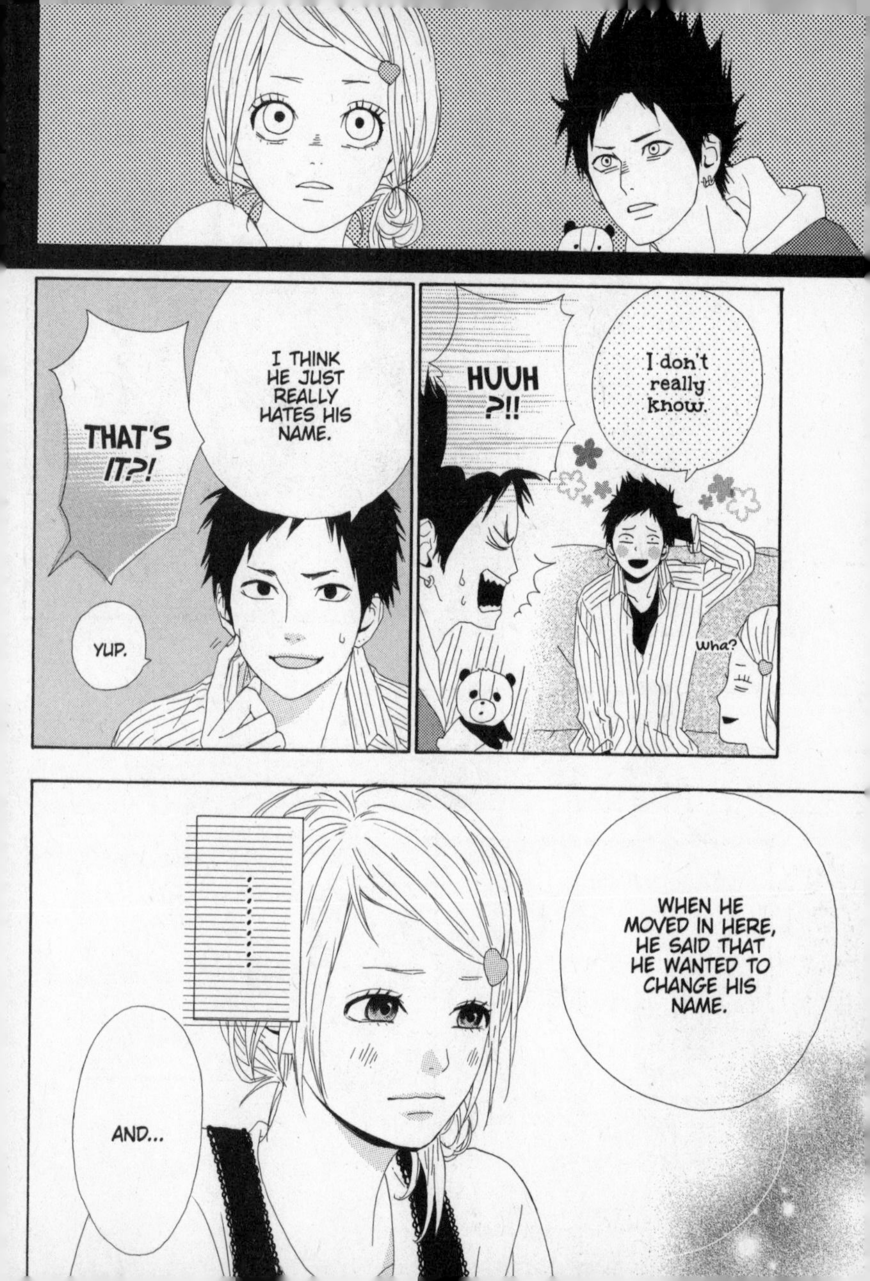

I don't really know.
HUUH ?!!
Wha?
I THINK HE JUST REALLY HATES HIS NAME.
THAT'S IT?!
YUP.
WHEN HE MOVED IN HERE, HE SAID THAT HE WANTED TO CHANGE HIS NAME.
......
AND...

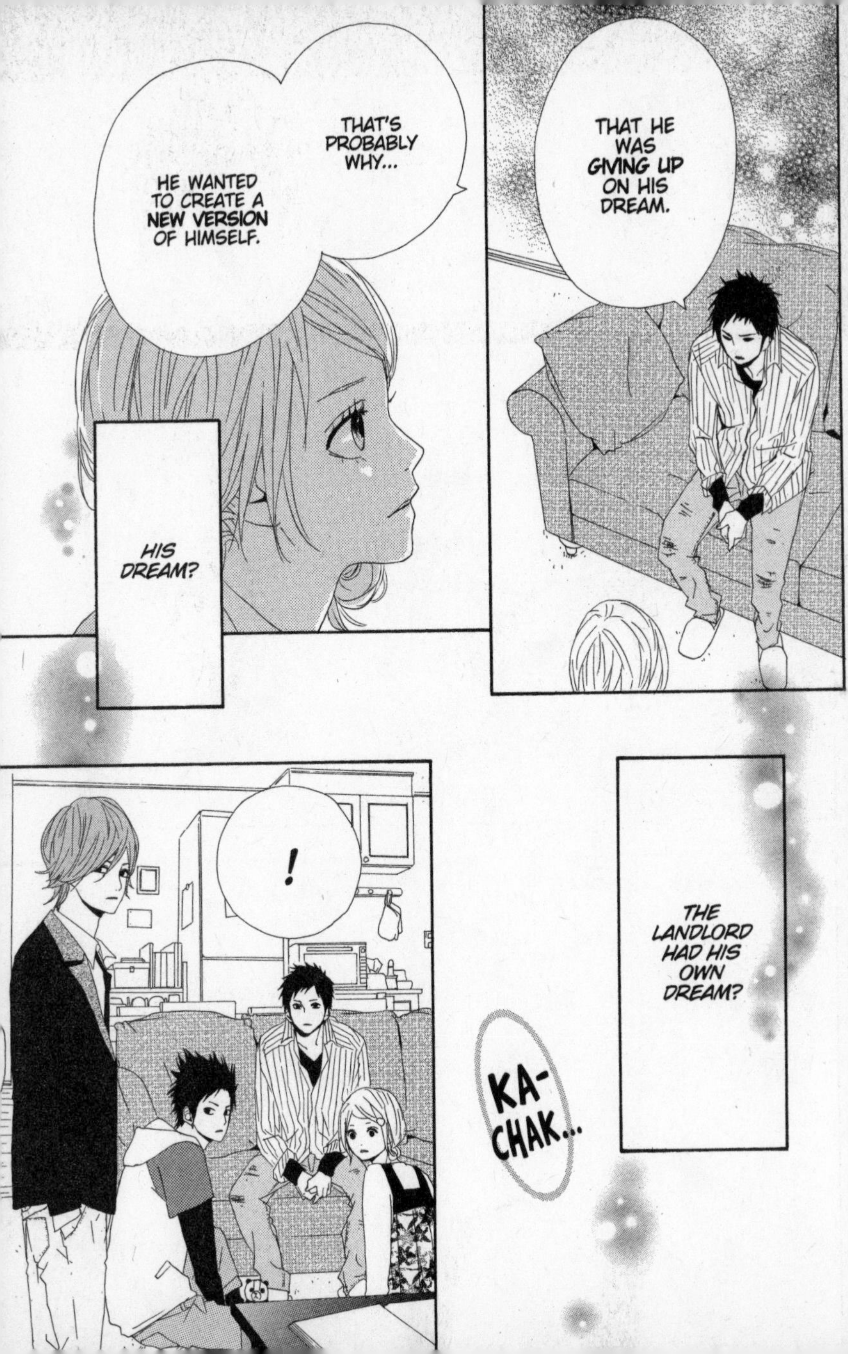
THAT HE WAS GIVING UP ON HIS DREAM.
THAT'S PROBABLY WHY...
HE WANTED TO CREATE A NEW VERSION OF HIMSELF.
HIS DREAM?
THE LANDLORD HAD HIS OWN DREAM?
KA-CHAK...
!

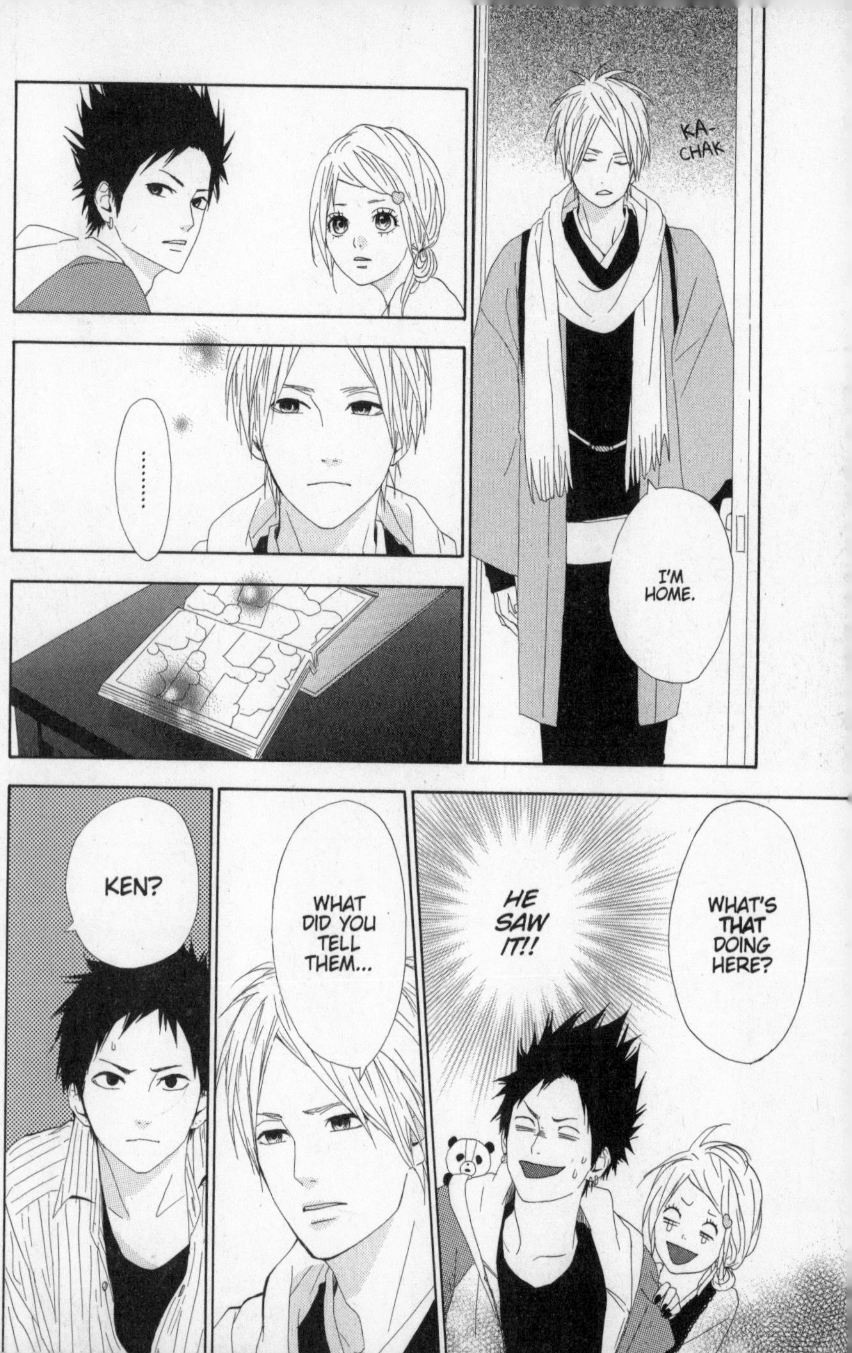
KA-CHAK
I'M HOME.
......
WHAT'S THAT DOING HERE?
HE SAW IT!!
WHAT DID YOU TELL THEM...
KEN?

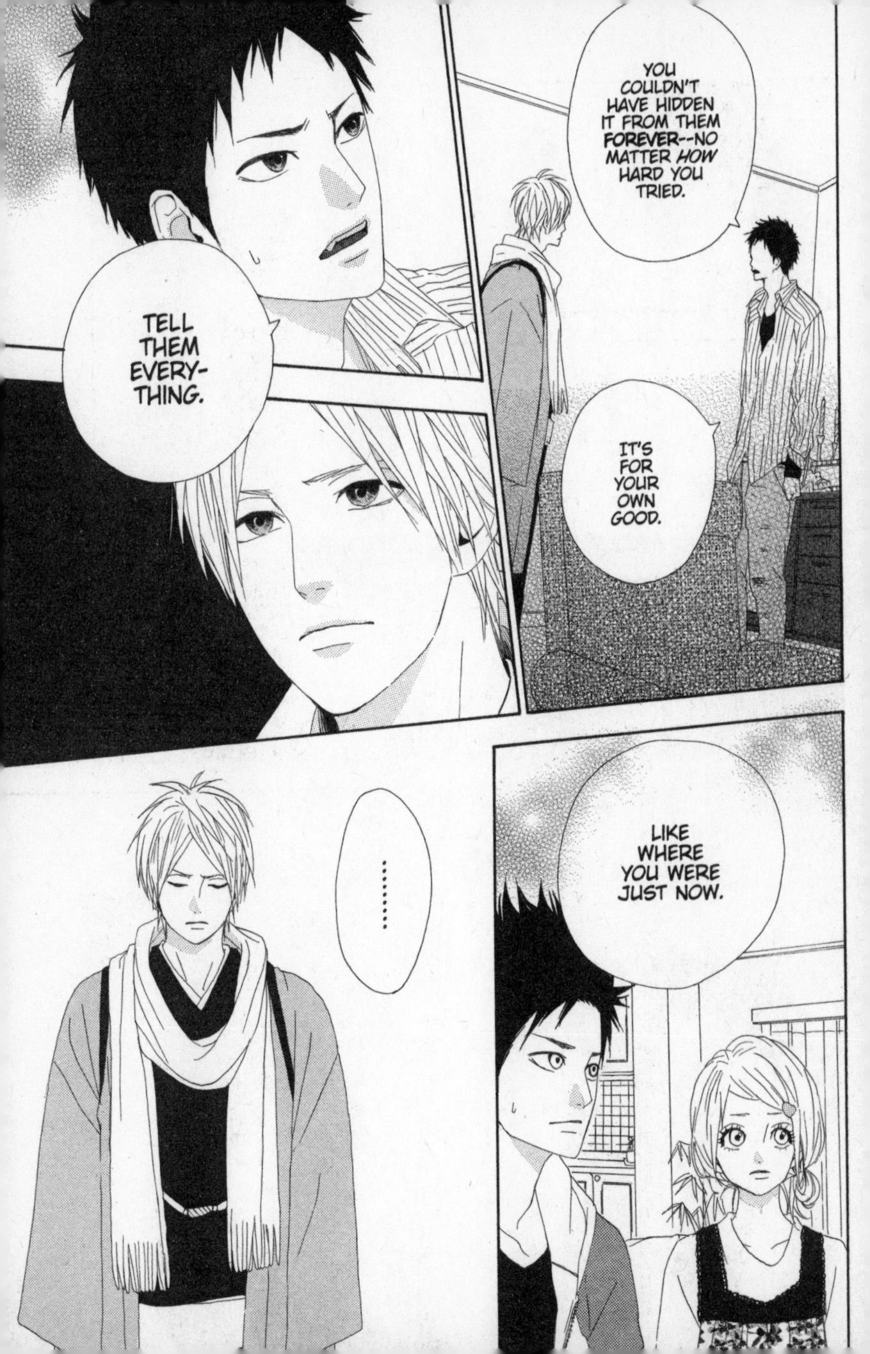
YOU COULDN'T HAVE HIDDEN IT FROM THEM FOREVER--NO MATTER *HOW* HARD YOU TRIED.
IT'S FOR YOUR OWN GOOD.
TELL THEM EVERY-THING.
LIKE WHERE YOU WERE JUST NOW.
......

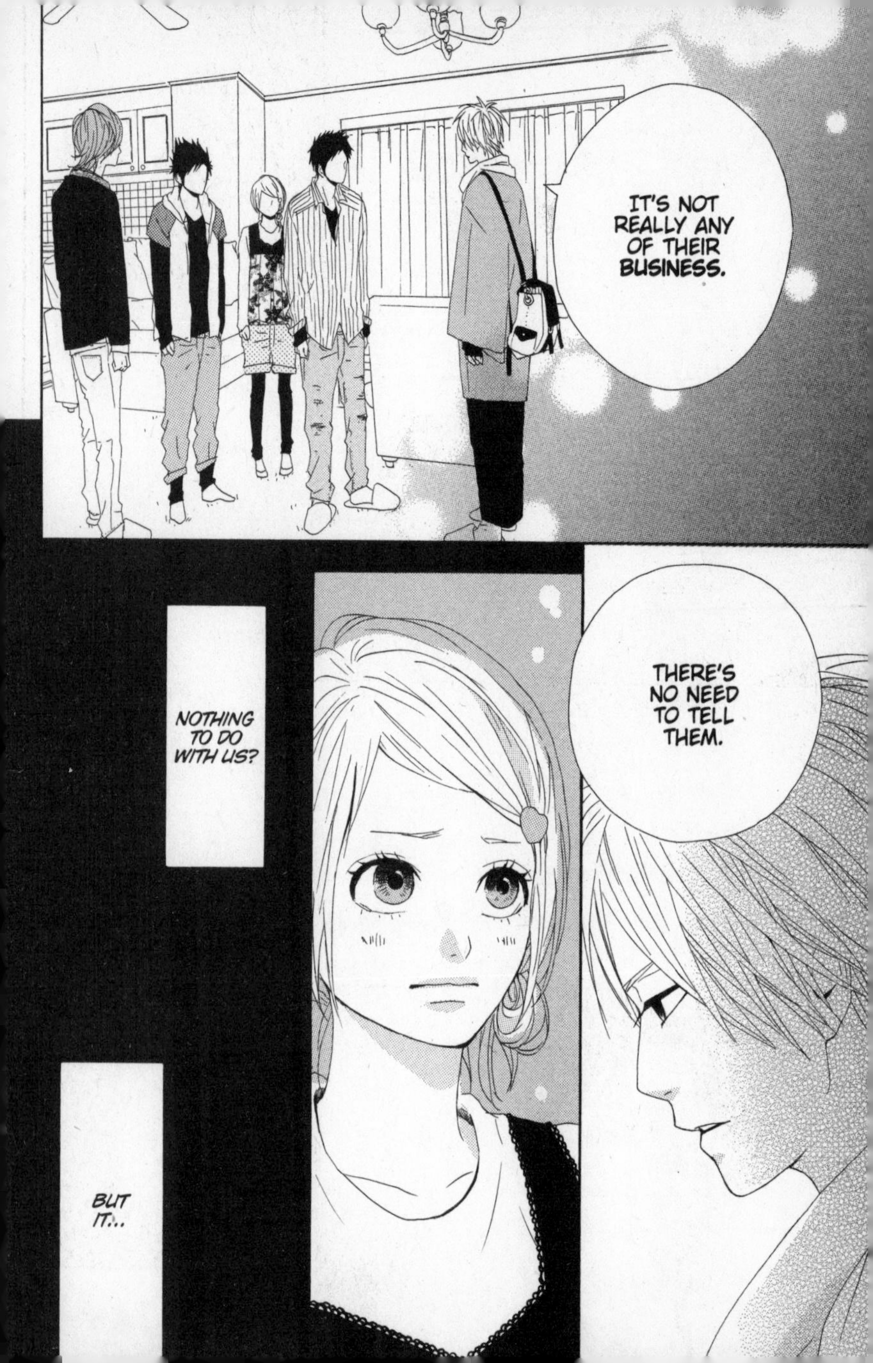
IT'S NOT REALLY ANY OF THEIR BUSINESS.
THERE'S NO NEED TO TELL THEM.
NOTHING TO DO WITH US?
BUT IT...

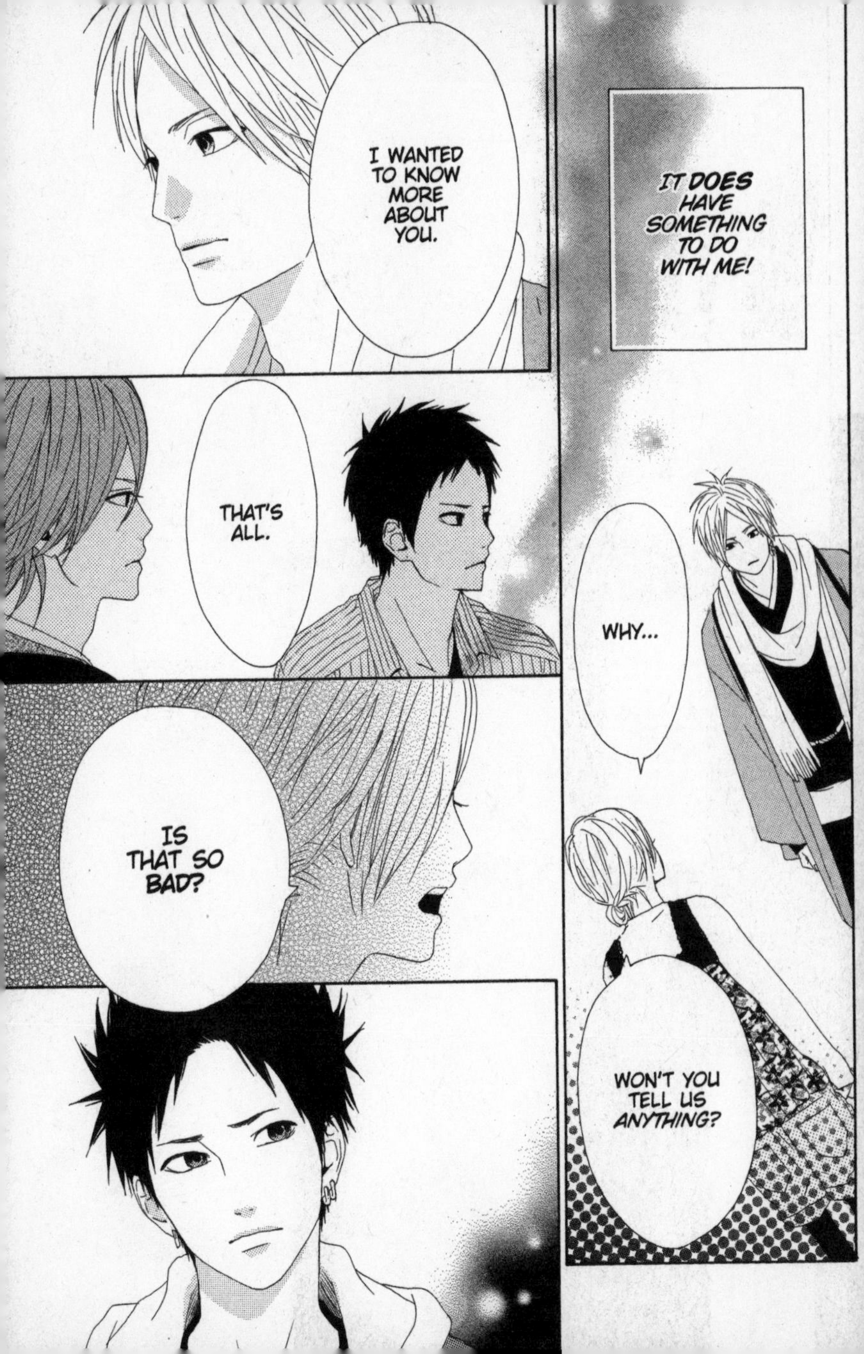
IT DOES HAVE SOMETHING TO DO WITH ME!
WHY...
WON'T YOU TELL US ANYTHING?
I WANTED TO KNOW MORE ABOUT YOU.
THAT'S ALL.
IS THAT SO BAD?

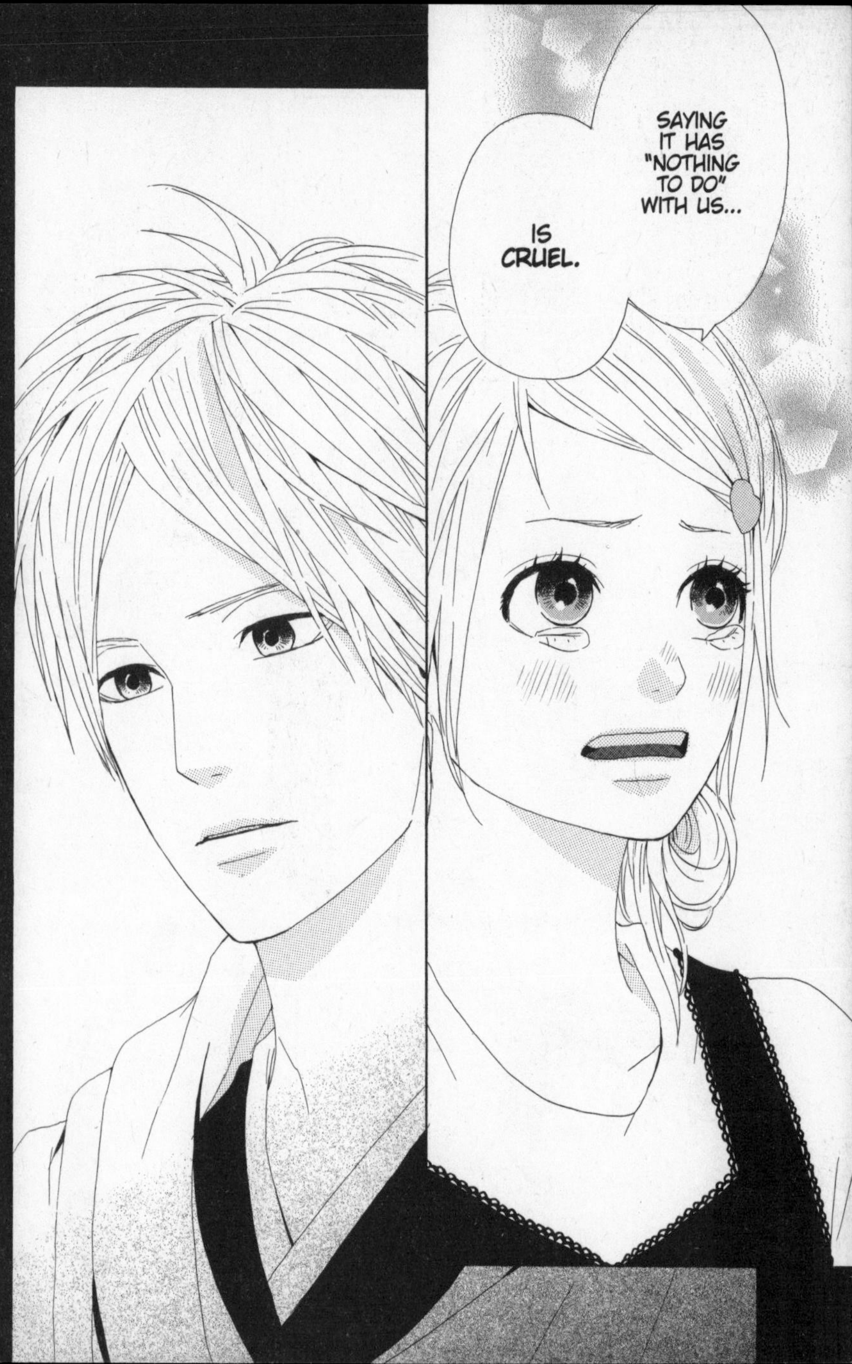
SAYING IT HAS "NOTHING TO DO" WITH US...
IS CRUEL.

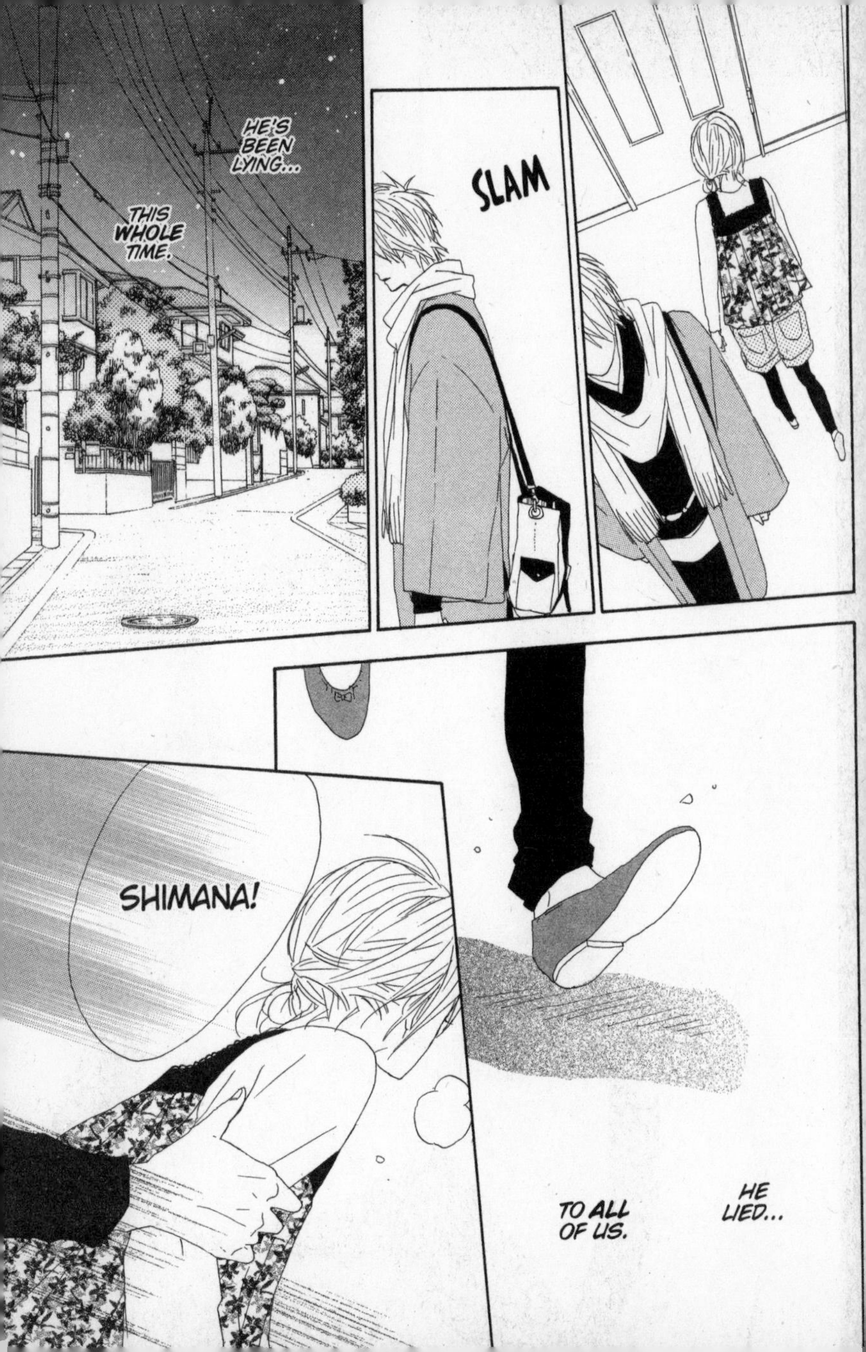
SLAM
HE'S BEEN LYING...
THIS WHOLE TIME.
HE LIED...
TO ALL OF US.
SHIMANA!

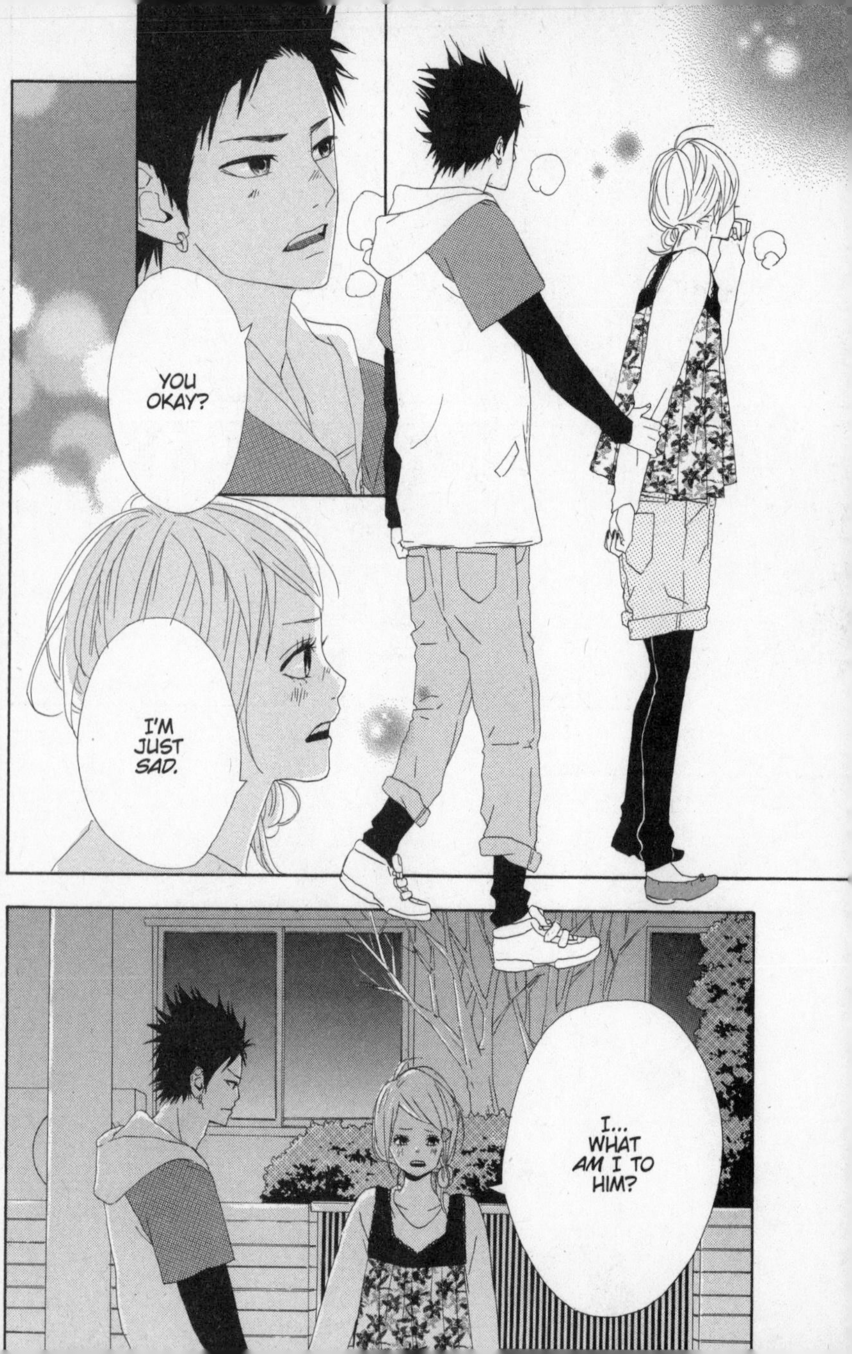
YOU OKAY?
I'M JUST SAD.
I... WHAT *AM* I TO HIM?

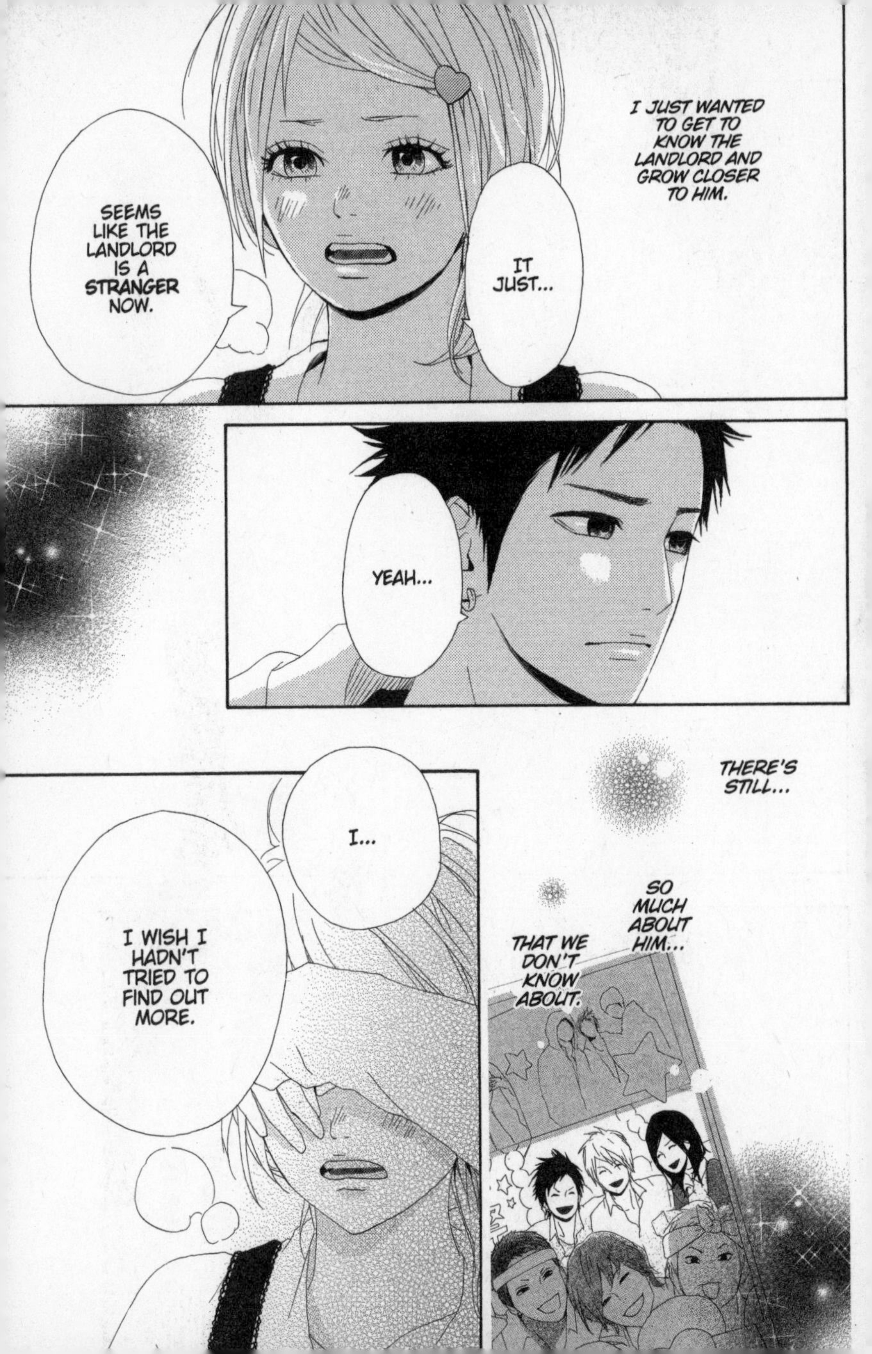
I JUST WANTED TO GET TO KNOW THE LANDLORD AND GROW CLOSER TO HIM.
IT JUST...
SEEMS LIKE THE LANDLORD IS A STRANGER NOW.
YEAH...
THERE'S STILL...
SO MUCH ABOUT HIM...
THAT WE DON'T KNOW ABOUT.
I...
I WISH I HADN'T TRIED TO FIND OUT MORE.

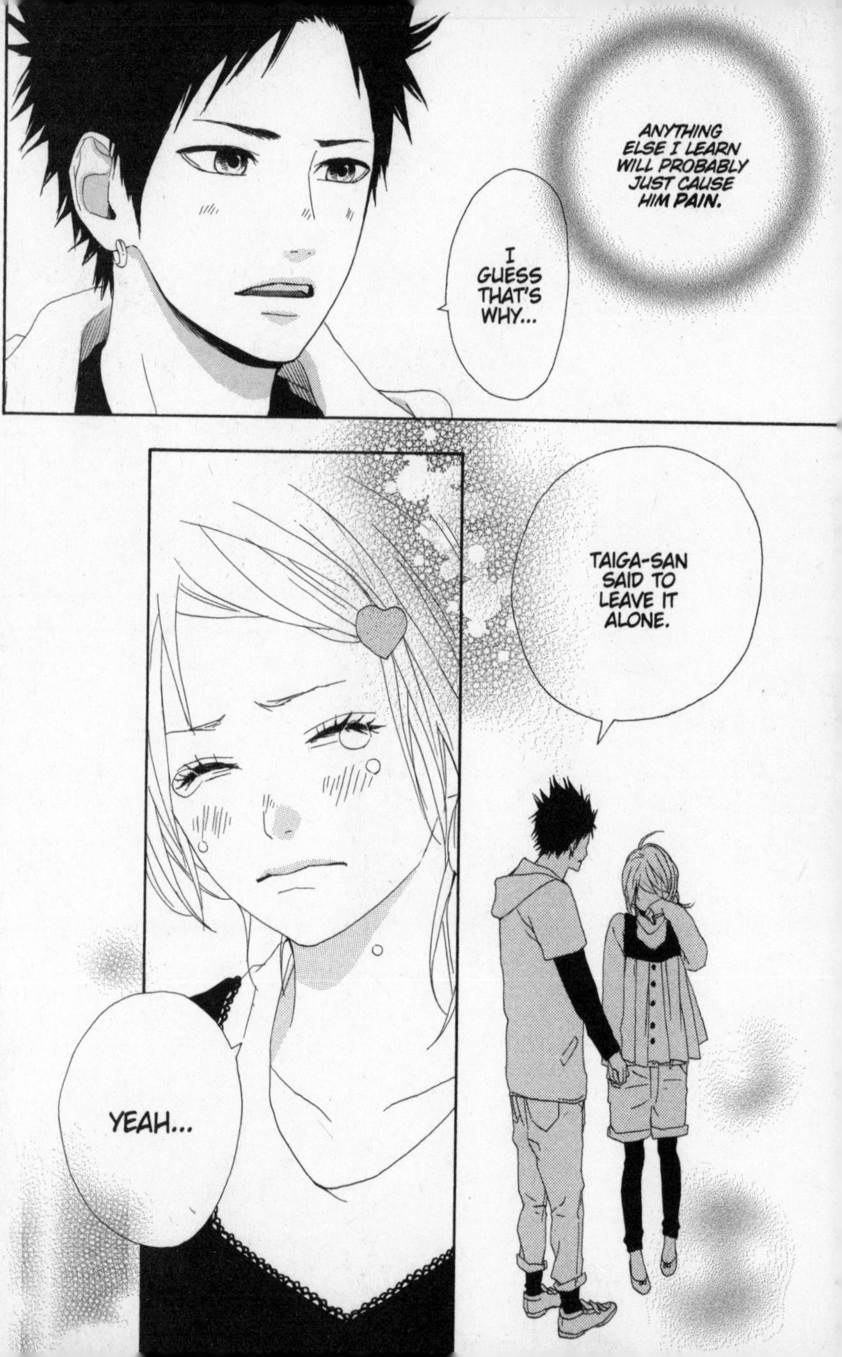
ANYTHING ELSE I LEARN WILL PROBABLY JUST CAUSE HIM PAIN.
I GUESS THAT'S WHY...
TAIGA-SAN SAID TO LEAVE IT ALONE.
YEAH...

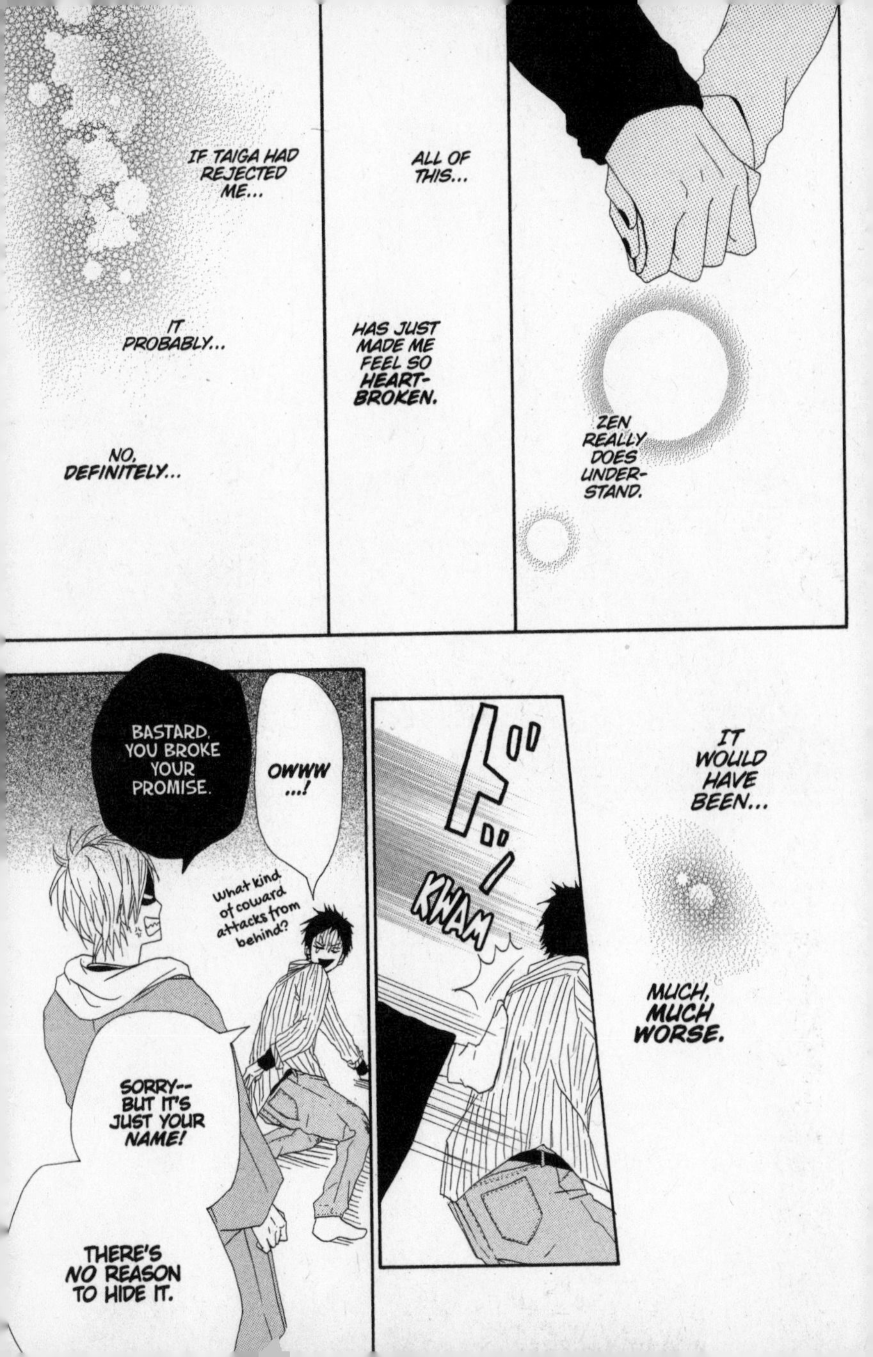
ZEN REALLY DOES UNDERSTAND.
ALL OF THIS...
HAS JUST MADE ME FEEL SO HEART-BROKEN.
IF TAIGA HAD REJECTED ME...
IT PROBABLY...
NO, DEFINITELY...
IT WOULD HAVE BEEN...
MUCH, MUCH WORSE.
KWAM
OWWW ...!
BASTARD. YOU BROKE YOUR PROMISE.
What kind of coward attacks from behind?
SORRY-- BUT IT'S JUST YOUR NAME!
THERE'S NO REASON TO HIDE IT.

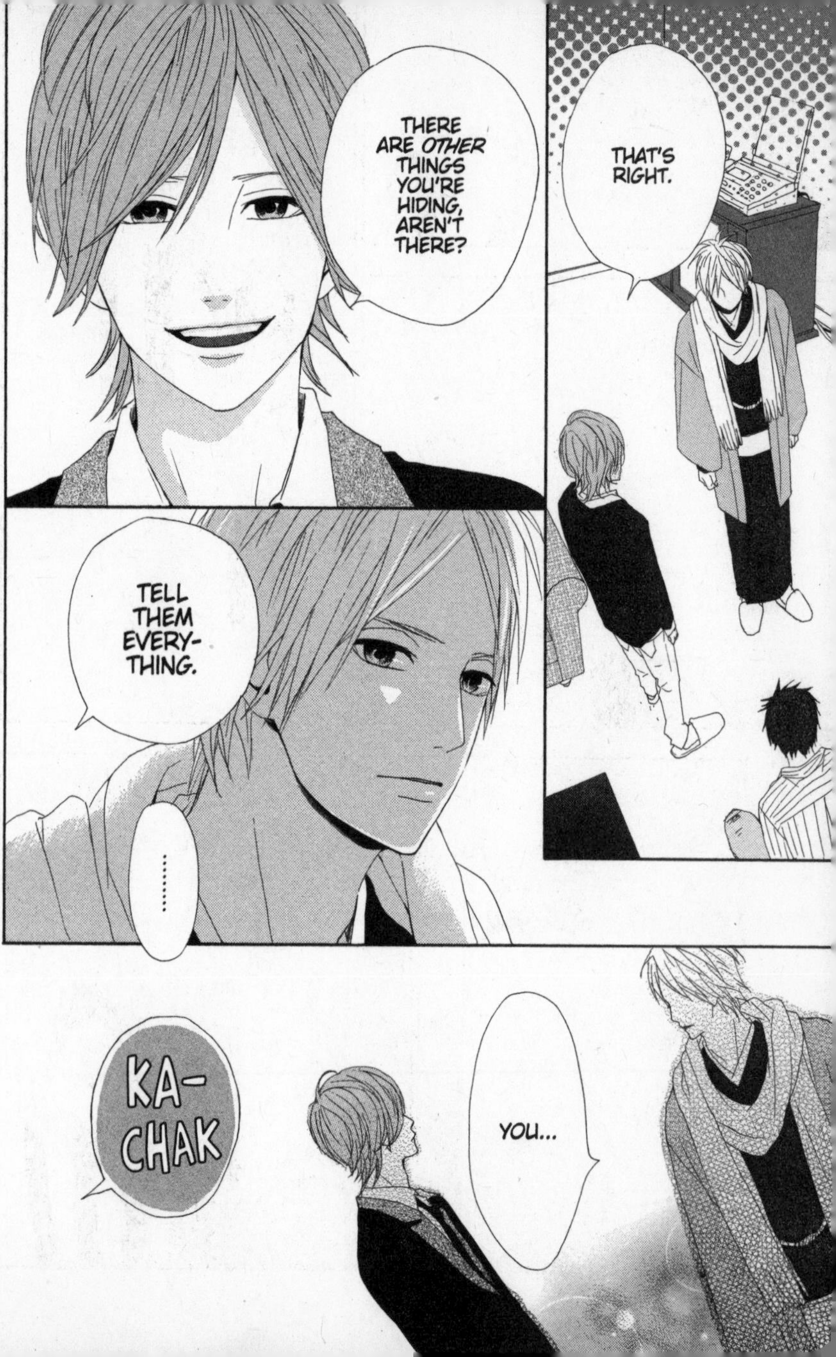

THAT'S RIGHT.
THERE ARE *OTHER* THINGS YOU'RE HIDING, AREN'T THERE?
TELL THEM EVERY-THING.
......
YOU...
KA-CHAK

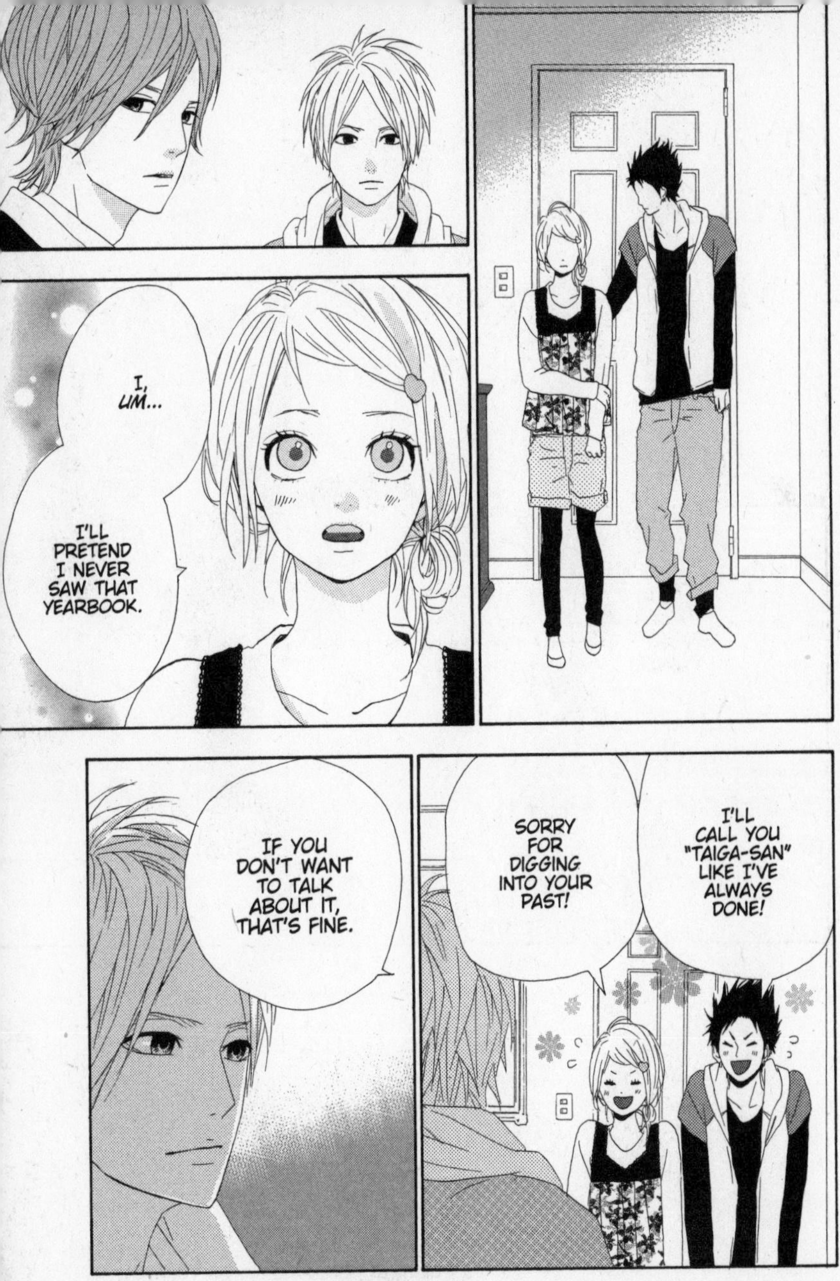
I, UM...
I'LL PRETEND I NEVER SAW THAT YEARBOOK.
I'LL CALL YOU "TAIGA-SAN" LIKE I'VE ALWAYS DONE!
SORRY FOR DIGGING INTO YOUR PAST!
IF YOU DON'T WANT TO TALK ABOUT IT, THAT'S FINE.

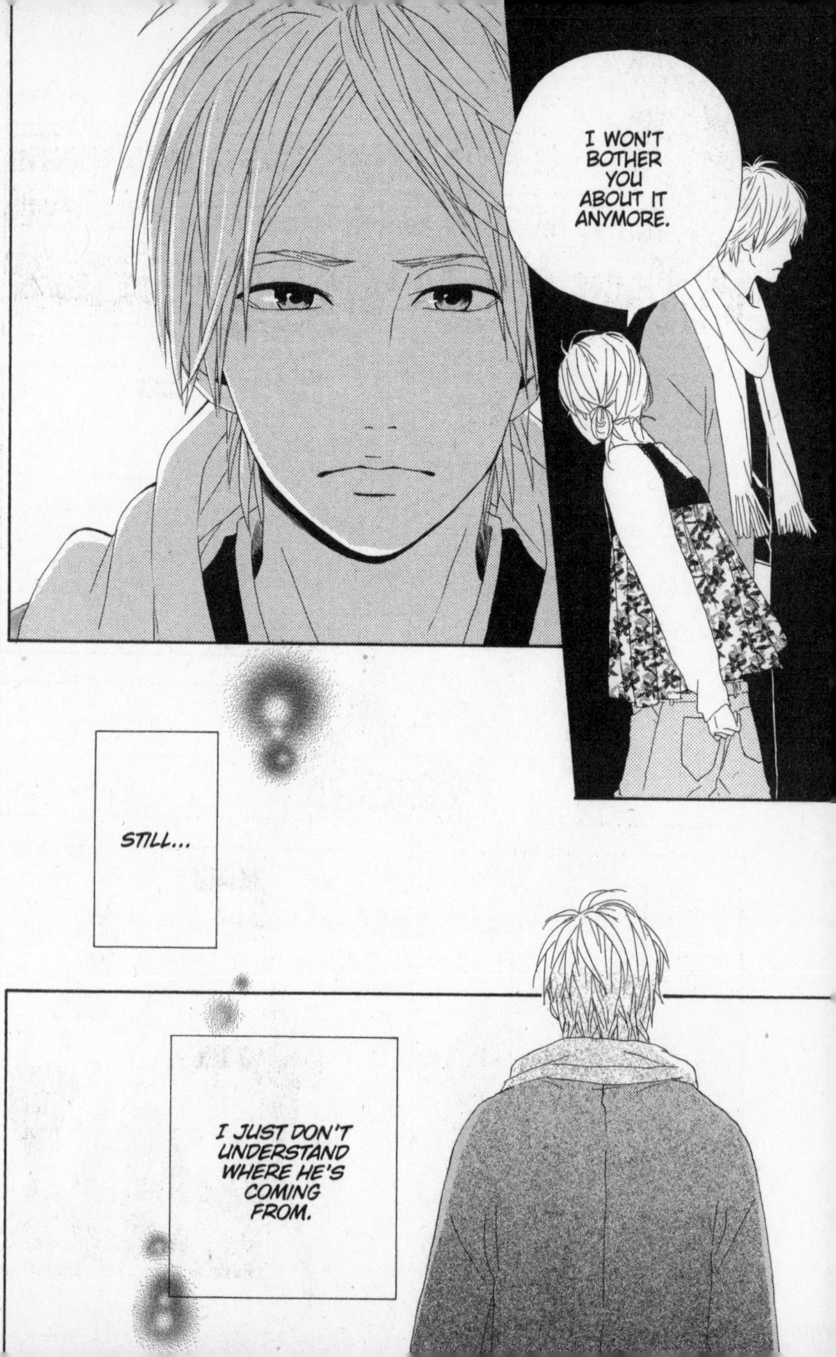
I WON'T BOTHER YOU ABOUT IT ANYMORE.
STILL...
I JUST DON'T UNDERSTAND WHERE HE'S COMING FROM.

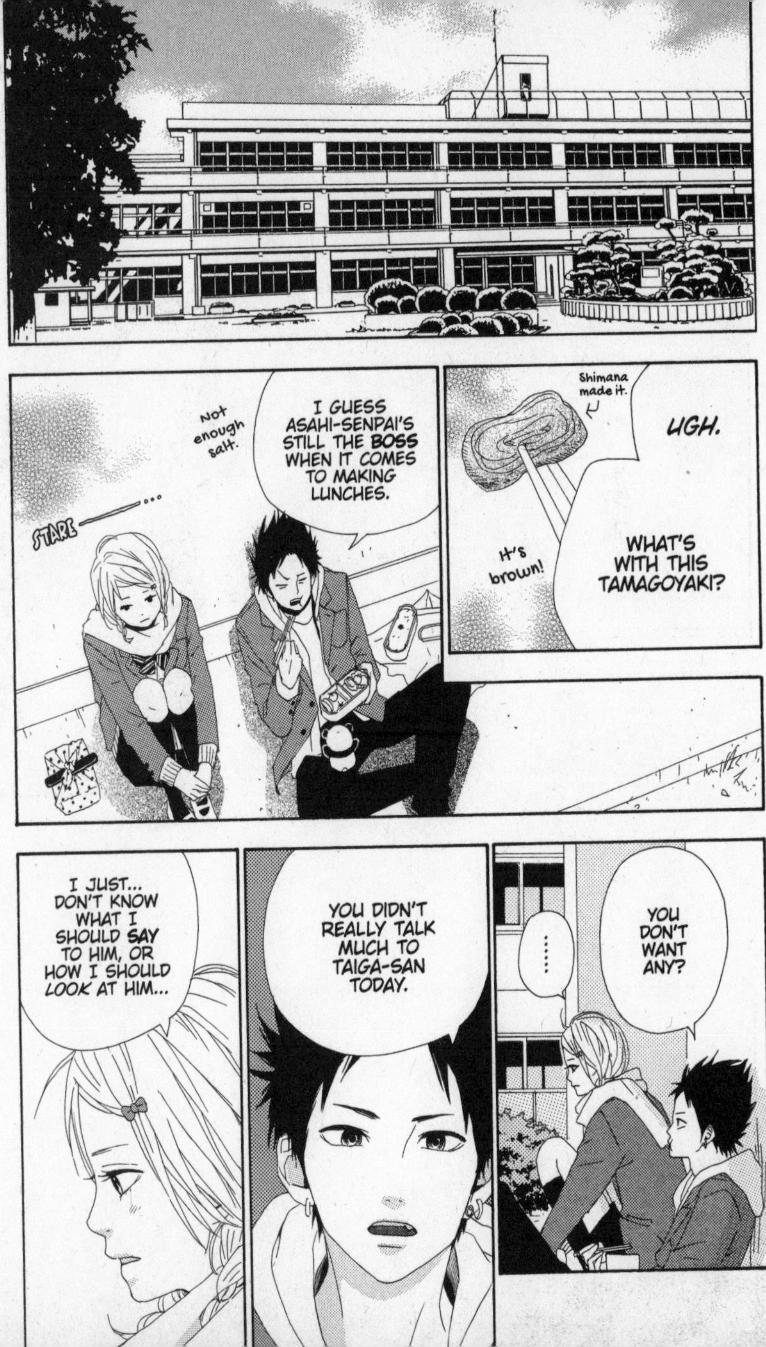
Shimana made it.
UGH.
WHAT'S WITH THIS TAMAGOYAKI?
It's brown!
I GUESS ASAHI-SENPAI'S STILL THE BOSS WHEN IT COMES TO MAKING LUNCHES.
Not enough salt.
STARE—...
YOU DON'T WANT ANY?
......
YOU DIDN'T REALLY TALK MUCH TO TAIGA-SAN TODAY.
I JUST... DON'T KNOW WHAT I SHOULD SAY TO HIM, OR HOW I SHOULD LOOK AT HIM...

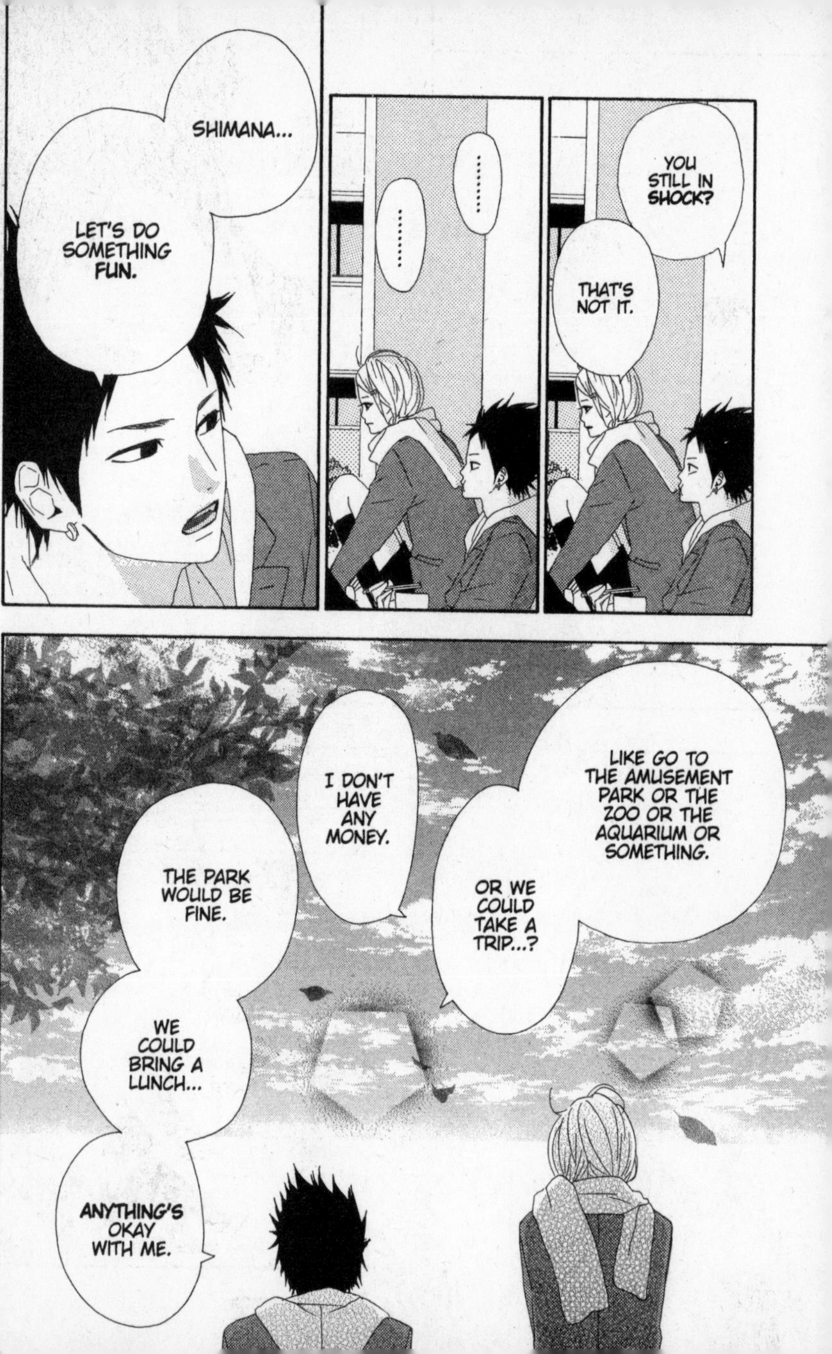
YOU STILL IN SHOCK?
THAT'S NOT IT.
......
......
SHIMANA...
LET'S DO SOMETHING FUN.
LIKE GO TO THE AMUSEMENT PARK OR THE ZOO OR THE AQUARIUM OR SOMETHING.
OR WE COULD TAKE A TRIP...?
I DON'T HAVE ANY MONEY.
THE PARK WOULD BE FINE.
WE COULD BRING A LUNCH...
ANYTHING'S OKAY WITH ME.

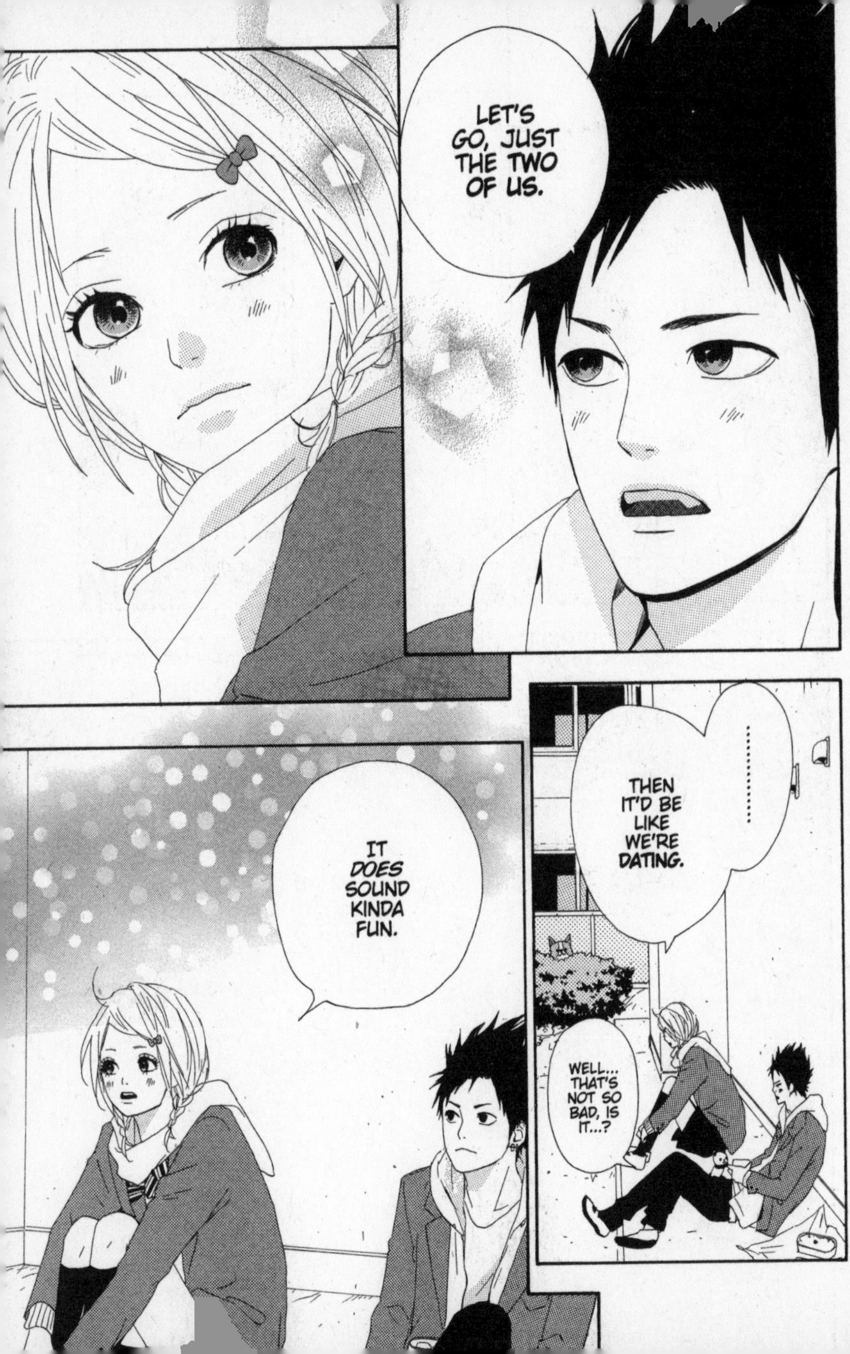
LET'S GO, JUST THE TWO OF US.
......
THEN IT'D BE LIKE WE'RE DATING.
WELL... THAT'S NOT SO BAD, IS IT...?
IT DOES SOUND KINDA FUN.

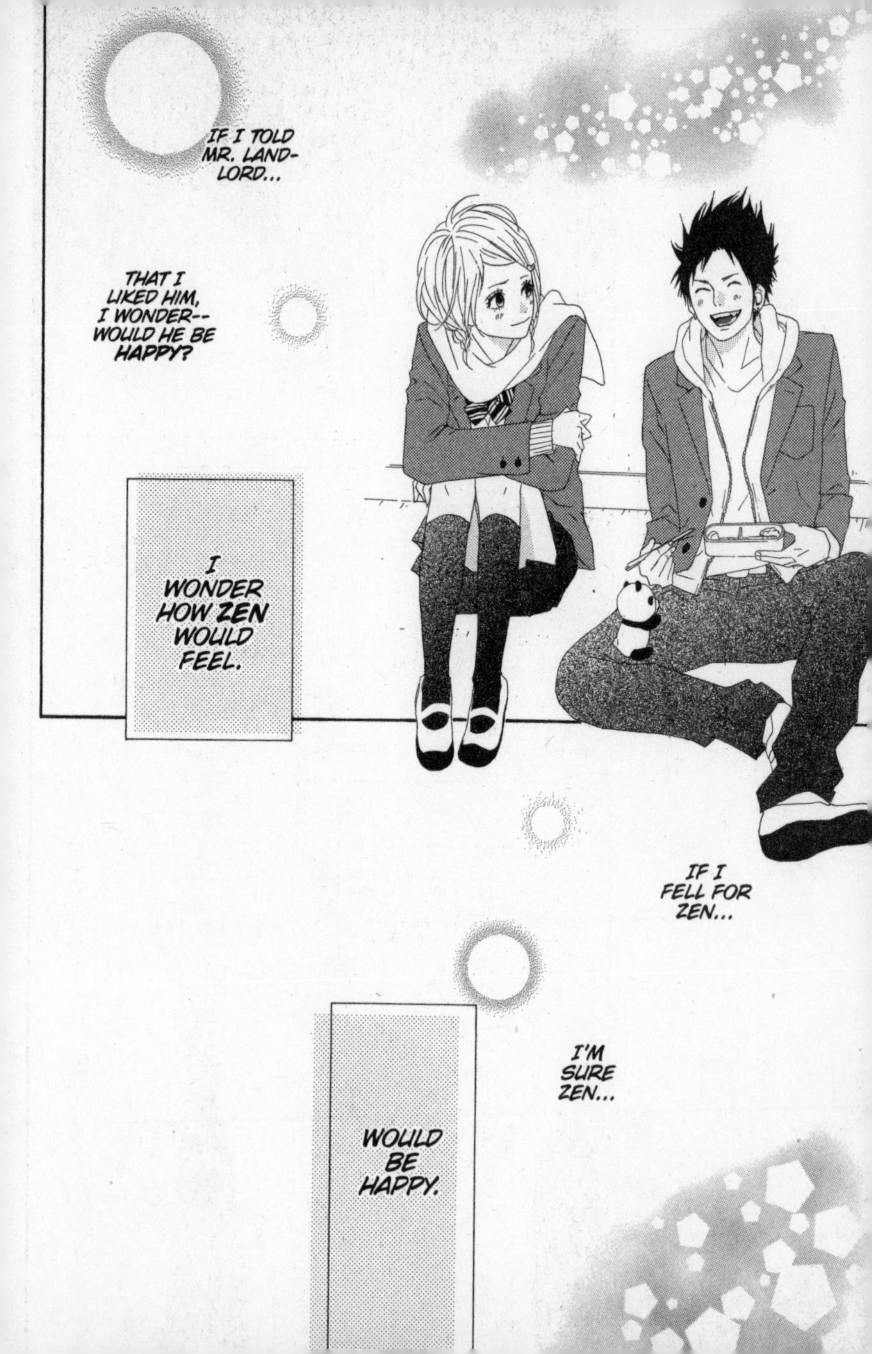

IF I TOLD MR. LANDLORD...
THAT I LIKED HIM, I WONDER--WOULD HE BE HAPPY?
I WONDER HOW ZEN WOULD FEEL.
IF I FELL FOR ZEN...
I'M SURE ZEN...
WOULD BE HAPPY.

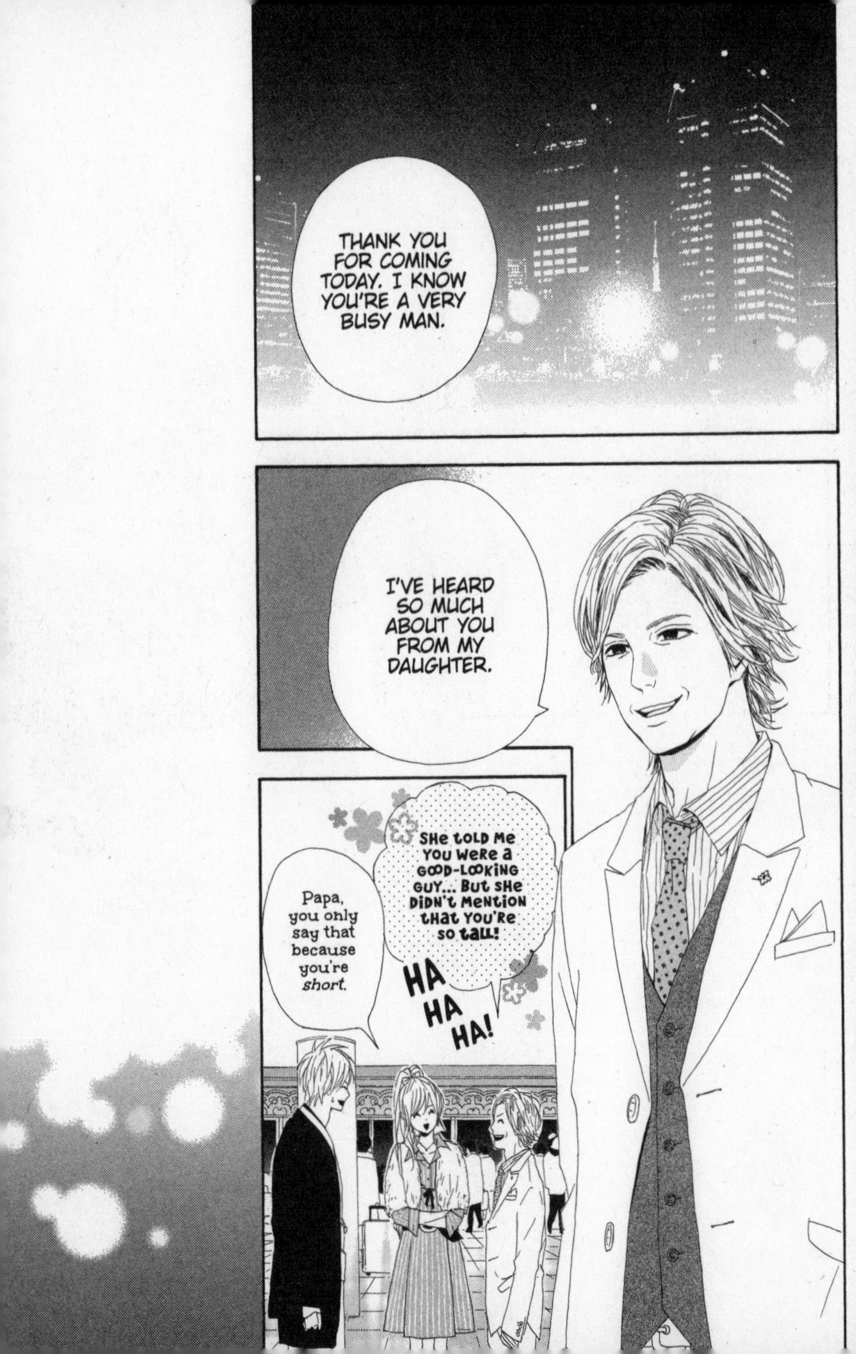
THANK YOU FOR COMING TODAY. I KNOW YOU'RE A VERY BUSY MAN.
I'VE HEARD SO MUCH ABOUT YOU FROM MY DAUGHTER.
SHE TOLD ME YOU WERE A GOOD-LOOKING GUY... BUT SHE DIDN'T MENTION THAT YOU'RE SO TALL!
HA HA HA!
Papa, you only say that because you're *short*.

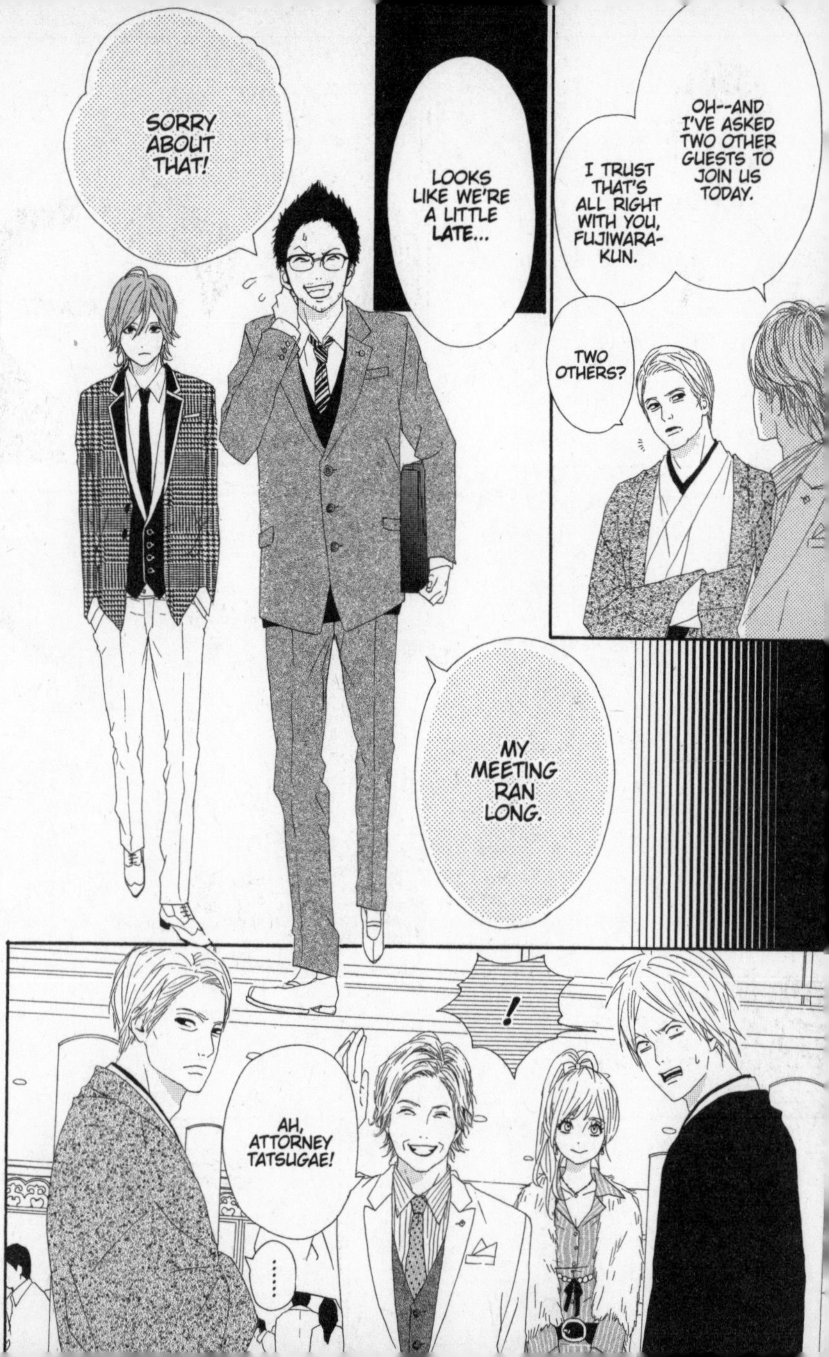
OH--AND I'VE ASKED TWO OTHER GUESTS TO JOIN US TODAY.
I TRUST THAT'S ALL RIGHT WITH YOU, FUJIWARA-KUN.
TWO OTHERS?
LOOKS LIKE WE'RE A LITTLE LATE...
SORRY ABOUT THAT!
MY MEETING RAN LONG.
!
AH, ATTORNEY TATSUGAE!
......

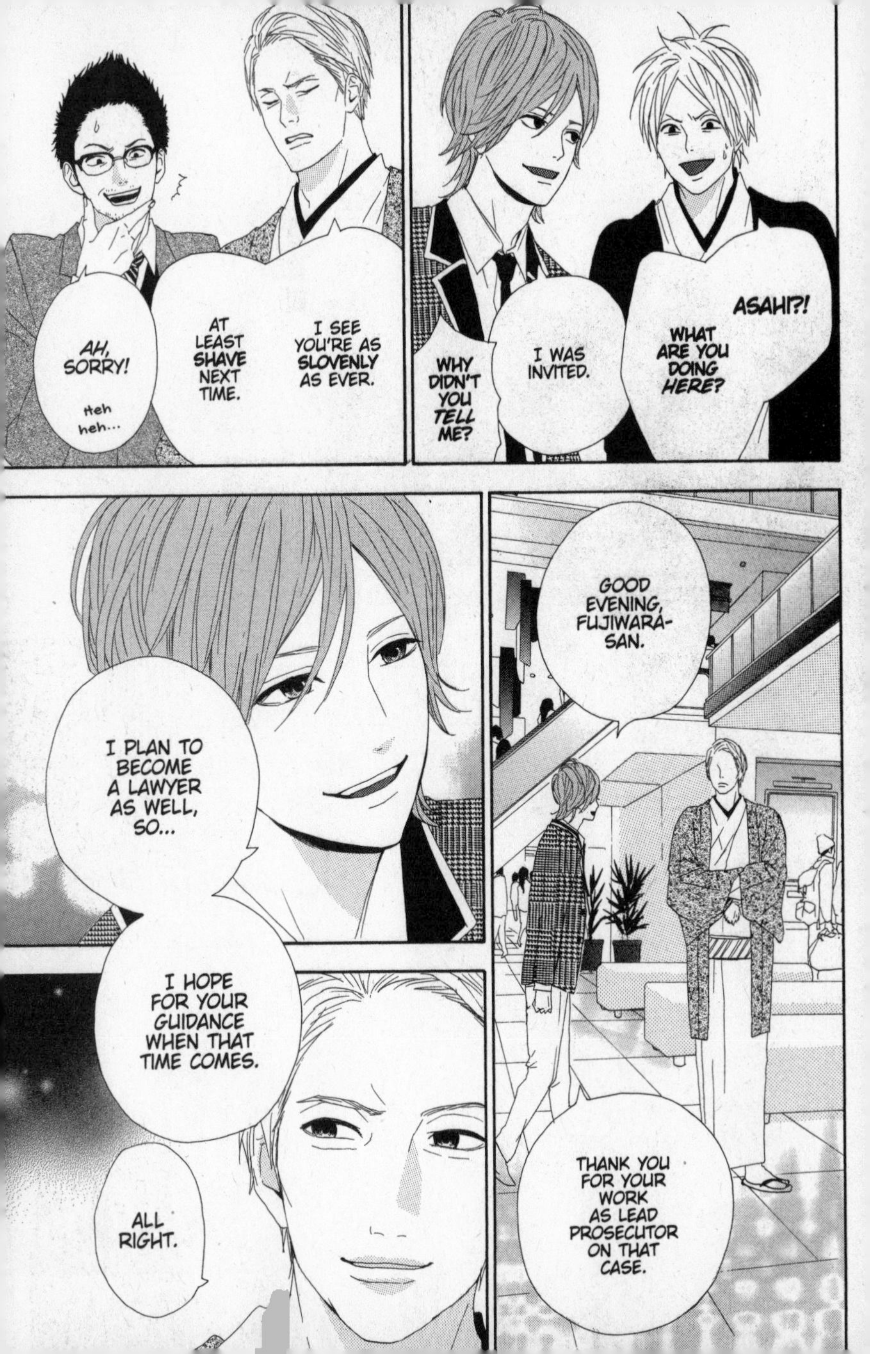
ASAHI?!
WHAT ARE YOU DOING HERE?
I WAS INVITED.
WHY DIDN'T YOU TELL ME?
I SEE YOU'RE AS SLOVENLY AS EVER.
AT LEAST SHAVE NEXT TIME.
AH, SORRY!
Heh heh...
GOOD EVENING, FUJIWARA-SAN.
THANK YOU FOR YOUR WORK AS LEAD PROSECUTOR ON THAT CASE.
I PLAN TO BECOME A LAWYER AS WELL, SO...
I HOPE FOR YOUR GUIDANCE WHEN THAT TIME COMES.
ALL RIGHT.

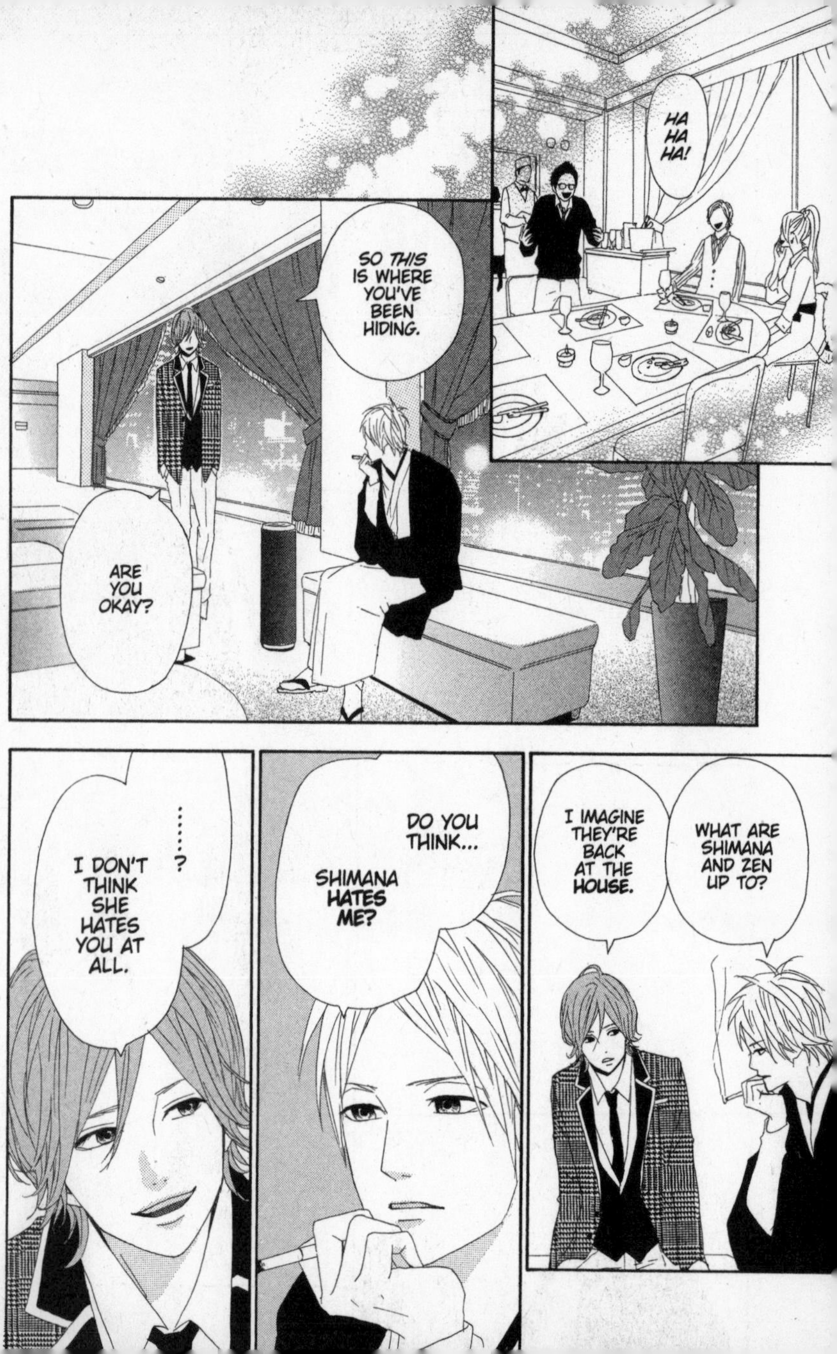
HA HA HA!
SO *THIS* IS WHERE YOU'VE BEEN HIDING.
ARE YOU OKAY?
WHAT ARE SHIMANA AND ZEN UP TO?
I IMAGINE THEY'RE BACK AT THE HOUSE.
DO YOU THINK...
SHIMANA HATES ME?
......?
I DON'T THINK SHE HATES YOU AT ALL.

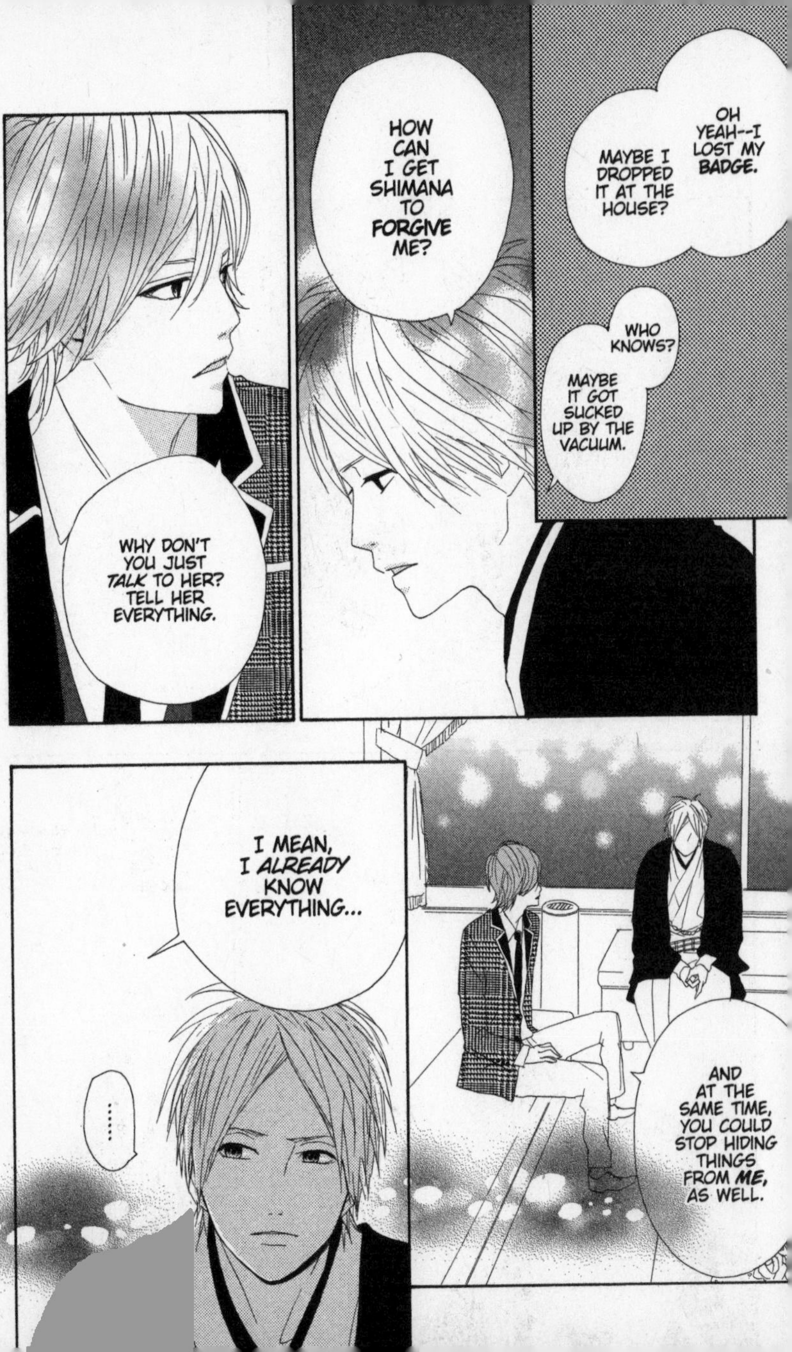
OH YEAH--I LOST MY BADGE.
MAYBE I DROPPED IT AT THE HOUSE?
WHO KNOWS?
MAYBE IT GOT SUCKED UP BY THE VACUUM.
HOW CAN I GET SHIMANA TO FORGIVE ME?
WHY DON'T YOU JUST *TALK* TO HER? TELL HER EVERYTHING.
AND AT THE SAME TIME, YOU COULD STOP HIDING THINGS FROM *ME*, AS WELL.
I MEAN, I *ALREADY* KNOW EVERYTHING...
......

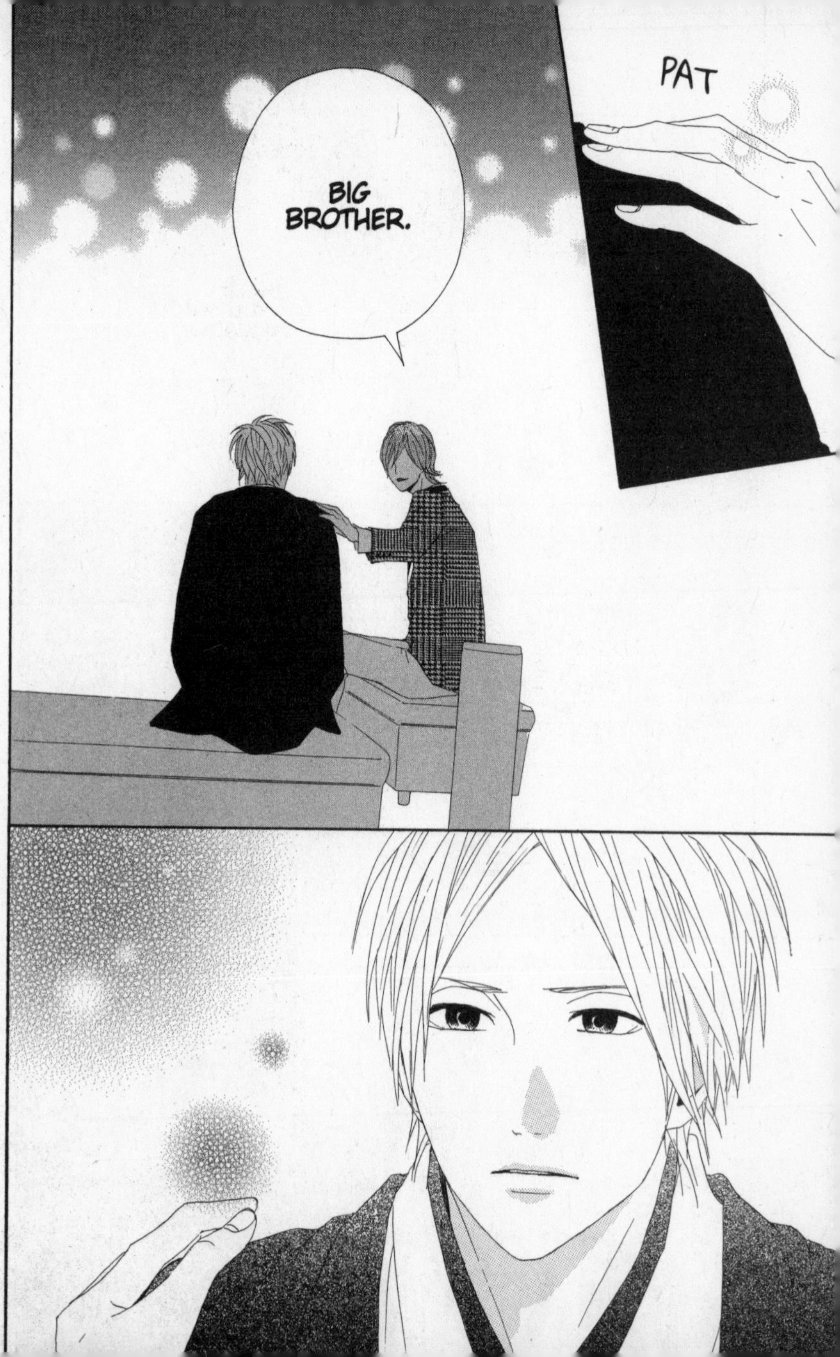
PAT
BIG BROTHER.

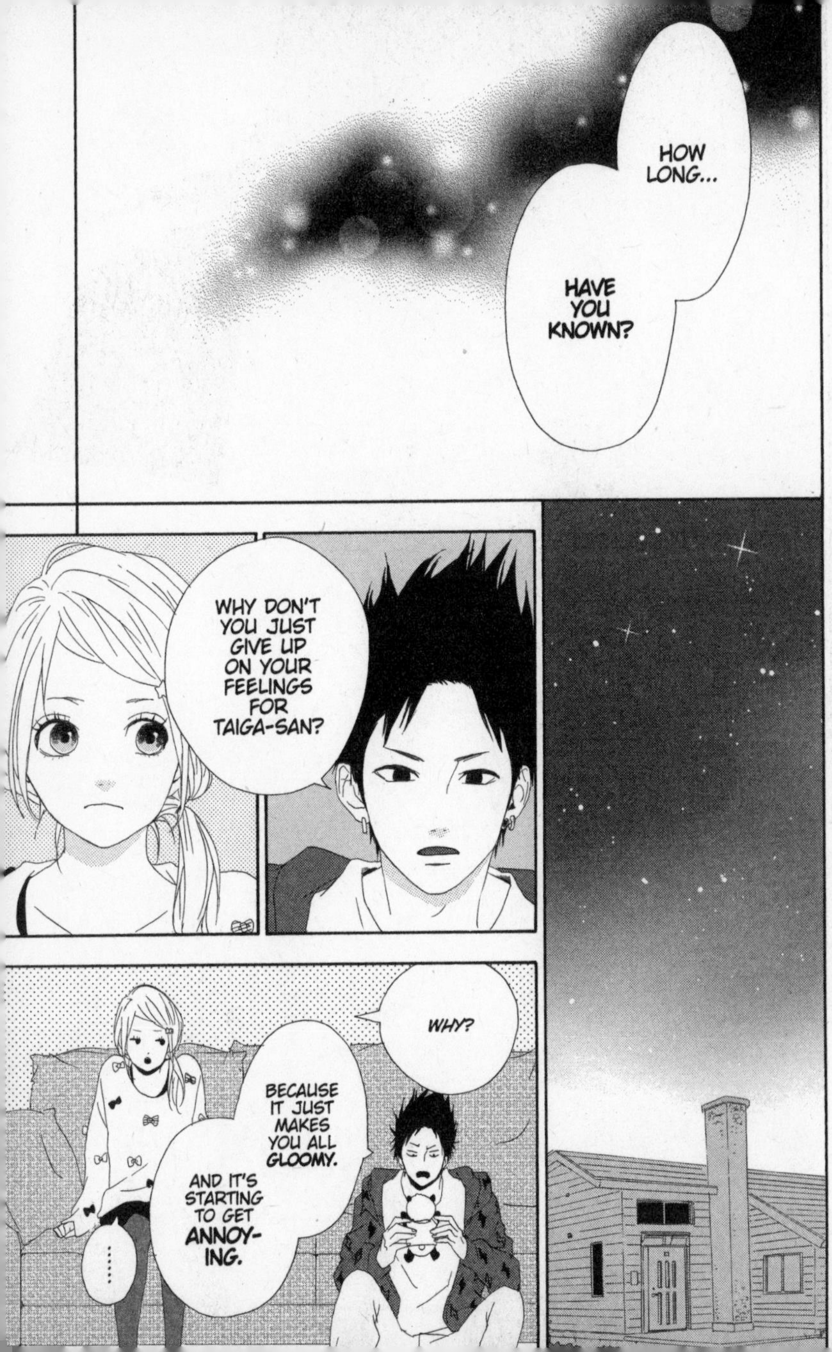
HOW LONG...
HAVE YOU KNOWN?
WHY DON'T YOU JUST GIVE UP ON YOUR FEELINGS FOR TAIGA-SAN?
WHY?
BECAUSE IT JUST MAKES YOU ALL GLOOMY.
AND IT'S STARTING TO GET ANNOY-ING.
......

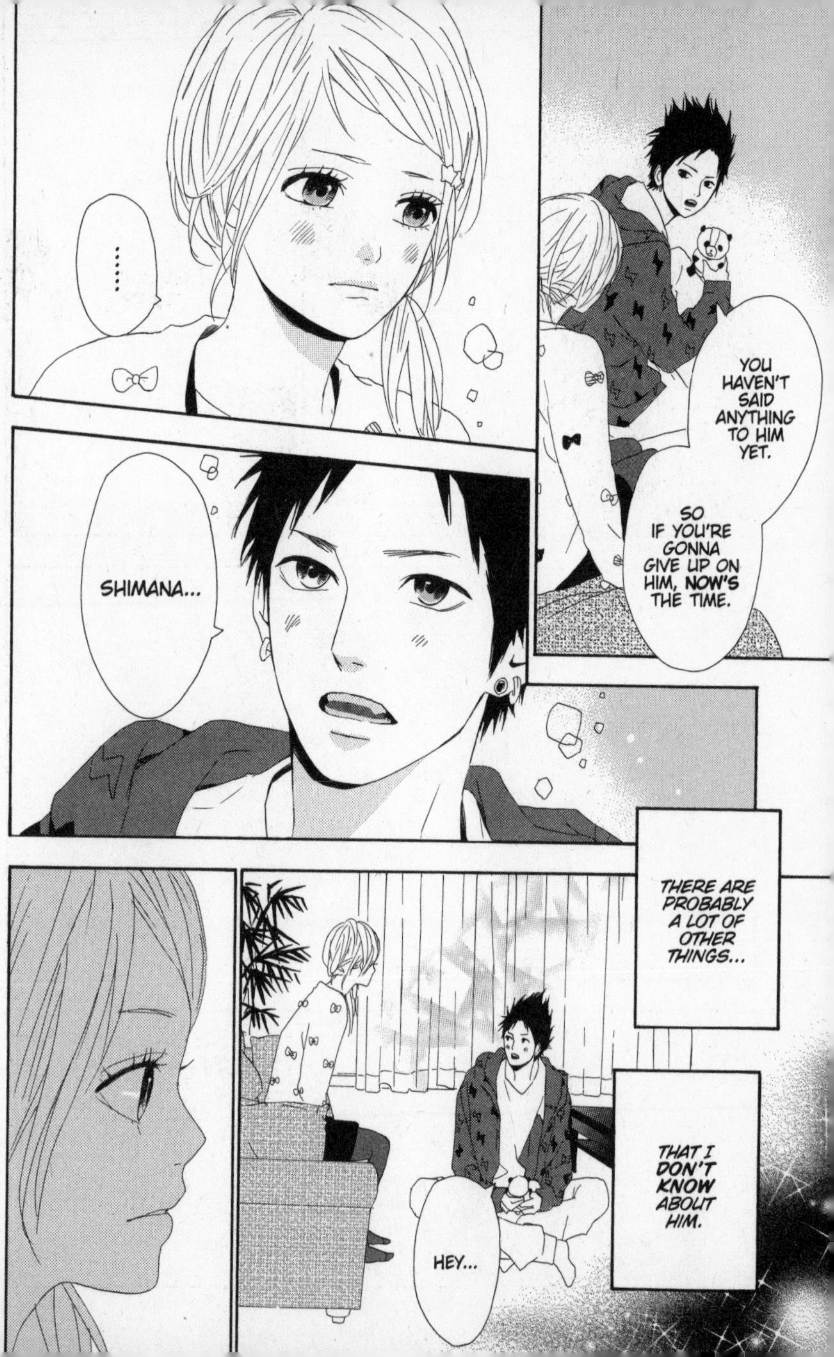
YOU HAVEN'T SAID ANYTHING TO HIM YET.
SO IF YOU'RE GONNA GIVE UP ON HIM, NOW'S THE TIME.
......
SHIMANA...
THERE ARE PROBABLY A LOT OF OTHER THINGS...
THAT I DON'T KNOW ABOUT HIM.
HEY...

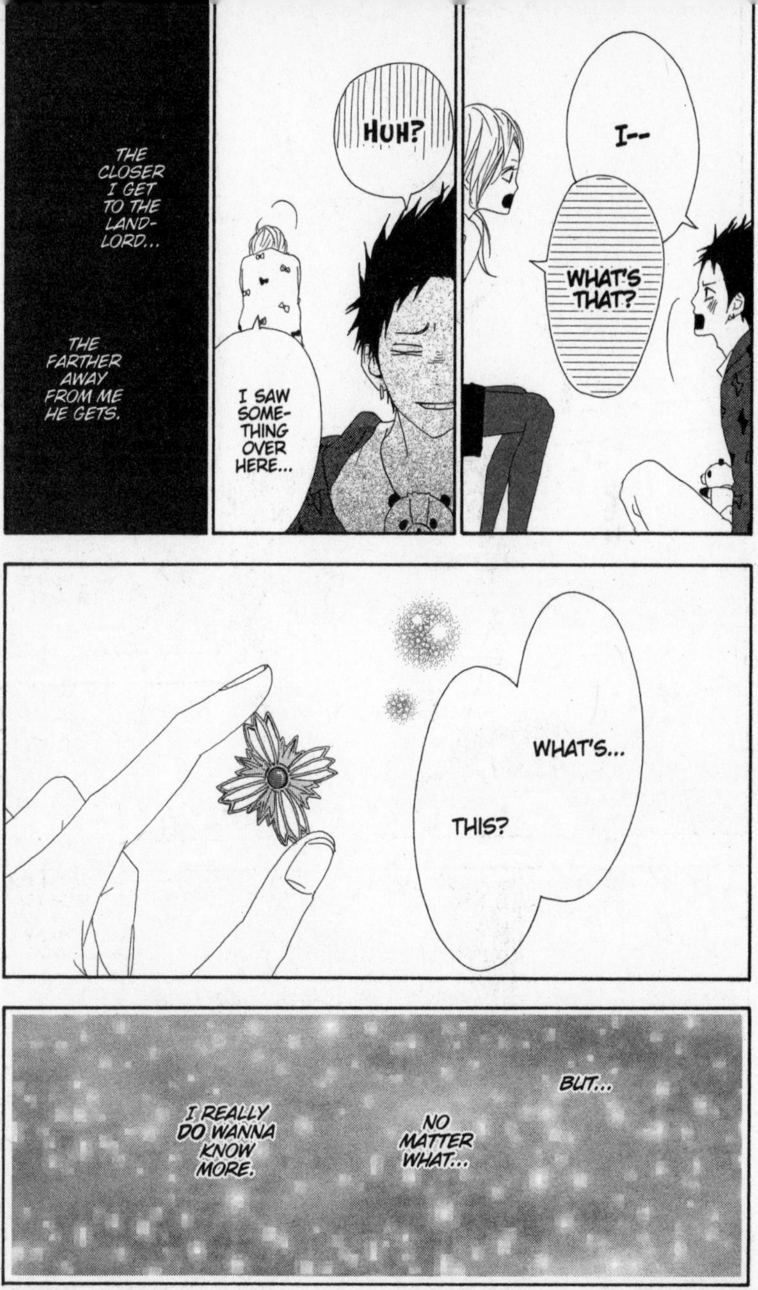
I--
WHAT'S THAT?
HUH?
I SAW SOMETHING OVER HERE...
THE CLOSER I GET TO THE LANDLORD...
THE FARTHER AWAY FROM ME HE GETS.
WHAT'S...
THIS?
BUT...
NO MATTER WHAT...
I REALLY DO WANNA KNOW MORE.

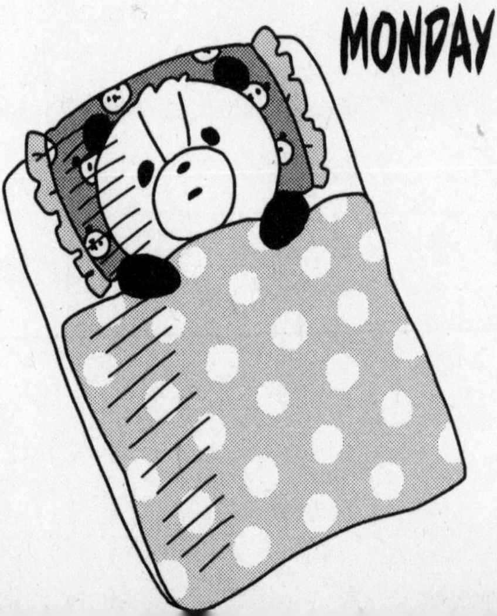
MONDAY

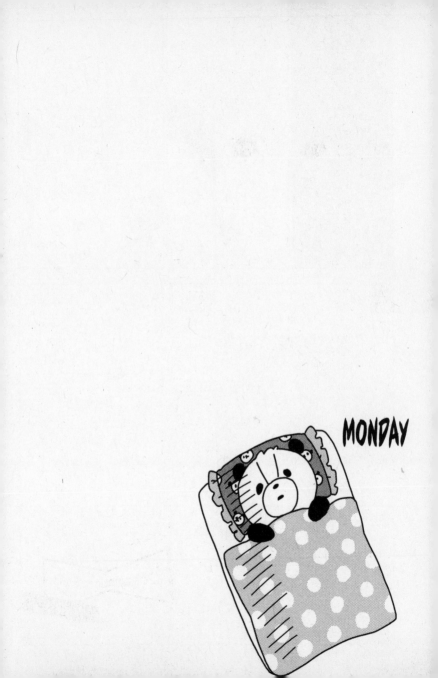

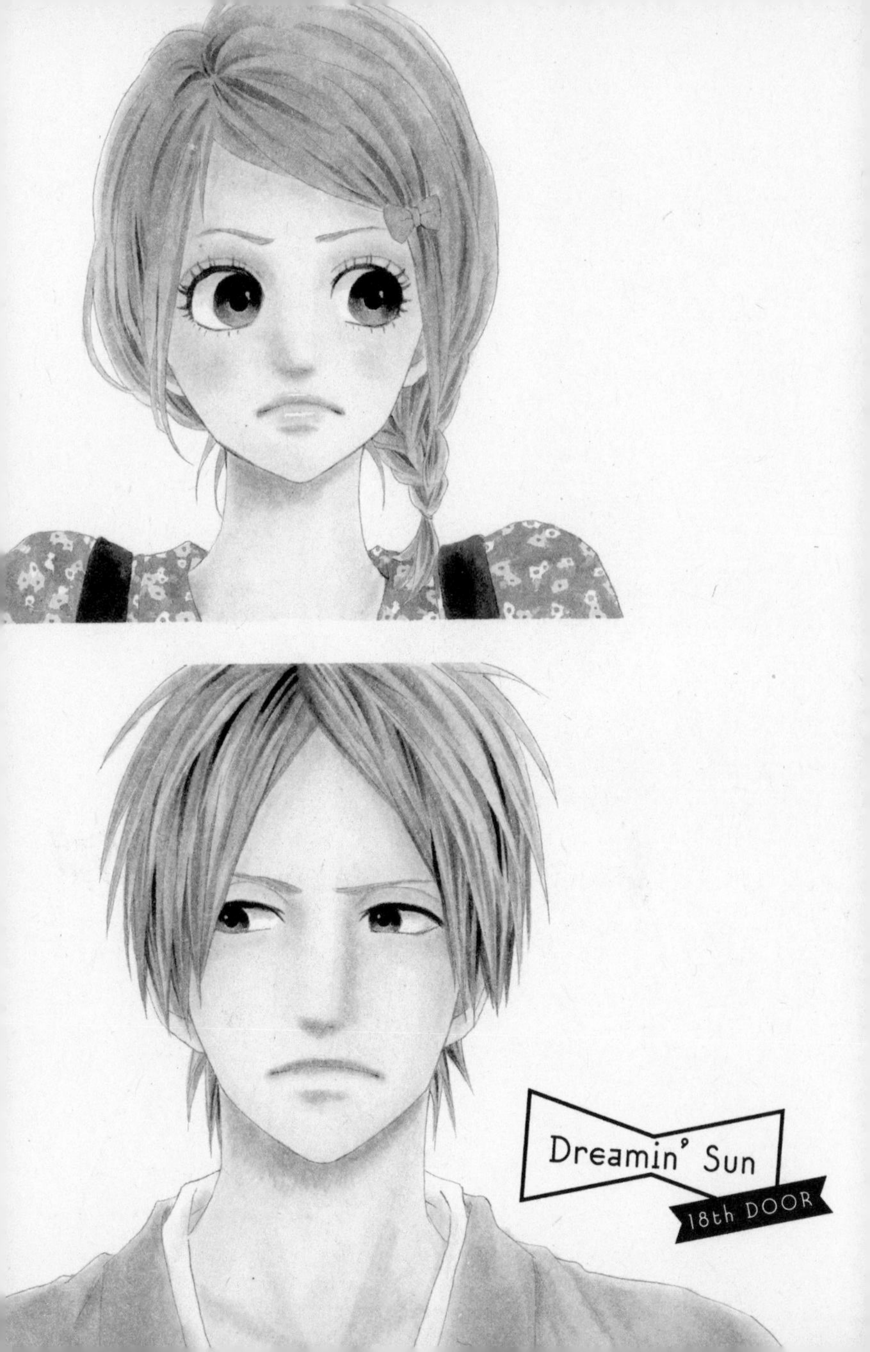
Dreamin' Sun
18th DOOR

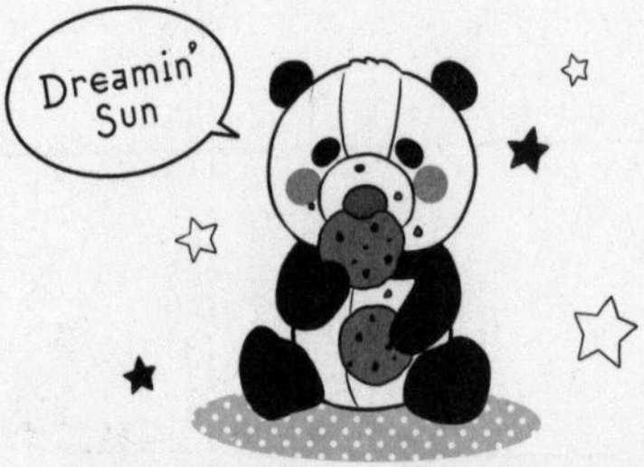
Dreamin' Sun

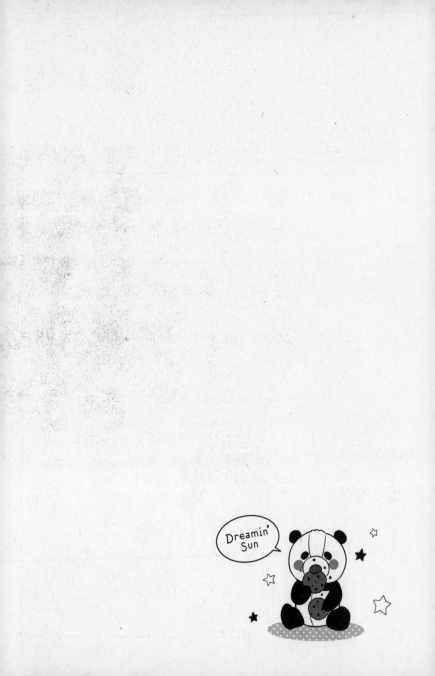

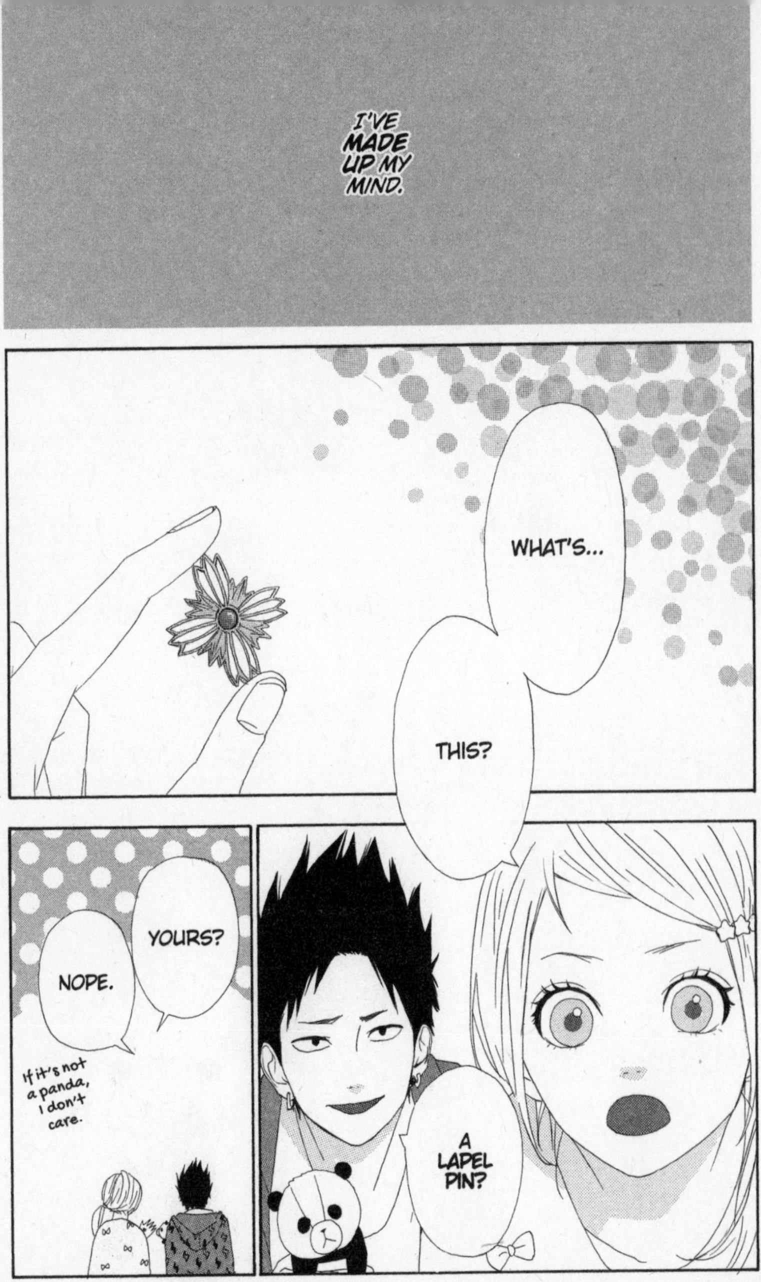
I'VE MADE UP MY MIND.
WHAT'S...
THIS?
A LAPEL PIN?
YOURS?
NOPE.
If it's not a panda, I don't care.

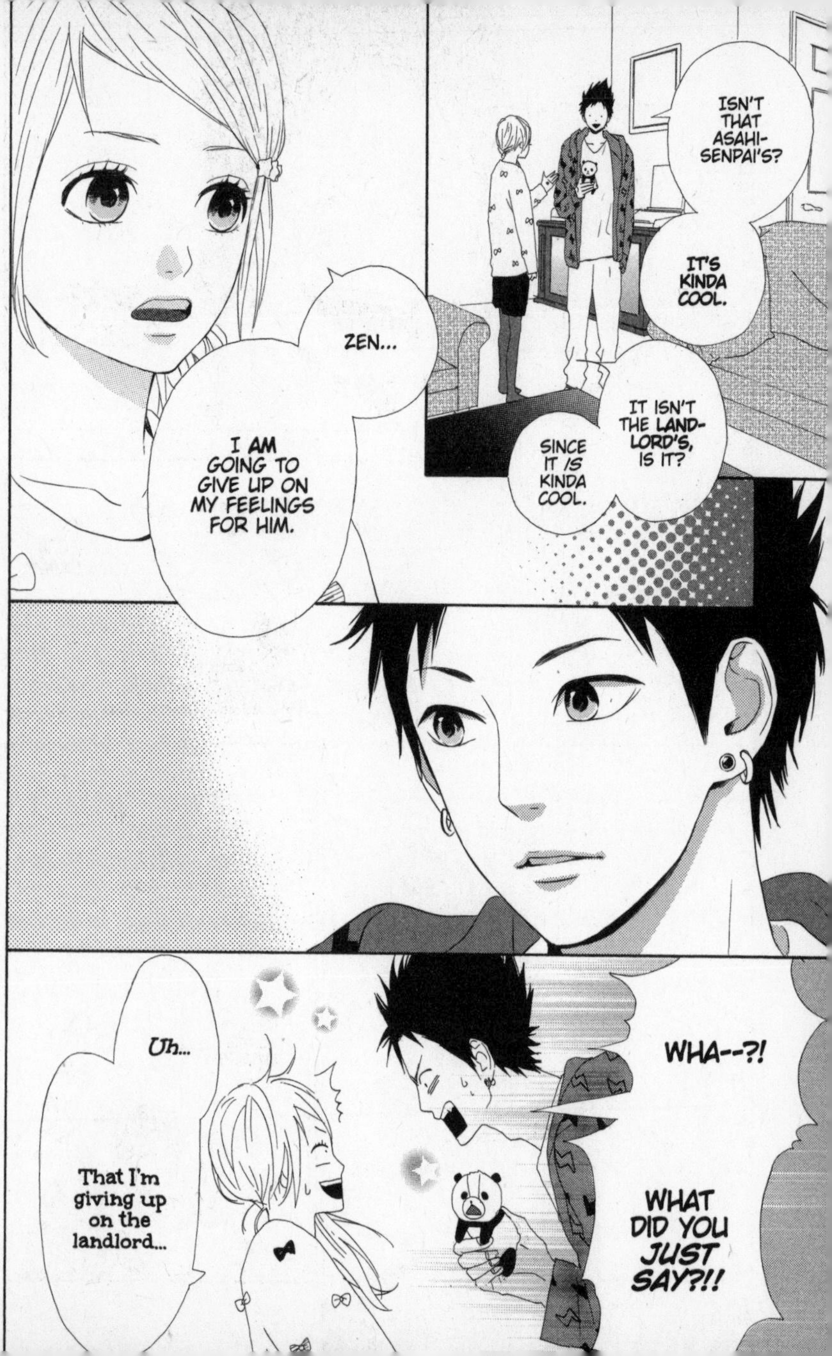
ISN'T THAT ASAHI-SENPAI'S?
IT'S KINDA COOL.
IT ISN'T THE LANDLORD'S, IS IT?
SINCE IT *IS* KINDA COOL.
ZEN...
I AM GOING TO GIVE UP ON MY FEELINGS FOR HIM.
WHA--?!
WHAT DID YOU *JUST* SAY?!!
Uh...
That I'm giving up on the landlord...

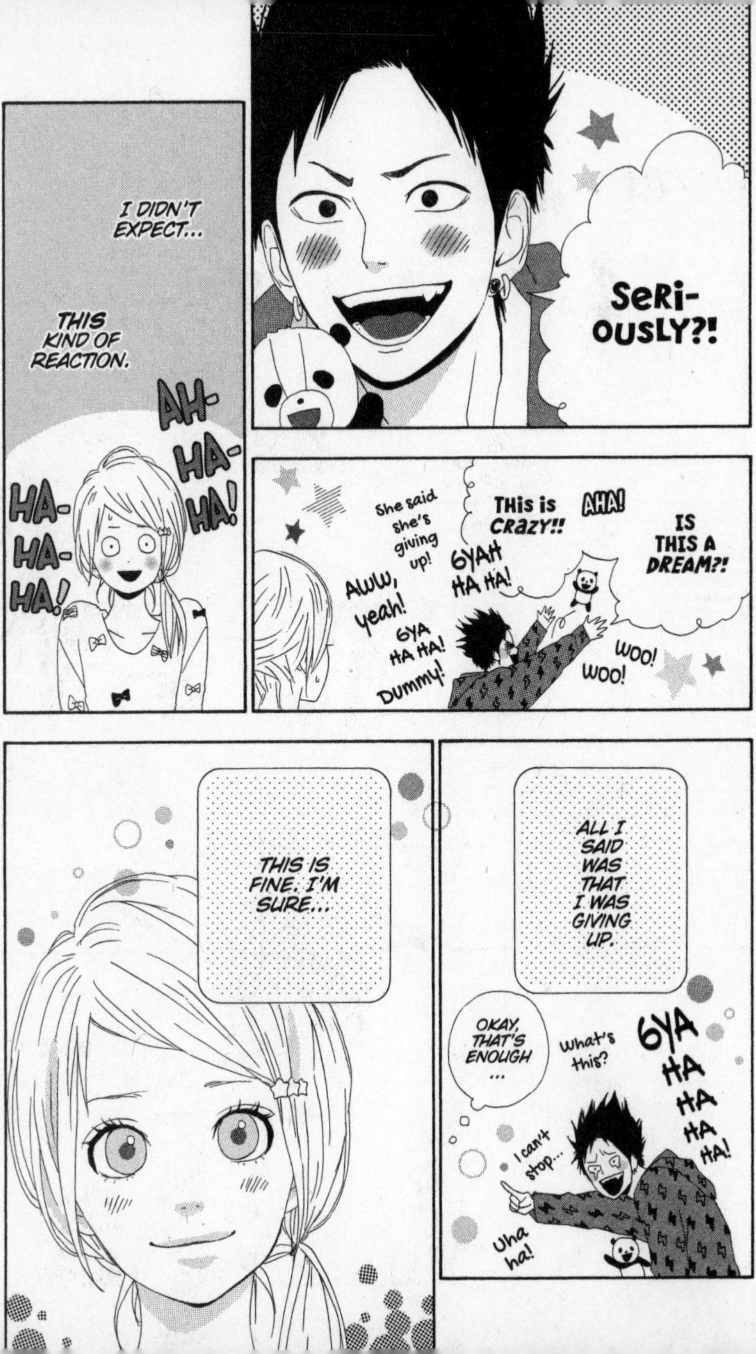
SERI-OUSLY?!
IS THIS A DREAM?!
AHA!
THIS IS CRAZY!!
She said she's giving up!
6YAH HA HA!
WOO! WOO!
AWW, yeah!
6YA HA HA!
Dummy!
I DIDN'T EXPECT...
THIS KIND OF REACTION.
AH-HA-HA!
HA-HA-HA!
ALL I SAID WAS THAT I WAS GIVING UP.
6YA HA HA HA HA!
What's this?
OKAY, THAT'S ENOUGH...
I can't stop...
Uha ha!
THIS IS FINE. I'M SURE...

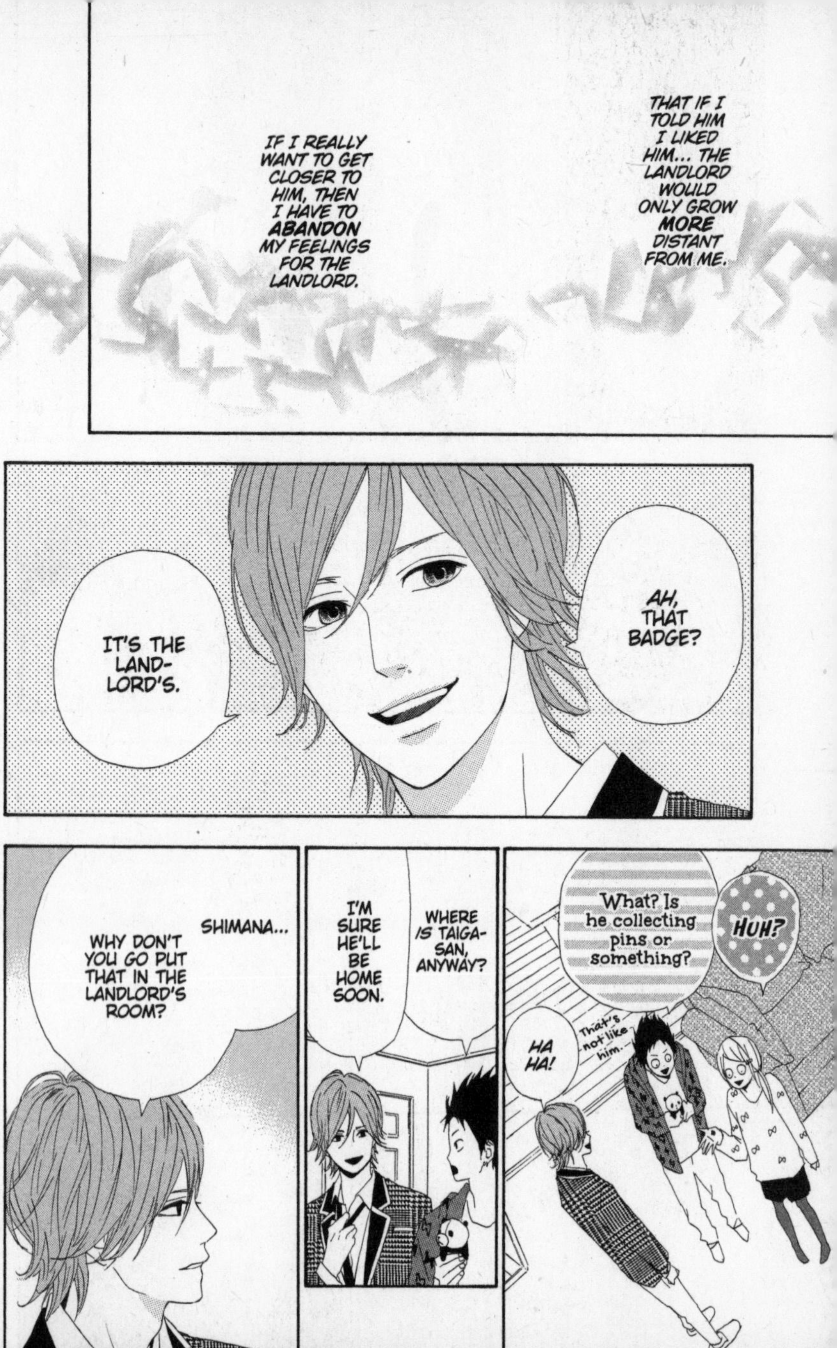
THAT IF I TOLD HIM I LIKED HIM... THE LANDLORD WOULD ONLY GROW MORE DISTANT FROM ME.
IF I REALLY WANT TO GET CLOSER TO HIM, THEN I HAVE TO ABANDON MY FEELINGS FOR THE LANDLORD.
AH, THAT BADGE?
IT'S THE LAND-LORD'S.
HUH?
What? Is he collecting pins or something?
That's not like him.
HA HA!
WHERE IS TAIGA-SAN, ANYWAY?
I'M SURE HE'LL BE HOME SOON.
SHIMANA...
WHY DON'T YOU GO PUT THAT IN THE LANDLORD'S ROOM?

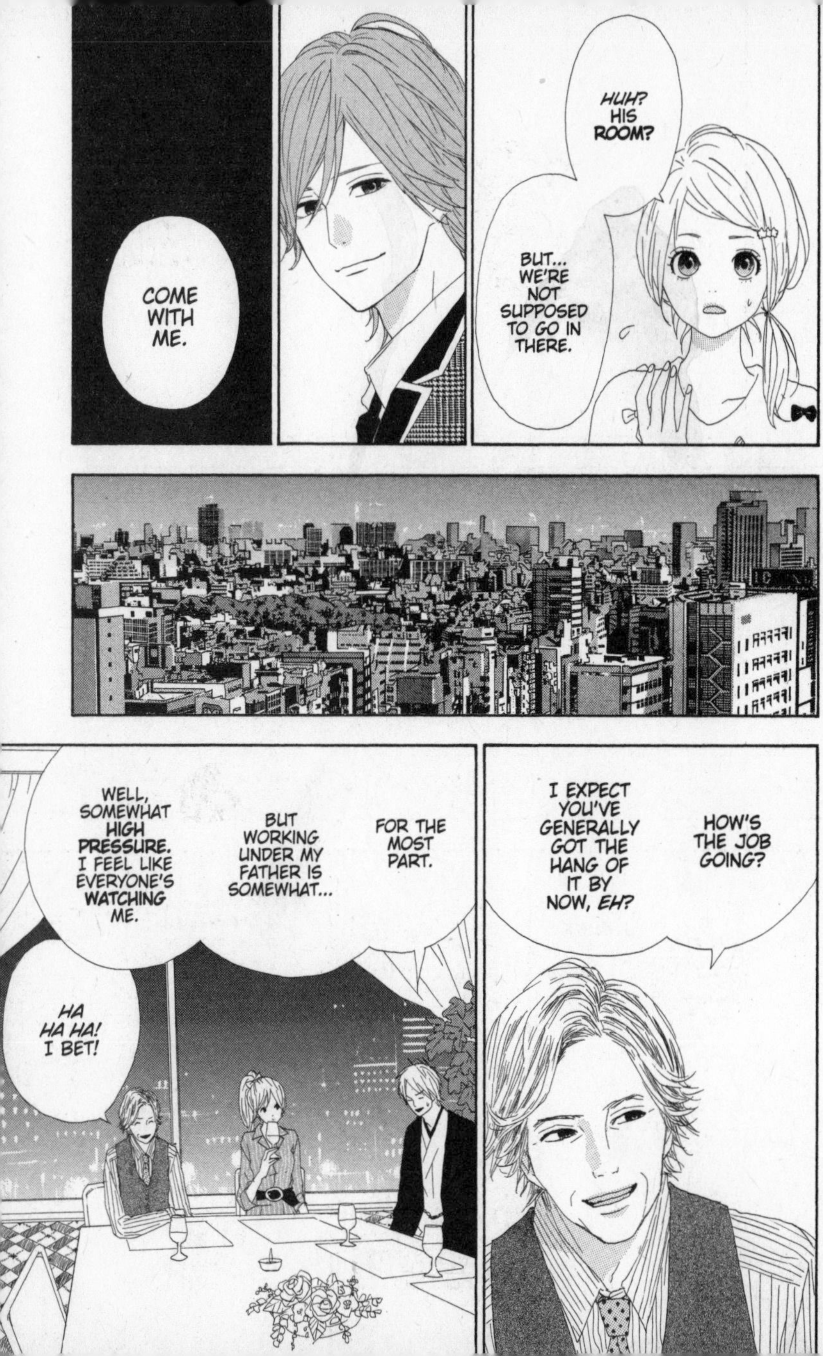
HUH? HIS ROOM?
BUT... WE'RE NOT SUPPOSED TO GO IN THERE.
COME WITH ME.
HOW'S THE JOB GOING?
I EXPECT YOU'VE GENERALLY GOT THE HANG OF IT BY NOW, *EH?*
FOR THE MOST PART.
BUT WORKING UNDER MY FATHER IS SOMEWHAT...
WELL, SOMEWHAT HIGH PRESSURE. I FEEL LIKE EVERYONE'S WATCHING ME.
HA HA HA! I BET!

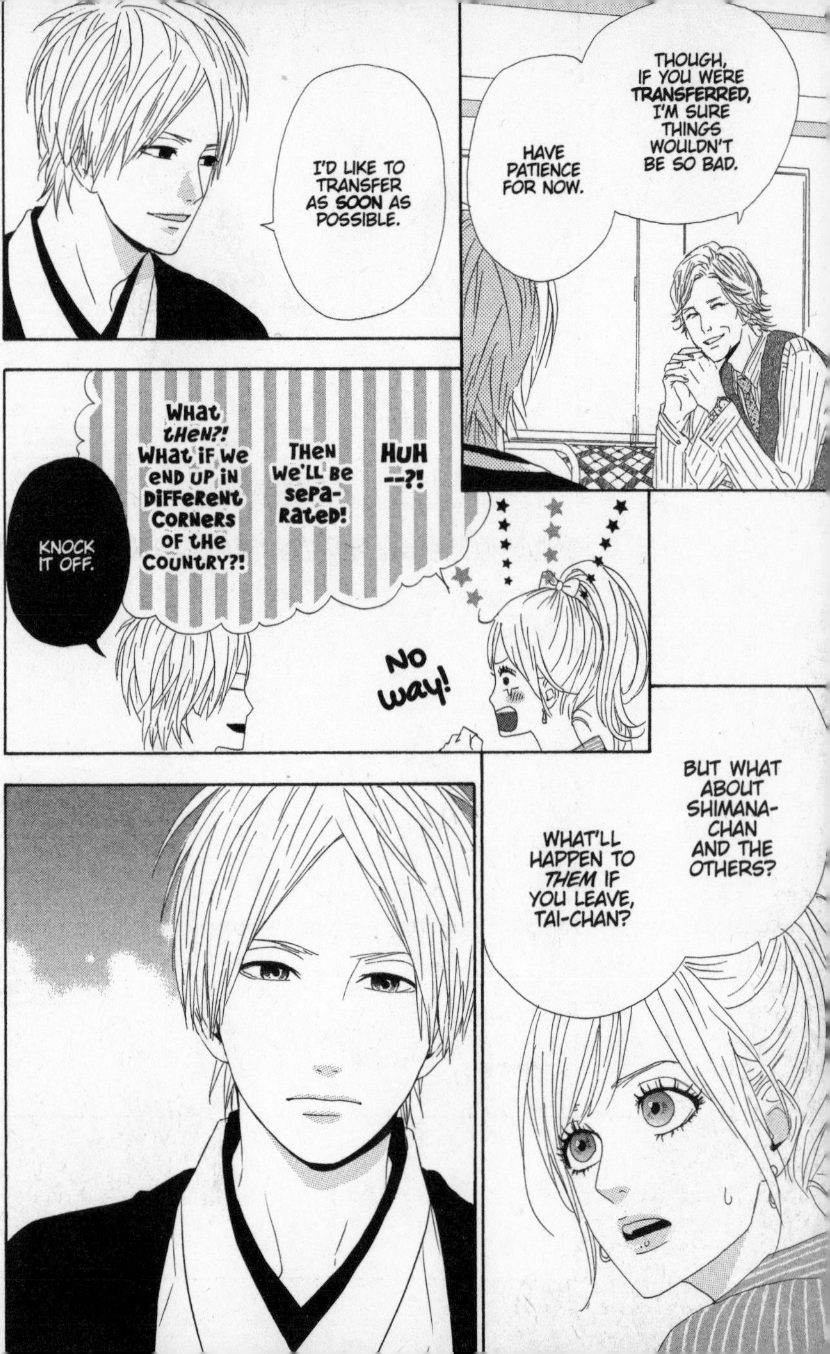
THOUGH, IF YOU WERE TRANSFERRED, I'M SURE THINGS WOULDN'T BE SO BAD.
HAVE PATIENCE FOR NOW.
I'D LIKE TO TRANSFER AS SOON AS POSSIBLE.
HUH--?!
THEN WE'LL BE SEPARATED!
WHAT THEN?! WHAT IF WE END UP IN DIFFERENT CORNERS OF THE COUNTRY?!
NO WAY!
KNOCK IT OFF.
BUT WHAT ABOUT SHIMANA-CHAN AND THE OTHERS?
WHAT'LL HAPPEN TO *THEM* IF YOU LEAVE, TAI-CHAN?

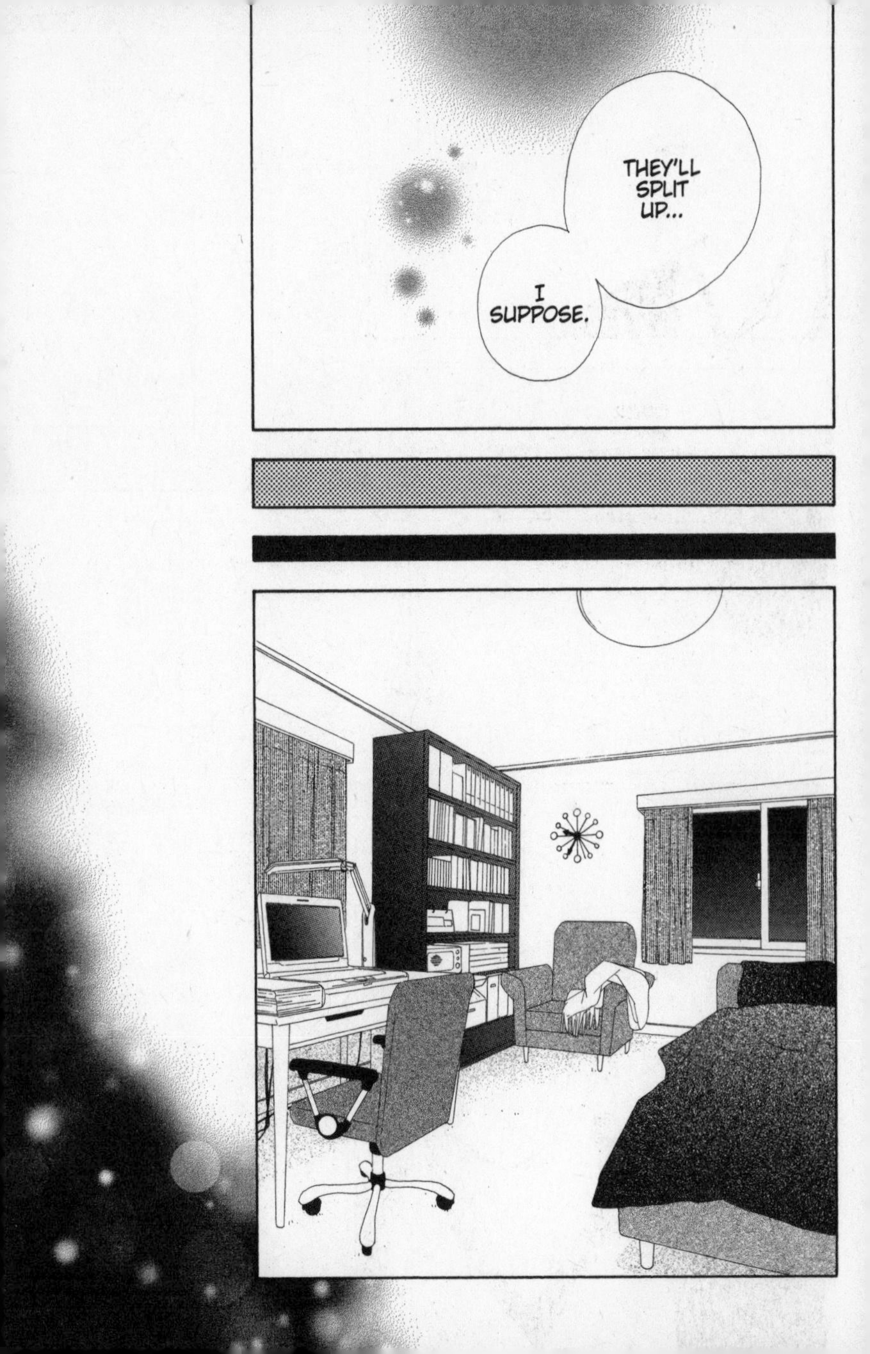
THEY'LL SPLIT UP...
I SUPPOSE.

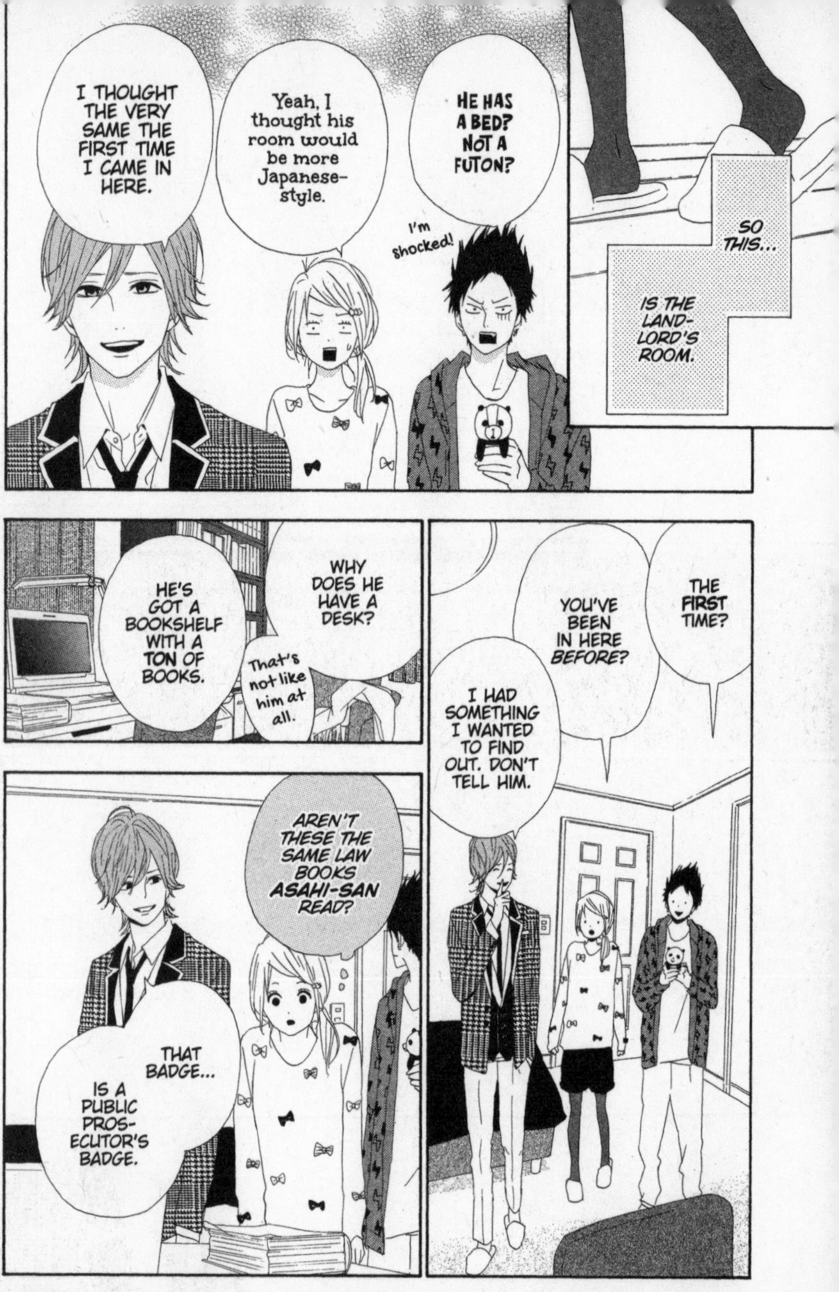
SO THIS...
IS THE LANDLORD'S ROOM.
HE HAS A BED? NOT A FUTON?
I'm shocked!
Yeah, I thought his room would be more Japanese-style.
I THOUGHT THE VERY SAME THE FIRST TIME I CAME IN HERE.
THE FIRST TIME?
YOU'VE BEEN IN HERE BEFORE?
I HAD SOMETHING I WANTED TO FIND OUT. DON'T TELL HIM.
WHY DOES HE HAVE A DESK?
HE'S GOT A BOOKSHELF WITH A TON OF BOOKS.
That's not like him at all.
AREN'T THESE THE SAME LAW BOOKS ASAHI-SAN READ?
THAT BADGE...
IS A PUBLIC PROSECUTOR'S BADGE.

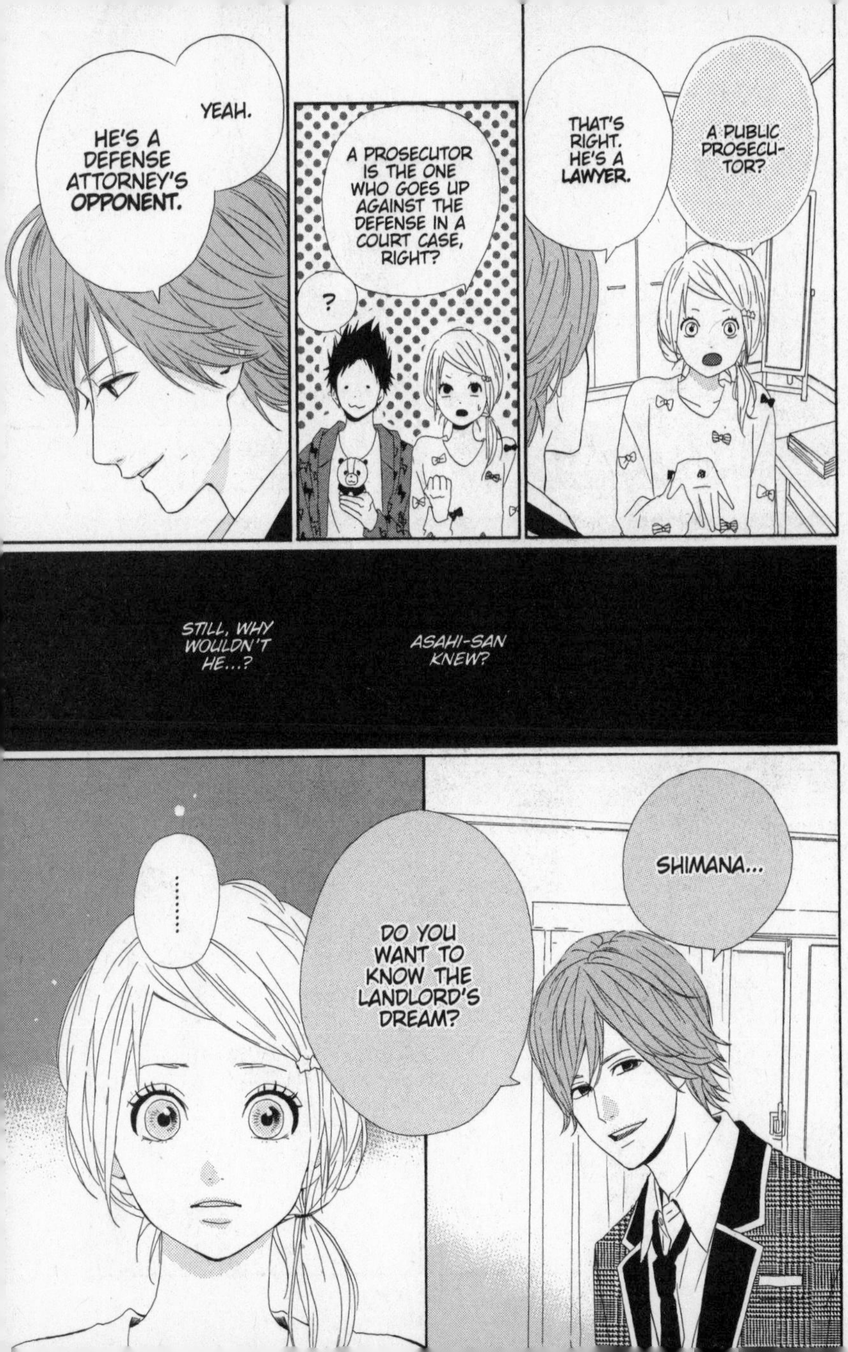
A PUBLIC PROSECUTOR?
THAT'S RIGHT. HE'S A LAWYER.
A PROSECUTOR IS THE ONE WHO GOES UP AGAINST THE DEFENSE IN A COURT CASE, RIGHT?
?
YEAH.
HE'S A DEFENSE ATTORNEY'S OPPONENT.
ASAHI-SAN KNEW?
STILL, WHY WOULDN'T HE...?
SHIMANA...
DO YOU WANT TO KNOW THE LANDLORD'S DREAM?
......

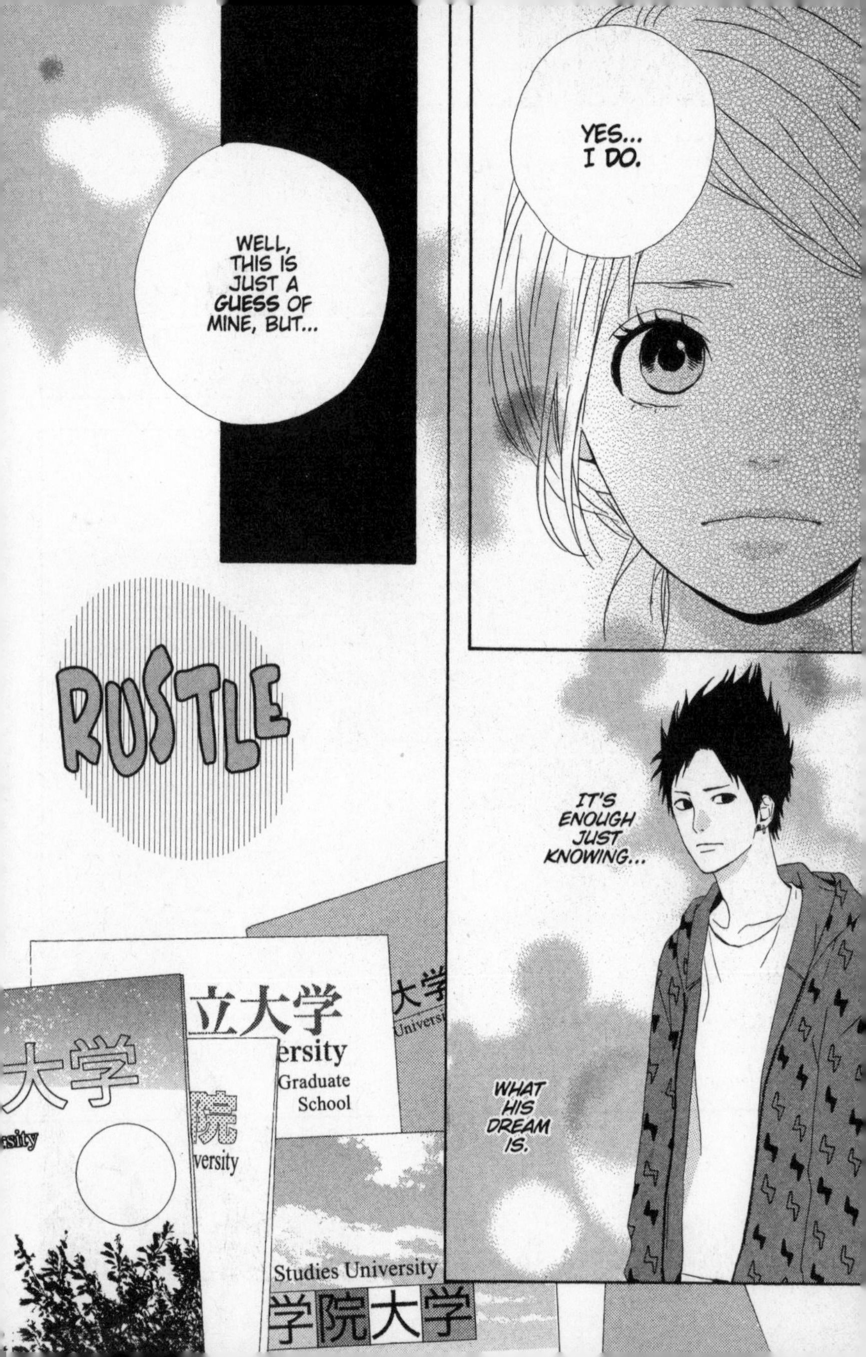
YES... I DO.
IT'S ENOUGH JUST KNOWING...
WHAT HIS DREAM IS.
WELL, THIS IS JUST A GUESS OF MINE, BUT...
RUSTLE
立大学
ersity
Graduate School
大学
院
versity
Studies University
学院大学

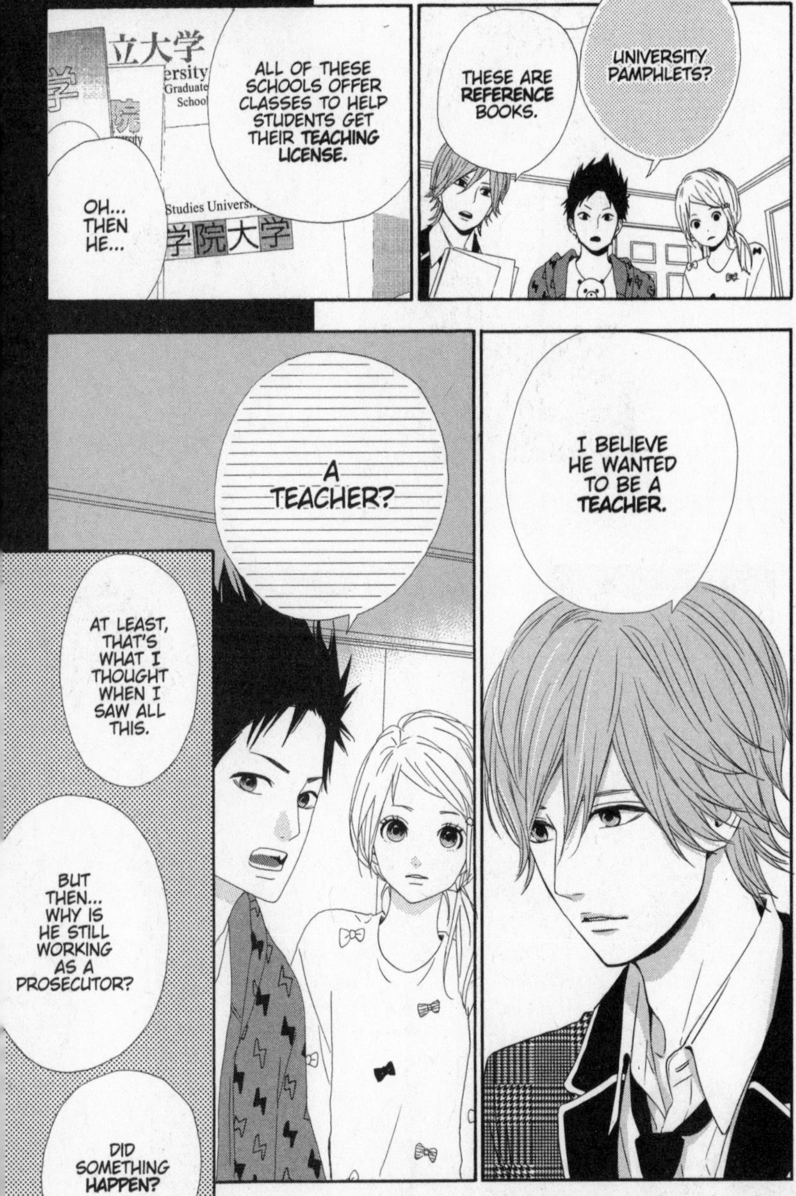
UNIVERSITY PAMPHLETS?
THESE ARE REFERENCE BOOKS.
ALL OF THESE SCHOOLS OFFER CLASSES TO HELP STUDENTS GET THEIR TEACHING LICENSE.
立大学
Graduate School
学院大学
OH... THEN HE...
I BELIEVE HE WANTED TO BE A TEACHER.
A TEACHER?
AT LEAST, THAT'S WHAT I THOUGHT WHEN I SAW ALL THIS.
BUT THEN... WHY IS HE STILL WORKING AS A PROSECUTOR?
DID SOMETHING HAPPEN?

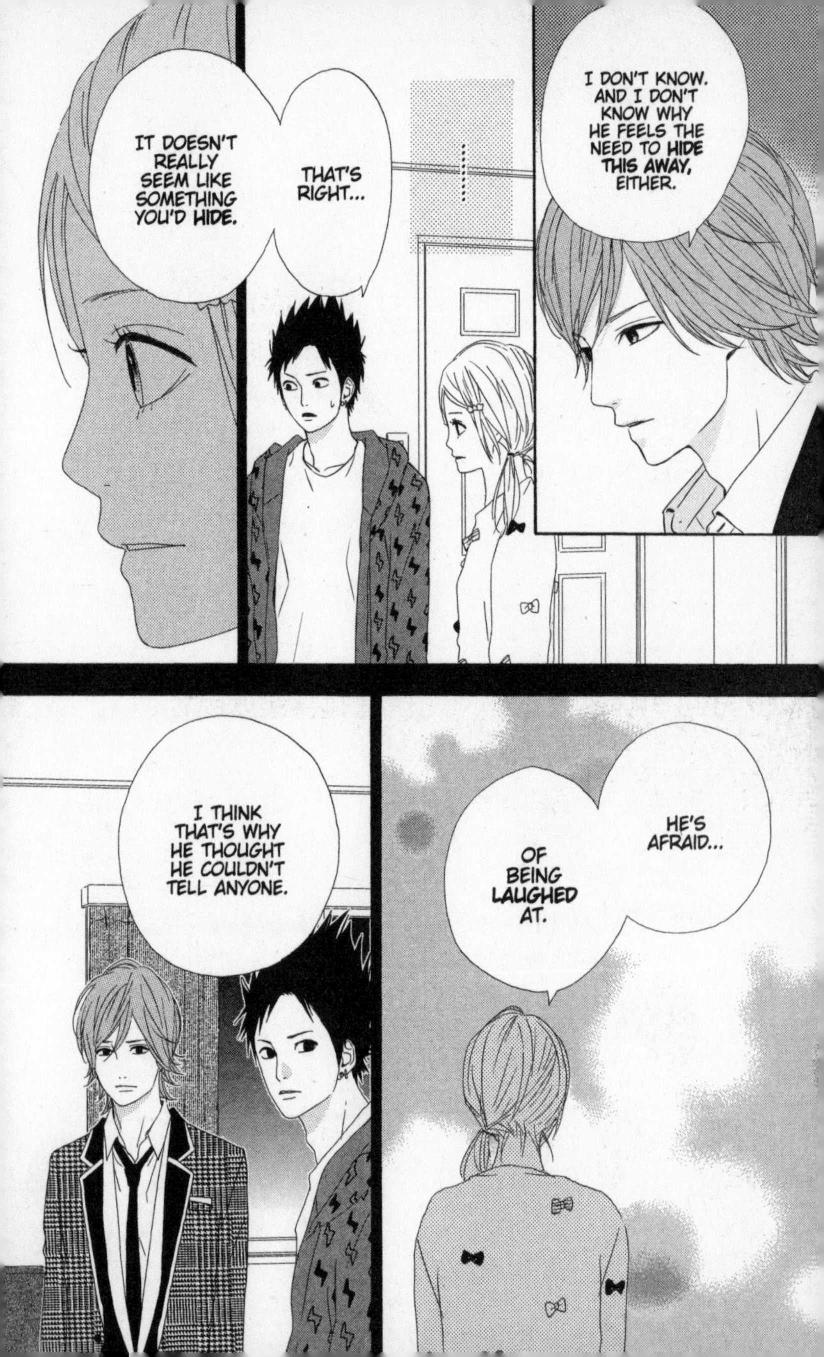
I DON'T KNOW. AND I DON'T KNOW WHY HE FEELS THE NEED TO HIDE THIS AWAY, EITHER.
......
THAT'S RIGHT...
IT DOESN'T REALLY SEEM LIKE SOMETHING YOU'D HIDE.
HE'S AFRAID...
OF BEING LAUGHED AT.
I THINK THAT'S WHY HE THOUGHT HE COULDN'T TELL ANYONE.

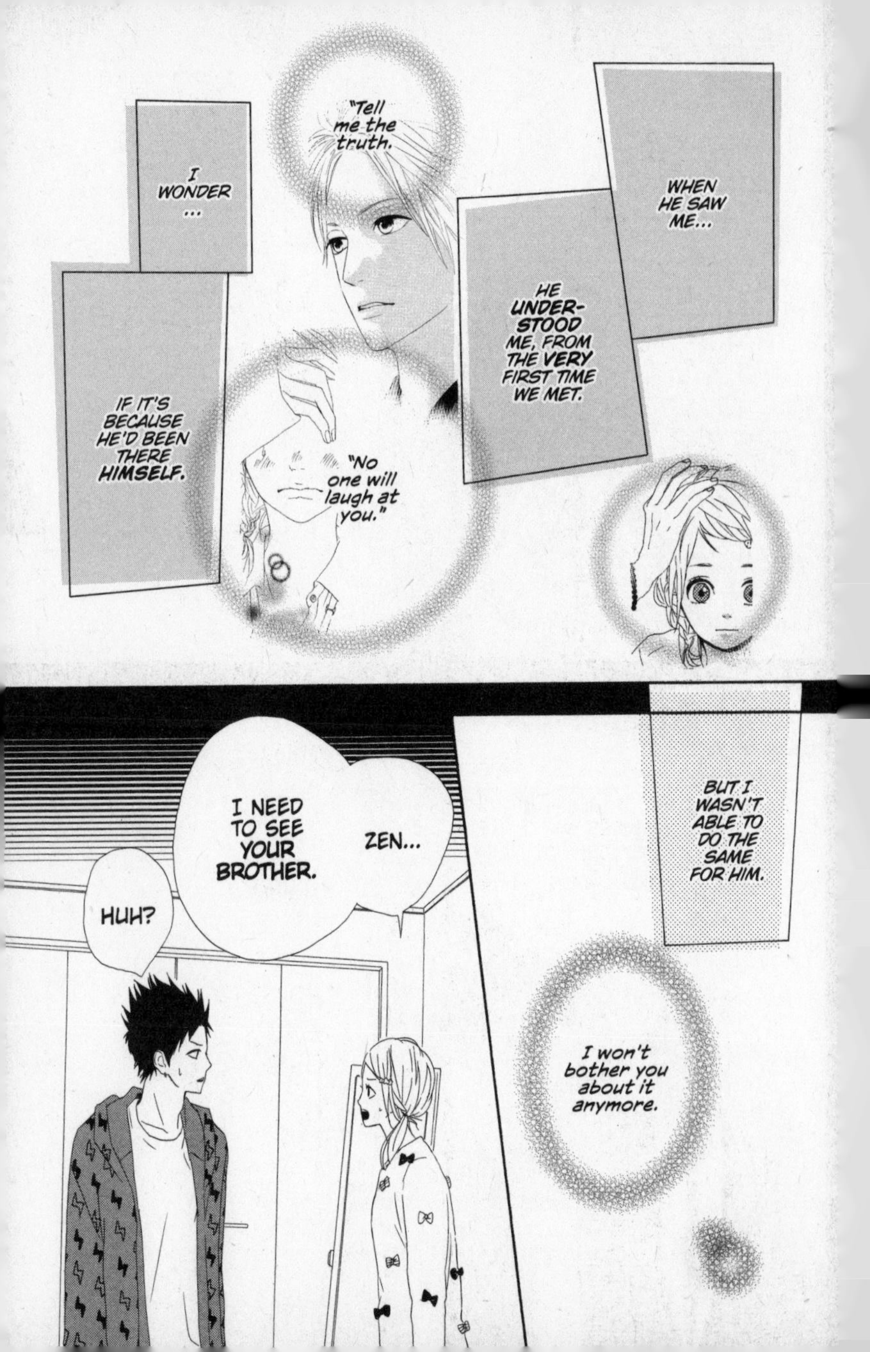
WHEN HE SAW ME...
HE UNDERSTOOD ME, FROM THE VERY FIRST TIME WE MET.
"Tell me the truth.
"No one will laugh at you."
I WONDER...
IF IT'S BECAUSE HE'D BEEN THERE HIMSELF.
BUT I WASN'T ABLE TO DO THE SAME FOR HIM.
I won't bother you about it anymore.
ZEN...
I NEED TO SEE YOUR BROTHER.
HUH?

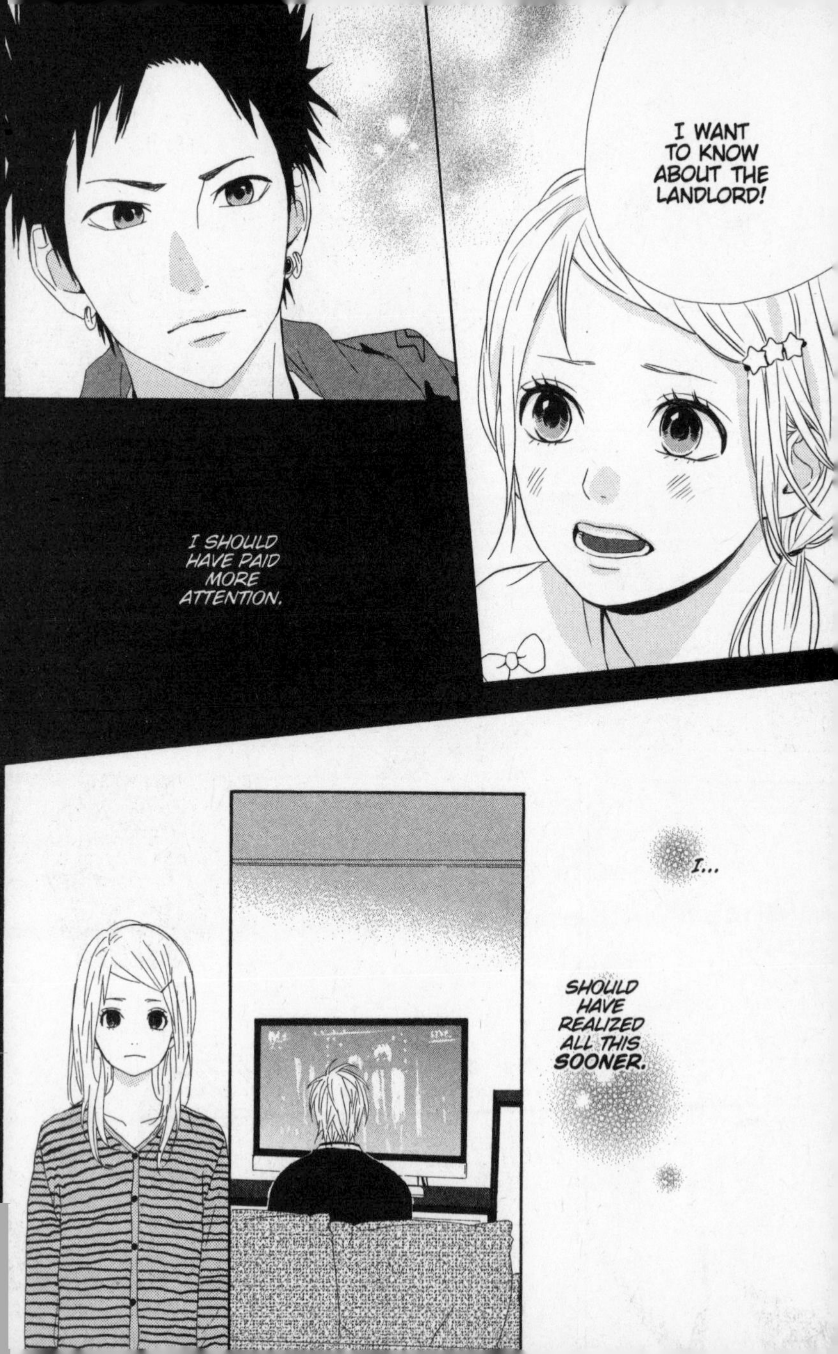
I WANT TO KNOW ABOUT THE LANDLORD!
I SHOULD HAVE PAID MORE ATTENTION.
I...
SHOULD HAVE REALIZED ALL THIS SOONER.

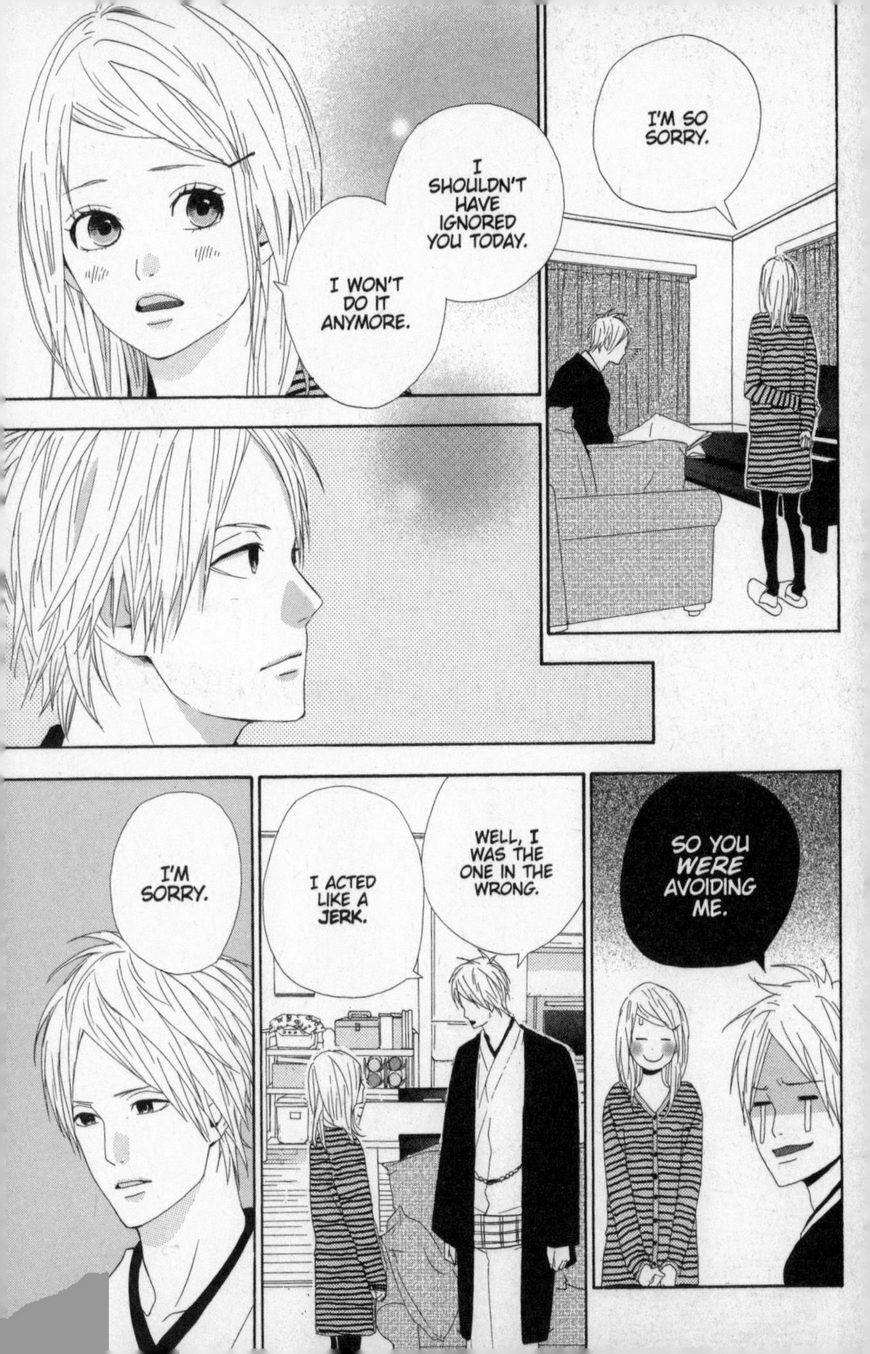
I'M SO SORRY.
I SHOULDN'T HAVE IGNORED YOU TODAY.
I WON'T DO IT ANYMORE.
SO YOU WERE AVOIDING ME.
WELL, I WAS THE ONE IN THE WRONG.
I ACTED LIKE A JERK.
I'M SORRY.

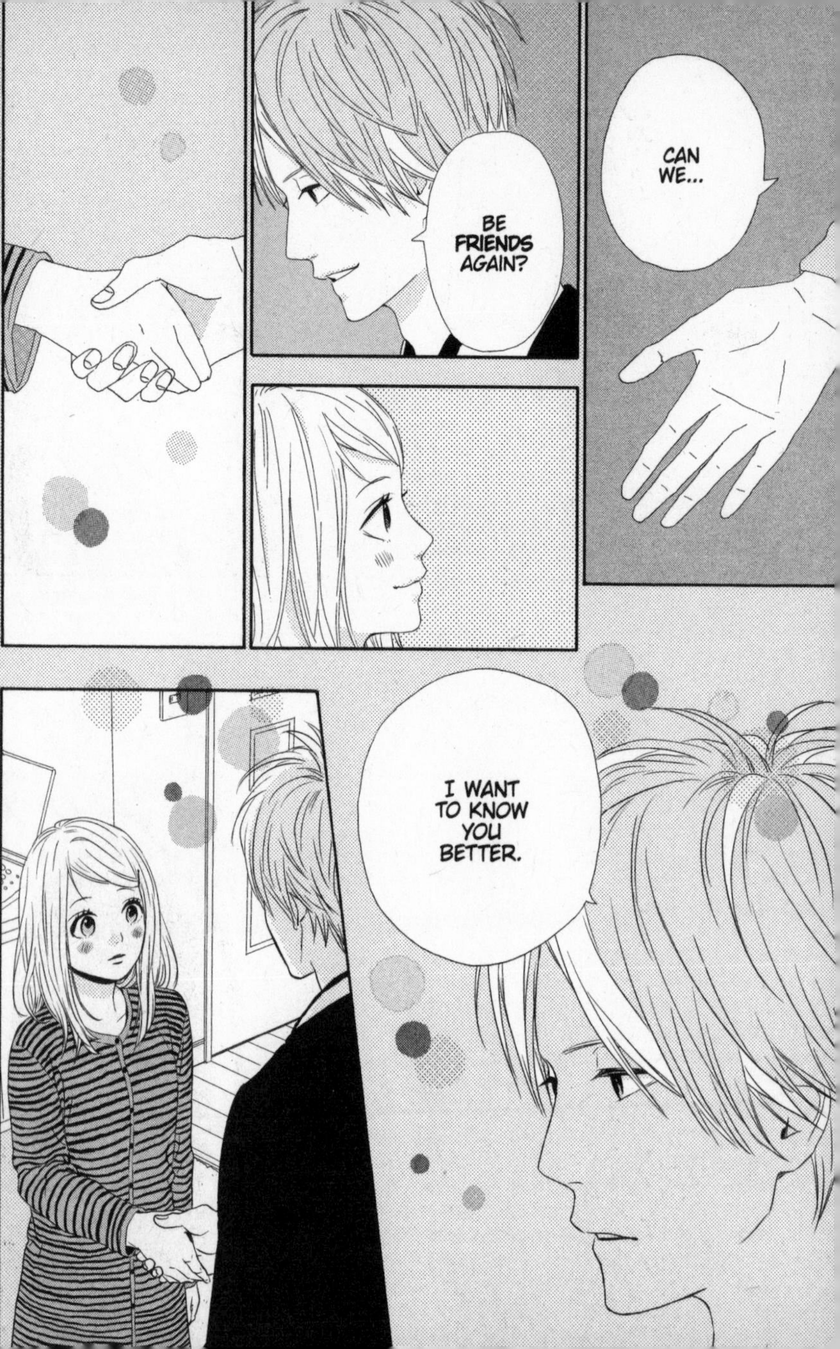
CAN WE...
BE FRIENDS AGAIN?
I WANT TO KNOW YOU BETTER.

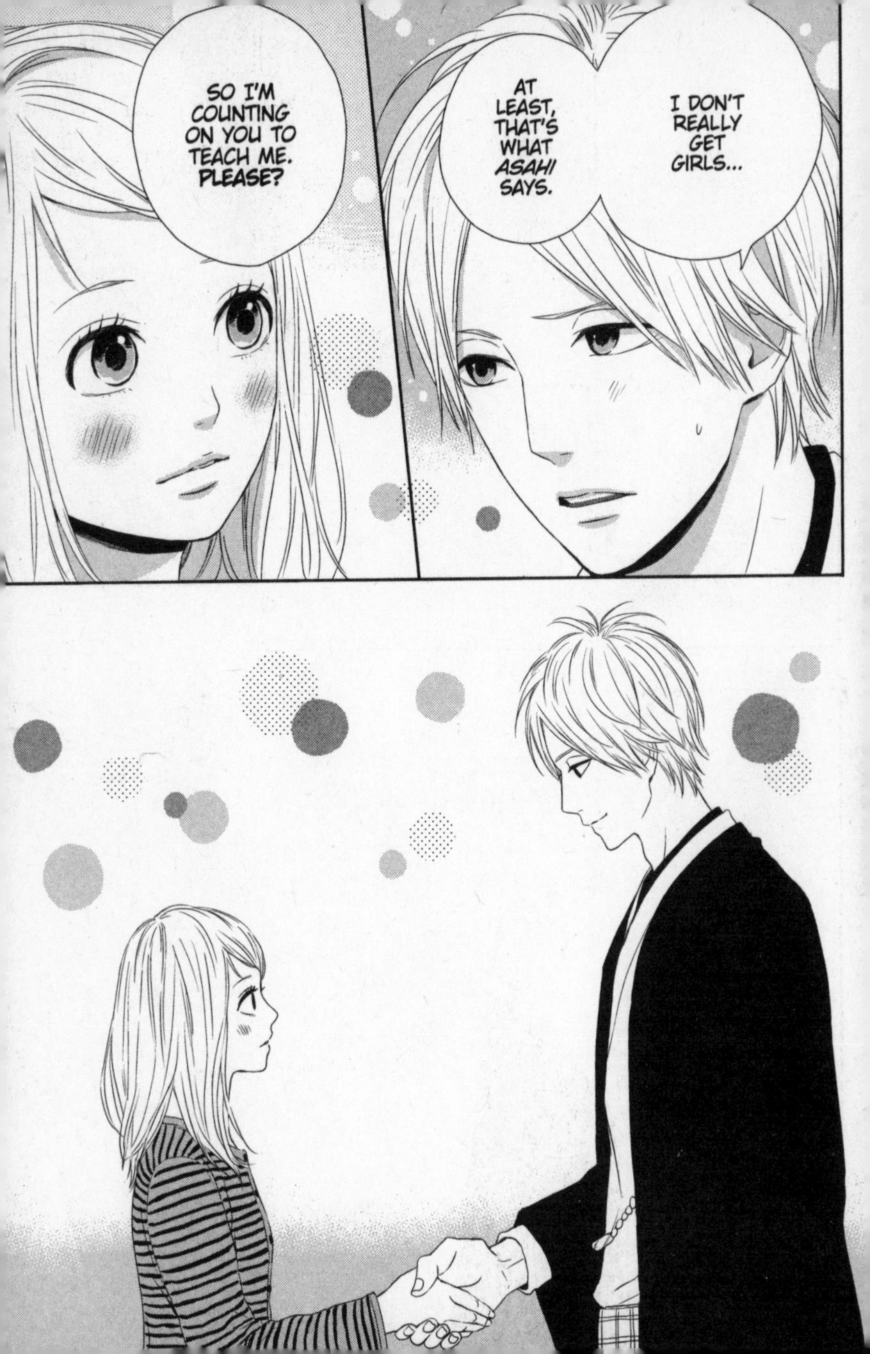
I DON'T REALLY GET GIRLS...
AT LEAST, THAT'S WHAT ASAHI SAYS.
SO I'M COUNTING ON YOU TO TEACH ME. PLEASE?

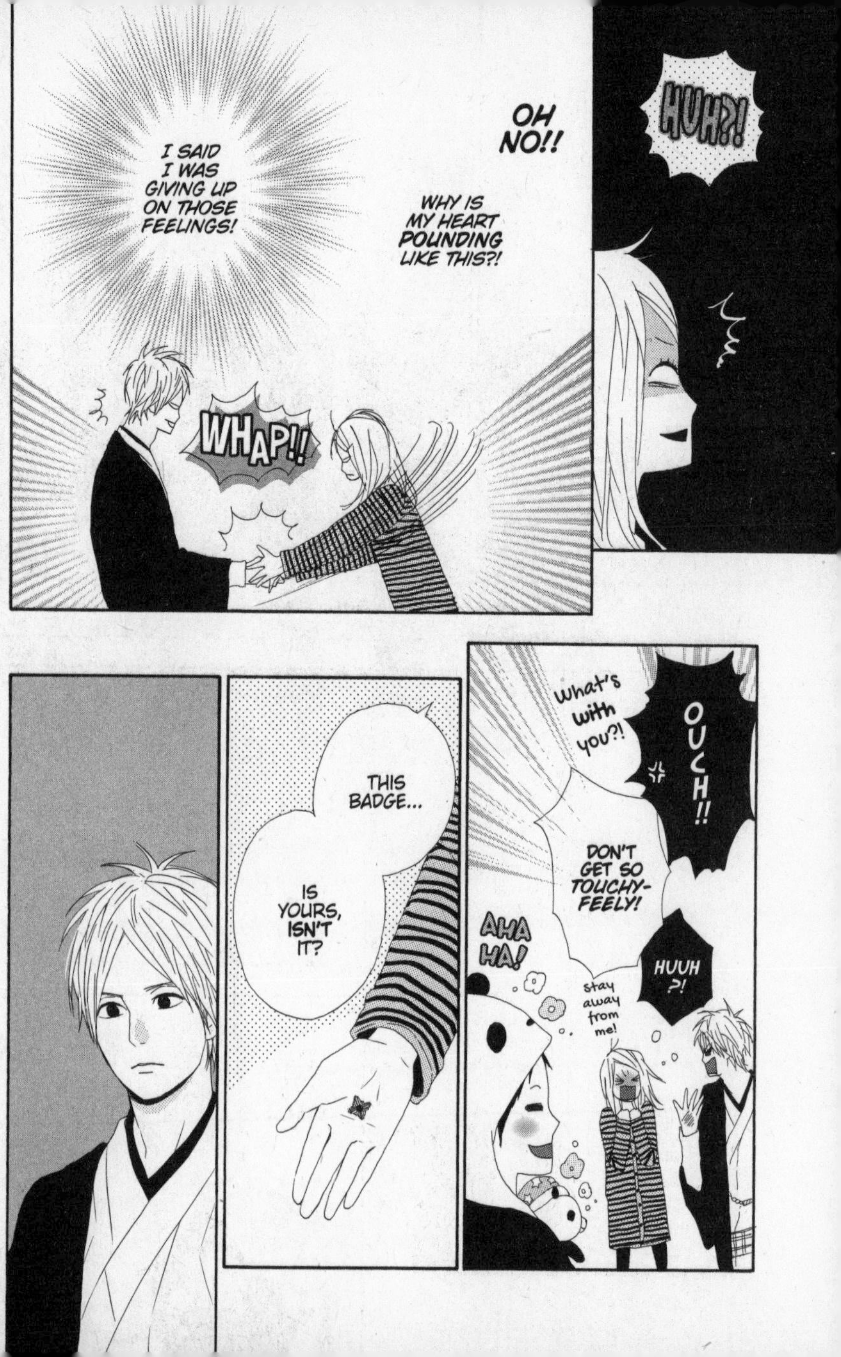
HUH?!
OH NO!!
WHY IS MY HEART POUNDING LIKE THIS?!
I SAID I WAS GIVING UP ON THOSE FEELINGS!
WHAP!!
What's with you?!
OUCH!!
DON'T GET SO TOUCHY-FEELY!
HUUH ?!
stay away from me!
AHA HA!
THIS BADGE...
IS YOURS, ISN'T IT?

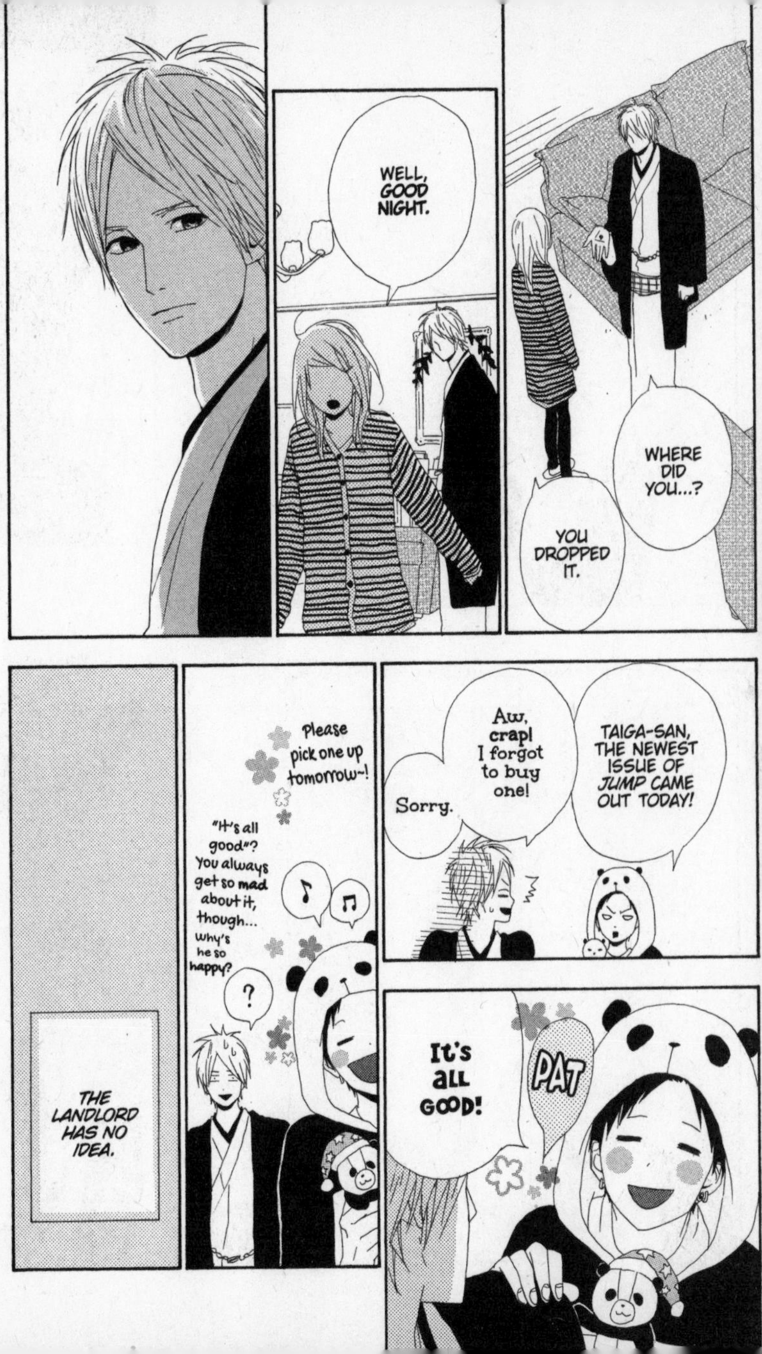
WHERE DID YOU...?
YOU DROPPED IT.
WELL, GOOD NIGHT.
TAIGA-SAN, THE NEWEST ISSUE OF JUMP CAME OUT TODAY!
Aw, crap! I forgot to buy one!
Sorry.
PAT
It's all GOOD!
Please pick one up tomorrow~!
"It's all good"? You always get so mad about it, though...
why's he so happy?
?
THE LANDLORD HAS NO IDEA.

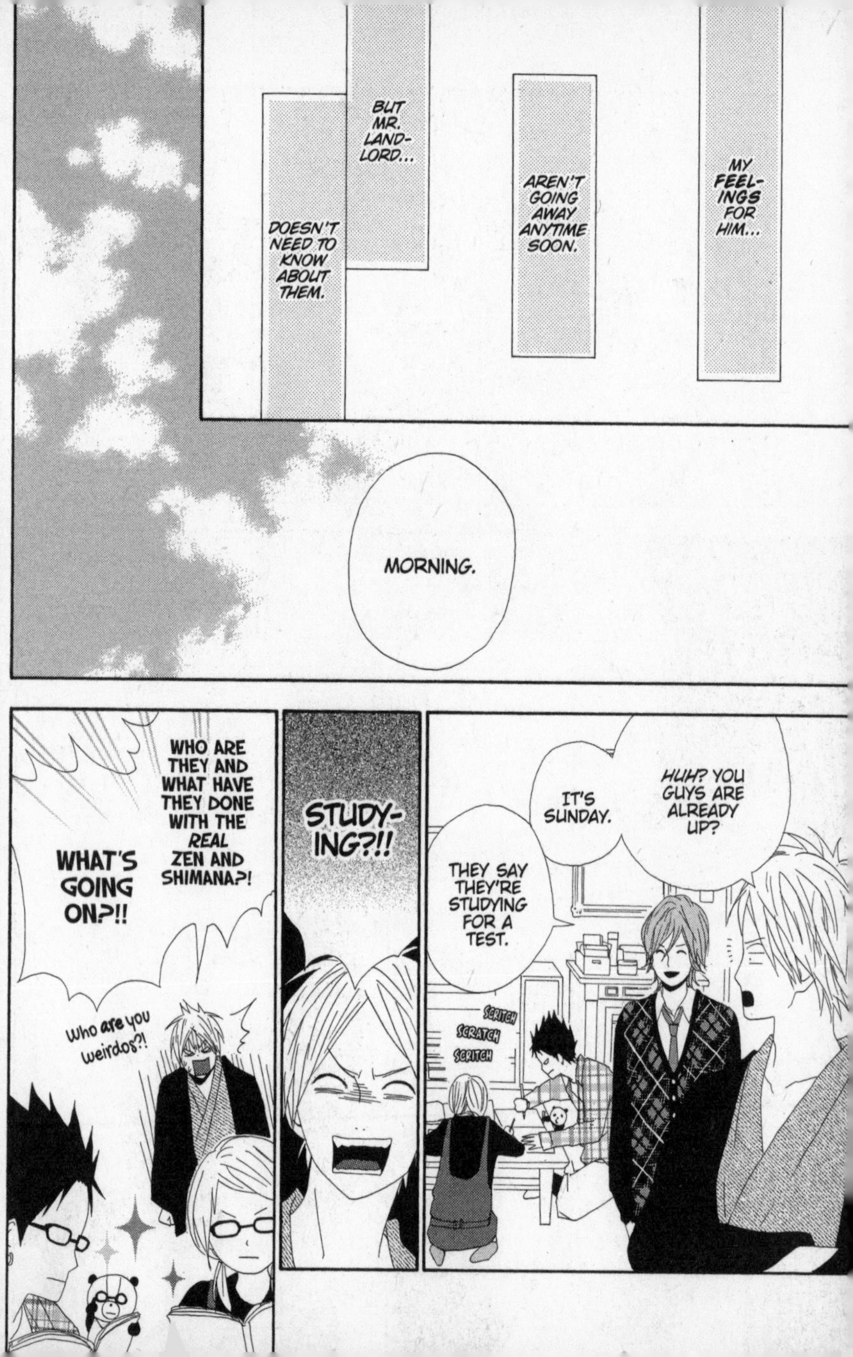
MY FEELINGS FOR HIM...
AREN'T GOING AWAY ANYTIME SOON.
BUT MR. LANDLORD...
DOESN'T NEED TO KNOW ABOUT THEM.
MORNING.
HUH? YOU GUYS ARE ALREADY UP?
IT'S SUNDAY.
THEY SAY THEY'RE STUDYING FOR A TEST.
SCRITCH
SCRATCH
SCRITCH
STUDY-ING?!!
WHO ARE THEY AND WHAT HAVE THEY DONE WITH THE *REAL* ZEN AND SHIMANA?!
WHAT'S GOING ON?!!
Who are you weirdos?!

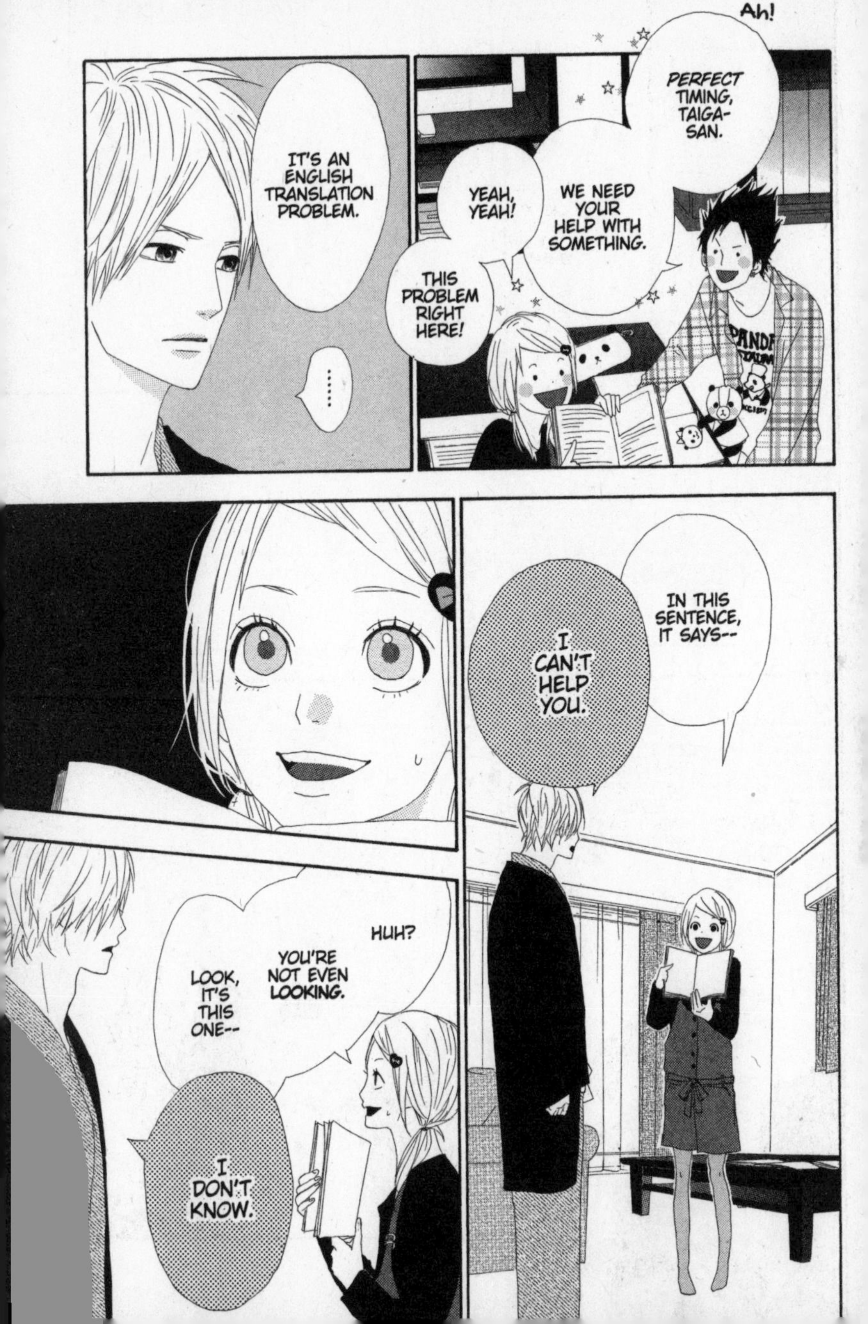

Ah!
PERFECT TIMING, TAIGA-SAN.
WE NEED YOUR HELP WITH SOMETHING.
YEAH, YEAH!
THIS PROBLEM RIGHT HERE!
IT'S AN ENGLISH TRANSLATION PROBLEM.
......
IN THIS SENTENCE, IT SAYS--
I CAN'T HELP YOU.
HUH?
YOU'RE NOT EVEN LOOKING.
LOOK, IT'S THIS ONE--
I DON'T KNOW.

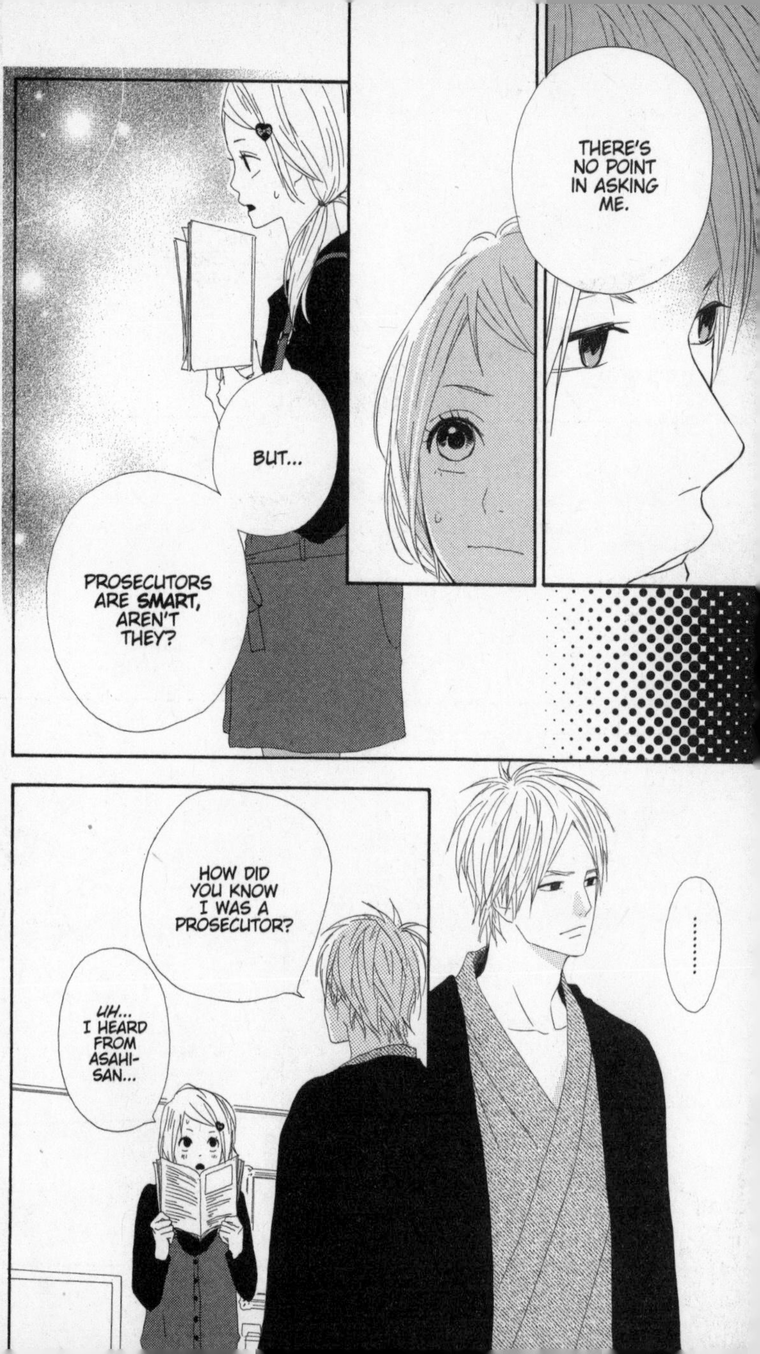
THERE'S NO POINT IN ASKING ME.
BUT...
PROSECUTORS ARE SMART, AREN'T THEY?
......
HOW DID YOU KNOW I WAS A PROSECUTOR?
UH... I HEARD FROM ASAHI-SAN...

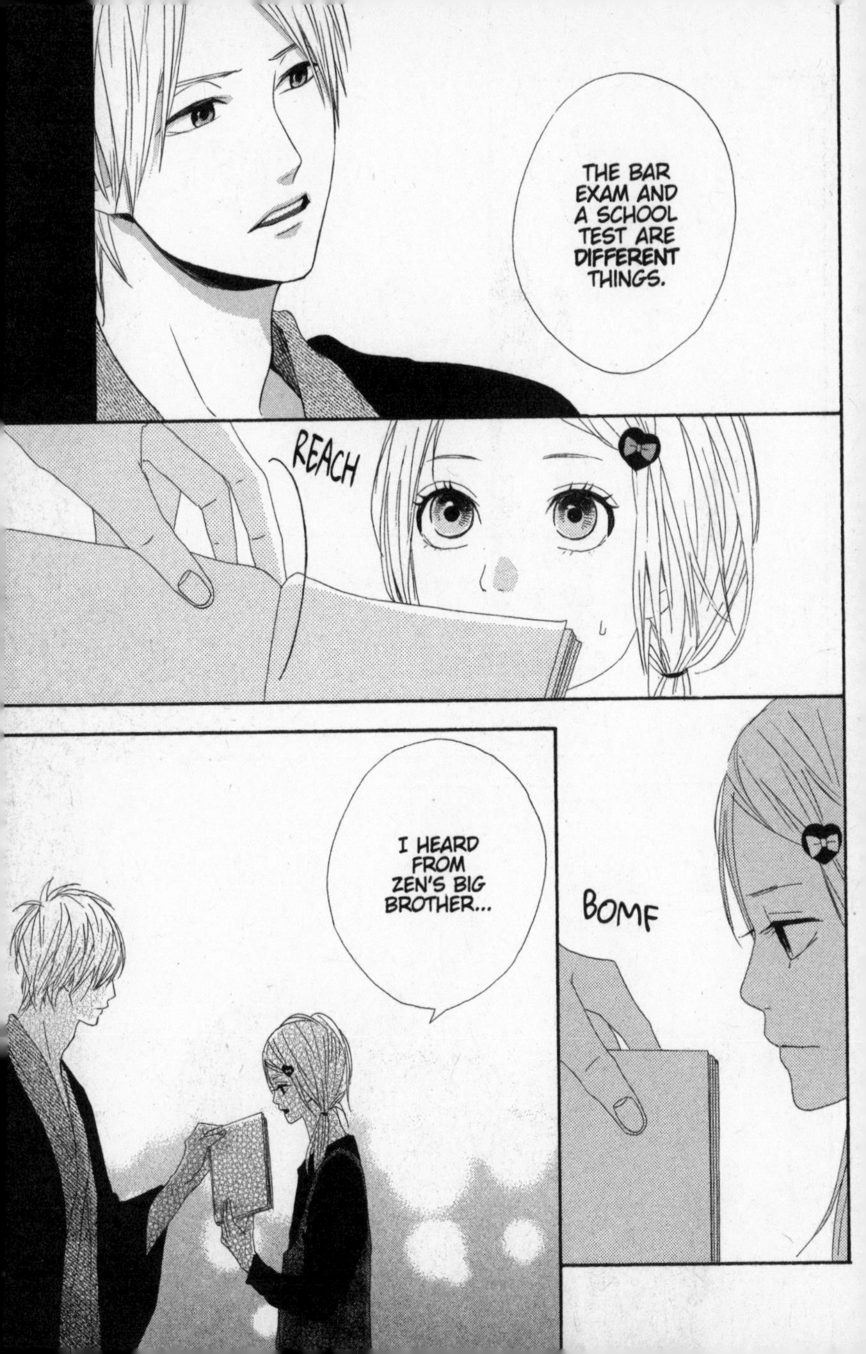
THE BAR EXAM AND A SCHOOL TEST ARE DIFFERENT THINGS.
REACH
BOMF
I HEARD FROM ZEN'S BIG BROTHER...

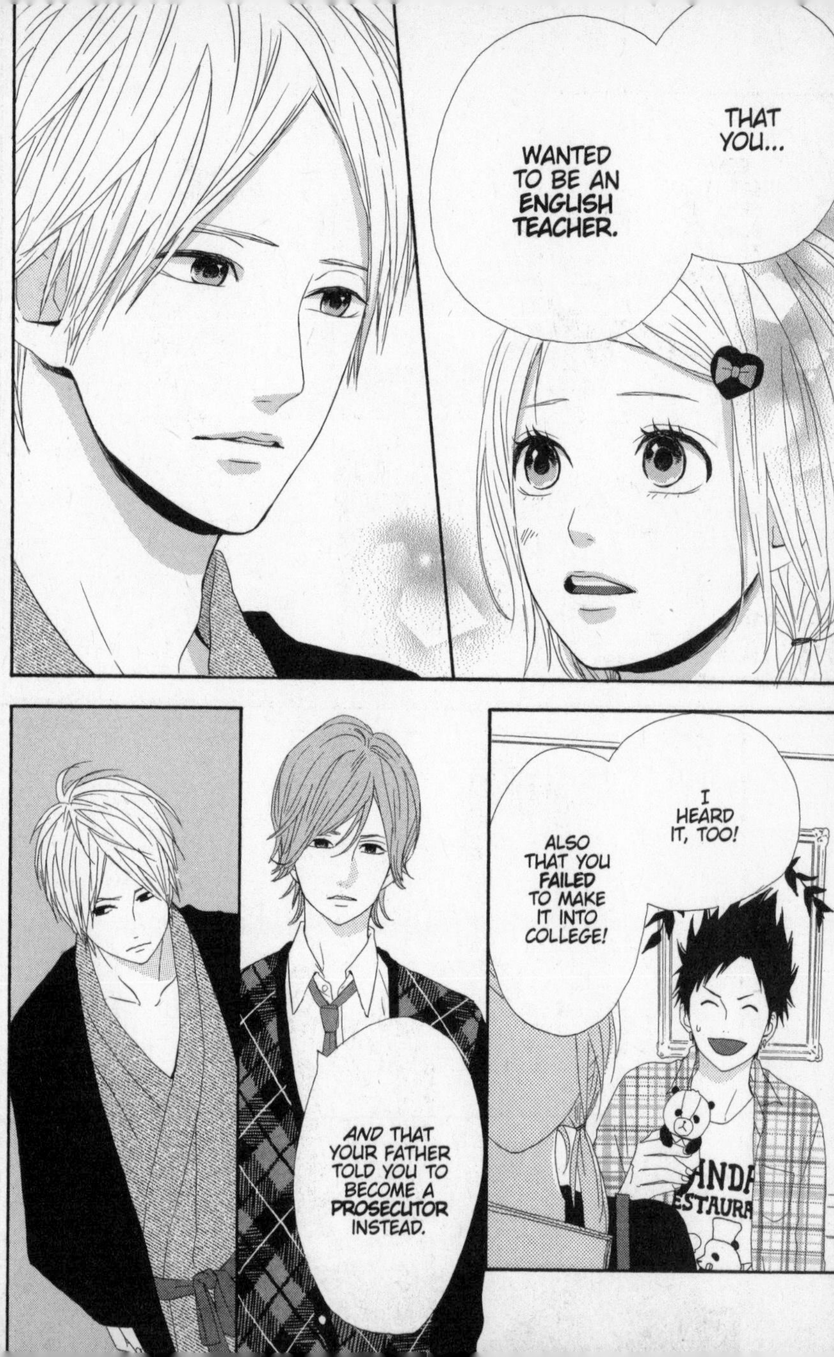
THAT YOU...
WANTED TO BE AN ENGLISH TEACHER.
I HEARD IT, TOO!
ALSO THAT YOU FAILED TO MAKE IT INTO COLLEGE!
AND THAT YOUR FATHER TOLD YOU TO BECOME A PROSECUTOR INSTEAD.

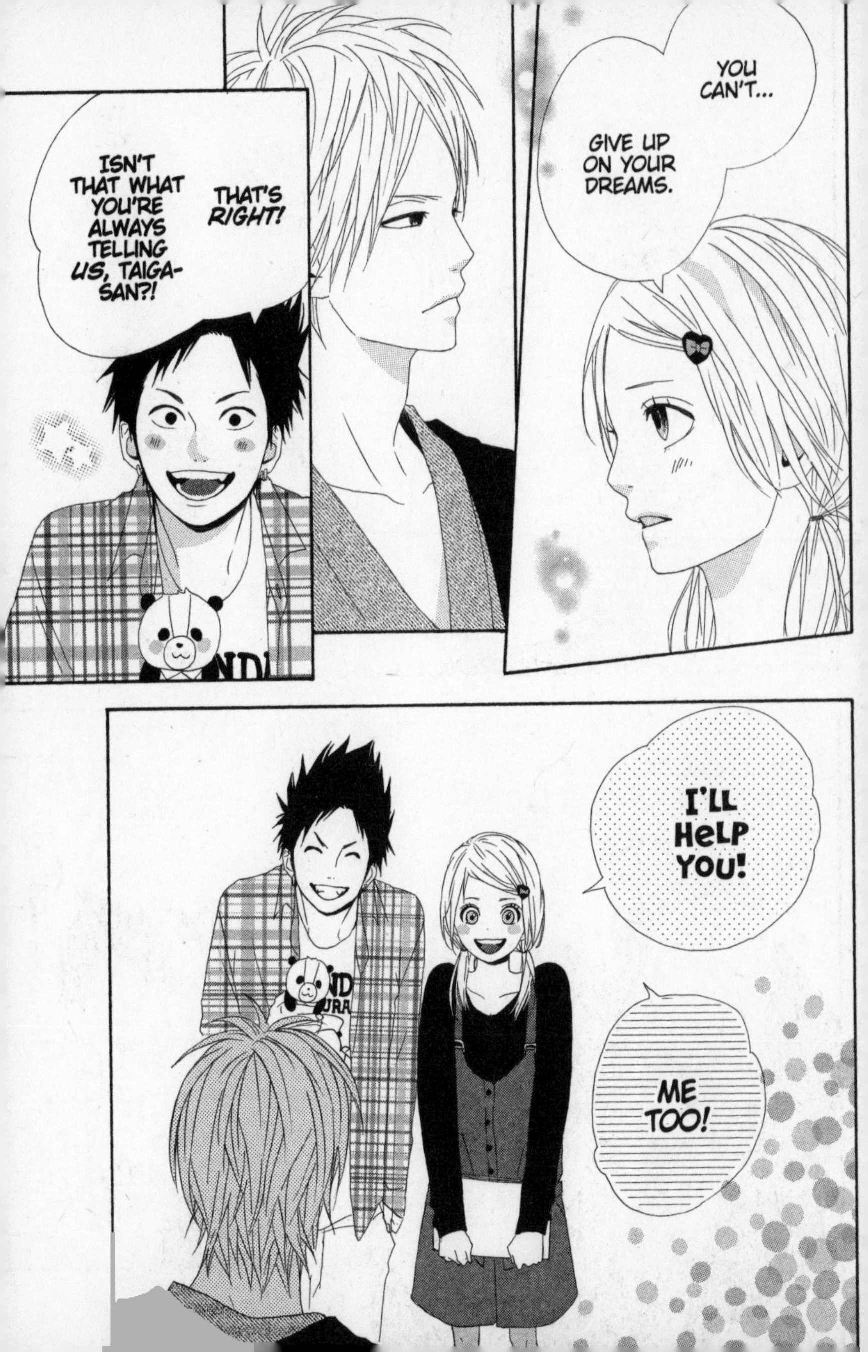
YOU CAN'T...
GIVE UP ON YOUR DREAMS.
THAT'S RIGHT!
ISN'T THAT WHAT YOU'RE ALWAYS TELLING US, TAIGA-SAN?!
I'LL HELP YOU!
ME TOO!

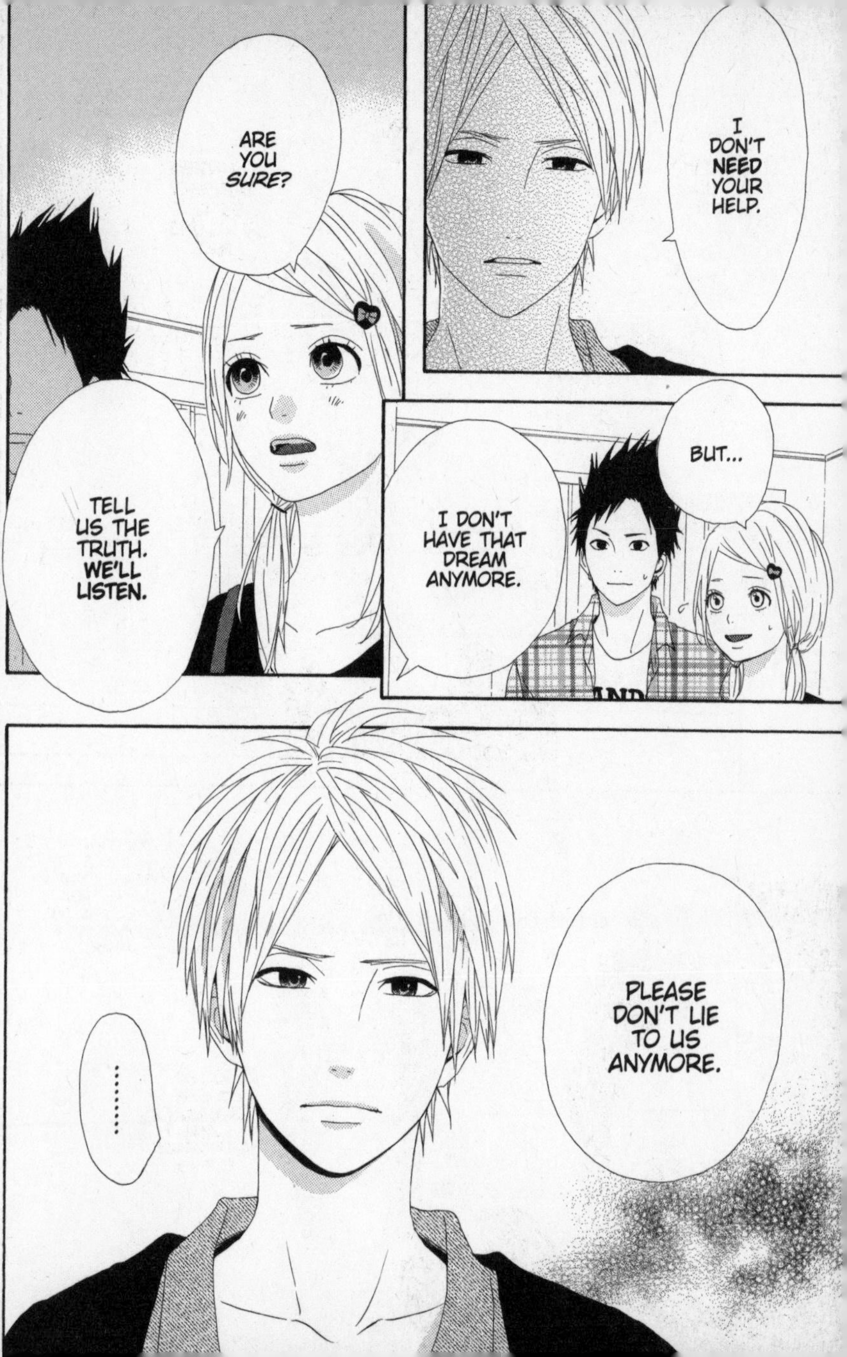

I DON'T NEED YOUR HELP.
BUT...
I DON'T HAVE THAT DREAM ANYMORE.
ARE YOU SURE?
TELL US THE TRUTH. WE'LL LISTEN.
PLEASE DON'T LIE TO US ANYMORE.
......

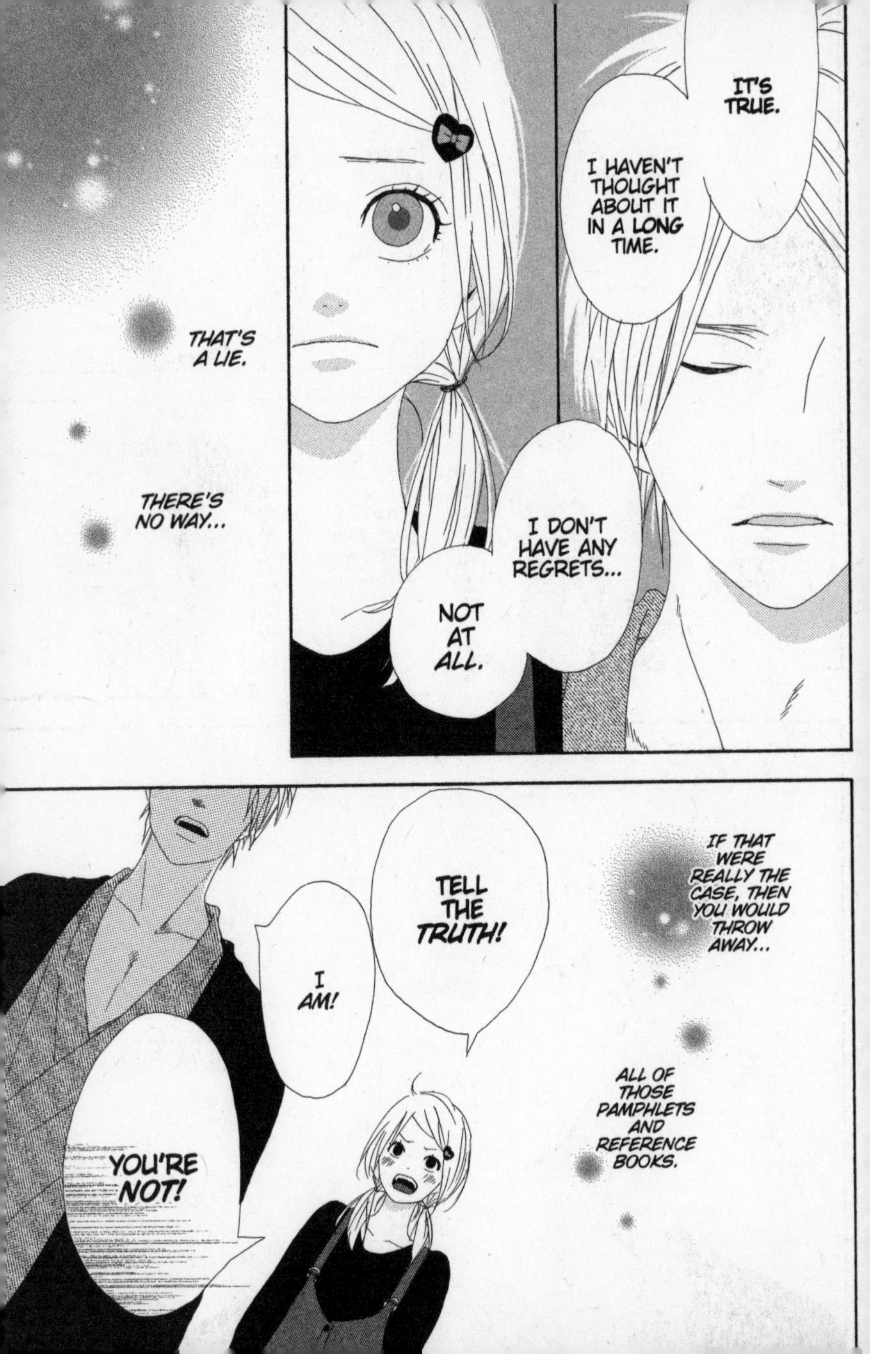
IT'S TRUE.
I HAVEN'T THOUGHT ABOUT IT IN A LONG TIME.
I DON'T HAVE ANY REGRETS...
NOT AT ALL.
THAT'S A LIE.
THERE'S NO WAY...
IF THAT WERE REALLY THE CASE, THEN YOU WOULD THROW AWAY...
ALL OF THOSE PAMPHLETS AND REFERENCE BOOKS.
TELL THE TRUTH!
I AM!
YOU'RE NOT!

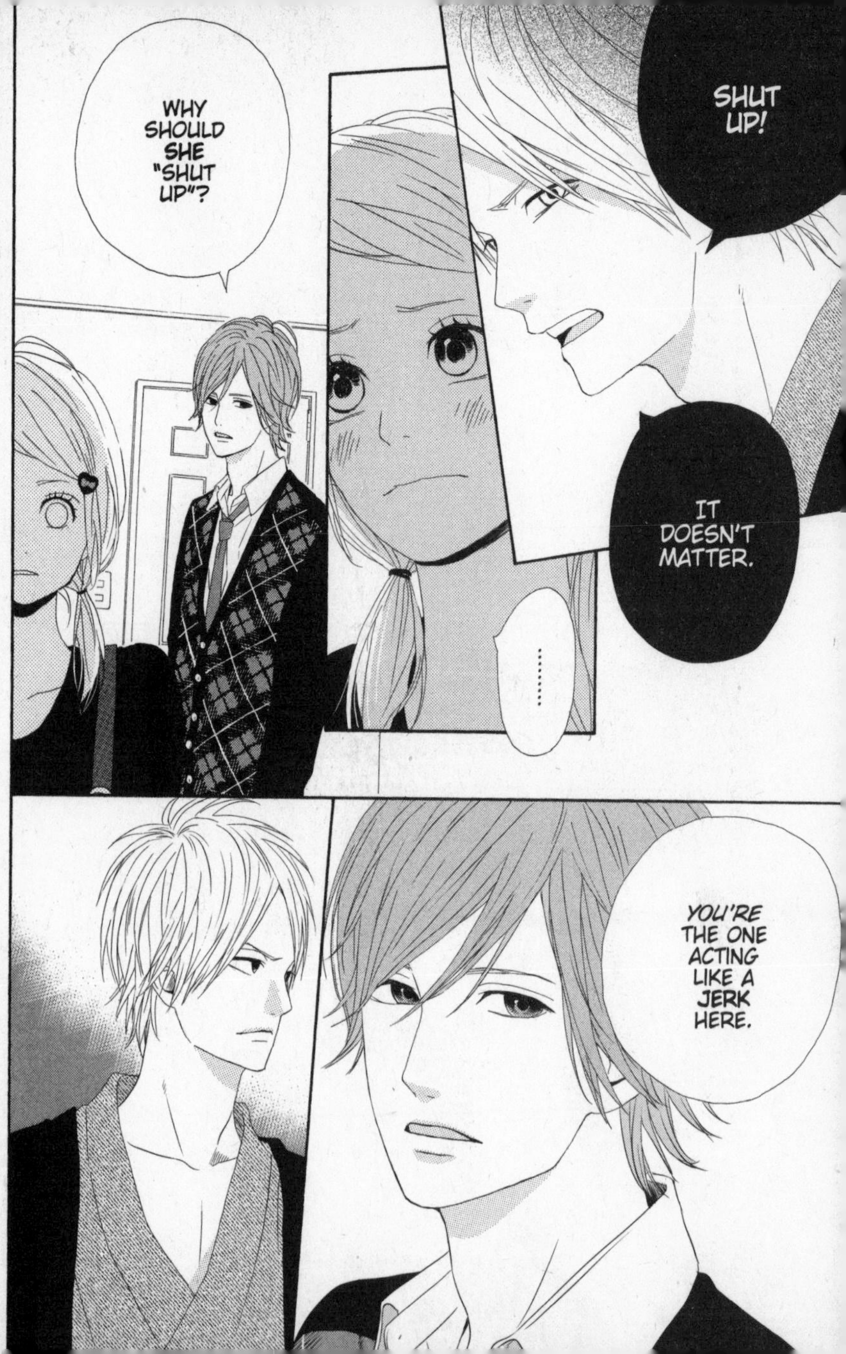
SHUT UP!
IT DOESN'T MATTER.
......
WHY SHOULD SHE "SHUT UP"?
YOU'RE THE ONE ACTING LIKE A JERK HERE.

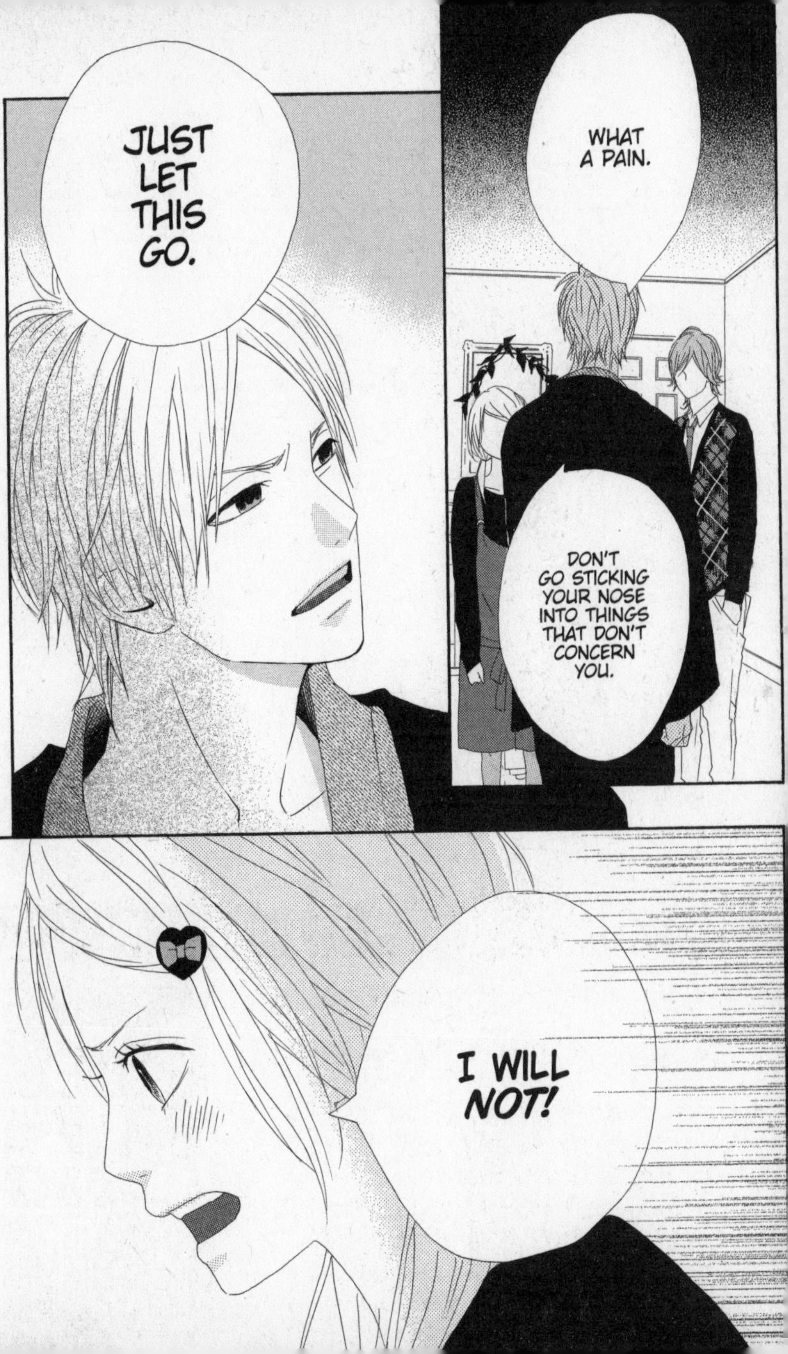
WHAT A PAIN.
DON'T GO STICKING YOUR NOSE INTO THINGS THAT DON'T CONCERN YOU.
JUST LET THIS GO.
I WILL *NOT!*

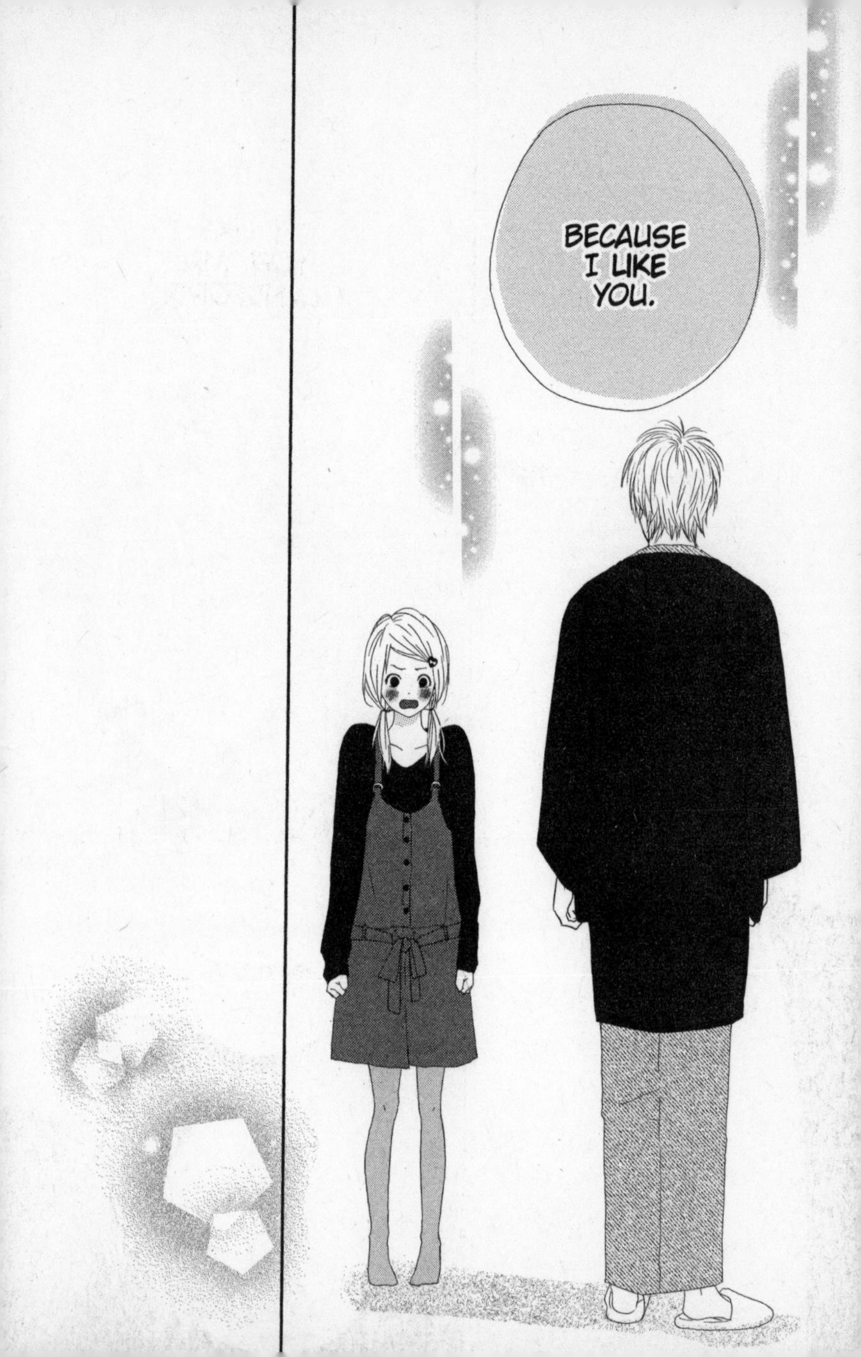
BECAUSE I LIKE YOU.

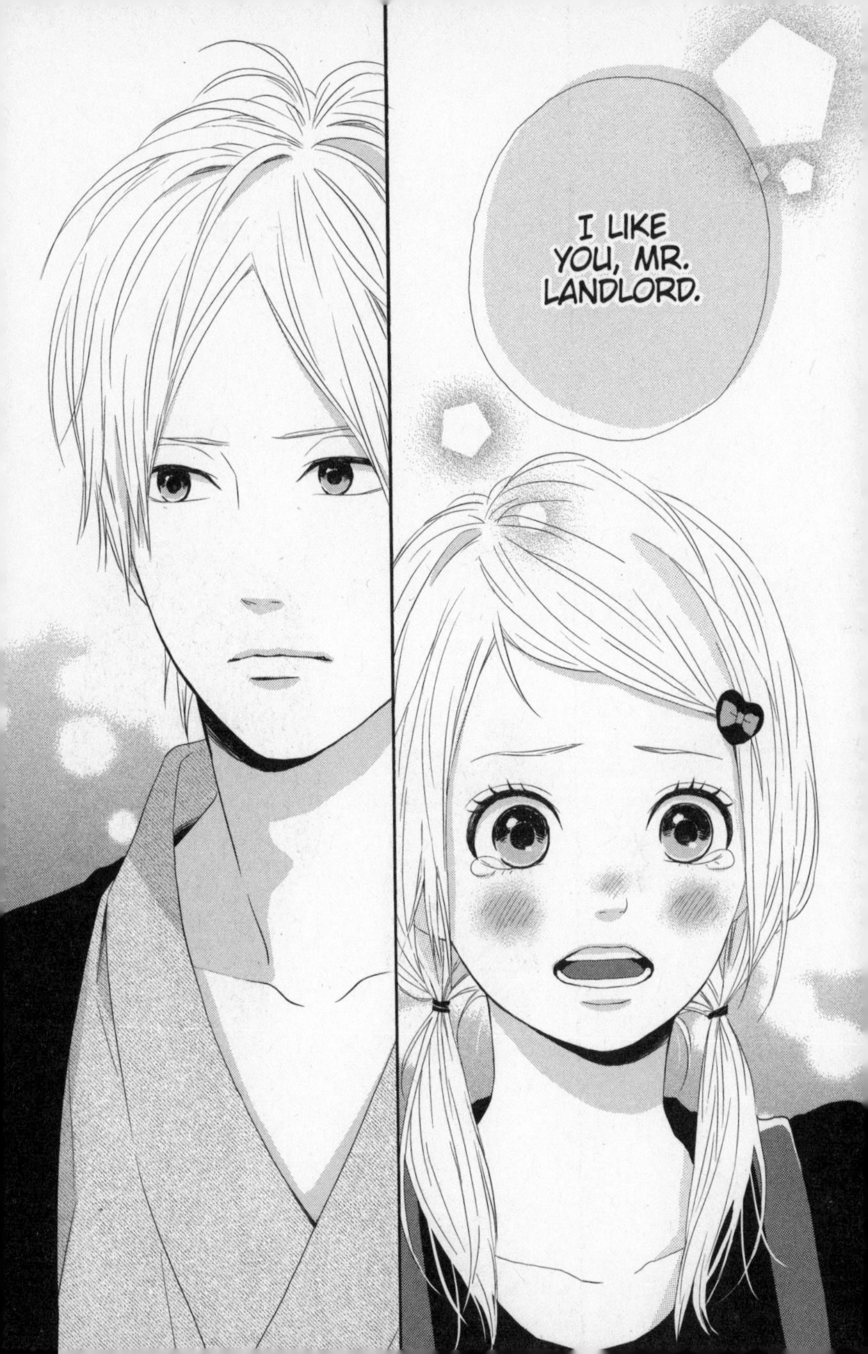
I LIKE YOU, MR. LANDLORD.

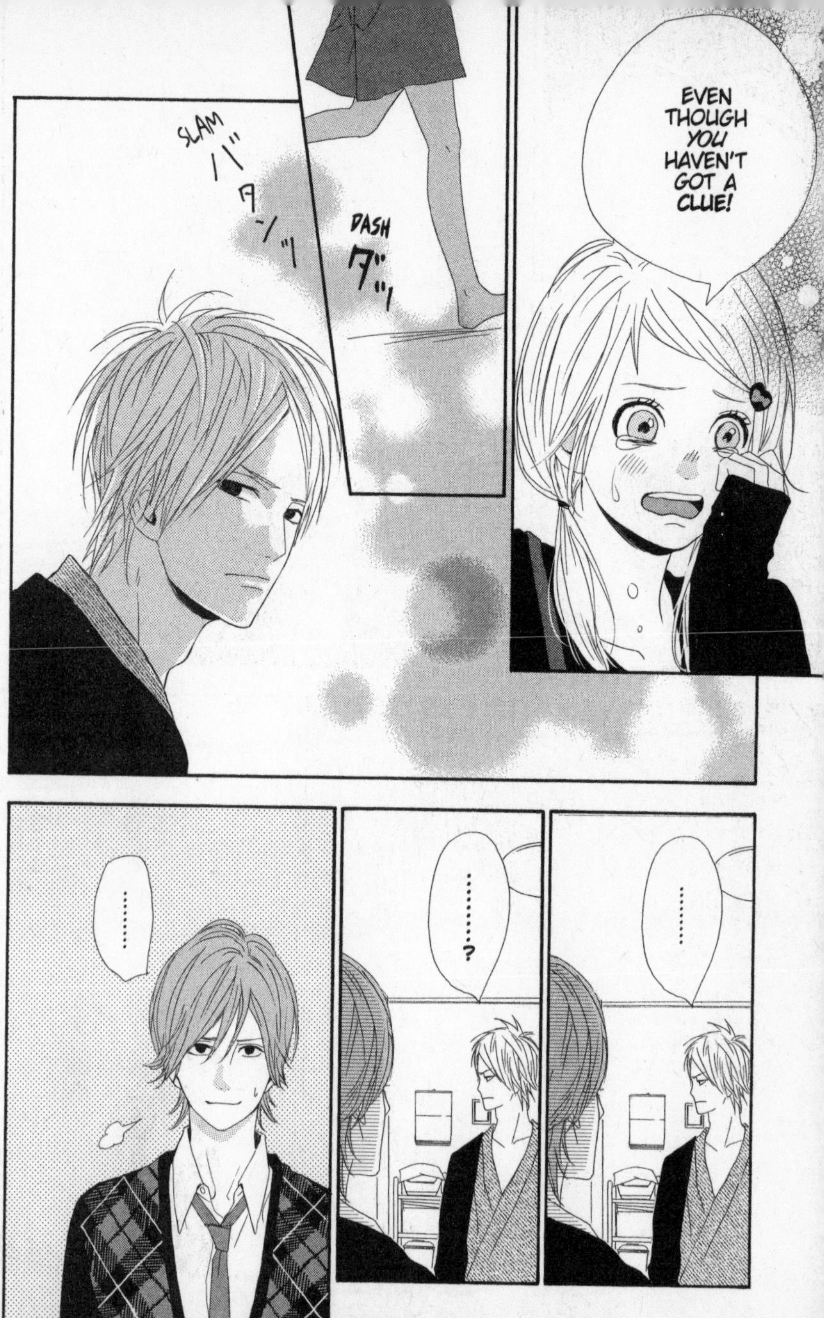
EVEN THOUGH YOU HAVEN'T GOT A CLUE!
DASH
ダッ
SLAM
バターンッ
......
......?
......

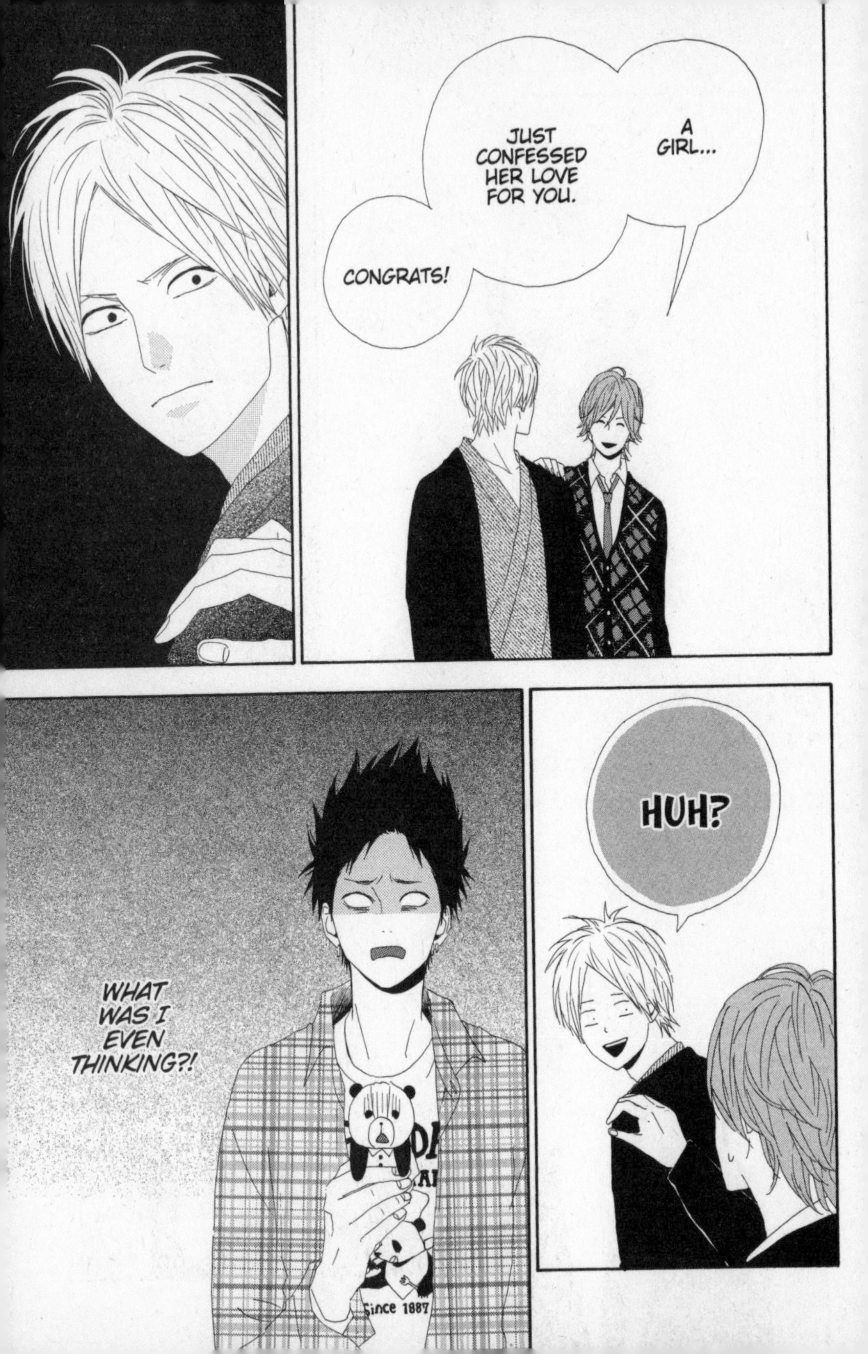
A GIRL...
JUST CONFESSED HER LOVE FOR YOU.
CONGRATS!
HUH?
WHAT WAS I EVEN THINKING?!
Since 1887

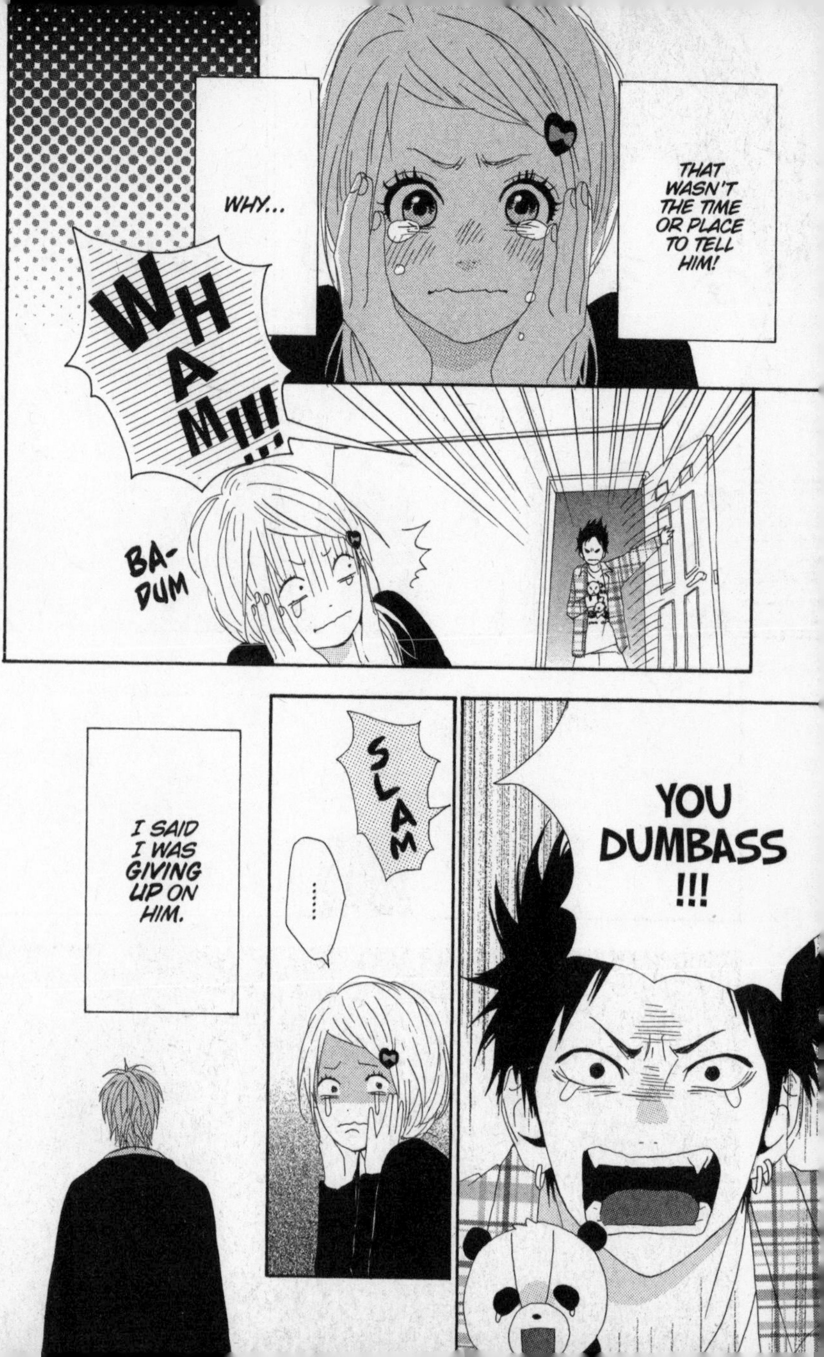
THAT WASN'T THE TIME OR PLACE TO TELL HIM!
WHY...
WHAM!!!
BA-DUM
YOU DUMBASS!!!
SLAM
......
I SAID I WAS GIVING UP ON HIM.

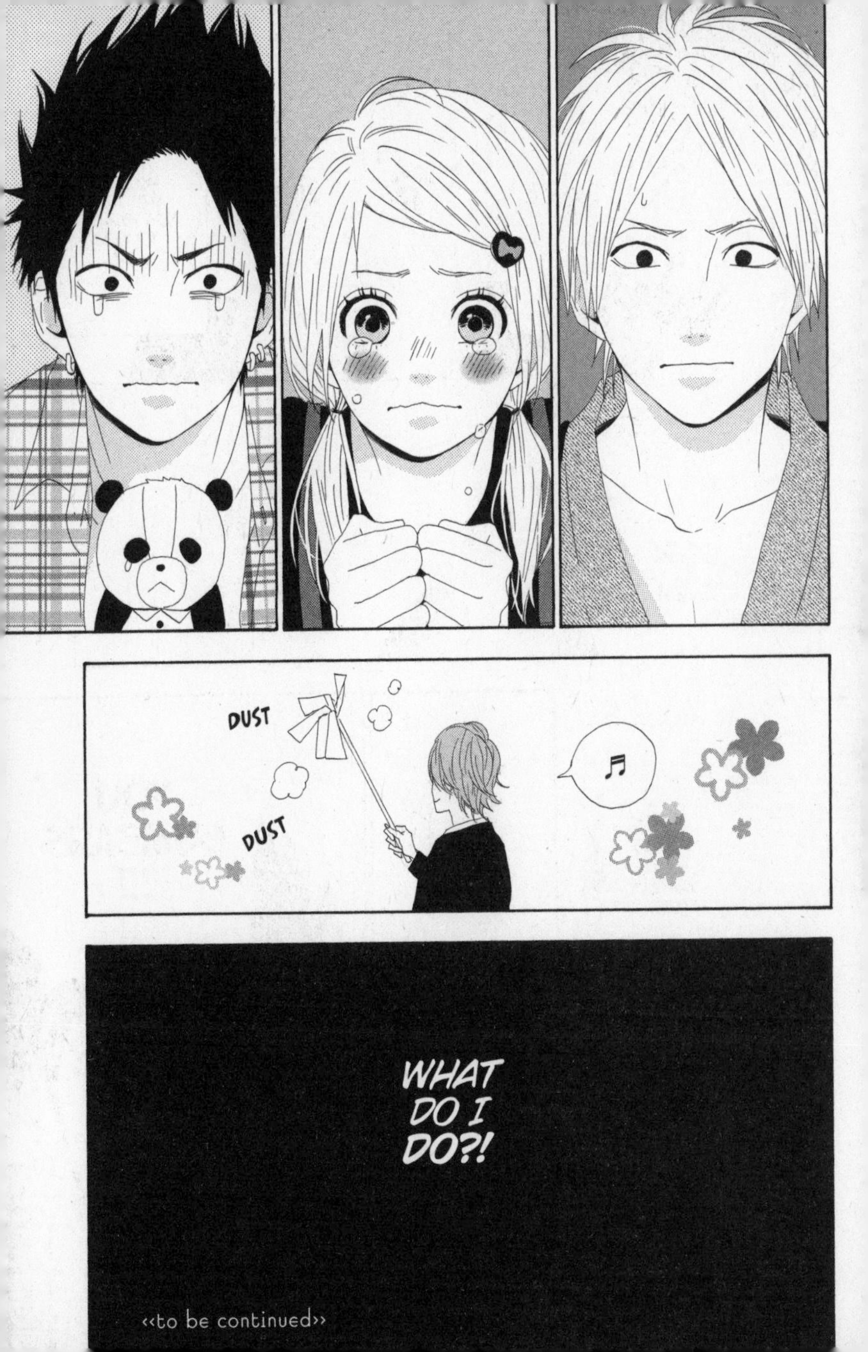
♬
DUST
DUST
WHAT DO I DO?!
‹‹to be continued››

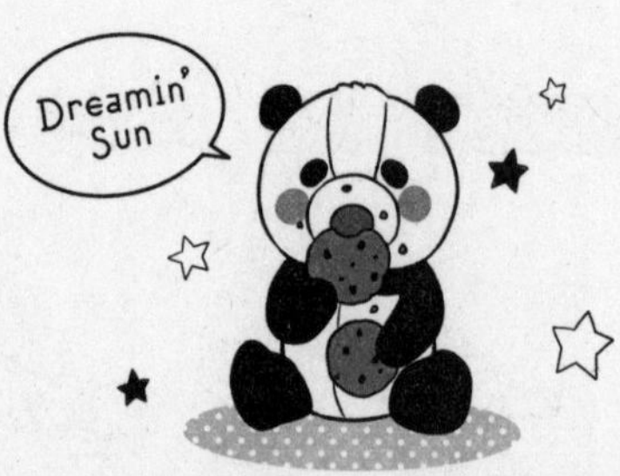
Dreamin' Sun

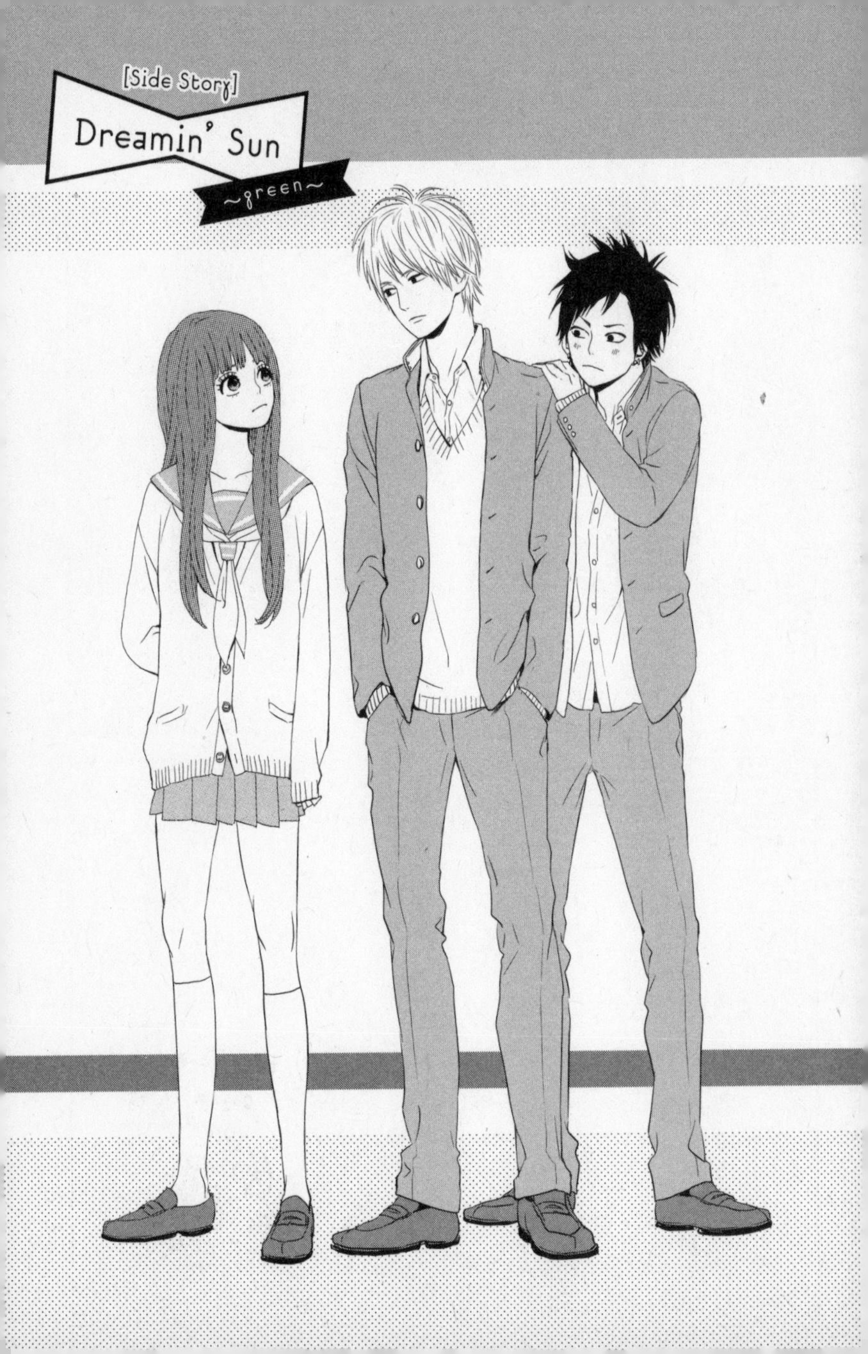
[Side Story]
Dreamin' Sun
~green~

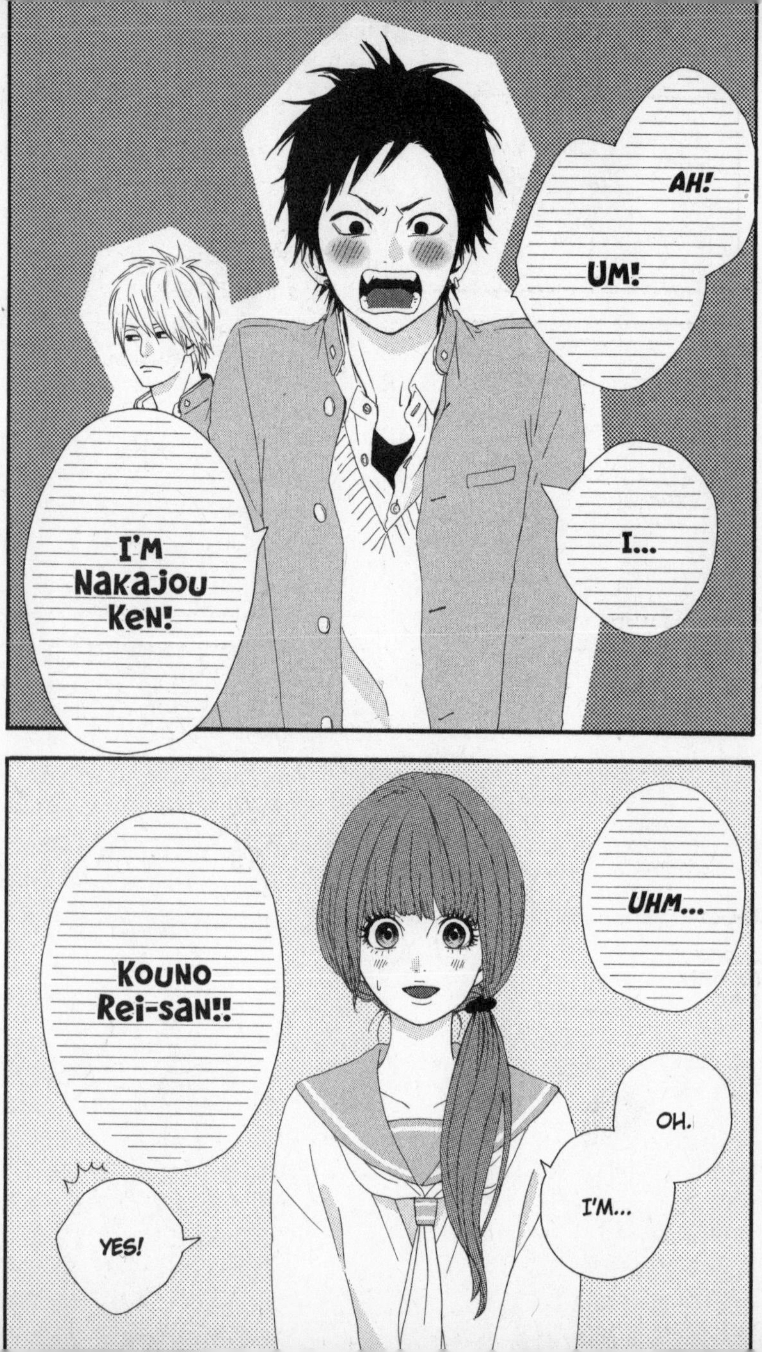
AH! UM!
I...
I'M NAKAJOU KEN!
UHM...
KOUNO REI-SAN!!
OH. I'M...
YES!

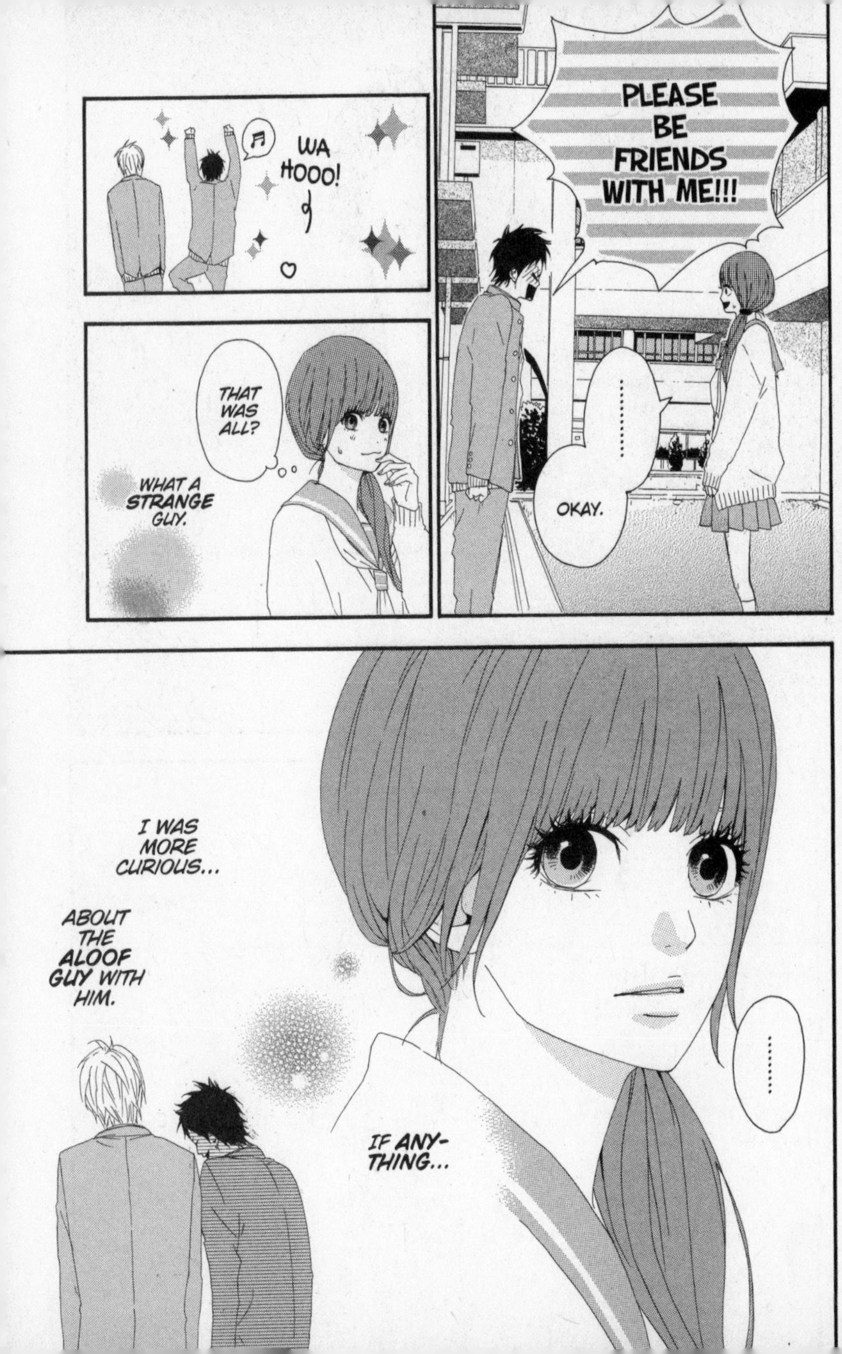
PLEASE BE FRIENDS WITH ME!!!
......
OKAY.
WA HOOO!
THAT WAS ALL?
WHAT A STRANGE GUY.
......
I WAS MORE CURIOUS...
ABOUT THE ALOOF GUY WITH HIM.
IF ANY-THING...

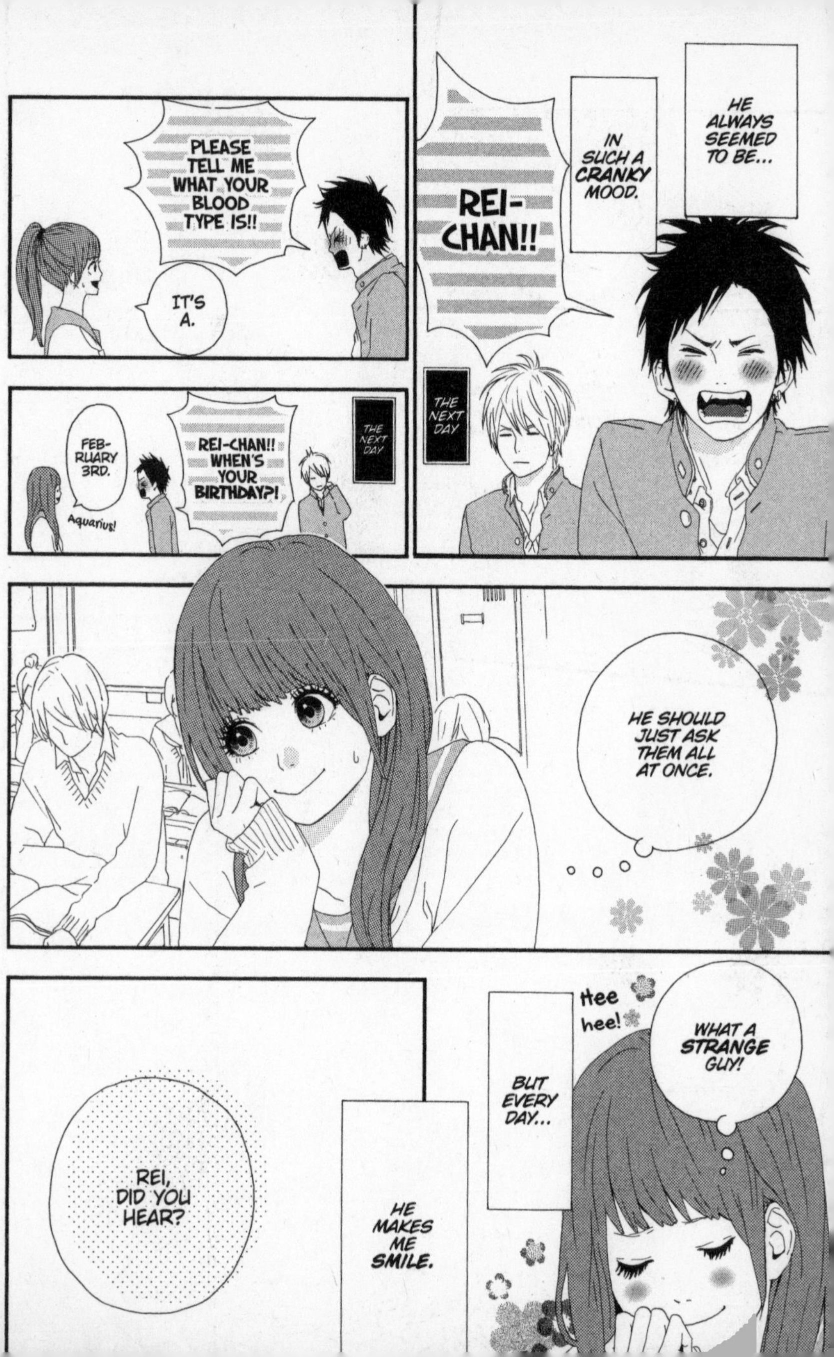
HE ALWAYS SEEMED TO BE...
IN SUCH A CRANKY MOOD.
REI-CHAN!!
THE NEXT DAY
PLEASE TELL ME WHAT YOUR BLOOD TYPE IS!!
IT'S A.
THE NEXT DAY
REI-CHAN!! WHEN'S YOUR BIRTHDAY?!
FEB-RUARY 3RD.
Aquarius!
HE SHOULD JUST ASK THEM ALL AT ONCE.
WHAT A STRANGE GUY!
Hee hee!
BUT EVERY DAY...
HE MAKES ME SMILE.
REI, DID YOU HEAR?

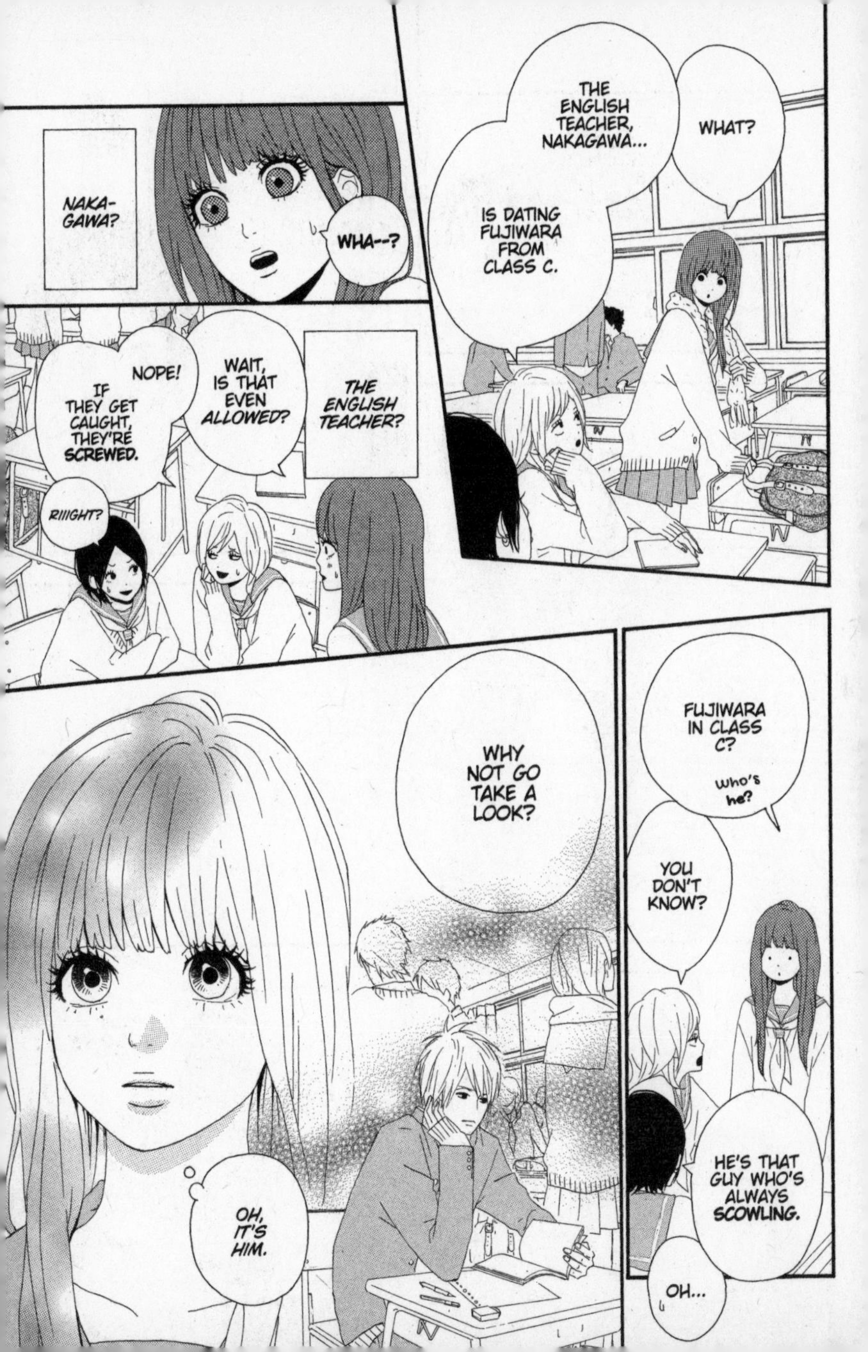
THE ENGLISH TEACHER, NAKAGAWA...
WHAT?
IS DATING FUJIWARA FROM CLASS C.
WHA--?
NAKAGAWA?
THE ENGLISH TEACHER?
WAIT, IS THAT EVEN ALLOWED?
NOPE! IF THEY GET CAUGHT, THEY'RE SCREWED.
RIIIGHT?
FUJIWARA IN CLASS C?
Who's he?
YOU DON'T KNOW?
HE'S THAT GUY WHO'S ALWAYS SCOWLING.
OH...
WHY NOT GO TAKE A LOOK?
OH, IT'S HIM.

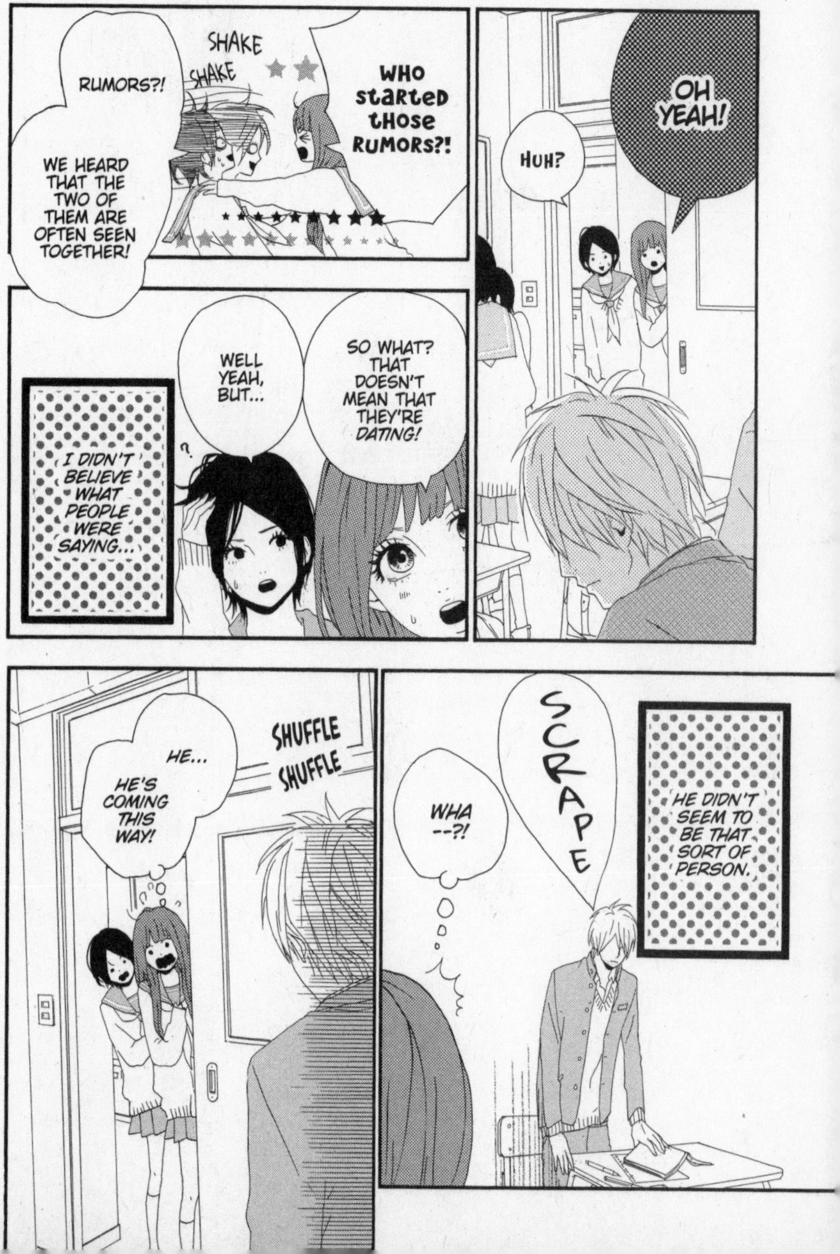
OH YEAH!
HUH?
WHO STARTED THOSE RUMORS?!
SHAKE
SHAKE
RUMORS?!
WE HEARD THAT THE TWO OF THEM ARE OFTEN SEEN TOGETHER!
SO WHAT? THAT DOESN'T MEAN THAT THEY'RE *DATING!*
WELL YEAH, BUT...
I DIDN'T BELIEVE WHAT PEOPLE WERE SAYING...
HE DIDN'T SEEM TO BE THAT SORT OF PERSON.
SCRAPE
WHA --?!
SHUFFLE
SHUFFLE
HE...
HE'S COMING THIS WAY!

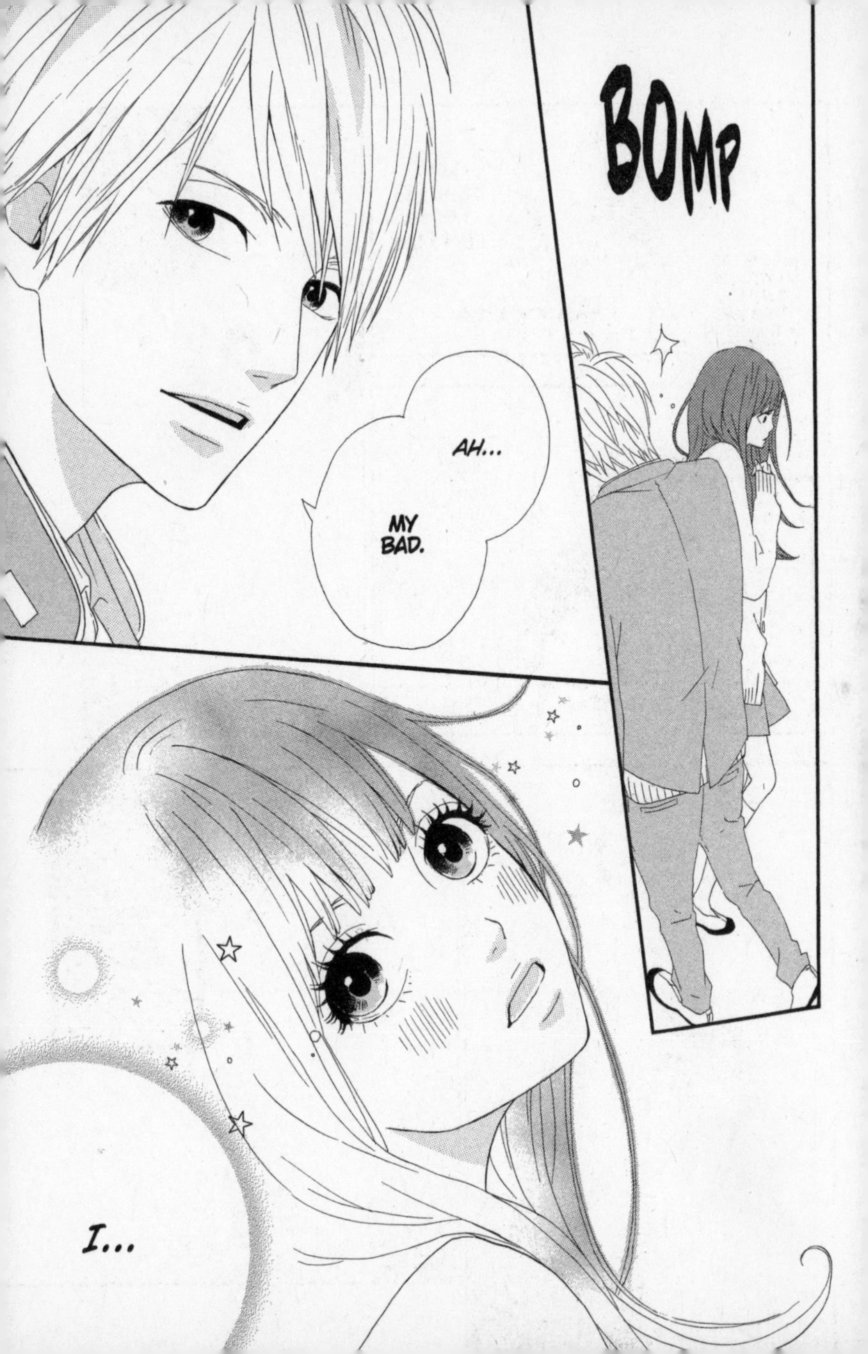
BOMP
AH...
MY BAD.
I...

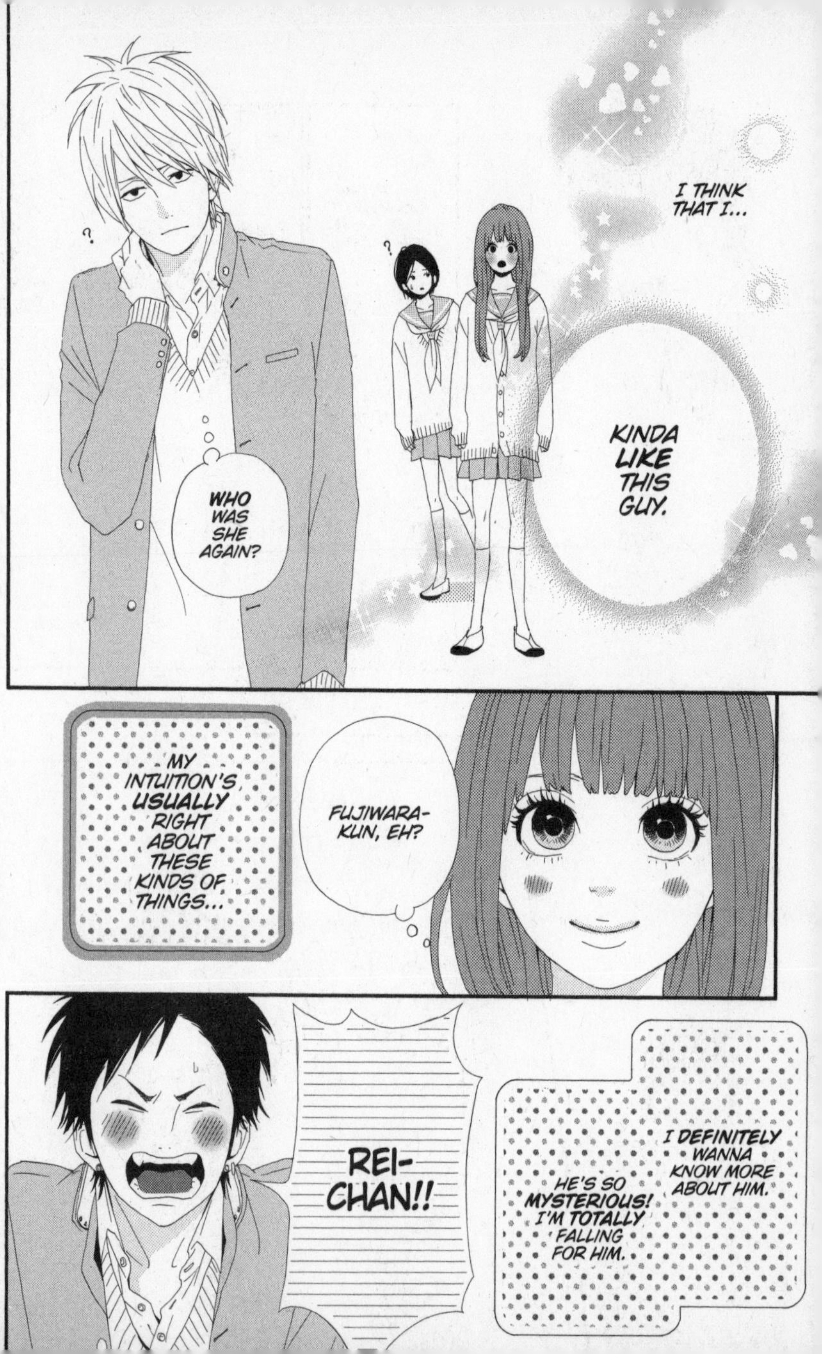
I THINK THAT I...
KINDA LIKE THIS GUY.
WHO WAS SHE AGAIN?
FUJIWARA-KUN, EH?
MY INTUITION'S USUALLY RIGHT ABOUT THESE KINDS OF THINGS...
I DEFINITELY WANNA KNOW MORE ABOUT HIM.
HE'S SO MYSTERIOUS! I'M TOTALLY FALLING FOR HIM.
REI-CHAN!!

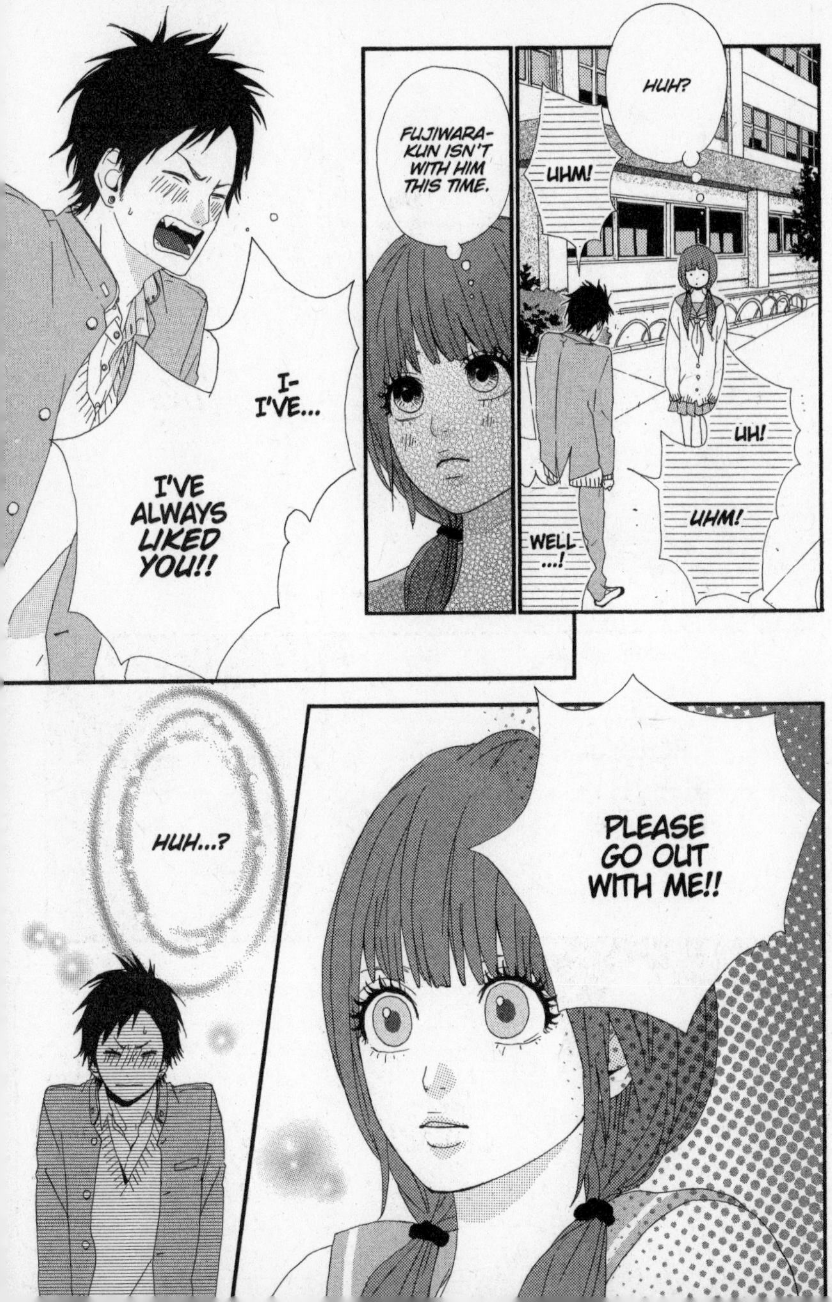
HUH?
UHM!
UH!
UHM!
WELL...!
FUJIWARA-KUN ISN'T WITH HIM THIS TIME.
I- I'VE...
I'VE ALWAYS LIKED YOU!!
PLEASE GO OUT WITH ME!!
HUH...?

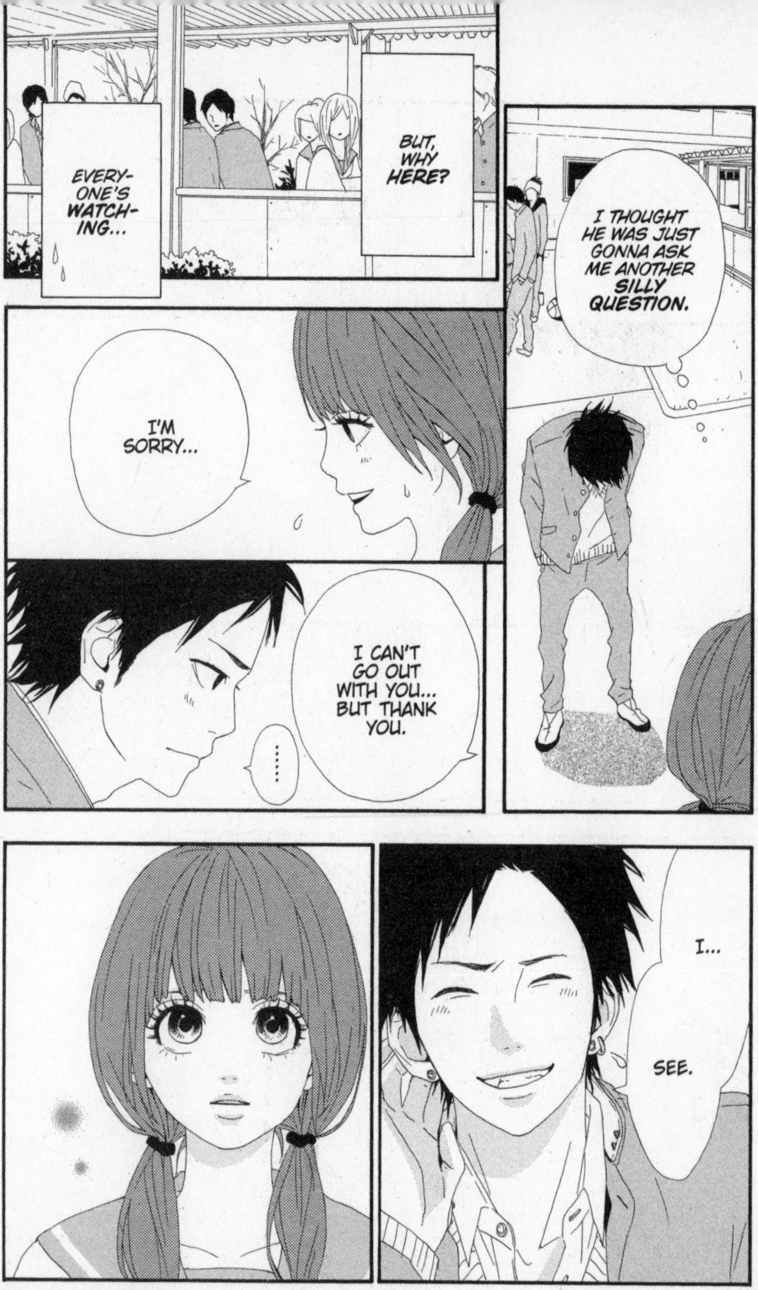

BUT, WHY HERE?
EVERYONE'S WATCHING...
I THOUGHT HE WAS JUST GONNA ASK ME ANOTHER SILLY QUESTION.
I'M SORRY...
I CAN'T GO OUT WITH YOU... BUT THANK YOU.
......
I...
SEE.

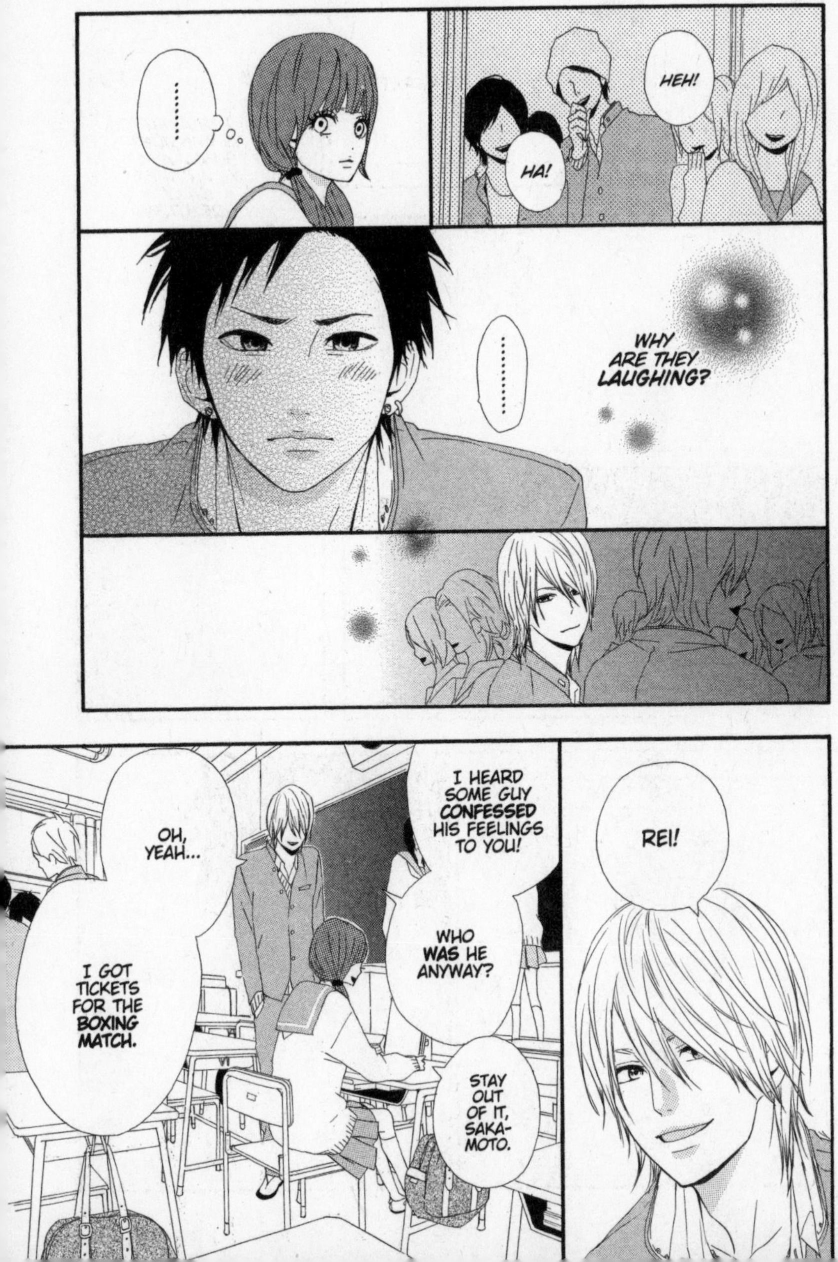
HEH!
HA!
......
WHY ARE THEY LAUGHING?
......
REI!
I HEARD SOME GUY CONFESSED HIS FEELINGS TO YOU!
OH, YEAH...
WHO WAS HE ANYWAY?
STAY OUT OF IT, SAKAMOTO.
I GOT TICKETS FOR THE BOXING MATCH.

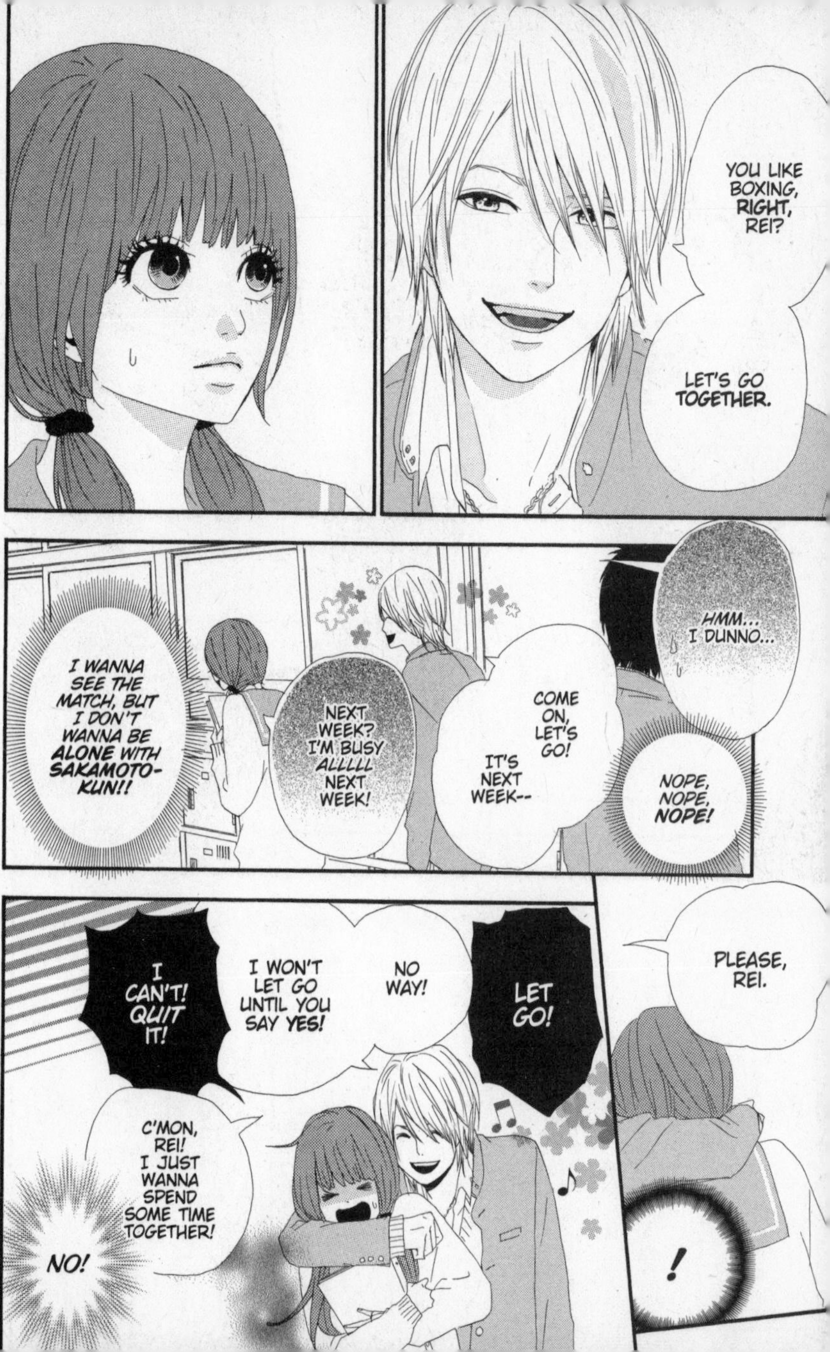
YOU LIKE BOXING, RIGHT, REI?
LET'S GO TOGETHER.
HMM... I DUNNO...
COME ON, LET'S GO!
NOPE, NOPE, NOPE!
IT'S NEXT WEEK--
NEXT WEEK? I'M BUSY ALLLLL NEXT WEEK!
I WANNA SEE THE MATCH, BUT I DON'T WANNA BE ALONE WITH SAKAMOTO-KUN!!
PLEASE, REI.
!
LET GO!
NO WAY!
I WON'T LET GO UNTIL YOU SAY YES!
I CAN'T! QUIT IT!
C'MON, REI! I JUST WANNA SPEND SOME TIME TOGETHER!
NO!

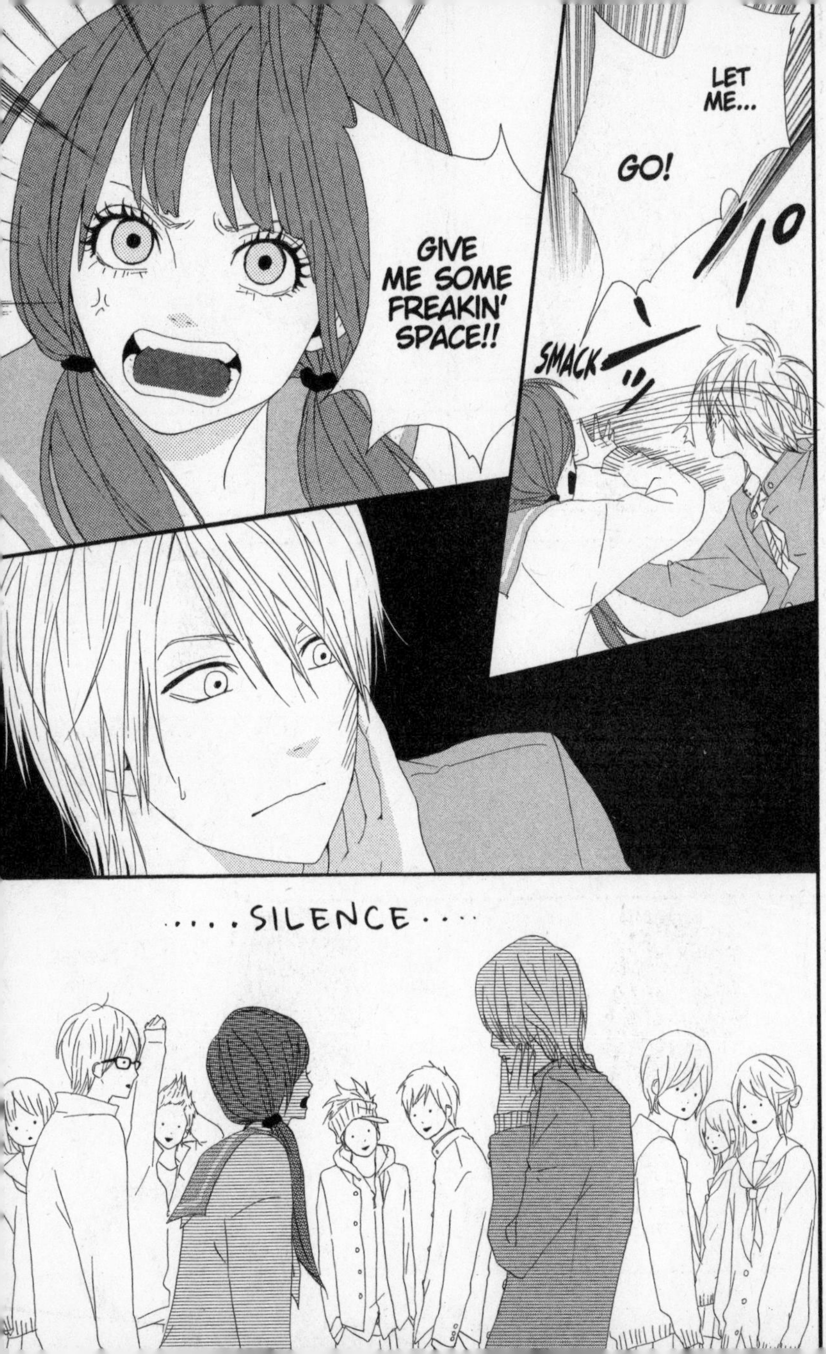
LET ME...
GO!
SMACK
GIVE ME SOME FREAKIN' SPACE!!
.....SILENCE....

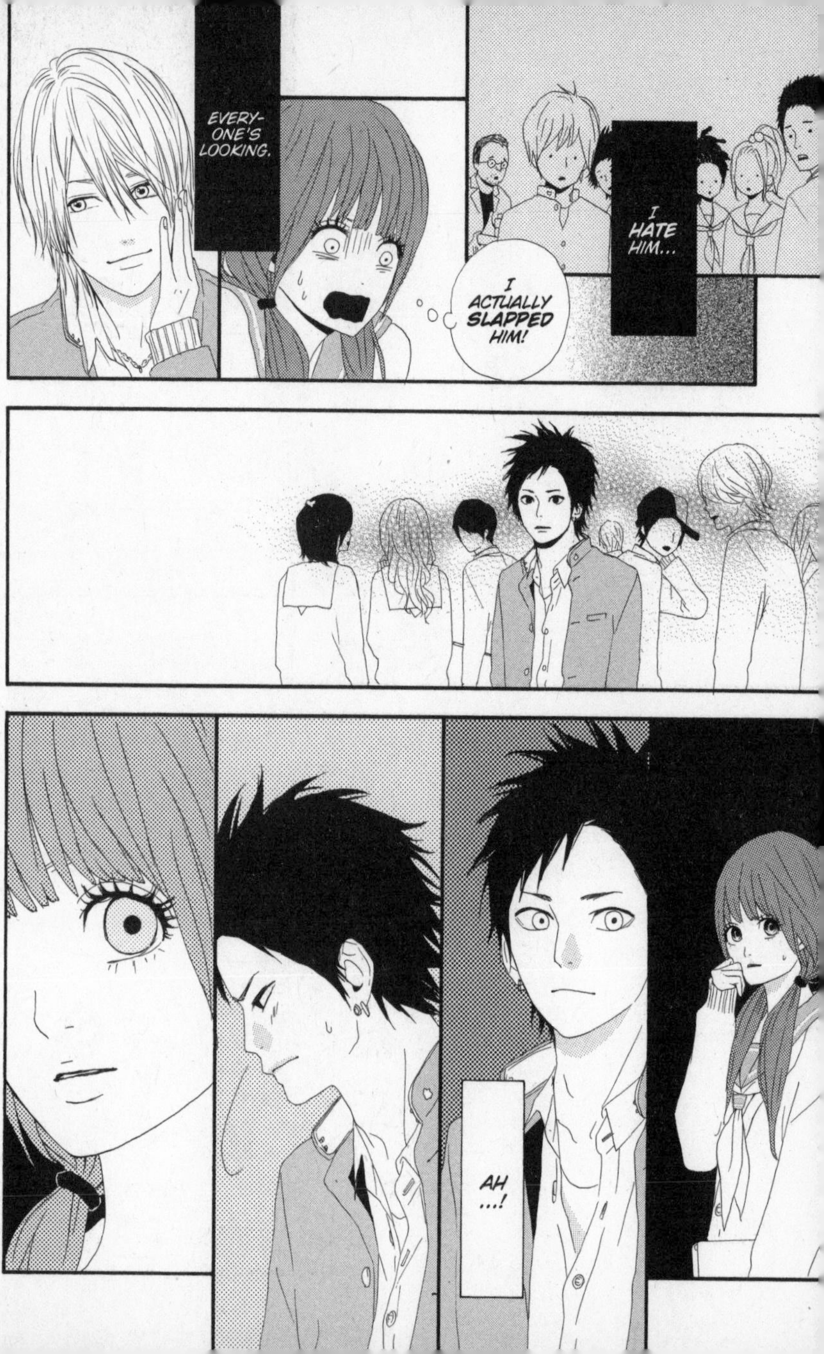
I HATE HIM...
I ACTUALLY SLAPPED HIM!
EVERY-ONE'S LOOKING.
AH ...!

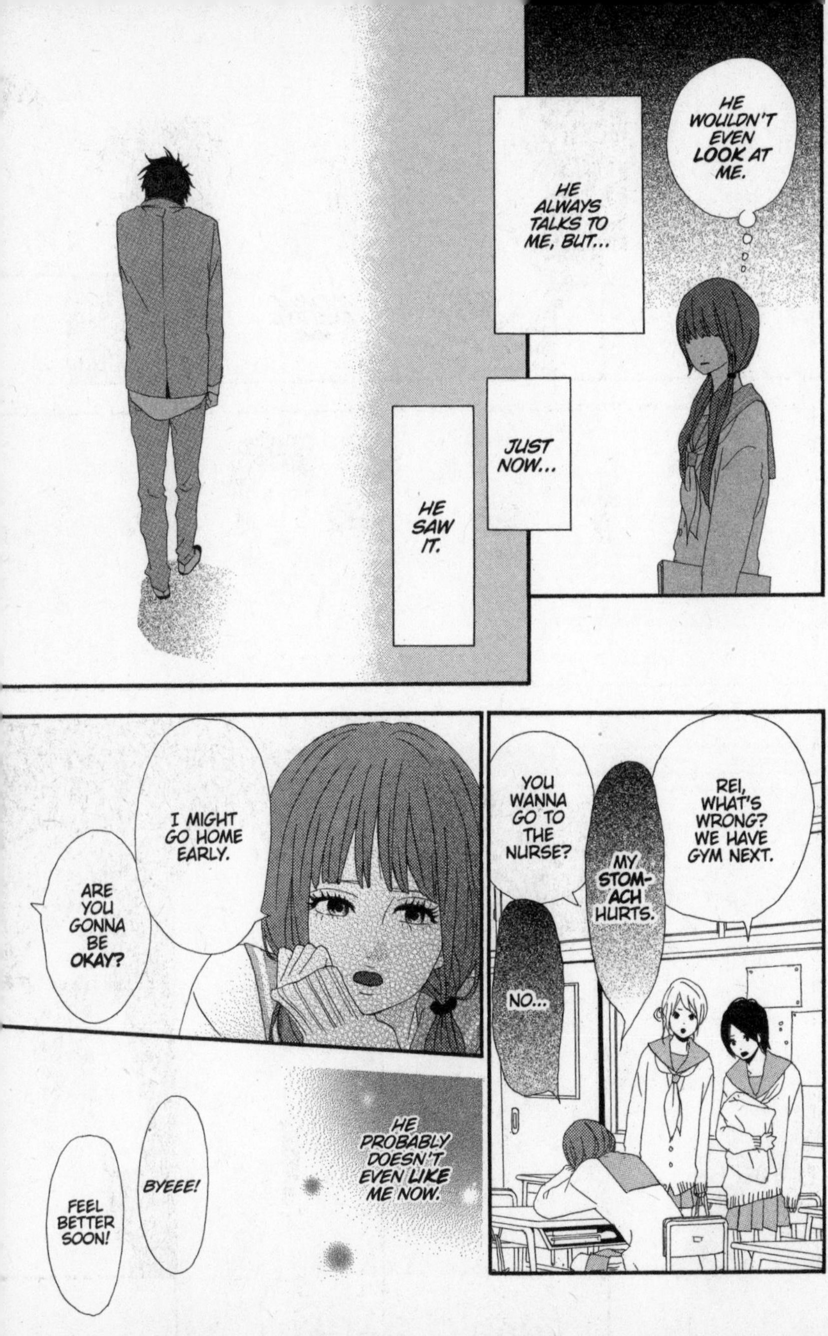
HE WOULDN'T EVEN LOOK AT ME.
HE ALWAYS TALKS TO ME, BUT...
JUST NOW...
HE SAW IT.
REI, WHAT'S WRONG? WE HAVE GYM NEXT.
MY STOM-ACH HURTS.
YOU WANNA GO TO THE NURSE?
NO...
I MIGHT GO HOME EARLY.
ARE YOU GONNA BE OKAY?
HE PROBABLY DOESN'T EVEN LIKE ME NOW.
BYEEE!
FEEL BETTER SOON!

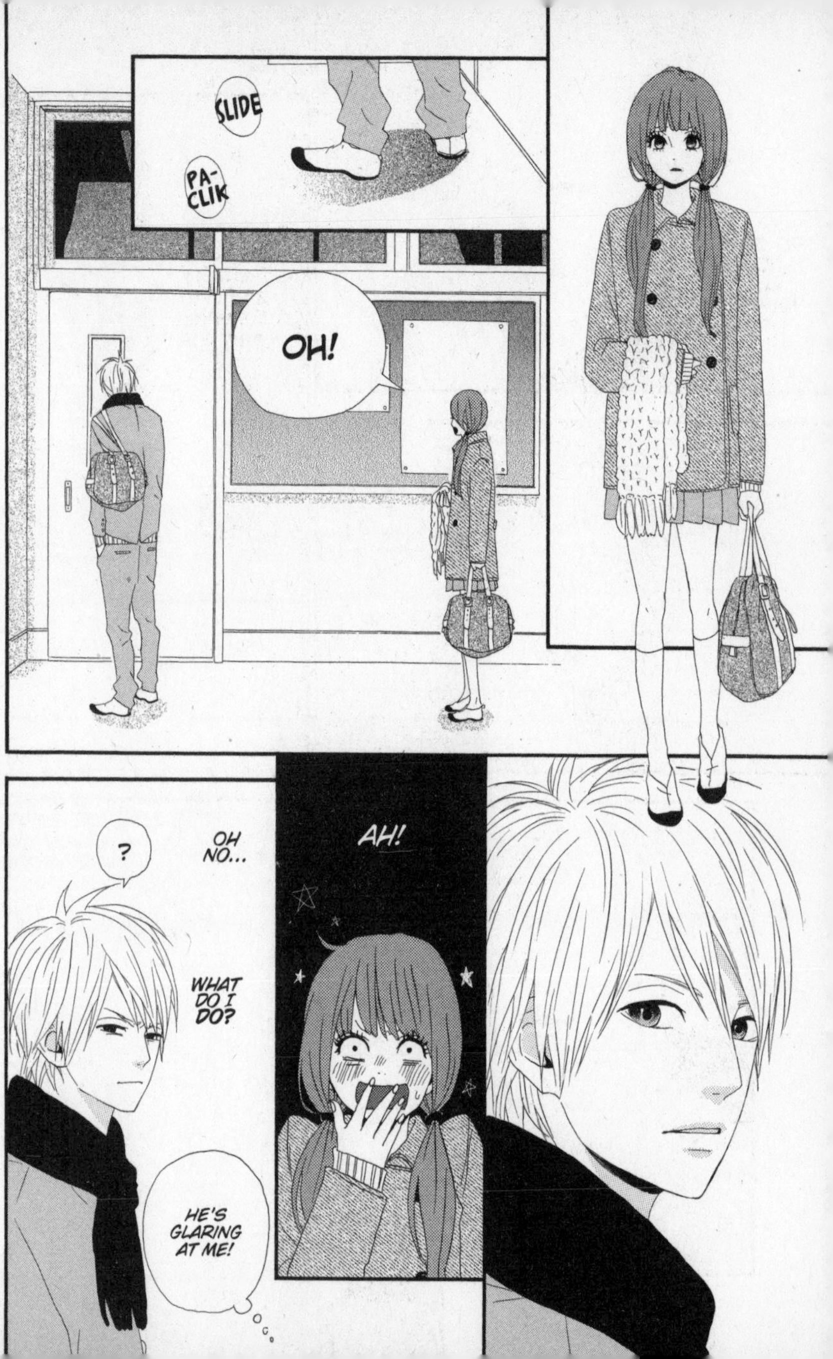
SLIDE
PA-CLIK
OH!
AH!
?
OH NO...
WHAT DO I DO?
HE'S GLARING AT ME!

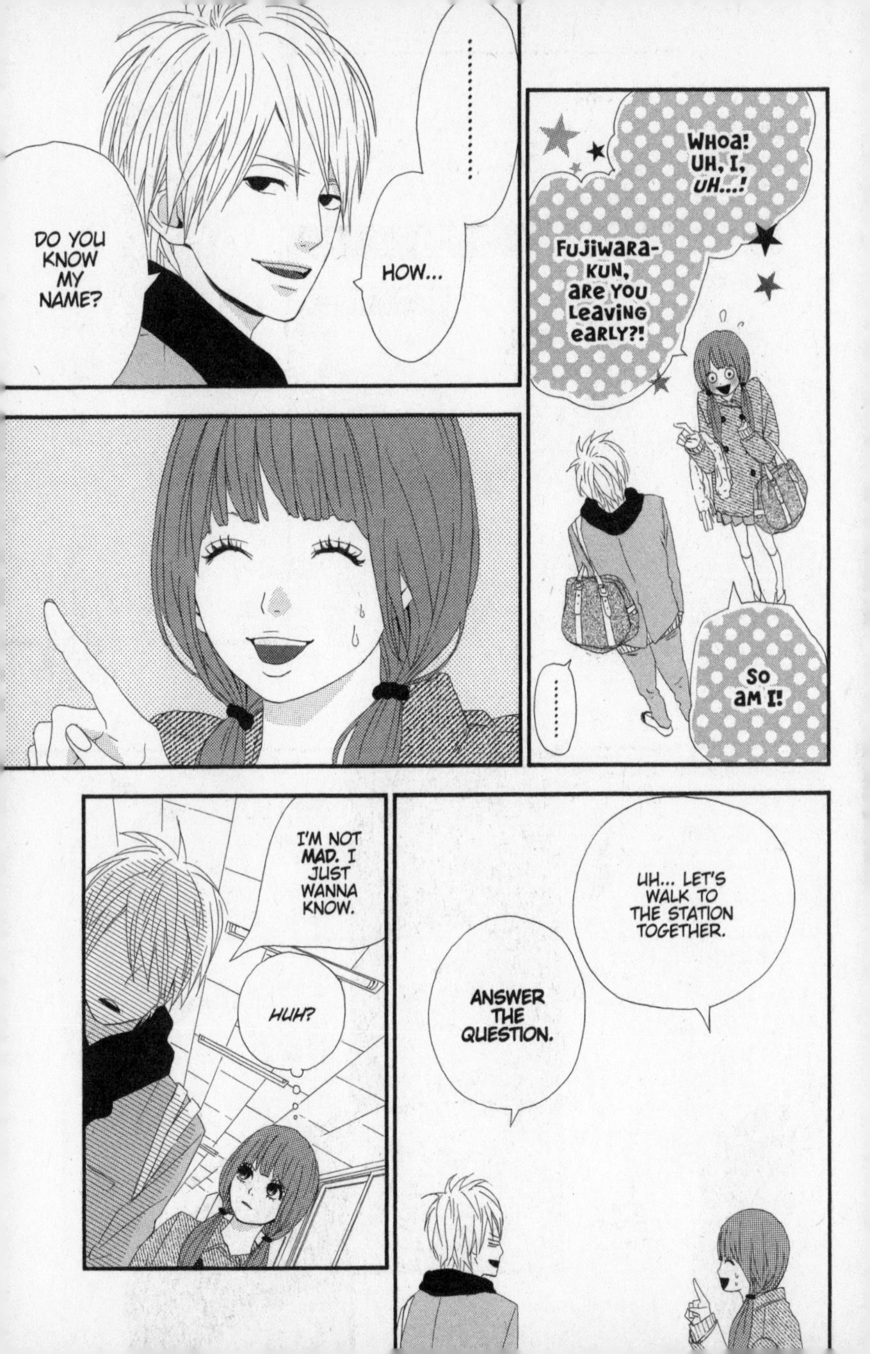
Whoa! Uh, I, uh...!
Fujiwara-kun, are you leaving early?!
So am I!
......
......
How...
Do you know my name?
Uh... let's walk to the station together.
Answer the question.
I'm not mad. I just wanna know.
Huh?

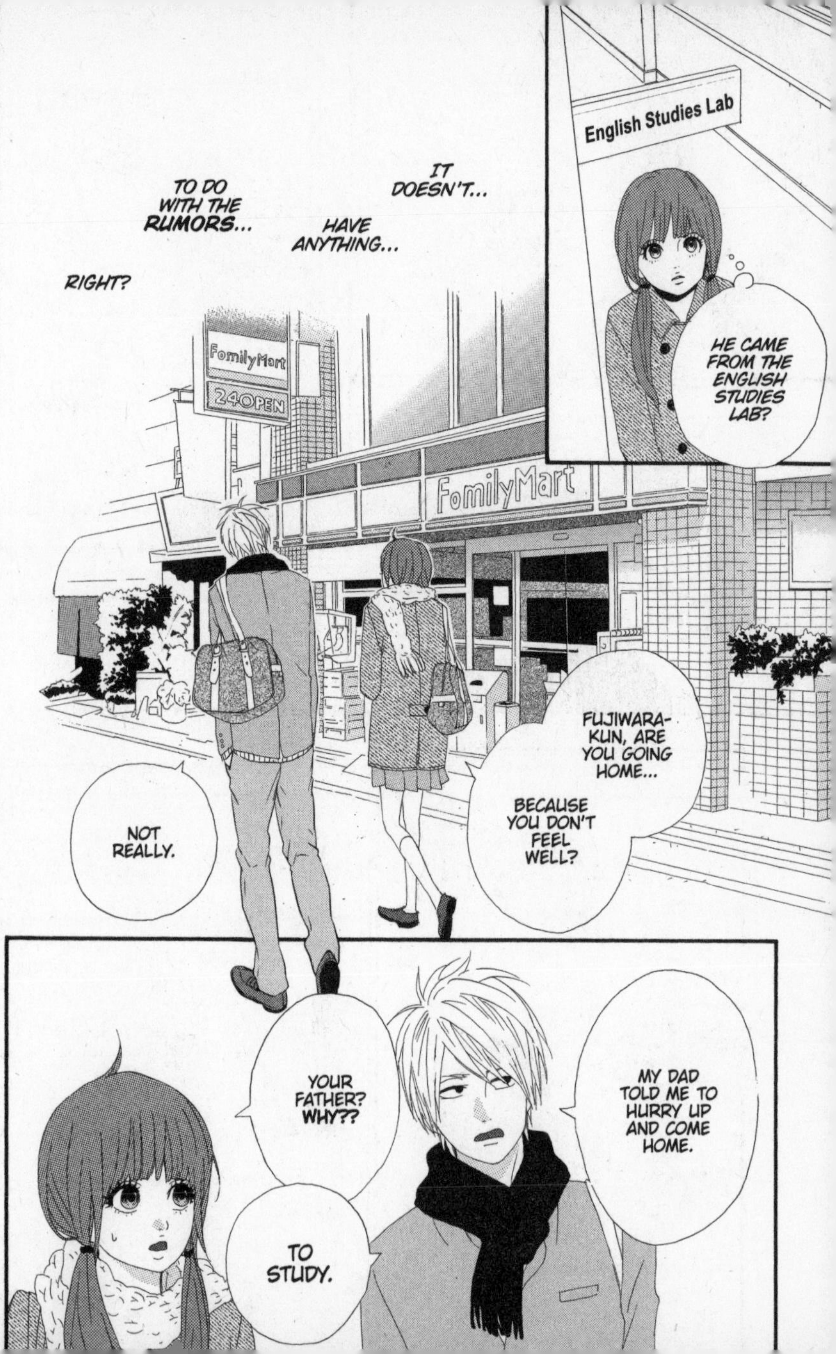
English Studies Lab
HE CAME FROM THE ENGLISH STUDIES LAB?
IT DOESN'T...
HAVE ANYTHING...
TO DO WITH THE RUMORS...
RIGHT?
FamilyMart
24OPEN
FamilyMart
FUJIWARA-KUN, ARE YOU GOING HOME...
BECAUSE YOU DON'T FEEL WELL?
NOT REALLY.
MY DAD TOLD ME TO HURRY UP AND COME HOME.
YOUR FATHER? WHY??
TO STUDY.

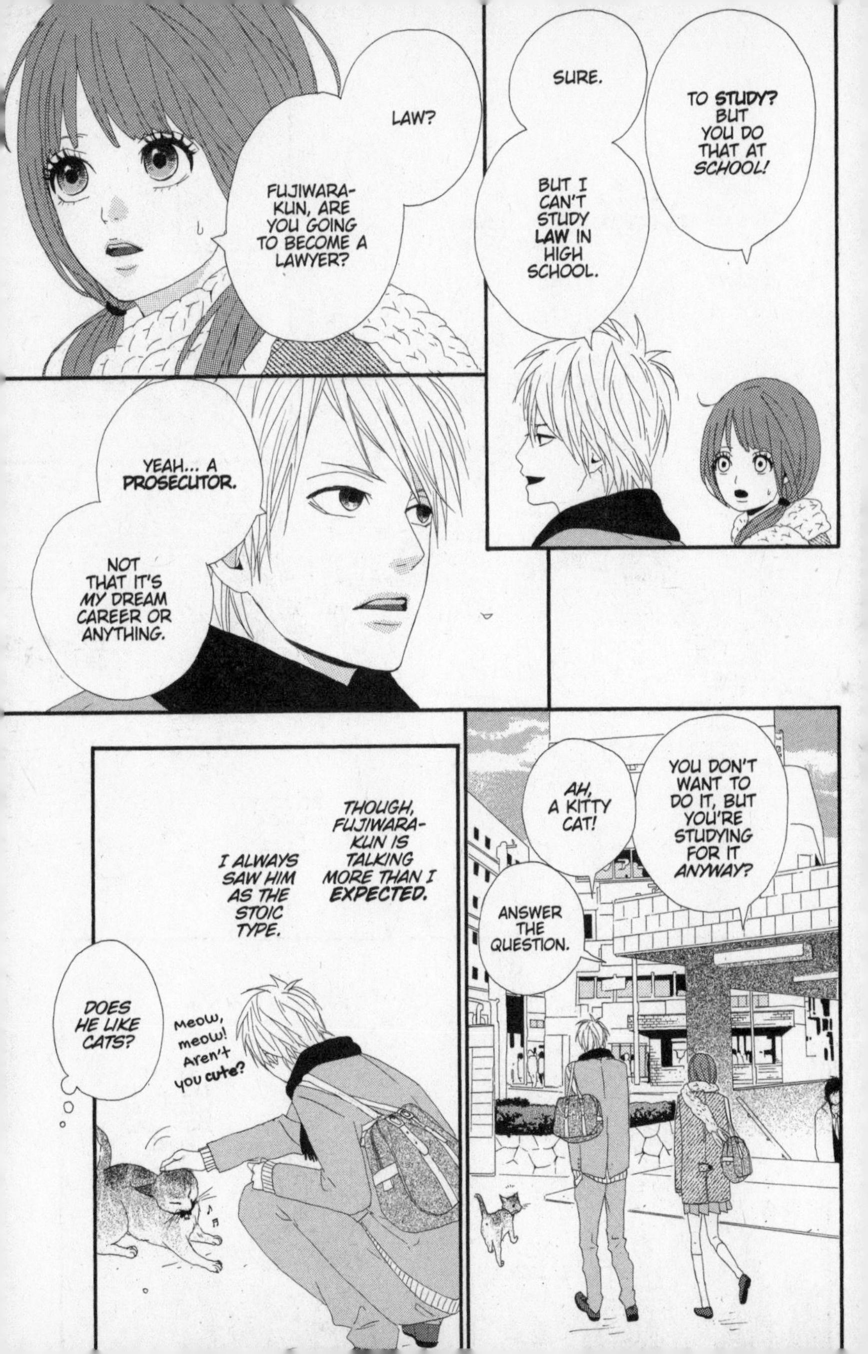
TO STUDY? BUT YOU DO THAT AT SCHOOL!
SURE.
BUT I CAN'T STUDY LAW IN HIGH SCHOOL.
LAW?
FUJIWARA-KUN, ARE YOU GOING TO BECOME A LAWYER?
YEAH... A PROSECUTOR.
NOT THAT IT'S MY DREAM CAREER OR ANYTHING.
YOU DON'T WANT TO DO IT, BUT YOU'RE STUDYING FOR IT ANYWAY?
AH, A KITTY CAT!
ANSWER THE QUESTION.
THOUGH, FUJIWARA-KUN IS TALKING MORE THAN I EXPECTED.
I ALWAYS SAW HIM AS THE STOIC TYPE.
Meow, meow! Aren't you cute?
DOES HE LIKE CATS?

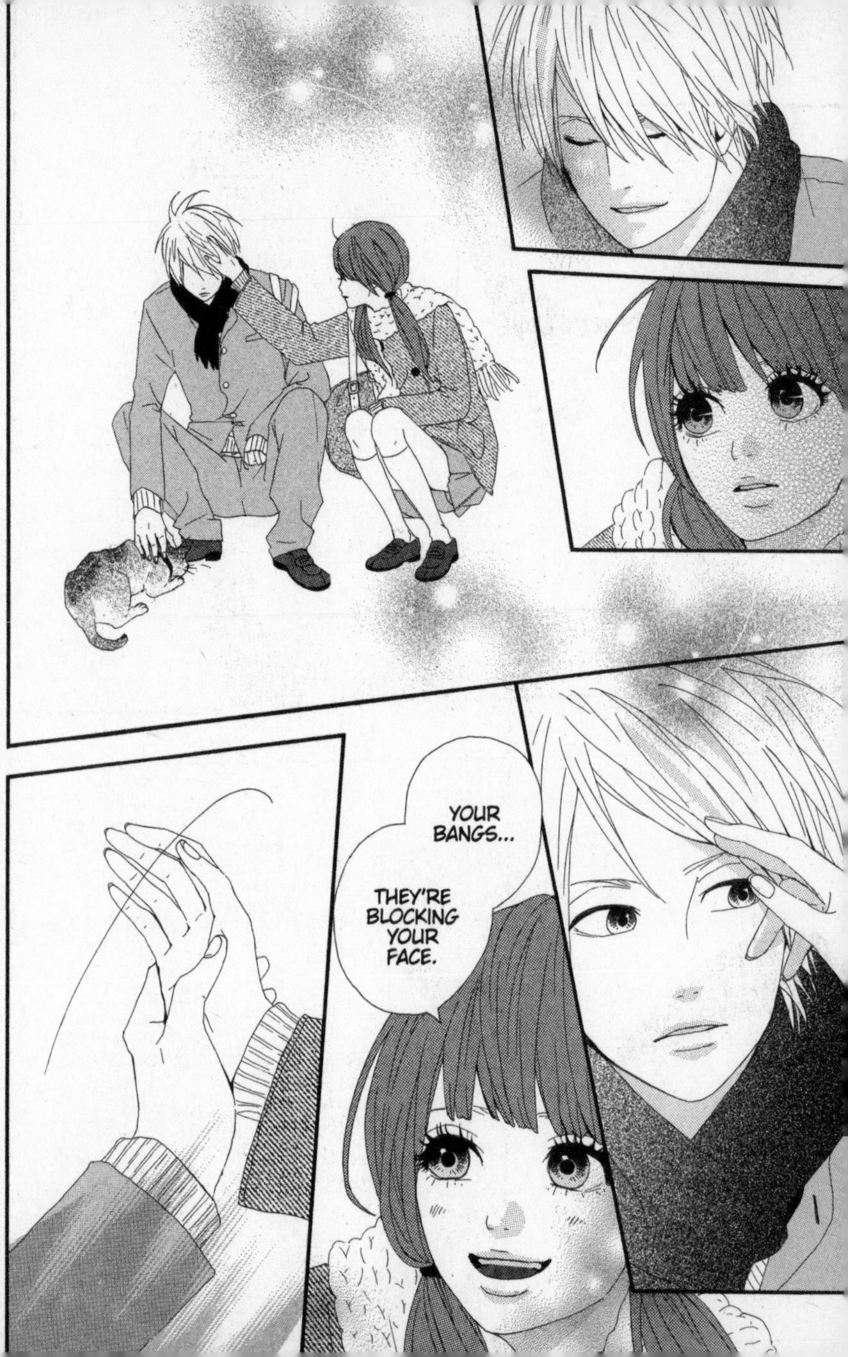
YOUR BANGS...
THEY'RE BLOCKING YOUR FACE.

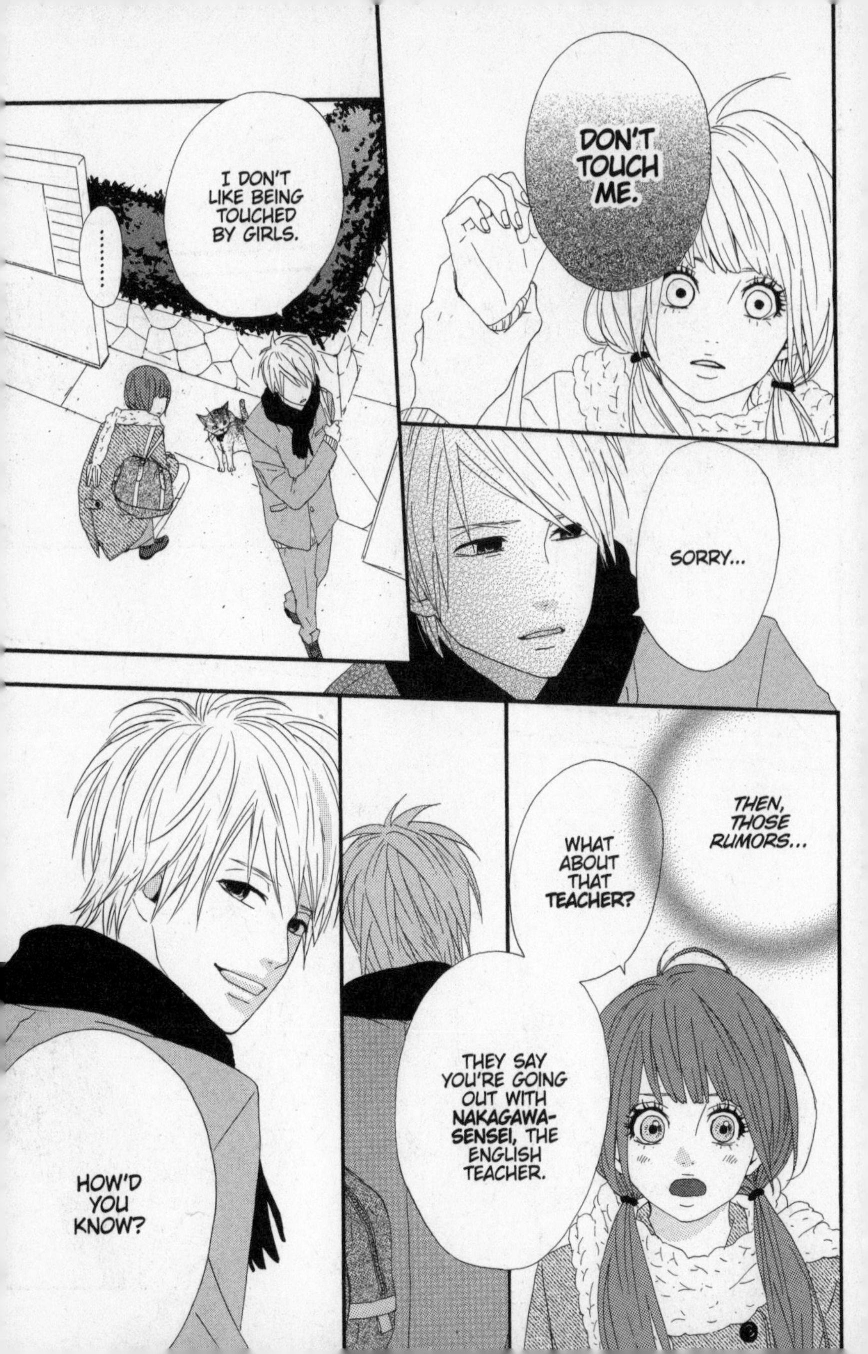
DON'T TOUCH ME.
SORRY...
I DON'T LIKE BEING TOUCHED BY GIRLS.
......
THEN, THOSE RUMORS...
WHAT ABOUT THAT TEACHER?
THEY SAY YOU'RE GOING OUT WITH NAKAGAWA-SENSEI, THE ENGLISH TEACHER.
HOW'D YOU KNOW?

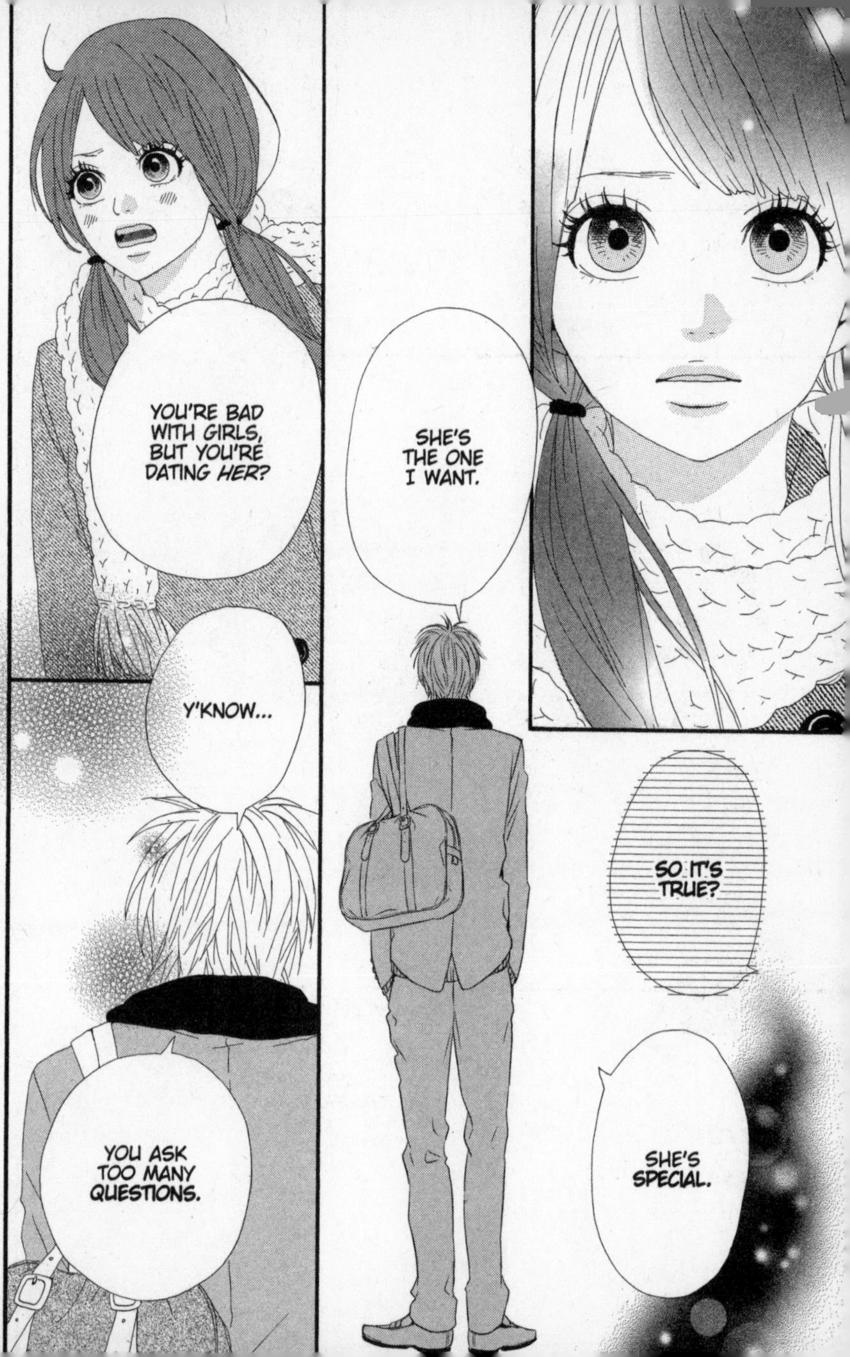
SHE'S THE ONE I WANT.
SO IT'S TRUE?
SHE'S SPECIAL.
YOU'RE BAD WITH GIRLS, BUT YOU'RE DATING *HER*?
Y'KNOW...
YOU ASK TOO MANY QUESTIONS.

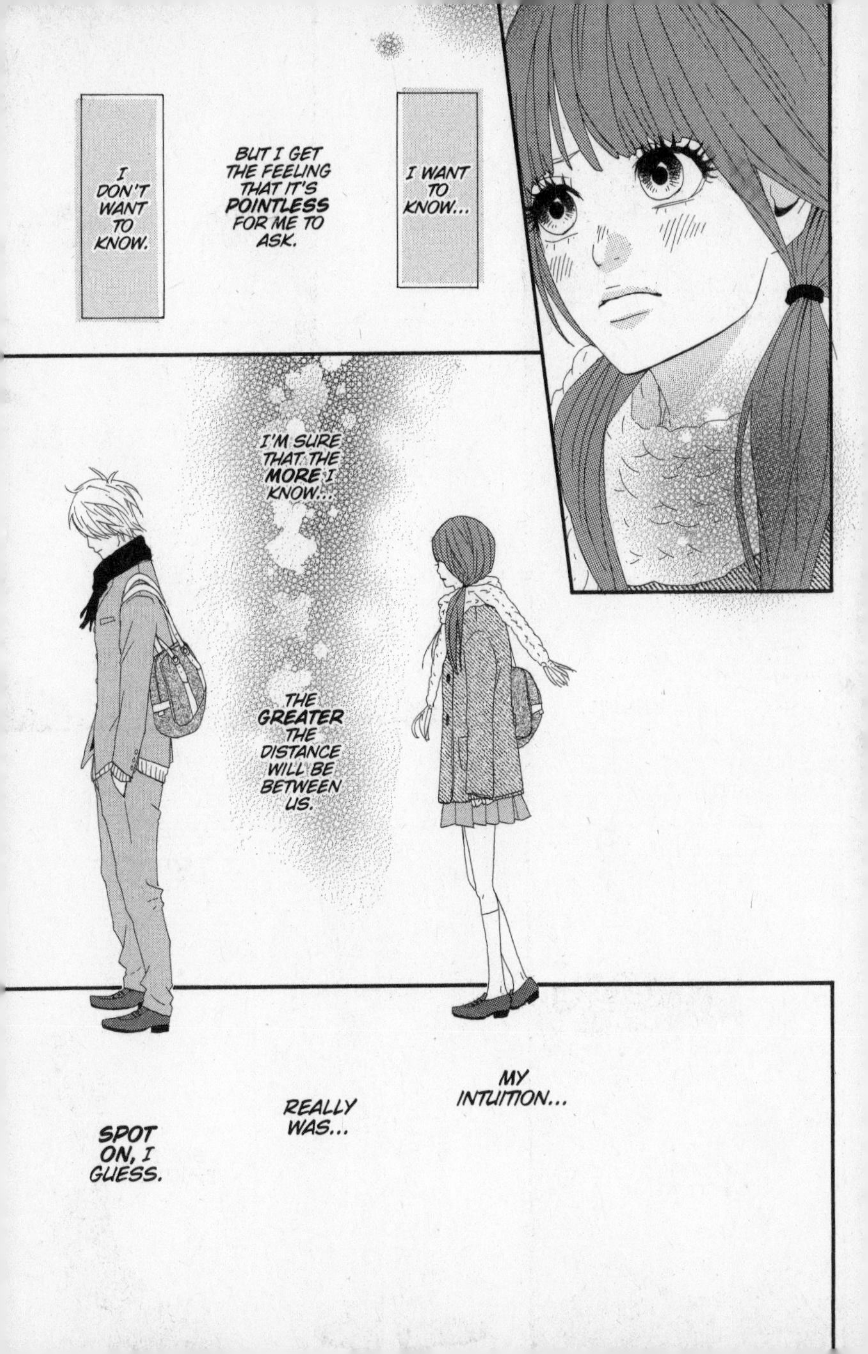
I WANT TO KNOW...
BUT I GET THE FEELING THAT IT'S **POINTLESS** FOR ME TO ASK.
I DON'T WANT TO KNOW.
I'M SURE THAT THE **MORE** I KNOW...
THE **GREATER** THE DISTANCE WILL BE BETWEEN US.
MY INTUITION...
REALLY WAS...
SPOT ON, I GUESS.

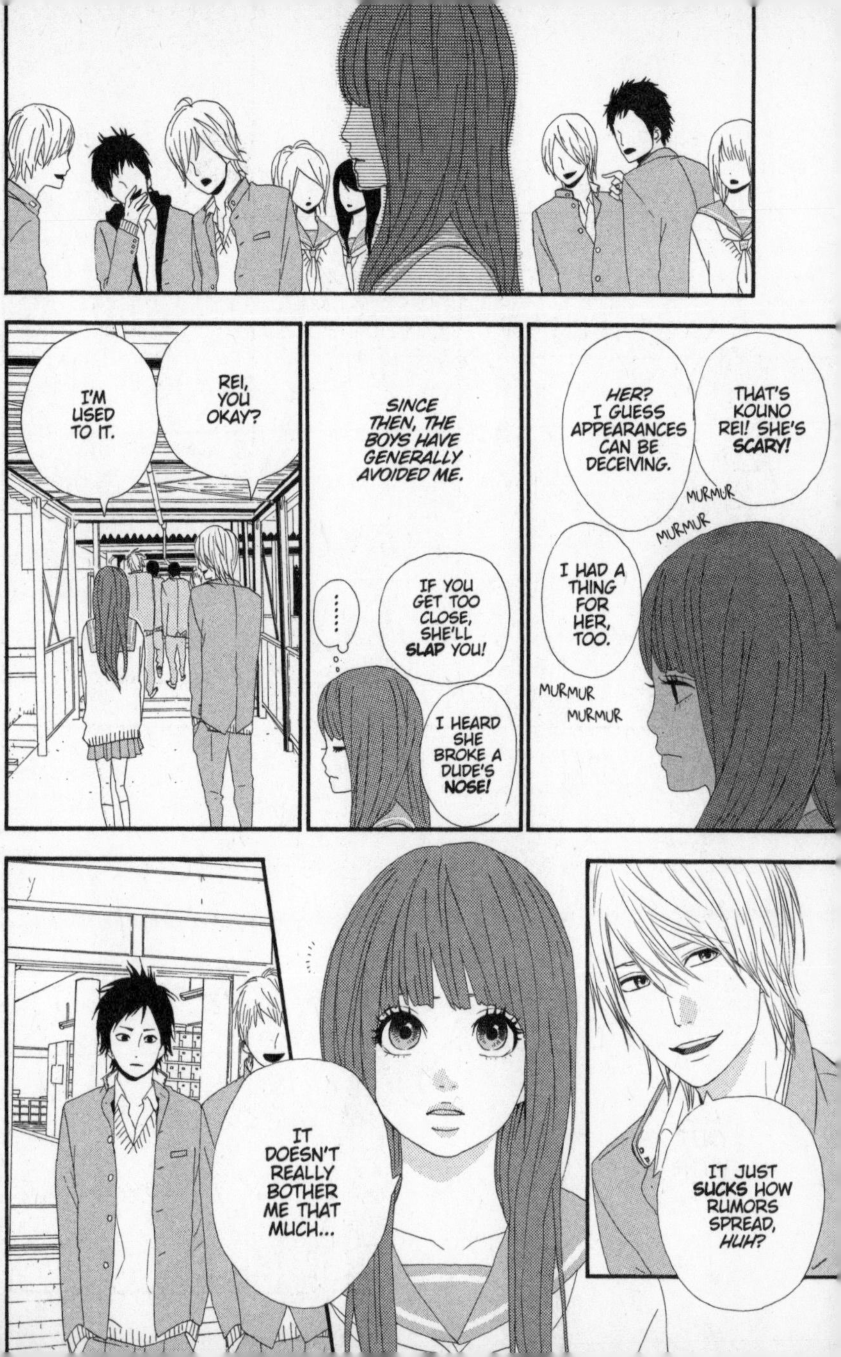
THAT'S KOUNO REI! SHE'S SCARY!
HER? I GUESS APPEARANCES CAN BE DECEIVING.
MURMUR
MURMUR
I HAD A THING FOR HER, TOO.
MURMUR
MURMUR
SINCE THEN, THE BOYS HAVE GENERALLY AVOIDED ME.
IF YOU GET TOO CLOSE, SHE'LL SLAP YOU!
......
I HEARD SHE BROKE A DUDE'S NOSE!
REI, YOU OKAY?
I'M USED TO IT.
IT JUST SUCKS HOW RUMORS SPREAD, HUH?
IT DOESN'T REALLY BOTHER ME THAT MUCH...

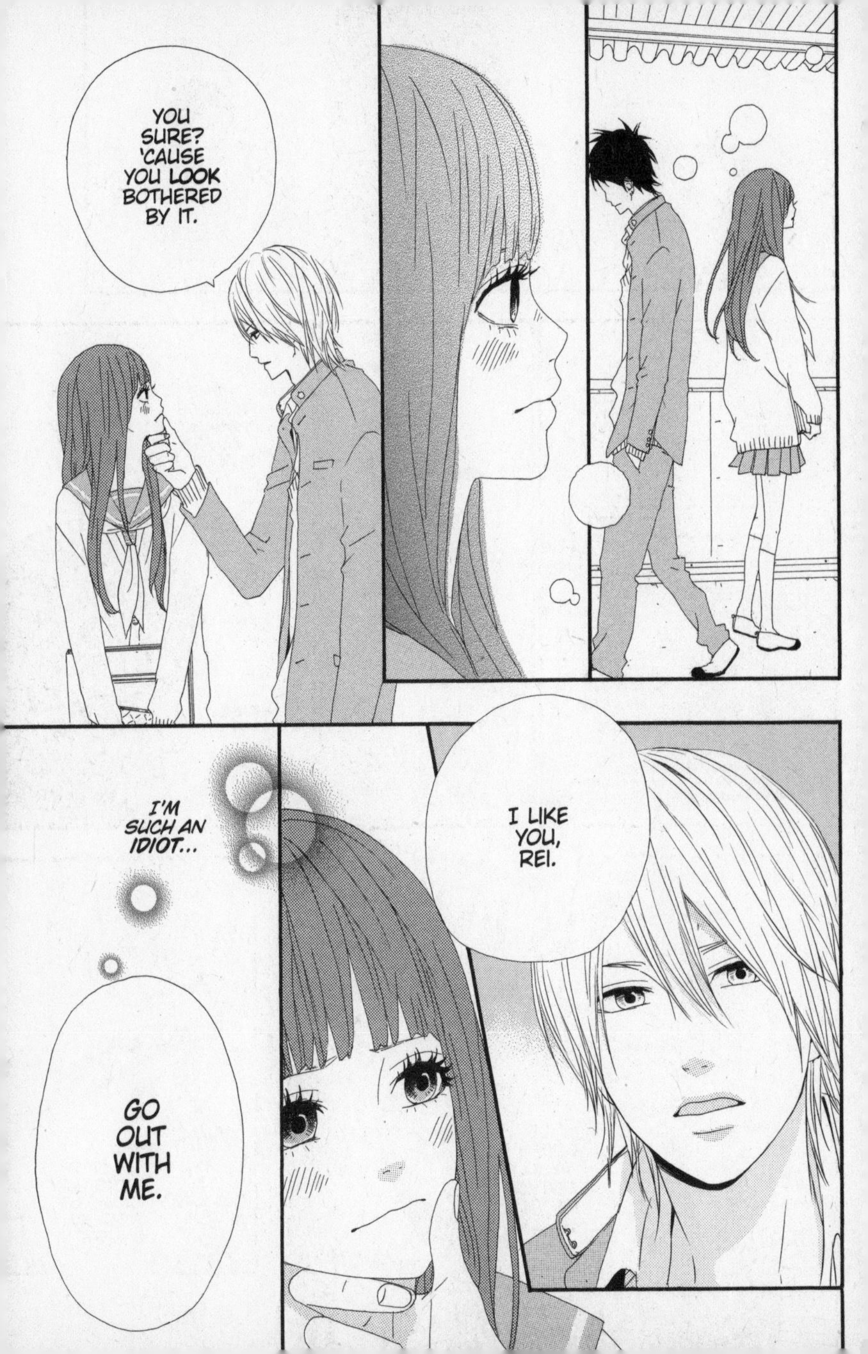
YOU SURE? 'CAUSE YOU LOOK BOTHERED BY IT.
I LIKE YOU, REI.
I'M SUCH AN IDIOT...
GO OUT WITH ME.

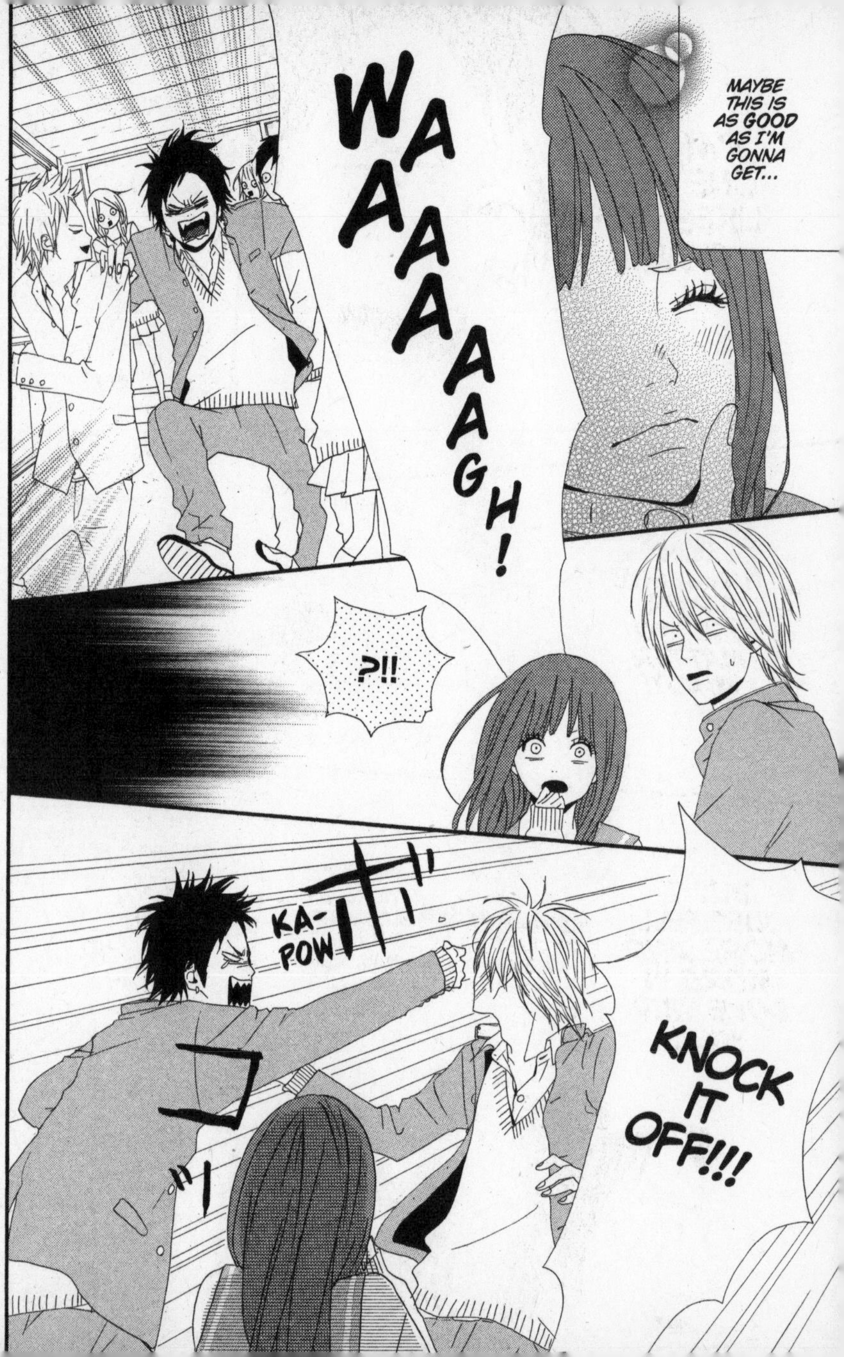
MAYBE THIS IS AS GOOD AS I'M GONNA GET...
WAAAAAAAGH!
?!!
KNOCK IT OFF!!!
KA-POW

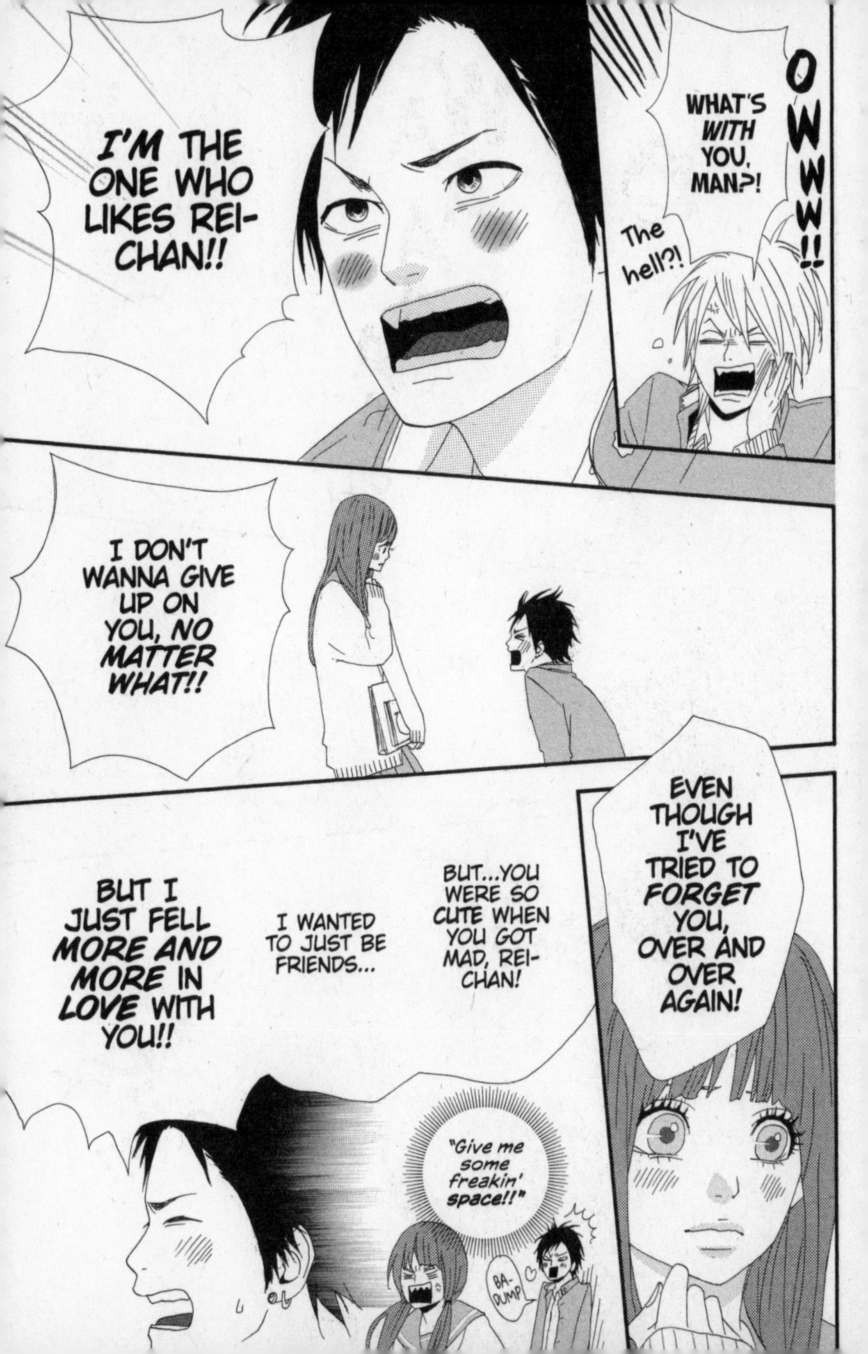
OWWWW!!
WHAT'S WITH YOU, MAN?!
The hell?!
I'M THE ONE WHO LIKES REI-CHAN!!
I DON'T WANNA GIVE UP ON YOU, NO MATTER WHAT!!
EVEN THOUGH I'VE TRIED TO FORGET YOU, OVER AND OVER AGAIN!
BUT...YOU WERE SO CUTE WHEN YOU GOT MAD, REI-CHAN!
I WANTED TO JUST BE FRIENDS...
BUT I JUST FELL MORE AND MORE IN LOVE WITH YOU!!
"Give me some freakin' space!!"
BA-DUMP

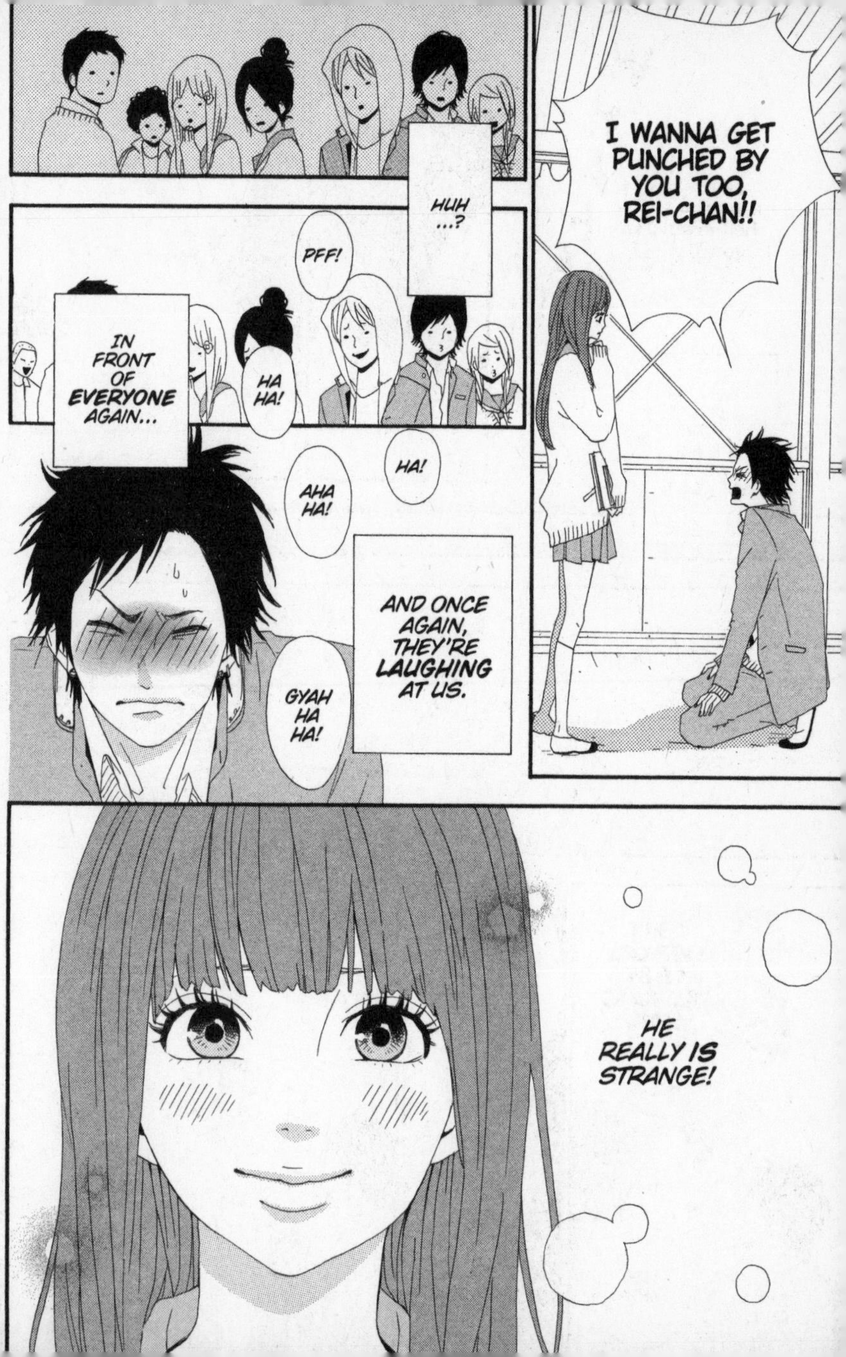
I WANNA GET PUNCHED BY YOU TOO, REI-CHAN!!
HUH ...?
PFF!
IN FRONT OF EVERYONE AGAIN...
HA HA!
HA!
AHA HA!
AND ONCE AGAIN, THEY'RE LAUGHING AT US.
GYAH HA HA!
HE REALLY IS STRANGE!

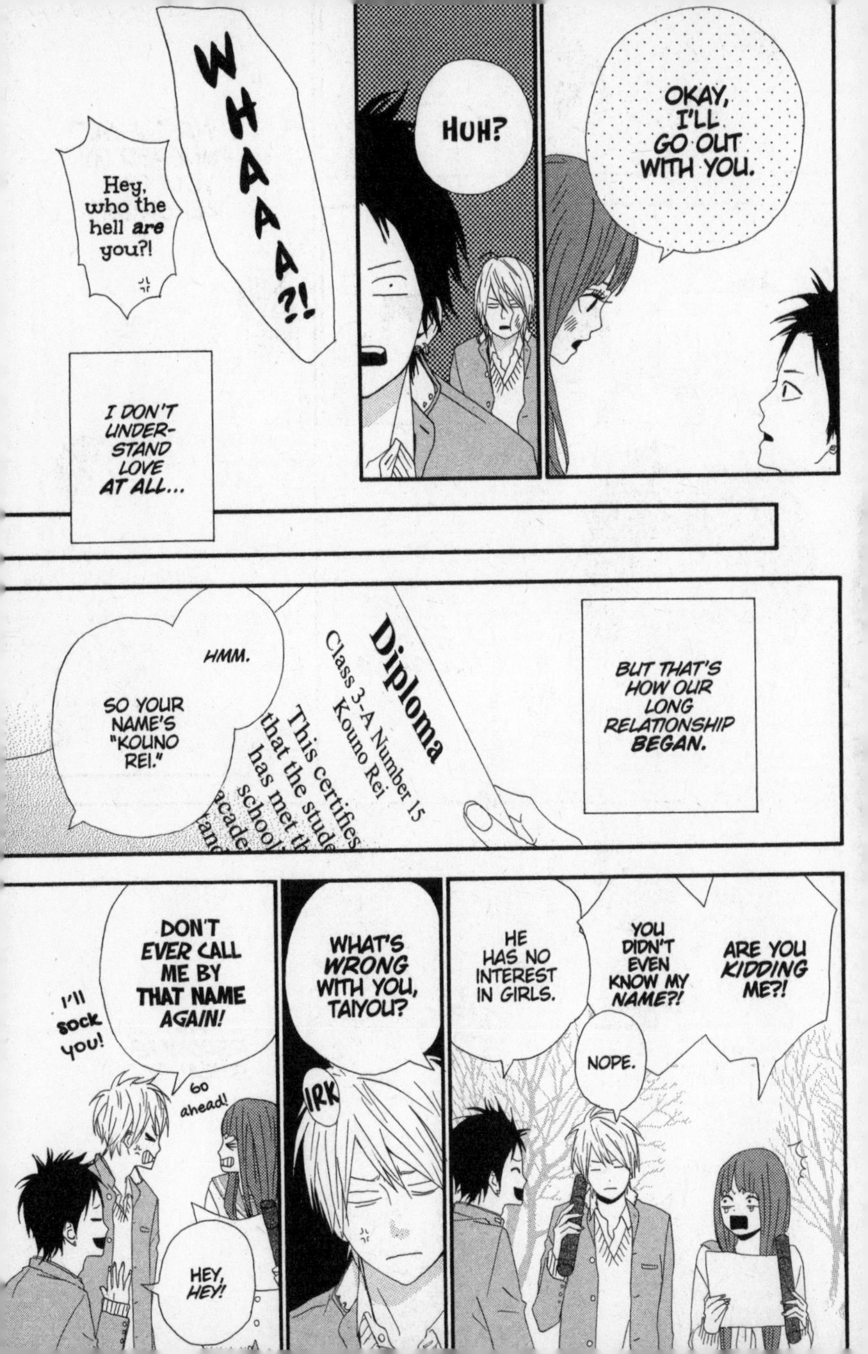
OKAY, I'LL GO OUT WITH YOU.
HUH?
WHAAAA?!
Hey, who the hell are you?!
I DON'T UNDERSTAND LOVE AT ALL...
BUT THAT'S HOW OUR LONG RELATIONSHIP BEGAN.
Diploma
Class 3-A Number 15
Kouno Rei
This certifies
HMM.
SO YOUR NAME'S "KOUNO REI."
ARE YOU KIDDING ME?!
YOU DIDN'T EVEN KNOW MY NAME?!
HE HAS NO INTEREST IN GIRLS.
NOPE.
WHAT'S WRONG WITH YOU, TAIYOU?
IRK
DON'T EVER CALL ME BY THAT NAME AGAIN!
I'll sock you!
Go ahead!
HEY, HEY!

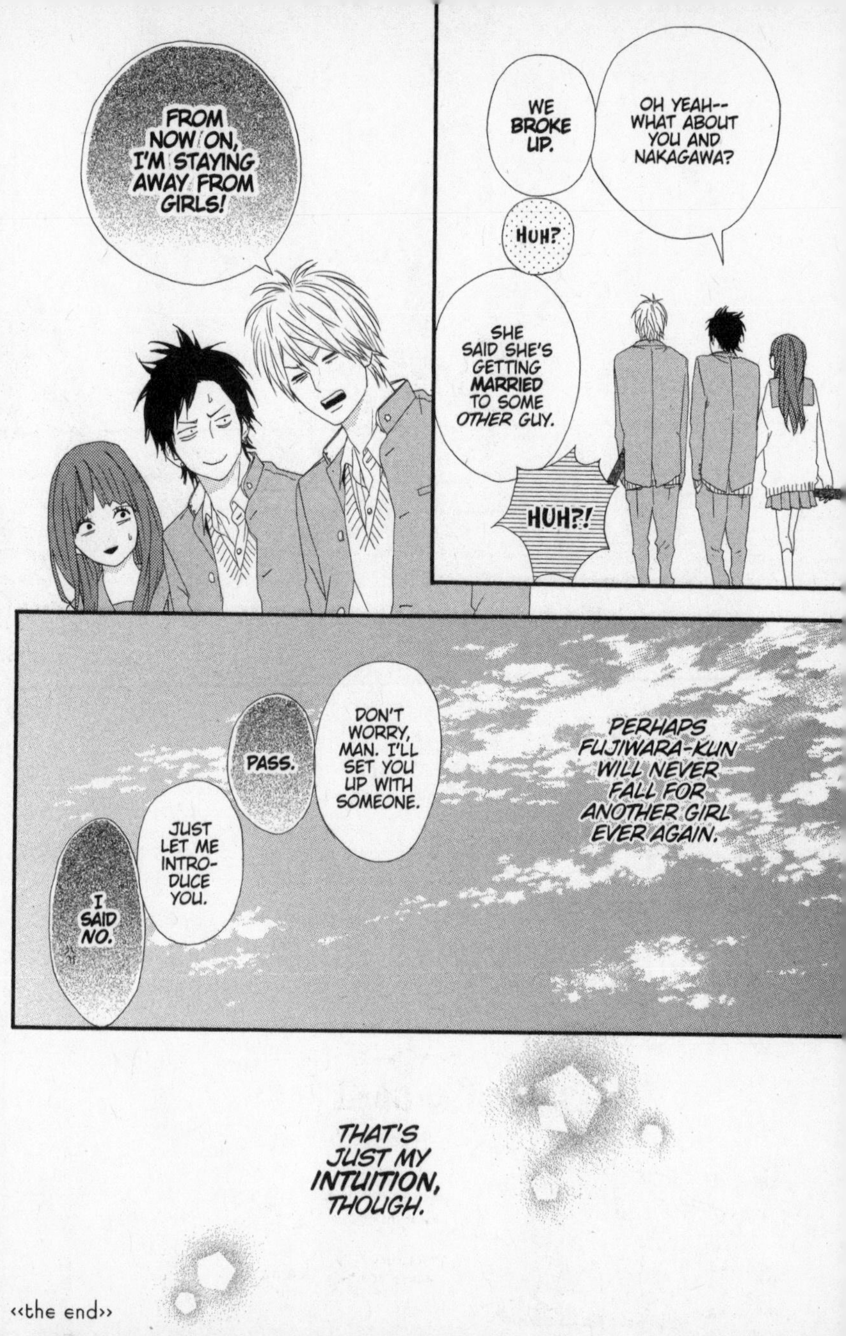
OH YEAH-- WHAT ABOUT YOU AND NAKAGAWA?
WE BROKE UP.
HUH?
SHE SAID SHE'S GETTING MARRIED TO SOME OTHER GUY.
HUH?!
FROM NOW ON, I'M STAYING AWAY FROM GIRLS!
PERHAPS FUJIWARA-KUN WILL NEVER FALL FOR ANOTHER GIRL EVER AGAIN.
DON'T WORRY, MAN. I'LL SET YOU UP WITH SOMEONE.
PASS.
JUST LET ME INTRODUCE YOU.
I SAID NO.
THAT'S JUST MY INTUITION, THOUGH.
‹‹the end››

THE FIND POKO GAME

Poko is hidden throughout the manga! Find him!

This time, there are **4** POKOS.

SNIFF
SNIFF

BONUS MANGA (After the Christmas Party)

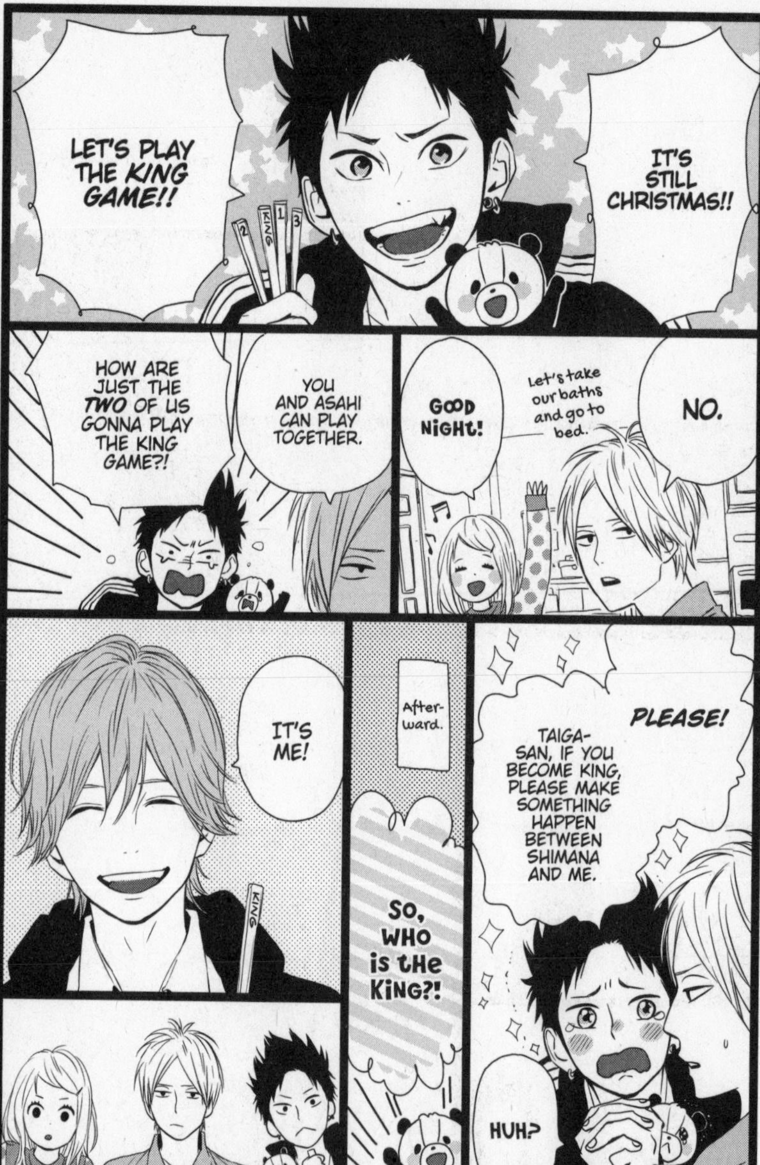
IT'S STILL CHRISTMAS!!
LET'S PLAY THE *KING* GAME!!
NO.
Let's take our baths and go to bed.
GOOD NIGHT!
YOU AND ASAHI CAN PLAY TOGETHER.
HOW ARE JUST THE *TWO* OF US GONNA PLAY THE KING GAME?!
PLEASE!
TAIGA-SAN, IF YOU BECOME KING, PLEASE MAKE SOMETHING HAPPEN BETWEEN SHIMANA AND ME.
HUH?
After-ward.
SO, WHO is tHe KiNG?!
IT'S ME!

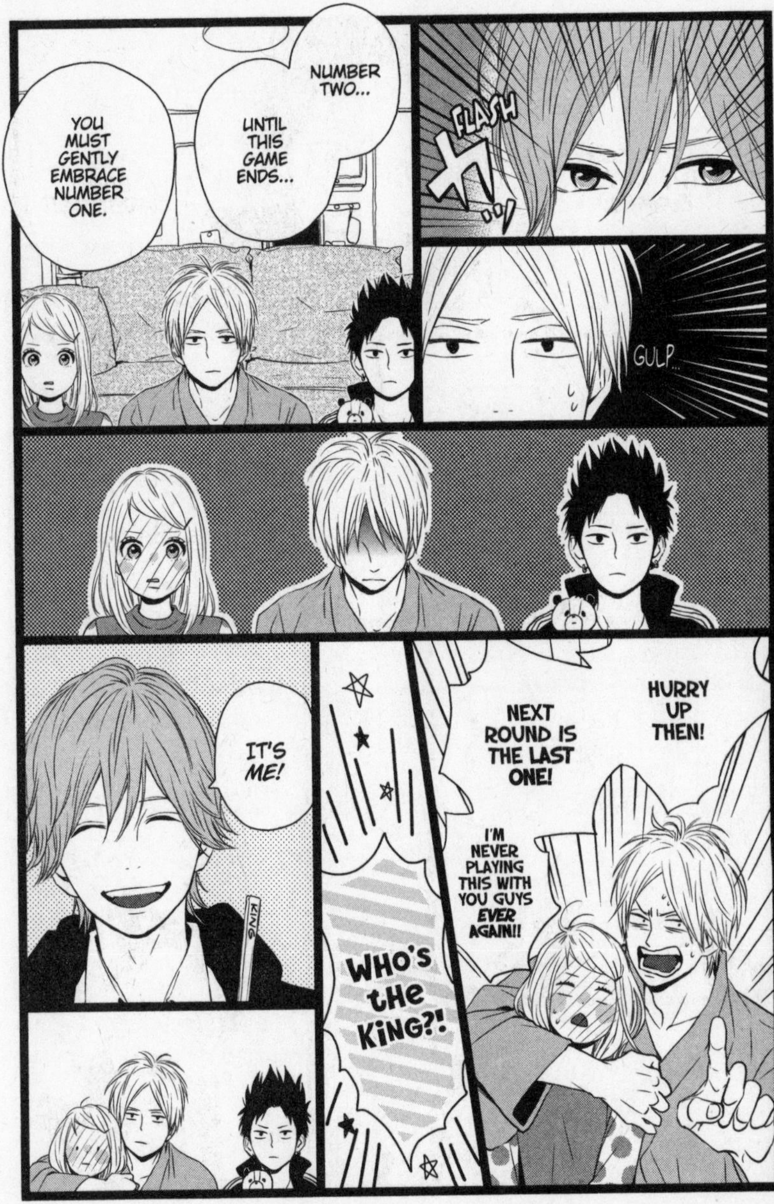
FLASH
GULP...
NUMBER TWO...
UNTIL THIS GAME ENDS...
YOU MUST GENTLY EMBRACE NUMBER ONE.
HURRY UP THEN!
NEXT ROUND IS THE LAST ONE!
I'M NEVER PLAYING THIS WITH YOU GUYS EVER AGAIN!!
WHO'S tHe KiNG?!
IT'S ME!
KING

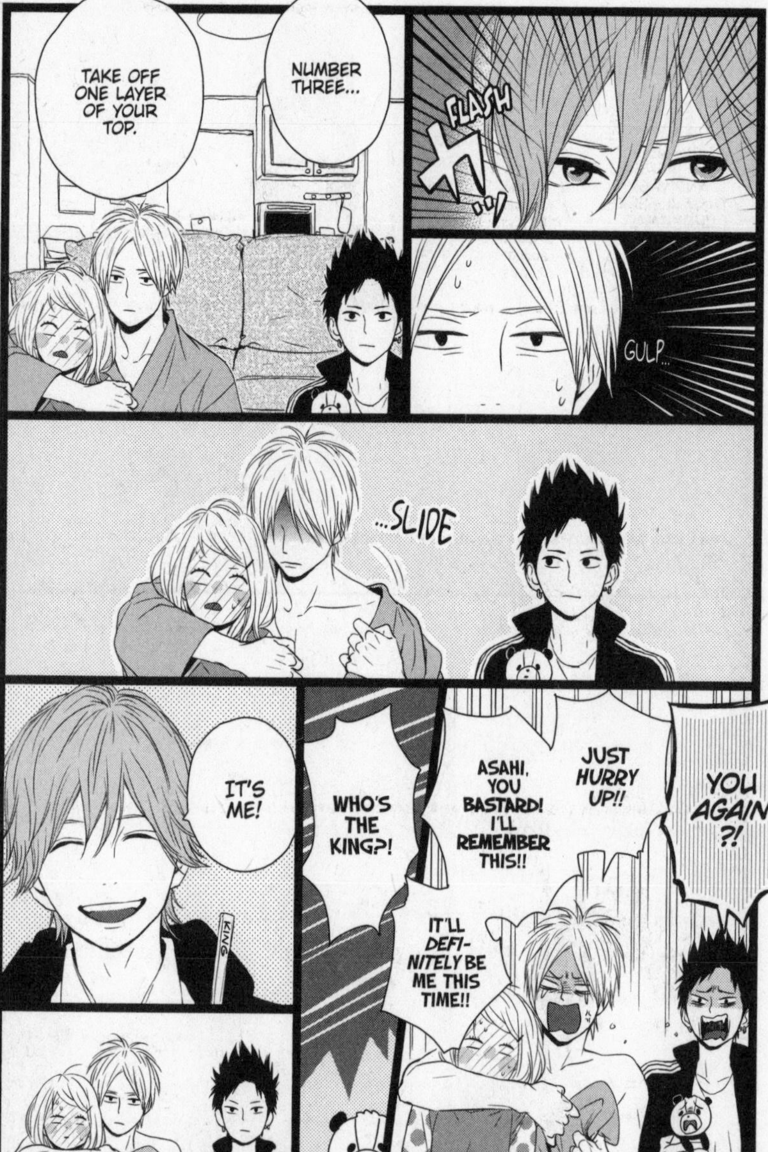
FLASH
GULP...
NUMBER THREE...
TAKE OFF ONE LAYER OF YOUR TOP.
...SLIDE
YOU AGAIN?!
JUST HURRY UP!!
ASAHI, YOU BASTARD! I'LL REMEMBER THIS!!
IT'LL *DEFI-NITELY* BE ME THIS TIME!!
WHO'S THE KING?!
IT'S ME!
KING

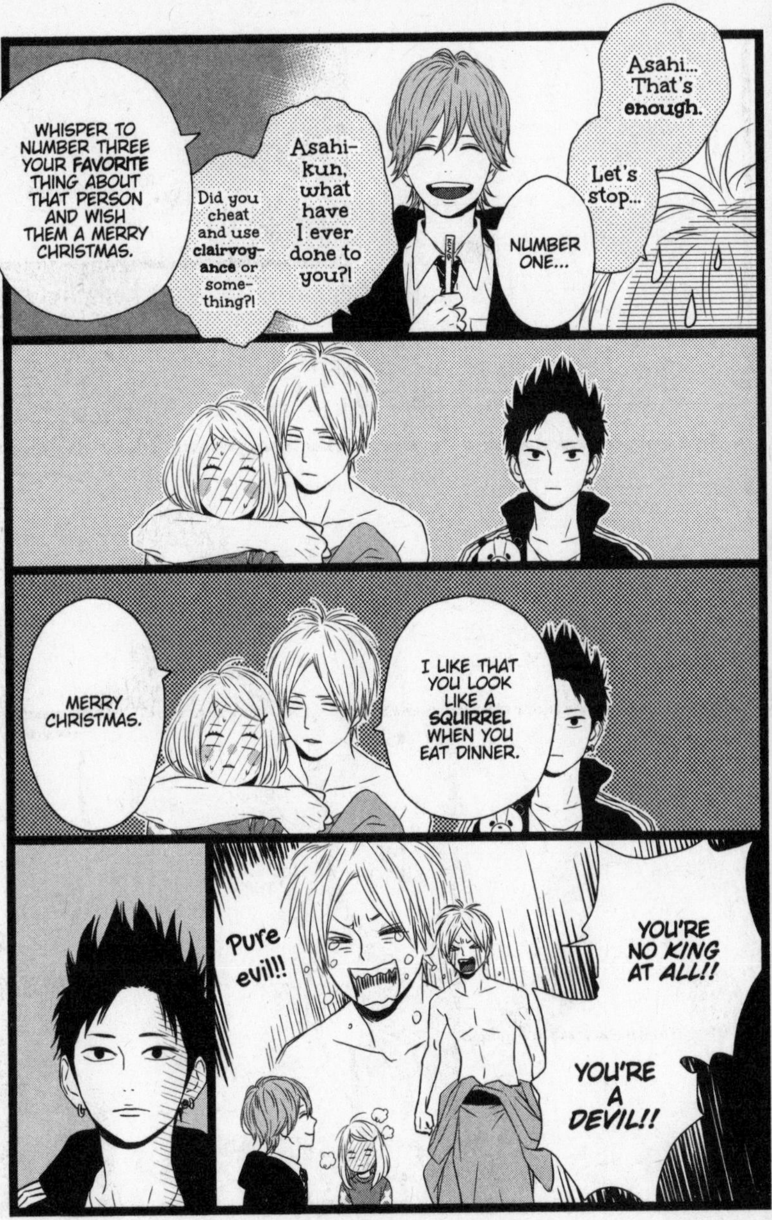
Asahi... That's enough.
Let's stop...
NUMBER ONE...
Asahi-kun, what have I ever done to you?!
Did you cheat and use clairvoyance or something?!
WHISPER TO NUMBER THREE YOUR FAVORITE THING ABOUT THAT PERSON AND WISH THEM A MERRY CHRISTMAS.
I LIKE THAT YOU LOOK LIKE A SQUIRREL WHEN YOU EAT DINNER.
MERRY CHRISTMAS.
YOU'RE NO KING AT ALL!!
YOU'RE A DEVIL!!
Pure evil!!

THE END

The New Release Version of the Hit Romantic Comedy!

With its redrawn artwork, it's even cuter than before!

**"If only I could at least...
control my *own* feelings."**

After the landlord refuses to divulge his past and the dream he gave up on, Shimana makes a confession in the heat of the moment. Though the landlord maintains his usual cool demeanor, Shimana invites him to the school's Founder's Day Festival and once again announces her feelings on stage. What will the landlord's response be?! And what will happen when the English teacher who might have been his old flame shows up?!

Includes *Dreamin' Sun* chapters 19~23, plus side story chapter 20.5 and a bonus manga!

Ichigo Takano presents
Dreamin' Sun 5

Coming Soon!

By Ichigo Takano, creator of the Eisner Award-nominated *orange*!

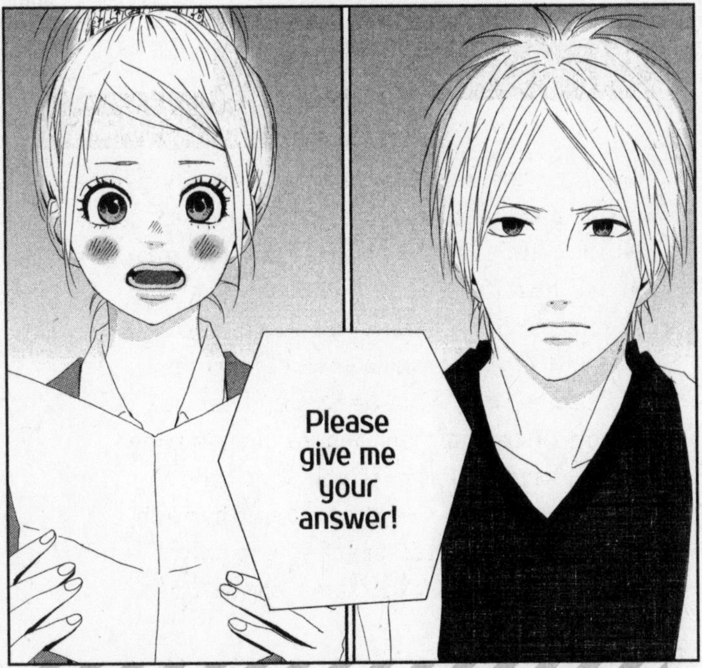
Please give me your answer!

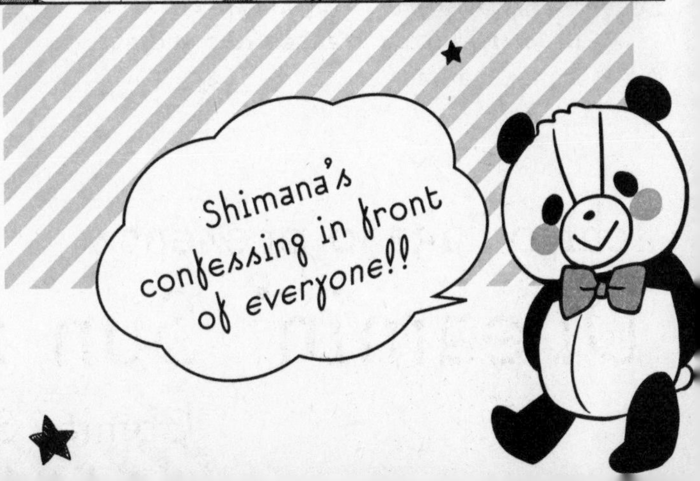
Shimana's confessing in front of everyone!!

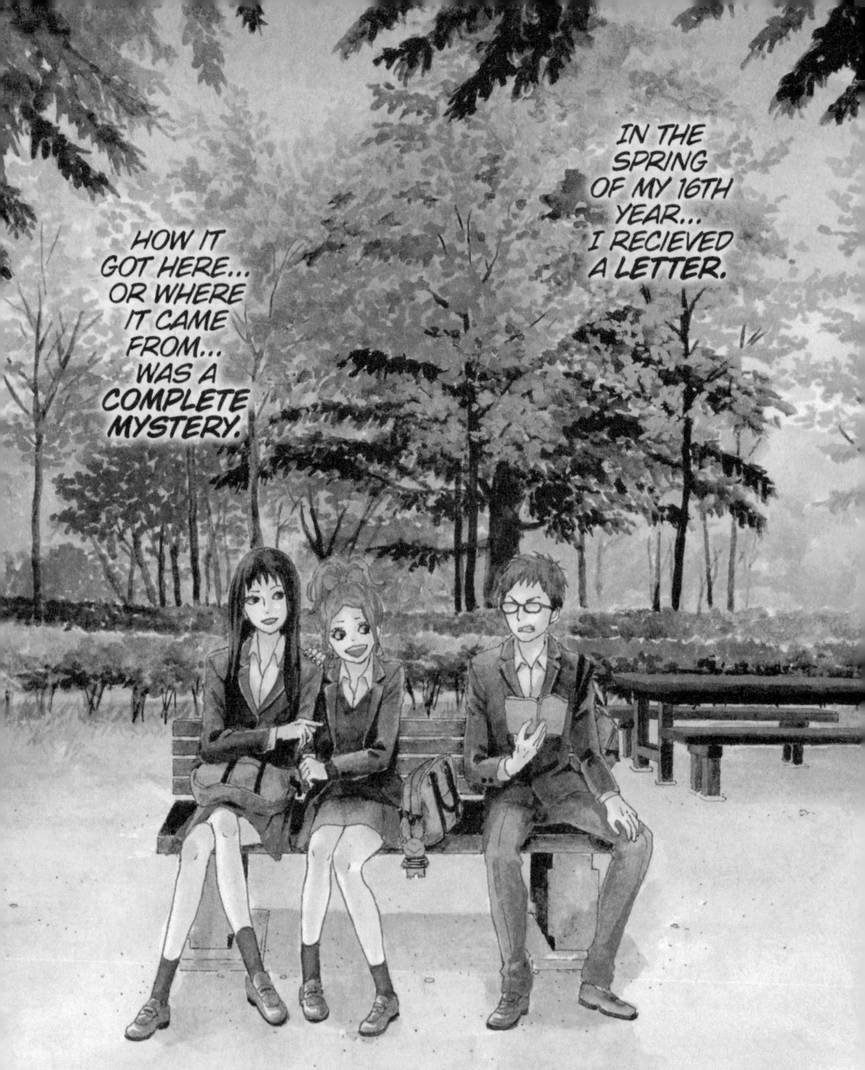
IN THE SPRING OF MY 16TH YEAR... I RECIEVED A LETTER.
HOW IT GOT HERE... OR WHERE IT CAME FROM... WAS A COMPLETE MYSTERY.

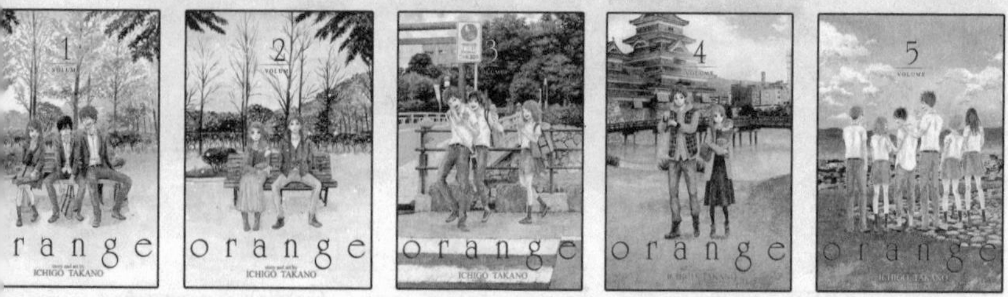
1
orange
ICHIGO TAKANO
2
orange
ICHIGO TAKANO
3
orange
ICHIGO TAKANO
4
orange
5
orange

SEVEN SEAS ENTERTAINMENT PRESENTS

Dreamin' Sun

story and art by **ICHIGO TAKANO** **VOLUME 4**

TRANSLATION
Amber Tamosaitis

ADAPTATION
Shannon Fay

LETTERING AND RETOUCH
Lys Blakeslee

COVER DESIGN
Nicky Lim

PROOFREADER
Danielle King
Holly Kolodziejczak

ASSISTANT EDITOR
Jenn Grunigen

PRODUCTION ASSISTANT
CK Russell

PRODUCTION MANAGER
Lissa Pattillo

EDITOR-IN-CHIEF
Adam Arnold

PUBLISHER
Jason DeAngelis

DREAMIN' SUN VOLUME 4

First published in Japan in 2015 by Futabasha Publishers Ltd., Tokyo.
English version published by Seven Seas Entertainment, LLC.
under license from Futabasha Publishers Ltd.

ISBN: 978-1-626925-75-5

Printed in Canada

First Printing: November 2017

10 9 8 7 6 5 4 3 2 1

READING DIRECTIONS

This book reads from ***right to left***, Japanese style. If this is your first time reading manga, you start reading from the top right panel on each page and take it from there. If you get lost, just follow the numbered diagram here. It may seem backwards at first, but you'll get the hang of it! Have fun!!

1
2
3
4
5
6
7
8
9

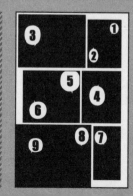

The *New York Times'* manga bestseller—a story of love and friendship that trancends time and tragedy.

orange

story & art by ICHIGO TAKANO

The complete five-volume series is available now in omnibus print and digital editions from **Seven Seas Entertainment**